Praise for *Miss Be[...]*

'Wonderfully fe[...]
***Platinum*, Book of the Month**

'Cosy crime at its finest' ***The Sun***

'The perfect cosy crime treat' ***Heat***

'Super-fun and super-readable' ***Fabulous***

'An absolute delight … witty, pacy and just a little
bit bonkers, it is fun and fabulous' ***My Weekly***

'Highly recommended' **Nuala McGovern, *Woman's Hour***

'An appealingly old-school protagonist, and I'm
sure it's going to be popular' ***Daily Mail***

'Mrs Beeton herself would be proud. A perfect
recipe, best devoured in one sitting between elevenses
and afternoon tea' **Ian Moore**

'A glorious new addition to the cosy crime genre with recipes
which will leave you wanting more' **Melanie Cantor**

'Witty, engaging, perfectly organised
sleuthing for the ages' **Sarah Lawton**

'A perfect Autumn crime read' ***YOURS***

'Miss Beeton truly stands out from the crowd' ***Sussex
Life Magazine*, Book of the Month**

'A wonderful cosy crime dish served up with humour,
warmth, satisfaction, a fabulous cast of characters to savour
and the lightest peppering of romance' **Hannah Dolby**

Josie Lloyd is the author of twenty-two novels (under various pen names) and her work has been translated into twenty-six languages. As well as the *Sunday Times* number one hit, *Come Together*, she's written several bestselling parodies with her husband, Emlyn Rees, including *We're Going on a Bar Hunt*. Their latest novel is *You & Me & You & Me & You & Me*. Josie lives in Brighton with Emlyn and when she's not writing, she likes cooking, sea-swimming, singing and walking on the Downs with her dog. She is the patron of the charity Lobular Breast Cancer UK and regularly runs wellbeing and creative writing workshops for people going through cancer treatment. She also co-hosts a podcast about the stories behind jewellery and keepsakes called 'Show Us Your Bits'.

The TV series of *Miss Beeton's Murder Agency* is currently in development with Escapade Pictures.

Also by Josie Lloyd and published by HQ
The Cancer Ladies' Running Club
Lifesaving for Beginners

MISS BEETON'S MURDER AGENCY

JOSIE LLOYD

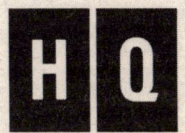

ONE PLACE. MANY STORIES

HQ
An imprint of HarperCollins*Publishers* Ltd
1 London Bridge Street
London SE1 9GF

www.harpercollins.co.uk

HarperCollins*Publishers*
Macken House, 39/40 Mayor Street Upper,
Dublin 1, D01 C9W8, Ireland

This paperback edition 2025

1
First published in Great Britain by
HQ, an imprint of HarperCollins*Publishers* Ltd 2024

PB ISBN: 9780008706654

This book is set in 11/15.5 pt. Bembo by Type-it AS, Norway

Printed and bound in the UK using 100% Renewable
Electricity by CPI Group (UK) Ltd

For more information visit: www.harpercollins.co.uk/green

For my great friend and source of all useful information, Shân Lancaster. With love.

1.

The kettle trilled like an old-fashioned police whistle. Still reading the open hardback library book, Alice Beeton walked across the small kitchen to turn off the gas, releasing the cap so that it gasped.

'I told you. It was the handsome professor.' Alice shut the book with a satisfied snap. 'Never trust a man with a dimple in his chin.'

Agatha barked once in reply, her bright brown eyes staring up at Alice who now took a china cup and two saucers from the cupboard, moving the remaining crockery a fraction to retain their pleasingly neat stacks. With a silver spoon, she measured out the precise amount of Earl Grey tea leaves from the caddy into the teapot, before filling it up from the kettle and placing a knitted cosy on top.

As a self-confessed addict of crime fiction, Alice loved the twisty plots, red herrings and scattered clues that invariably resulted in her outsmarting most fictional detectives – with the exception of Miss Marple, of course. She had a prized set of all eighty Agatha Christies (after whom she'd named her dog), but she'd run out of space for any more books.

Alice's basement flat was never at its best early in the day, only brightening up when the sun was above the buildings opposite.

Pulling up the Roman blind above the sink and peering up through the barred windows to street level, she noticed the weak grey shimmer of the December sky, but the 'beast from the east' that was predicted had yet to arrive. It really didn't look like it was going to snow, but you could never be too sure. Nevertheless, it was definitely a day for a thermal vest.

On the table the trumpets of the orange amaryllis that one of her grateful clients had sent her filled the kitchen with a cheery dash of exotic colour, but despite everything being just right in her flat, it was hard to ignore the loud neighbours upstairs. She winced as that dratted son of theirs bounced a ball across her ceiling. She flicked on the radio, which was set permanently to Classic FM, and turned up the blast of Vivaldi as a riposte.

Agatha barked again and tipped her head to one side.

'I'm doing it,' Alice said. 'Be patient.'

She poured the tea from the dainty spout into one of the saucers, topped it up with cold milk from the jug and placed it on the floor where Agatha lapped at it. But just as she was pouring her own cup, the ancient egg-shaped timer pinged. Alice jumped and put the teapot down. It got her every time.

She thought, as she often did, of how this small object brought her back to sitting on the bowed wooden counter in the kitchen of Hawthorn Hall, as Mrs Doulton taught her chapter and verse about running a kitchen and a household. Her memories had the same quality as those kodak prints of the time – faded and most definitely of a different era – but Mrs Doulton remained more like a feeling. The person who felt like home. Even now, five years after she'd passed on, Alice missed her old mentor and the person who'd been more like a mother than anyone else with an ache that she knew would never subside.

She slid on her oven gloves and peered through the clear glass door, but even without the timer she could tell from the delicious aroma that the biscuits were done to perfection. They were made to the precise recipe of her Victorian ancestor, the very famous Isabella Beeton – she of the *Book of Household Management* fame. Alice liked to live by the standards of her long-lost relative: neatness, orderliness, punctuality, and hard work. And of course, the satisfaction and comfort of home-baking.

Lemon Biscuits

INGREDIENTS – 1 1/4 lb of flour, 3/4 lb of loaf sugar, 6 oz of fresh butter, 4 eggs, the peel of 2 lemons, 2 dessertspoonfuls of lemon-juice.

METHOD – Rub the flour into the butter; stir in the pounded sugar and very finely minced lemon-peel, and when these ingredients are thoroughly mixed, add the eggs, which should be previously well whisked, and the lemon-juice. Beat the mixture well for a minute or two, then drop it from a spoon on to a buttered tin, about 2 inches apart, as the biscuits will spread when they get warm. Place the tin in the oven, and bake the biscuits to a pale brown from 15 to 20 minutes.

Time – 15 to 20 minutes.

Average cost, 1s. 6d.

Seasonable at any time.

Dressed in her usual uniform of a sensible knee-length skirt, the thermal vest, a crisp white shirt and one of her many neutral cashmere V-necks, and her most treasured accessory – her Victorian spinner necklace – Alice prepared to leave the flat. Given the weather, she added a jacquard silk scarf for a touch of colour and warmth, wondering, as she often did, why it was that people always bought her scarves as presents. Was she really that boring? If her sister-in-law Sassy gave her another this Christmas, she was determined to actually say something for once.

She took a tin from her large collection in the kitchen cupboard and lined it with crinkly greaseproof paper before placing the cooled biscuits carefully inside. Whistling along to the cheery Handel melody, she stowed the tin in her leather satchel, then turned off the radio and put her slippers in the shoe rack by the door. She laced up her leather brogues, shrugged on her trustworthy Burberry mac and checked herself in the gilt oval mirror by the front door, raking her fingers through the fringe of her neat brown bob. She was perfectly presentable. But hang on . . . Alice did a double take. Was that the faint outline of a . . . good heavens! A moustache?

Unlike so many of the women she met, she didn't engage in the lengthy and, in her opinion, mostly futile pursuit of fighting time. On the other side of fifty, but still feeling very much in her forties, she'd decided to make peace with her face shape changing, her waistline thickening, her hair showing off rather more than the odd strand of silver now. But whilst she wouldn't consider herself old, or vain by any stretch of the imagination, this new development simply wouldn't do.

If she could muster the courage, she'd ask Jinx how to get rid of it. Although, once she gave her best friend even an inkling of an 'in' when it came to Alice's appearance, she suspected the floodgates would open. Jinx had more lotions and potions and 'hacks' for beautifying oneself than Alice dared to count.

She took a deep breath and opened the door, steeling herself for the inevitable sight of discarded takeaway wrappers at the bottom of her steps, but for once the terracotta plant-pot-lined route up to the gate was clear.

Mr Mantis, the building manager, was coming down the wide stoop of the red-brick mansion house above her flat, sprinkling anti-slip salt onto the steps from a container that looked like a giant tube of Pringles. He was a little man – wiry and suspicious and always stooped over in his tatty leather jacket. He stank of cigarettes and cheap aftershave, and Alice didn't trust him one little bit.

'Miss Beeton,' he said, elongating the 'e' with his whiney voice. 'I've had a complaint, see. About your dog. Specifically about its barking.' He looked pointedly at Agatha and then flicked his head in the direction of the ground-floor window above them, the slatted blinds of which now flicked closed.

'Agatha doesn't *bark*. She *communicates*,' Alice replied, tightening the belt of her mac. 'And, anyway, *his* son bounces his ball across the floor. You can't imagine the noise. Consider the complaint doubled and sent back.'

'If you don't like living here, you could sell. I know people—'

'I've told you before, Mr Mantis,' she said, curtly, 'I'm not selling. Now, good day,' she added as she turned away, but not before noticing Mr Mantis's eyeroll. *The bloody cheek of it.*

2.

Alice walked her usual route to Kensington Gardens, releasing Agatha from her lead, so that she could sniff her favourite spots along the avenue of sycamore trees. She found comfort in the familiar morning commute: the runners, the young mothers with their pushchairs, the scooter kids and a gentleman Sikh who she often saw walking with his stick. In the distance, the ducks took off, skimming the surface of the pond and up towards the sprawling branches of the bare elms and the white sky above. There was an icy chill in the air, and Alice shivered, retrieving her woolly beret from her pocket and pulling it low over her ears.

She didn't usually allow rude people to bother her, but her encounter with Mr Mantis smarted. She'd dearly wanted to buy the ground-floor flat herself when it had come onto the market eighteen months ago, but the property had rocketed in value, and it was completely out of her budget. She'd re-mortgaged too many times and taken out too many loans over the years to help Jasper, and her line of credit was running out.

But it irked her that the spacious flat, with its stately period features, had been sold to such thoughtless neighbours who'd ripped the guts of it out, the endless building work causing no end of dust and noise. It puzzled Alice that they'd managed to get such a modern refurbishment in a listed building past the planning department. She didn't trust for a second that they had the right permissions. And now, having removed all of the insulation, they had the gall to complain about Agatha. Agatha was a *dream* compared to most dogs. Well, compared to any dog, as far as Alice was concerned. It was most discombobulating to be complained about for just living one's own life in one's own home. It was most un-neighbourly. People just didn't have any manners these days and, as Mrs Doulton had always insisted, manners were *everything*.

Sometimes, it felt as if the world was just changing far too fast. Take her neighbourhood, for instance. Alice had bought the bohemian basement flat before Notting Hill and its environs had become full of rich bankers. At the time, the half-derelict mansion block flat had been a bargain and she'd paid for it outright in cash from the sale of her mother's jewellery. She'd kept only the Victorian spinner necklace from the box of shiny baubles she'd inherited and tried to stop minding so very much that Jasper, her younger brother, had got the whole family estate. She couldn't fathom why her free-spirited parents had kept such an antiquated clause in their will, passing Hawthorn Hall down the male line. But then, they probably hadn't expected to die in a helicopter crash, after one of their legendary parties, causing Jasper to inherit when he'd been a clueless eighteen-year-old. Thank God for Mrs Doulton, who'd stayed on to run the whole place.

The pull of Hawthorn Hall was always there, but it would never be Alice's. And anyway, what would she do with it if it were? She wouldn't want to rattle around in Sussex all by herself. Hawthorn was more suited to Jasper and his boys, although Sassy (or @yummymummyinthehall as she apparently called herself on Instagram) had no clue how to run the place.

Besides, Alice loved London. Though, at this time of year with the Christmas decorations up, it was hard to combat the feeling that her life hadn't quite panned out as she'd hoped. As she crossed through the ornate, rusty-red Queen's Park gate and waited at the lights, a threesome of London buses squished together at the stop opposite, the sides of each decorated with a variation of the same advert for the latest movie romcom, depicting a perfect family opening presents next to a roaring fire.

She'd always assumed that she'd have her own luxury house like the one in the advert by now. In her mind's eye, she could perfectly envisage a hallway, a massive tree, the bannisters up the stairs decorated with ivy and lights, her brood of talented children jumping around in excitement; the comfortable, stylish drawing room filled with eclectic, arty friends; and in the centre of them all, pouring champagne, her husband, who she imagined was tall and mysterious – like a friendlier Captain von Trapp.

But this fantasy had somehow failed to materialise in any shape or form. She rarely pondered the fact that she was childless and single, but Christmas did rather serve to rub it in. Not for the first time, she wondered how it had all happened so fast – that her fertile years had passed in a flash whilst she'd been working. She'd assumed that if love were to find her, then it just *would*, despite Jinx telling her repeatedly that it wasn't how it worked these days. She'd steadfastly refused to put up her profile online, finding the whole idea of dating a stranger utterly distasteful and embarrassing. But having failed over the last twenty years to meet even one single, eligible man, Alice had reluctantly concluded that Jinx might have been right all along.

The buses were on the move now and they drove off in unison on their route towards Clapham. The pedestrian crossing flashed, breaking her out of her reverie. She walked determinedly forward, pulling Agatha who wanted to say hello to a Labrador going the other way.

Her life was perfectly satisfactory, Alice reminded herself. Besides, in her experience, children were totally overrated and not nearly as rewarding as a dog. And she had her business.

Yes, right foot forward, she thought. There was work to be done.

Ten minutes later, Alice arrived at a cream Regency building. Its glossy black door had once been the portal to a gentlemen's club, but the building was now full of offices. Like everyone else who crammed their businesses into the tiny spaces inside, Alice had chosen it solely for its prestigious postcode, just a stone's throw from Berkeley Square.

Inside was far more utilitarian than the Doric columns outside might have suggested. Walking two at a time up the grey stairs with their reinforced steel treads, Agatha panting and hopping up beside her, Alice passed several offices until she got to the door with the frosted glass, which read, 'The Good Household Management Agency'.

It had been Mrs Doulton who'd suggested the name for the agency since a book with 'good', 'household' and 'management' in the title had done very well for her distant relative. Alice knew that her old mentor would have been very proud that she'd been in business for over twenty-five years. Though probably, like Alice, she'd also be a little disappointed that in that time she'd failed to move into better, more brightly lit and spacious offices. They'd come close, of course, when the agency was doing well in the boom of the two-thousands, but the rent had sky-rocketed. And in recent years, the Covid pandemic certainly hadn't helped.

It was a non-stop job supplying the carefully vetted domestic staff for her clients' extravagant townhouses and sprawling country piles. Running the kind of high-end, event-filled life of the uber rich required good staff and Alice prided herself on supplying only the very best. Her old-fashioned Rolodex was stuffed with everyone from chefs, nannies, chauffeurs, estate managers, PTs and PAs, to mixologists, maids, gardeners and housekeepers, many of whom had been on her books for years.

She understood that for her clients, exceptionally high standards needed to be maintained and her staff knew that discretion was the key. No matter what the problem behind closed doors, staff from Alice's agency were always on-hand to fix it.

'Morning,' she said, entering. 'How are we?'

The cramped office contained two desks in the reception area – one for Helly and one for Jinx, and a green sofa. Alice's office was through a glass divide, but she rarely ever closed the door.

Helly put down her knitting, the ball of purple wool falling off the front of her desk and spinning towards Alice's feet.

'Oh, Alice, quick,' Helly said, and Alice grabbed the wool before Agatha got hold of it. Agatha considered Helly's knitting to be a particularly fun game and had once managed to unravel a whole jumper.

Helly was in her early twenties and had the kind of modern

cropped haircut that Alice had always wanted at her age but had never quite mustered the nerve to get. She had multiple piercings in her ears and a nose stud, although Alice had drawn the line at Helly's septum ring in the office. With her deadpan voice and all the piercings, Jinx had worried Helly wouldn't take to the work, but Alice had spotted a well-brought-up, organised young person with an old soul. And, despite Jinx's initial misgivings, she had turned out to do her job surprisingly well.

Jinx was warming herself against the fan heater, and now turned around in a way that a starlet from an old movie might, her arms outstretched.

'There you are. My baby, my baby,' she said in a silly voice, scooping up Agatha and nuzzling her.

'Good morning to you too,' Alice said, pointedly, making Jinx laugh – the same deep, raucous laugh she'd had since they were children at school together. The kind of laugh that had got them into trouble with their teachers.

After their A levels, when Jinx had been off on multiple gap years, they'd lost touch, and in her early twenties, when Alice had been dealing with the fall-out of her parents' sudden demise, she'd watched from afar as Jinx, armed with that very laugh and a swagger to match, had become an 'It' girl in London in the mid Nineties.

Always pictured in the gossip columns on the arm of some minor prince or playboy, Jinx's first celebrity wedding to an oil magnate's son had lasted all of six months. When Jinx had called out of the blue from the South of France, in floods of tears, explaining that she was penniless and humiliated, Alice hadn't hesitated in helping her out. Husband number two had seemed a better prospect, but he'd turned out to be a rotter too. Husband number three had hardly been any better. And when husband number four had died unexpectedly in a hot tub – which Jinx *hadn't* been in at the time – Jinx had cleaned up her act and declared that she was off men forever. It was then Alice had invited her to come aboard to help run the agency. From day one she'd been a natural, and in recent years had really come into her own, branching out into a very successful concierge service for their clients.

'What on earth are you wearing?' Alice asked, squinting at Jinx's stripey taffeta dress with puffed sleeves. She looked alarmingly like a deckchair.

'Don't you love being old enough for things to come back into fashion?'

'It's very Princess Diana,' Alice ventured, knowing the compliment would land with her friend, who loved the royals and had never really stopped being a Sloane Ranger – for whom the iconic Princess had, of course, been the main torchbearer. 'But maybe one for spring? Didn't you hear we're expecting snow?'

'Hasn't the royal family been cancelled? I don't know why you two still harp on about them,' Helly said, not looking up from her knitting.

Alice, who along with Jinx had mourned profoundly the passing of the late Queen, was saved from entering a debate about loyalty and service when the buzzer sounded.

Helly leant into the comms screen.

'It's that girl for the interview,' she said. 'She's early.'

'Good,' Alice said. 'Bring her in.'

3.

Alice prided herself on being able to get the cut of someone's jib (a favourite saying of Mrs Doulton's) in lightning quick time. Her instincts were rarely wrong. You only ever had one chance to make a good first impression, and so far, this young woman, Enya Fischer, had done a superb job.

She was tall and dressed in a pinstriped, double-breasted charcoal-grey suit. The skirt was maybe a little on the short side, but paired with just the right denier black stocking. Not too thick, not too thin. Her hair – long and blonde – was tied back in a ponytail, but with care. Not a strand out of place, and expertly teased, Alice noted, no doubt in the correct way – with the pointed end of a comb. She had high cheekbones and the kind of dewy complexion that the young have but never appreciate, and large, serious grey eyes.

'I love the way she has one black ear and one tan. What kind of dog is she?' Enya asked, nodding down towards Agatha.

'I've never been exactly sure,' Alice replied, always charmed by people who took the time to notice her beloved dog. 'We call her a Cojack – mostly Jack Russell, with a dash of corgi, I suspect.'

She didn't mention that when she'd found Agatha, she had

been the size of Alice's hand, abandoned next to a large black bin. The fact that the bin had been on Buckingham Palace Gate had always made her entertain the fantasy that one of the royal corgis might have been in some way responsible for her existence.

But this morning, Agatha was acting far from royal and seemed to have completely lost her manners. As Enya reached out to pet her, she emitted a low growl and Alice looked sharply in her direction, noticing that the small dog was baring her teeth.

'I'm so sorry. She's never normally like this. Agatha!' Alice said, picking her up. 'Whatever's got into you?'

She marched to the office door and put Agatha down, booting her gently towards Helly.

'I'm so sorry,' she apologised again, but Enya only smiled, revealing perfect white teeth.

'Agatha. That's an unusual name for a dog.'

'Oh, after Christie. I'm an addict of crime fiction,' Alice confessed. 'Do you like to read?'

'Oh yes, of course. Whenever I can,' Enya said, and slid across her professionally printed CV.

The first big tick, Alice thought, as she put on her thick-framed reading glasses. Helly said that they made her look like Velma from *Scooby-Doo* but Alice liked them. She scanned the impressive list of Enya's credentials and nodded thoughtfully.

'You went to school in Switzerland?'

'Yes, my parents lived there for a while. My father was German and my mother French, so I'm fluent in both,' the young woman said, confidently, with only the very merest hint of an accent.

'Good, good,' Alice said, mentally adding some more ticks, before moving on. She'd been around the block long enough to spot when someone was fluffing up their CV like a feather pillow, but Enya seemed to have excellent experience under her belt. Placements that had undoubtedly given her that very refined, implacable demeanour. She was respectful and polite and not at all showy. An ideal candidate.

But at the same time, she was surprised that a woman like Enya would want to have a position as domestic staff, rather than a position in, say, a business of her own. Not that there was anything wrong with being in domestic service, and most of the people on Alice's books were equally highly educated, but this Enya just seemed so very switched on.

That said, these days it was hard getting jobs that were well paid enough to allow a person to live in the lowliest of London postcodes, let alone the most prestigious. Being a live-in house-keeper came with many high-end perks as well as a very decent salary. And she wouldn't mind betting Enya knew that.

'Oh, and here are my references,' Enya said, reaching into a smart Smythson attaché case.

One was from The Dorchester hotel on headed paper, the second sheet from an upscale ski resort in Klosters.

'You ski?'

'Almost since before I could walk.'

'I've never been myself. I'm hopeless with heights,' Alice said with a chuckle.

The phone on her desk now unexpectedly rang and she looked through the glass towards Helly, who shrugged, holding out the receiver. Helly knew full well that it wasn't polite to disturb her during an interview.

'What is it?' Alice said rather snappily into the receiver.

'Sorry, it's just I have a call for you. She says it's urgent and won't be put off.'

Alice put her hand over the mouthpiece and smiled at Enya.

'Would you excuse me, just a moment.'

She nodded to Helly to put the call through. 'Alice Beeton speaking.'

The woman on the other end of the line – Camille Messent, as she now introduced herself – spoke good English, but so fast and in such a heavy French accent that Alice had to concentrate to keep up.

She smiled at Enya, who, politely pretended not to listen as she stood up and examined the framed illustrations from Mrs Beeton's *Book of Household Management*.

From what Alice could surmise, the Messents' current house-keeper had right this moment and wholly unexpectedly quit for personal reasons, which from Madame Messent's tone didn't qualify as a suitable reason at all. Left in a bind, she seemed rather frantic. Laura, her teenage daughter was already home from boarding school for the holidays and she had absolutely no time to supervise her, busy as she was with her charitable foundation for refugees and her husband abroad on business. The Good Household Management Agency had come highly recommended and, as she finally drew a breath, she asked if Miss Beeton could possibly help.

Alice was always glad when the agency had been personally recommended. There was no substitute for word of mouth. Jinx had been saying for years that they should advertise and expand, but Alice maintained that small and exclusive was her business plan, and she was sticking to it.

Alice assured Madame Messent that she'd see what she could do and put down the phone before apologising to Enya for the interruption.

'I couldn't help overhearing some of that,' Enya said.

'She was rather desperate. Being let down by staff at short notice is simply awful.'

'I quite agree,' Enya said. There was a small pause. 'Miss Beeton, I hate to be presumptuous, but I'm free. Perhaps I could go? Didn't she say she wanted someone right away?'

'I'm not sure, I mean, it's most irregular—'

'Oh, I'm sure it is, but as you know I'm quite up to the task and I do speak French after all?' Enya suggested, with a disarming smile. 'Perhaps just a case of being in the right place at the right time? Aren't you a believer in serendipity? I certainly am.'

Alice twisted her lips, feeling unusually put on the spot. Of course, Enya was right, there was a great deal in this life that relied on people being in the right place at the right time, but she and Jinx had put in strict protocols over the years to thoroughly vet their staff and there simply wasn't the time to go through all the checks if Enya were to go to the Messents' right away. But on the other hand, it was Christmas and as she quickly ran through the staff on her books who'd be available, everyone who sprung to mind was either already in a placement or on holiday.

'I'm not promising anything. I need to make a few calls and to check out these references, so perhaps you wouldn't mind waiting out there for a moment or two . . . ' Alice said.

'Of course,' Enya said, again with her lovely smile.

She really was very charming, Alice thought, smiling back and watching her close the door respectfully.

She logged onto her computer and checked the database, but Susie McTeary was with the family in Dubai and Paulette Cobin? Damn it, she was with her family in Antibes. So, actually Enya *was* looking like a very good candidate to send to the Messents.

She dialled the number on Enya's CV and as she waited for an answer, turned her chair away and looked up at the framed needlepoint on the wall – one of the only things she'd rescued from Mrs Doulton's room at Hawthorn. It had a picture of a home and in cursive writing was a famous quote of Mrs Beeton's: *A place for everything, and everything in its place.*

Five minutes later, Alice joined Enya, Helly and Jinx in the reception area. Jinx had obviously told Agatha to stay in her basket, as Agatha gave Alice a distinctly ashamed look, then shuffled round and turned her bottom to the room.

'They couldn't have been more enthusiastic about you,' Alice said, referring to the two calls she'd just made. The woman at The Dorchester, and indeed the woman at Klosters, had been very complimentary. 'To be honest, I'm not really sure why you left either job?'

'I want to run a proper household,' Enya said. 'Or run a houschold the proper way, to be precise. I can't help noticing these lovely pictures everywhere,' she continued, looking round. 'They're from Mrs Beeton's book, aren't they? I adore everything she wrote. Forgive me, but are you related?'

'Distantly,' Alice said, feeling a little flush of pride.

'My grandmother had her book. She was given it as a wedding present. I think most women were in those days.'

Alice caught Jinx and Helly exchange a look. Alice could extol the virtues of her distant relative for hours and she knew it bored them both. It was rather an unexpected pleasure to encounter a fellow Beeton-ite.

'You know, she was the first person to write out recipes with the ingredients, method and cost,' Enya said.

'I know!' Alice exclaimed, possibly a little too enthusiastically.

'Here we go,' Helly muttered.

'Before then, it must have been so hard to follow all those fancy French chefs,' Enya went on. 'She was very in tune with the times. Thanks to her, women everywhere were able to plan their weekly meals and budgets.'

Helly muttered something else, but Alice only caught the word 'patriarchy' and shot her a sharp look.

'Such a shame that she was only twenty-eight when she died,' Enya said. 'That's the same age as me.'

Alice looked Enya over again – a woman entering her prime – and felt a wave of sadness for poor Isabella Beeton. She'd been a businesswoman and entrepreneur and had written one of the most enduring, bestselling books of the twentieth century, but her husband had got all the credit at the time. She'd been the eldest of twenty-one siblings, so most of her childhood had been spent caring for them. In fact, there was no real evidence that she'd had the time to cook, or had particularly enjoyed it even, but that didn't diminish her huge legacy and the book that Arthur Conan Doyle described as having more wisdom per square inch than any ever written by a man.

'I never normally do this,' Alice said, 'but as your references are so good and as you're here, perhaps, as you say, we should embrace the serendipity and you should go to the Messents'.'

Jinx raised her eyebrows in surprise. 'That's the easiest ride anyone has got from Alice,' she said to Enya. 'It must be Christmas. Let's sort out that paperwork, shall we?'

Half an hour later, as Jinx gave Enya the Messents' address, they all waved her goodbye, though Agatha slightly dampened the moment, by letting out a long, low growl, like a distant rumble of thunder. The silly old sausage.

4.

At eleven on the dot, Alice retrieved the tin of lemon biscuits from her satchel and declared it time for their morning coffee break.

As Helly put the kettle on for coffee, Jinx started opening the large pile of Christmas cards on her desk, carefully scrutinising each one. Alice often thought that she could probably offer a whole open university degree course on the etiquette of card-giving.

'One from Terry, the window cleaner. Isn't he sweet? He always sends a card. Oh, and look, here's one from Shelley Van Oostrasburger, but not starring her in a full photoshoot this year . . . disappointing. In fact, I'd say a lot of these cards are decidedly less bling than usual.'

'Glitter is really bad for the environment,' Helly said, filling the cafetiere in the small kitchenette. 'Plus, why use trees for something so pointless? Especially when no one believes in Christmas anymore.'

'Bah humbug,' Alice said, although perhaps Helly did have a point. Alice had received several half-arsed round robin Christmas emails, which really weren't the same as a handwritten card. But Helly looked a bit put out, so Alice said more softly, 'Have you decided what you're doing for Christmas?'

'Back to see my folks,' Helly replied, unenthusiastically. 'It'll be a nightmare on the train to Leeds. *If* I can get there. There'll probably be strikes. All the travelling makes me anxious.'

'It won't be that bad, surely?' Alice said, trying to cajole her. 'Once you're there?'

Helly gave her a 'you've-got-to-be-joking' look. 'You know my brother's an idiot. I can't stand him for more than a day.'

'Talking of brothers, I take it you've been summoned to Hawthorn, Alice?' said Jinx, propping up each card on the office shelves.

'Yes. You don't want to come with me, do you?'

'I'm afraid I can't get out of Richard's shindig. Besides, you have no idea how irritating I find Sassy online. I don't think I could manage her in real life.'

'Her Insta is like, *totally* delulu,' Helly said.

Alice grimaced.

'If you won't enter the twenty-first century and get on the socials, Alice, it's your own fault you're missing out on the goss,' Jinx said as she took one of the lemon biscuits from the tin. Alice knew she ought to heed Jinx's advice and get onto social media, but she really couldn't see that any good would come of it. She liked her life being private. In Alice's opinion, there was something so vulgar about people sharing the details of their daily lives, filtering pictures of their coffees, editing and cropping out anything realistic and saying that they were constantly 'humbled' and 'blessed'. The world would be a much better place if people stopped navel gazing so much and got on with things that actually mattered.

'So? Has Jasper made any money yet? Like he promised?' Jinx asked pointedly, refusing to let the subject go, despite Alice's best efforts. 'Wasn't Christmas the cut-off?'

There weren't any secrets in the office, but it was uncouth to talk about money and Alice didn't approve of washing one's dirty linen in public, however upsetting and gossip-worthy Jasper's antics might be. And anyway, Jinx hardly knew the half of it. She'd be horrified if she realised that Alice had taken out yet another loan to 'tide Jasper over'.

'I'm sure he's got good news,' Alice said, as if it were no big deal, hoping to God it was true. Fortunately, the door buzzer rang, saving Alice from another dressing-down from Jinx about how Jasper was her one weak spot and she needed to take a firmer stance. As if Alice didn't know that already. She wasn't stupid.

'Oh!' Helly clapped her hands and pressed the entry button.

Jinx glanced at Alice. They both knew that there was only one person who could raise a smile like that from Helly. And sure enough, a moment later, a young man came bounding through the door, holding his moped helmet and shaking out his dreadlocks.

Agatha jumped out of her basket, barked twice in greeting and ran little circles of joy as Jacques Lourdan bent down and gave her a tickle behind the ears.

'Ah, so the wanderer returns?' Jinx said, kissing him on both cheeks. 'Let me look at you,' she said, holding him by the shoulders. She towered above him in her tall heels, and Alice saw the lascivious glint in her eye. He was handsome and cute at the same time, and he damned well knew it.

'Thought I'd swing by,' Jacques answered, ducking out of her grip, smiling at Alice as he dipped his hand into the tin. 'What have we here?' He took a considered bite of the lemon biscuit as he kicked back on the sofa and put his feet up on the arm. It was no coincidence that he'd turned up at this time. Helly fetched him the best mug from the cupboard and poured him a coffee.

'Nothing that will delight your sophisticated palette,' Alice said.

'*Au contraire*, these are very good, Miss B.' He raised his eyebrows at her, and she felt a warm glow of pride. She was merely an amateur, but it was always gratifying when people – especially ones as talented as Jacques – liked her baking.

'Was Japan as wonderful as you'd hoped?'

'Did you really go to Kyoto?' Helly asked, in an awe-laden voice. 'Was it incredible?'

'You'd love it,' Jacques said, as ever, basking in being centre of attention. 'I did this insane cookery course. *The* most amazing ingredients. Here, let me show you.'

He swung around off the sofa and retrieved his backpack, still chattering on about his travels and his course, and Alice smiled to herself.

He'd been the same since she'd first met him three years ago in the check-out queue in Harrods' food hall. She vividly recalled how a man had pushed in front of him and when Jacques, rightfully put-out, had challenged him, in a firm, but charming way, the man had uttered a nasty racist slur. Jacques, unflustered, had issued forth a spectacularly articulate take-down involving an explanation of his French and Guianese roots, his classical training and his love of world travel, arguing in fact that he had much better reasons for being in the food hall – ones connected to passion, rather than snobbery – and Alice, along with everyone else in the queue had burst into a round of applause. The old duffer had left and Alice had enrolled Jacques right there and then on her books as a freelance chef. She only hoped that one day he'd fulfil his potential and run his own restaurant. Or even just work on her books full time, instead of working for one of her rivals, Elite, as well.

'Aha, here,' he said, pulling out a leather pouch, bound with leather ties. He carefully unwrapped it, revealing a row of bottles, each in its own, even smaller, pouch. He gently pulled one out, the label of which was covered in Japanese writing.

'Smell this.' He wafted it under Alice's nose.

'Oh, goodness,' Alice exclaimed at the pungent smell.

'Concentrated lobster essence. It just takes a couple of drops, but the depth of flavour is . . . ' He kissed his fingertips.

Helly giggled as he put some on his little finger and let her taste it. Jinx rolled her eyes at the very obviously flirty move. Jacques had no idea of the erotically charged effect he had on Helly – indeed, the whole office. Alice suspected he left a trail of broken hearts behind him, but food was always going to be his first love.

'Oh, wow,' Helly exclaimed, covering her mouth at the shock of the taste.

'Oh, I forgot – you're not vegan, are you?' he asked.

'I am. Or was. I'm pescetarian,' she blustered.

This was news to Alice. Helly didn't seem to mind any of the ingredients Alice used in her culinary offerings. She'd snaffled half a tin of sausage rolls just last Friday. Jacques held eye contact with Helly for just the right amount of time to make her blush, then clapped his hands together and turned to Alice.

'So, I was wondering, are there any jobs going?' Jacques said, looking expectantly at Alice. 'I am . . . how should I put this? A bit *low* after my trip.'

'Nothing, right at this moment, but consider yourself officially on standby,' Alice reassured him. 'There's always last-minute problems with Christmas parties.'

'Yes, you'll be top of our list,' Helly said dreamily, before blushing again and turning away. Alice raised an eyebrow at Jinx, who smirked and Alice had to press her lips together to smother her own smile.

5.

It was already dark and cold when Alice slipped out with Agatha for an afternoon walk around the block. The fuggy London air she was used to had a sharp metallic tinge to it and her breath clouded in front of her.

She headed to the corner past the old school where, for a long time, the little girls in their boaters always used to run down the stoop and make a fuss of Agatha. But like everything else, the lovely building had been bought by developers and now had a gold plaque on the front wall in Russian.

It often seemed to Alice that the people on the streets in this square of the A–Z were from every corner of the globe. On any walk, she might hear one of a dozen different languages – Korean, German, Spanish, Arabic. The Koreans in their platform trainers and puffa coats, the older European businessmen in long camel coats talking into their cell phones, the younger ones in brogues with their bare ankles showing (a pet hate of Alice's). But they all had one language in common: money.

The shops here were exclusive and expensive. Places that she, even with the fortunate background she'd had, could never afford to shop. But she knew many of the staff and drew a nod from Karl, a security doorman standing in a smart black coat outside a jeweller.

She ducked down a side street, passing a dry cleaner. She cupped her face against the window and waved to her friend inside. Shilpa waved back and slipped around the counter, past the rails of plastic-covered clothing, and opened the door.

'Alice,' she said, 'what a delightful surprise.'

'I'm not stopping,' Alice said, hugging her old friend. 'How are you?'

'Oh, the usual,' Shilpa explained, with an exasperated sigh. Alice wondered how she could cope with the smell of chemicals, or the noise of the key cutting machine on one wall, which Agatha now took exception to, whining and hiding behind Alice's legs.

Shilpa called across to where her husband was grinding the metal and he stopped and waved to Alice.

'You busy?' Alice asked.

'Run off our feet. Everyone wants everything yesterday. I swear they get ruder. I'll be on my knees by Christmas.'

Alice knew what Shilpa meant. Plenty of the very rich people she'd met could be charming, but some, including lots of those who'd recently snapped up prime real estate around here, expected their whims to be catered for without realising that greasing the way with common courtesy was the most efficacious way to get things done in a hurry. The sense of entitlement some of these people had, in Alice's view, was an outrage.

She continued on her walk towards the library, shops giving way to grand houses, and played the nosy game that always amused her – rating the wreaths on each door and the Christmas trees in the front windows. In one garden, a cherry tree was lit up with thousands of lights, which Alice stopped to admire as Agatha sniffed around the base of the plane tree set into the wide pavement. The shutters in the bay window were open and there was an equally impressive sparkly tree inside. Her imagination was already racing ahead with the different scenarios she could imagine for the occupants: getting ready for their Christmas parties, concerts and ballets, the excitement building.

She still craved that magical feeling she'd had as a child, when the anticipation of Christmas had given her stomach aches and sleepless nights, which had, over time, evaporated to something ephemeral and hard to grasp – like a remembered smell. She still sought out a whiff – a wisp of something she could hold onto – because she still believed. Not necessarily in all the religious stuff, although she liked singing carols, but in that magical feeling of Christmas, of being safe and warm and cosy and part of a family.

She would start on her baking for her trip to Hawthorn tonight, she decided, pulling on Agatha's lead. That would undoubtedly put her in the Christmas spirit. Because, as her great ancestor always said:

In December, the principal household duty lies in preparing for the creature comforts of those near and dear to us, so as to meet old Christmas with a happy face, a contented mind, and a full larder; and in stoning the plums, washing the currants, washing the citron, beating the eggs, and MIXING THE PUDDING, a housewife is not unworthily greeting the genial season of all good things.

She must remember to pick up the spices on the way home. And after their annual Christmas lunch, Jinx had promised to help her shop for her nephews. Unlike Alice, who second-guessed her decisions the whole time, Jinx was an expert when it came to present shopping – especially if she was spending someone else's money – and in particular when she'd had a few glasses of wine.

A sleek black Bentley drew up beside her and its window slid down.

'I thought it was you,' said the driver. 'Do you fancy a lift?'

Alice smiled. Massoud had been on her books almost since the day she'd started the agency.

'Oh, how lovely to see you,' she said. 'And thank you, but I'm only walking Agatha to the library.'

'Hop in.'

'It's only around the corner.'

'It'd be a pleasure. Come on.'

He got out to open the passenger door for Alice and Agatha with a flourish. Alice laughed, seeing that he'd put on his cap just for her. His bushy black moustache hid his smile, but his eyes twinkled as he touched the peak of his cap.

'Ma'am,' he joked.

Scooping Agatha up, she climbed in. 'You behave,' she whispered to her dog.

She'd been in Massoud's limo a few times, but it never failed to make her feel special. The sudden silence, the plush leather seats, the perfect air temperature. It was like being hermetically sealed against the elements the moment the door was closed.

Massoud got back into the driver's seat and pulled out easily into the traffic on the main road. In this part of town, people always gave way to cars like his.

'Everything still going well with the Jerrards?'

'Yes, they're in the Caribbean for Christmas.'

Alice smiled, glad that Massoud had some time off.

'They might stay there for a few months, so I may need some ad hoc work.'

'Consider it done,' Alice said. She'd be able to find no end of jobs for him. 'I never get over how quiet it is inside here.'

'I've just had her serviced,' he said, tapping the wheel. 'She's good as new. Oh, by the way, when I was in Seb's garage, I saw your MG. They say it's ready.'

'Is it? Oh, right,' Alice said, thinking how she'd entirely forgotten that Massoud had arranged the service for her.

She knew that there was no particular reason to have a car in London these days – especially because of the congestion charge and the criminally high parking fees – but since Massoud housed it for free in his mews garage, she'd hung onto the soft-top British racing green MG Midget for sentimental reasons.

The classic sports car had been a present from her brother Jasper. In a typically flamboyant gesture he had surprised her with it on the morning of her thirtieth birthday, honking the horn outside her flat. When she'd gone outside, Alice had found the ridiculous car with a giant white bow wrapped all the way around it and Jasper dangling the keys from his fingertips, looking like the cat that had got the cream. It remained the most extravagant gift she'd ever received. And expensive . . . from her point of view. Not only had she subsequently probably ended up re-lending Jasper the money he'd initially spent on it, it had cost her thousands over the years to make it remotely roadworthy.

'How much do I owe you?' she asked, steeling herself for the answer. Another bill for the car was the last thing she could do with.

'Nothing.'

'But—'

'Miss Beeton, I won't hear of it,' Massoud said. He'd never addressed her as Alice – even though she'd asked him to a hundred times.

They chatted easily, as Massoud stopped at the lights, Alice happy to catch up on his family news. Dora, his wife, was sadly suffering from multiple sclerosis and now mostly confined to a wheelchair but still worked full time as a translator.

'Wisam takes after her,' Massoud said, tapping the side of his head. 'The one with the brains.'

Alice smiled but shot Massoud a reproving glance. He was no weakling in the brains department either. The rumour was that he'd worked for the Egyptian security services a lifetime ago. As he indicated and turned down another shortcut, Alice wished the library was a bit further away. She didn't want this lovely journey to end.

'Wisam? Your grandson, right?'

Massoud nodded. 'He's a wizard with computers and especially phones. Not that the poor kid can get a job. Had a spot of bother at school and his report was bad. I worry he's had too many knockbacks.'

'Oh dear.'

'He's online all the time. Tapping away at his keyboard. He hardly sees daylight. When I was his age, I was always outside.'

'Children are resilient,' Alice assured Massoud, but she was only paying lip service to the problem. She didn't have the faintest clue how to deal with troubled young people, whose lives seemed to have been ruined in so many ways by the invention of the internet.

'I hope so. Oh, look, we're here.'

Alice thanked him for the lift.

'Are you still baking?' he asked, suddenly.

'Goodness, yes. I have a whole list to make for Hawthorn.'

'Then I shall drop you round some of my cousin's currants and dates. A box just arrived from Cairo with more in it than we can possibly use.'

'Oh, that would be wonderful,' Alice said. 'And thanks.'

She alighted onto the pavement, feeling momentarily like a celebrity author might. She closed the door and watched Massoud's hazard warning lights flash twice as a goodbye as he drove away.

She looked down at Agatha who shook herself, then peed on the empty bike bars set into the pavement. Alice shivered. She'd only been in Massoud's limo for five minutes, but she could swear the temperature had dropped even further.

6.

Barney was at the counter and waved when he saw Alice. He was in his late sixties, with a mop of white hair, and wore his usual soft cotton plaid shirt under a woollen cardigan with leather buttons that reminded Alice of toffees.

For some years, Barney had run a financial consultancy in Alice's office building, and when they'd discovered a mutual love for Scrabble, they'd become Scrabble partners – and in time – good friends. It was years before she'd discovered that he'd been high up at GCHQ. Jinx was still convinced that Barney's job at the library was an elaborate cover and that he was still some kind of spy, but Alice was fairly sure he was retired from all of that.

Like her, Barney was single. He had, until quite recently, been married to the formidable Honey, who had been, when Alice had met her, a lot less sweet than her name had implied. In fact, she'd been so scary that Alice had wondered if her name had been some sort of ironic joke. Sometimes Barney would recount a story that seemed straight out of the pages of the books Alice like to read – about him and Honey escaping from 'a scrape' in a sewer in Moscow in the early Eighties, or crash-landing a private plane in Marrakech. They were outlandish stories that fascinated Alice, but also made her feel incredibly boring by comparison.

She'd spent the last twenty years placing staff who facilitated other people's fun-filled lives, assuming that, at some point, she'd have adventures herself. But she always seemed to be several steps removed from the action. It was why, she guessed, she liked reading so much. At least in a book, she could put herself centre stage.

After exchanging pleasantries, Alice handed over her last library book and Barney lifted it close to his face, looking over the top of his rectangular glasses. For a librarian, he had possibly the worst eyesight of anyone Alice had ever met.

'Ah yes. The professor,' he said.

'It was obvious.' Alice smiled. 'Never trust a man with a dimple in his chin, I say.'

Barney laughed.

'Did you save the next one?'

'Of course,' he said, lifting it from beneath the desk. 'Not as good. Great cliff-hangers though.'

'You're always saying you're going to write a book yourself. Have you started it yet?' Alice asked.

'No,' Barney said with an embarrassed shrug. 'I can't seem to motivate myself to do anything. I actually hate this time of year.'

Alice rarely got an insight into his inner emotions and the little comment wrenched at her.

'What are you doing for Christmas?'

'My sister's. You?'

'I'm going to Hawthorn.'

'I wish I could stay at home by myself and wait until the whole thing is over. Christmas is no fun when you're single.'

He looked up and pulled a face. 'Sorry. Don't mean to rub it in.'

Suddenly, there was a whoop, and she and Barney looked towards the door. A little boy ran in through the doors.

'It's started,' he shouted. 'It's snowing.'

Barney stood up and came around the desk to walk with Alice to the door, where they all stood watching the fat flakes fall from the sky. There were few things that stopped people in their tracks in London – the death of a celebrity, the birth of a royal baby, and this: the arrival of snow. Even a smattering of flakes was an event. Alice smiled at Barney as three children ran out into the spill of light from the library doors, and Agatha barked and ran bravely after them, before rapidly chickening out and running back inside.

'Here,' Barney said, taking a treat from his cardigan pocket and feeding it to Agatha, who took it daintily.

'She doesn't deserve it,' Alice said. 'She growled terribly at a new employee earlier. I was most embarrassed.'

'Was there something wrong?'

'What do you mean?'

'With the client?'

'No, quite the opposite. She was absolutely perfect.'

'Well, Agatha might have a point. I find perfection to be most overrated,' Barney said.

Alice shrugged Barney's words off, but as she walked back to the office, her beret pulled down low over her head, the fat snowflakes pricking her eyes, she remembered Jinx's surprised look and felt a nagging doubt that she'd acted hastily. Gut instinct was all very well, but she was in the business of crossing the T's and dotting the I's so perhaps, just to be on the safe side, she'd pay Enya a visit in the morning to see for herself how she was getting on.

Back at home, determined to summon the Christmas spirit, Alice changed into her cosy cashmere sweatpants, put a Michael Bublé CD on in the ancient sound system and rolled up her sleeves to start on her cake mixture. She lifted down her ancient *Book of Household Management* from the shelf in the cupboard, careful to keep all the cut-out recipes from magazines and the ones she'd handwritten and printed out over the years that lived amongst its pages. She carefully placed the thick tome onto an old wooden pulpit stand in the kitchen and put on her glasses.

Mrs Doulton used to make a large traditional cake weeks ahead of Christmas, which she'd feed with brandy and cover in thick curved white icing like ceiling cornicing. Alice could remember the almondy smell of the marzipan and how she'd cut out holly leaves and paint them green with a fine-tipped paintbrush then fashion the leftovers into little marzipan berries and fake oranges in little baskets.

But the cake itself was stodgy and heavy, and in later years when Mrs Doulton would bring Alice a cake in London, there'd rarely been takers for it in the office and Alice had often ended up throwing it away rather than eating it, much to her upset.

This recipe was far lighter and contained no alcohol. Lord knows Jasper imbibed enough over Christmas and extra brandy was the last thing he needed. Besides, her nephews Baxter and Woody liked this version better. It was a more like a treacle and ginger cake than a fruit cake. As Alice found the recipe and started gathering together the ingredients, the smell of the powdered ginger gave her the shot of Christmas oomph she was missing.

Christmas Cake

INGREDIENTS – 5 teacupfuls of flour, 1 teacupful of melted butter, 1 teacupful of cream, 1 teacupful of treacle, 1 teacupful of moist sugar, 2 eggs, 1/2 oz of powdered ginger, 1/2 lb of raisins, 1 teaspoonful of carbonate of soda, 1 tablespoonful of vinegar.

Method—Make the butter sufficiently warm to melt it, but do not allow it to boil; put the flour into a basin; add to it the sugar, ginger, and raisins, which should be stoned and cut into small pieces. When these dry ingredients are thoroughly mixed, stir in the butter, cream, treacle, and well-whisked eggs, and beat the mixture for a few minutes. Dissolve the soda in the vinegar, add it to the dough, and be particular that these latter ingredients are well incorporated with the others; put the cake into a buttered mould or tin, place it in a moderate oven immediately.

Bake for 1 3/4 to 2 1/4 hours.

She hummed along to cheesy Christmas favourites as she stirred the mixture, feeling a fuzzy warm glow. Her mind filled with flashes of childhood memories of Christmases at Hawthorn.

When Pop-Pop and GG, her grandparents, had been alive,

Christmas had been magical, but she'd been seven when Pop-Pop had died, and GG had gone into a nursing home where she had died of a broken heart a few months later. And that's when her parents had inherited Hawthorn.

For a very long time, she'd tried not to think too much about this period of her life, those happy memories so tinged with what happened next, but she remembered her parents revelling in the house and how they'd flung open their doors to their London friends, and how the house had been full of strangers, especially at Christmas, with the festivities seeping well into the new year.

Even now, Alice couldn't wrap her head around exactly who her mother Beatrice Beeton had been. The memory of her seemed so out of reach and exotic. She'd been the daughter of a diplomat and a celebrated ballet dancer and had fallen hopelessly in love with Alice's father, Henry, a confirmed bachelor, when she'd been in her early twenties. Henry had been twenty years her senior and a whole foot shorter. But their love had been real. Of that, Alice had no doubt. When they'd been together, Alice had always felt like an outsider.

In her mind's eye now, she pictured her mother, lolling on her father's shoulder, both looking down at her, her mother in a long, shimmering dress, her huge eyes smudged with the previous night's mascara, her manicured finger absently flipping the dangling spinner necklace. She remembered how they'd giggled at Alice in her school uniform, as if it were a funny quirk to see her dressed that way at 7.30 a.m. on a Wednesday, and how it had made her sure that adults were a different species altogether.

But now, with her grandparents, parents and Mrs Doulton gone, Hawthorn Christmases had an altogether different vibe.

But her remaining family would all be together and that was all that mattered, Alice thought as she carefully tipped the Christmas cake onto the wire rack and pressed its steaming surface, feeling for the springiness that meant it was done to perfection. She placed it on the table to cool and stood back, satisfied. The first big tick off her Christmas list.

In the bathroom, after a long soak with her library book propped up on the wooden rack, she consulted the packet of bleach she'd bought in the chemist and gingerly applied it to her top lip. She caught her own eye in the magnifying mirror – giving herself a sharp look of reproach for her vanity.

She left the cream on as she went into the kitchen to put the kettle on for a soothing cup of camomile. But as she stood at the sink, she heard an odd noise. A faint *plink, plink*.

'What's that, Agatha? Can you hear something?' she said.

Agatha barked.

'Shush,' Alice said, holding up her finger and they both cocked their heads to listen.

Plink, plink, plink.

Alice turned and stared at the cake, noticing a damp sheen on its surface. As she got closer, she felt a drop of cold water on the back of her head.

'What on earth . . .'

Looking up, she moved away just in time, as another drop fell from the ceiling. She snatched away the cake, but she could tell from the weight of it that it must already be infused with dripping, dirty water.

'You have *got* to be joking,' she fumed, staring up at the ceiling. 'Right.'

She would never normally consider going out in her casual wear, but this was an emergency. She pulled on her Ugg boots and a long coat in a furious rush.

She stomped up her steps and through the gate, up the stoop and pressed hard on the buzzer for the ground-floor flat. The chill snaked through her coat. The snow was falling thickly now, muffling everything, and the buzzer sounded urgent and loud.

'Who is it?' A male voice came through the speaker. Him. The nasty neighbour. Mr whatever his name was, with the awful son.

'It's Miss Beeton – Alice – from the flat downstairs. There's a leak in my ceiling. Coming from your flat. Whatever you're running . . . you must turn it off immediately. Immediately!'

'There's nothing on.' His tone was dismissive, bored even.

'But there *must* be. I'm telling you . . . there's water dripping through the ceiling. It's ruined my cake.' Her voice rose slightly hysterically.

'Oh, piss off, lady,' he said, and she heard that he'd hung up the entry phone.

'Well,' she said, furiously walking back down the steps and slipping on the snow, only just managing to grab the rail and right herself in time.

Back in her flat, she was shaking. And not just from the cold. She was so incensed she was tempted to call the police, but she was stopped by the thought of trying to explain that the ruined cake might be a crime. Instead, realising she'd left her mobile phone at the office on the charger, she went to her padded Liberty address book and looked up Mr Mantis's number.

She enjoyed still having her old-fashioned rotary phone, which Jinx roundly mocked, but it was rather inconvenient to have to dial the numbers so slowly when one was in such a furious hurry. When Mr Mantis answered his mobile, Alice surmised from the music and clatter of cutlery that he must be in a restaurant, and from his slurred greeting, had clearly had a few glasses of wine. She told him all about the drip through the ceiling and how rude the neighbour had been.

'I don't need trouble. Not this close to Christmas,' he said, clearly annoyed.

Alice watched the damp patch spread across her ceiling.

'But you've got to come. Right now,' Alice demanded. 'It's an emergency.'

'Put a bowl down to catch the drips. I'll come in the morning.'

She was still furious as she finally got into bed, huddling under her ancient eiderdown. The top of her lip was sore where she'd left the bleach on for too long, her moustache problem a whole lot worse than it had been. She thought of what Mrs Doulton might have said – undoubtedly a quote such as 'vanity is the quicksand of reason'.

With a harrumph, she wrapped her duvet even more tightly around her, but no matter what she did she couldn't stop hearing the *plink, plink, plink* into the washing-up bowl on the table in the kitchen.

And suddenly it was if she could see herself from the ceiling, like a little lonely mouse in her bed, in her basement flat, in the dark, and that wave of sadness that rarely came washed over her and filled her eyes with tears.

'Oh, for heaven's sake,' she said aloud, wiping her eyes before they fell.

7.

The Messents' home was an imposing white building in a terrace built along the west side of a handsome Kensington Square. The traffic-calming bumps had stopped it being a cut-through for cabs so the road was pleasantly quiet. There was a parking bay along the black railings opposite and a view from the stoop onto the nicely laid out trees and rose beds in the private garden in the centre of the square.

Built in the late 1750s, the house sported an English Heritage blue plaque detailing the life of a French composer Alice had never heard of. Perhaps it was this link to French cultural heritage that had drawn the Messents to this particular house. Or perhaps it was the fact that in 2010 a footballer had completely refurbished the property, excavating the basement to make room for a Turkish bath, sauna and a professionally equipped kitchen.

Alice rang the old-fashioned bell and rubbed her leather gloves together, looking down the street and noticing that many of the luxury cars that usually graced squares like these were absent. This close to Christmas, Knightsbridge emptied, its residents taking off for their ski chalets, country piles, or to warmer climes.

Dropping in on her staff wasn't unusual, but Alice knew that

Enya might be busy so she resolved not to outstay her welcome. She often thought being a housekeeper must be so satisfying and she hoped that Enya had taken to it. She found herself thinking of a passage about the duties of a housekeeper from Mrs Beeton's book, which she often held up as a benchmark with which to judge her employees.

> Like 'Caesar's wife', she should be 'above suspicion', and her honesty and sobriety unquestionable; for there are many temptations to which she is exposed. In a physical point of view, a housekeeper should be healthy and strong, and be particularly clean in her person, and her hands, although they may show a degree of roughness, from the nature of some of her employments, yet should have a nice inviting appearance. In her dealings with the various tradesmen, and in her behaviour to the domestics under her, the demeanour and conduct of the housekeeper should be such as, in neither case, to diminish, by an undue familiarity, her authority or influence.

The heavy front door now opened. 'Miss Beeton?' Enya said, uncertainly. She was dressed in black trousers and a black smock. It was clearly a uniform but it made her look a little like a beautician at a spa. 'I wasn't expecting you.'

'I was just passing,' Alice lied with a smile. 'A courtesy call. Nothing more. I came to see how you're getting on. Is Madame Messent at home?' She stepped towards Enya, already nosing inside the house.

'No, no. She's out. And Monsieur is busy.'

There was an awkward moment when Enya looked as if she were tempted to close the door on Alice, but instead, flustered, she stood back further. Alice smiled and advanced towards her.

'Um . . . then come in,' Enya said, clearly unsure whether this was etiquette, but Alice stepped gratefully into the ambient warmth of the Messents' mansion.

'Oh, just for a little bit. If you're having a coffee, then I wouldn't say no,' Alice said presumptuously, peering past Enya into the hallway. Its sweeping stairs had been remodelled with glass panels but several of its original features were intact.

'Um,' Enya began, 'there's still some in the pot.'

'Marvellous.'

Alice followed Enya as she walked briskly past a plinth display-ing a bust of Napoleon and turned to look through the door of the drawing room to one side.

It was a beautiful space, Alice thought, noticing the modern glass chandelier, antique bevelled mirrors, bookcases filled with an array of antique tomes, large sofas upholstered in salmon pink, and two atlas globes. On one side was a shiny grand piano with the lid open. Houses like these always benefited from a piano and she wondered how Albert the piano tuner was keeping these days now that Mortimer, his guide dog, had sadly passed away. She hoped he'd received the card Jinx had sent.

'One always forgets the scale of these properties,' Alice said, as they passed an enormous set of double doors. 'What's in there, I wonder?'

'Oh . . . er . . . the ballroom.'

Alice pulled an impressed face. 'How grand. Can I peek?'

Enya looked confused but did not express an opinion. Alice

put her hand on the door. She allowed Enya a moment more to protest, then opened it a fraction. On the other side was a beautiful parquet floor and a pink and grey silk Persian rug that was by far and away the largest Alice had ever seen. At one end a painting covered nearly the entire wall and Alice cocked her head trying to make sense of it. Was it some sort of seascape?

'That's quite a piece,' she said, sensing Enya next to her and clearly wanting her to close the door.

'There are lots like it throughout the house.'

'Monsieur Messent is an art dealer, isn't he?' Alice said.

'He has a gallery not far from here. But I've hardly seen him. He's always out. Everyone is very busy. There's a lot to do. Madame's throwing a big party on New Year's Eve, you see. She's given me a list of tasks. They both seemed a little stressed, so I offered to help.'

'Both?'

'Oh, Madame Messent has a secretary, Thérèse.'

Of course, they'd have utilised clever Enya. She felt confident that Madame Messent would be reporting back very favourably about her new member of staff.

At that moment, the phone Enya was carrying rang and she looked at the screen.

'Oh, I have to take this,' she said. 'It's the photographer.'

It was now Alice's turn to eavesdrop on Enya's conversation and it wasn't long before she realised that Enya was talking to Charles Tavistock. She brought to mind the celebrity photographer, with his shaggy collar-length dark hair and ubiquitous leather trousers. He'd been around for years, and Alice had employed him on several occasions in the past. She couldn't be sure, but she was pretty certain that he and Jinx had had a brief fling once.

She took the opportunity to study the photographs on the marble console table at the bottom of the staircase, looking at the array of tasteful silver frames. She noted a classically beautiful woman in most of them, Camille Messent, she assumed. The largest showed her with the French president, her lustrous chestnut hair styled falling over slim shoulders, a sheath dress of shimmering material hugging her enviably perfect figure. A tall man with dark hair stood on the other side of the president. He appeared in the next photograph too. This must be Camille's husband, Alex Messent, Alice thought, picking up the photograph to stare more closely at his inscrutable gaze. As someone who had never looked good in photographs, she was always intrigued by people who had cultivated a 'photo face', like Alex Messent clearly had. The kind of neutral look that seemed the same in every shot and one that gave no clue as to his mood or temperament. But he was undeniably good-looking, with fine, Gallic, symmetrical features, but . . . Alice peered in closer, was that a *dimple* in his chin?

Enya now came and stood beside her, clutching the phone. She shimmied in between Alice and the table so that Alice had to step away, placing the photo back down.

'That must be Monsieur Messent,' Alice said. 'And Laura? The daughter?'

'She's upstairs. Actually, Miss Beeton, I must go and check on her. I really don't have time to stop for a coffee . . . '

'Oh, of course. I didn't mean to disrupt your morning. You're clearly busy.'

'I am,' Enya said, relieved. She moved the photograph back to where it had been in its previous position, adjusting it just so.

She held out her hand for Alice to guide her back towards the front door. The perfect etiquette for getting rid of unwanted visitors. Alice couldn't have done better herself.

'I appreciate you coming,' Enya said, as they got to the door, 'but really, everything is fine. There's no need to worry.'

'Do let me know if there's anything I can do to help,' Alice offered, warmed by Enya's charming smile. She really had such a lovely manner.

'Of course.'

A second later, Alice was out through the front door, which closed abruptly. She could hear Enya walking away quickly back inside the house.

Smoothing down her jacket, Alice put on her gloves. 'Just as it should be,' she said to herself, 'she's perfect after all.'

8.

Alice went back to the office to pick Agatha up and to check for messages. Helly had left yesterday for Leeds and today would be the last day the office was open.

She answered a few enquiries and emails, then, still at Helly's desk, did an internet search on Alex Messent. A Wikipedia page revealed that, until recently, he'd been the director of a huge gallery in Paris but had come to London to set up on his own. She opened up the website for the Swan Gallery, looking at the glossy pictures of the modern art pieces and reading the incomprehensible explanations that accompanied them.

Alice appreciated that art had its own language, but there was something rather 'emperor's new clothes' about it, to quote Mrs Doulton. Not that you could ever voice such a heretical view in this neck of the woods. Art and its value were subjective and if people were willing to pay, then let them pay. These billionaires and multi-millionaires had to spend their money on something, although it seemed unfair to Alice that, in her experience, very few of the artists were ever as rich as the dealers and gallerists who promoted them.

'Let's go and have a look, shall we?' she said to Agatha, before redirecting the office phone to her mobile. It would be the last time she'd be here in the office – probably until the new year and, as she locked up, she rested her hand on the glass panel of the front door and gave a silent little thank you to the business for seeing her through another year.

After a brisk fifteen-minute walk, she and Agatha reached the black marble frontage of Alex Messent's art gallery. It had that hiding-in-plain-sight kind of anonymity – a place for people in the know.

She walked slowly past, peeping in through the tinted glass windows as Agatha took a pee on its black marble step, before she pulled her away, embarrassed. The gallery was clearly filled with the kind of art that graced the walls of the Messents' home. She was tempted to go inside. She doubted somewhere so high end would allow dogs, but what was the harm in brazening it out and just having a look?

But the sign on the door was switched round to closed, which struck Alice as odd, as it was the Friday before Christmas, and so surely the perfect time to be open, when the rich, always pressed for time, liked to flash their money around.

'Come on, Agatha,' she said, tugging the lead.

It was only then that she caught a glimpse of someone at the back of the gallery. A man in a suit – tall with black hair. Perhaps Alex Messent? She couldn't tell. But now, as he turned around, laughing, she saw that it was indeed the man from the photo in the house, and he was holding out a glass of champagne towards someone. Alice could only see the bottom half of this second person – a woman in white trousers. So, Monsieur Messent was indeed *busy*, Alice thought, but not necessarily in the way

Enya had assumed. Just as soon as she'd had this slightly sala-cious thought, Alice checked herself. She mustn't go jumping to conclusions. This could even be Madame Messent inside. Or it might well be the case that he'd closed the gallery in order to sell a painting to a private client.

A text pinged in her pocket. It was Jinx telling her to pick her up from Tiffany's. Her beautician, not the jeweller.

Alice smiled. It wasn't the first time that Jinx had been waylaid at Tiff's where she loved to gossip, and it almost certainly wouldn't be the last.

I hope you don't mind, but I brought the Tiffin from the freezer, Jinx texted. **She was delighted. Tiffin for Tiffany!** Alice rolled her eyes.

Tiffin was one of the first recipes Mrs Doulton had taught her as a child. Alice had written out the recipe in an exercise book and the chocolate-daubed paper still lived between the leaves of her Mrs Beeton. It was really just a case of melting chocolate and mixing in the other ingredients, but it was always a crowd pleaser.

Tiffin

INGREDIENTS – 2½ oz golden syrup, 3½ oz unsalted butter, diced, 6 oz milk chocolate roughly chopped, 4½ oz dark chocolate, roughly chopped, 8 oz crisp amaretti biscuits, crushed, 3½ oz Maltesers, 2½ oz raisins, 2 oz dates finely chopped, 1 oz candied peel, handful of chopped pistachio nuts.

METHOD – *Line the base and sides of 8in cake tin with baking paper. Combine the golden syrup, butter, milk chocolate and dark chocolate in a medium-large heat-proof bowl set over a pan of barely simmering water. Stir from time to time until the ingredients are nearly all melted and smooth. Remove from the heat, stir until smooth and leave to cool for 5 minutes. Meanwhile, combine the crushed biscuits with the Maltesers and fruit in a large mixing bowl. Pour the melted chocolate mixture into the bowl and, using a rubber spatula, mix to combine thoroughly. Scoop the mixture into the prepared tin and spread level using the back of a spoon. Chill for one hour until firm and then cut into portions to serve.*

Makes ten to twelve pieces.
Store in the freezer.
Seasonable at any time, but particularly at Christmas.

Tiffany's salon was on a lovely parade of shops in the heart of Belgravia, and this close to Christmas, they'd all gone to town with glorious decorations in their shopfront displays.

Alice stopped to admire an arch of blue and silver lights in a winter wonderland-themed window, gazing in delight at a crystal-covered princess dress on a mannequin below, whilst at the same time thinking how impractical a dress like that would be to move in. She caught sight of her reflection in her trusted, ancient Burberry mac in the window and wondered when was the last time she'd had reason to wear anything at all apart from her bland sensible clothes? Wouldn't it be wonderful to have somewhere swanky to go to? To actually dress up for once, but as quickly as she'd had it, she dismissed the thought. There was no good in envying other people's lives, hard as it was not to sometimes.

Tiffany's salon was at the end of the parade and Alice spotted Jinx in the seat nearest the window. She waved enthusiastically at Alice to come inside, and Alice didn't need a second invitation, grateful to be out of the cold.

'What do you think?' Jinx asked, spinning around in the old-fashioned barber's chair and cupping her hand under her hair, which to Alice's mind looked exactly the same as it had yesterday.

'It's lovely.'

'Not too blonde?'

'Is there such thing?' Alice asked, making Jinx laugh. A lot. Ah, she'd been drinking, Alice deduced, seeing two empty champagne glasses on the counter below the huge round mirror surrounded by movie-star lightbulbs.

'Tiff!' she called. 'Alice is here.'

A petite, buxom, black-haired woman at the back of the salon, who was busily inspecting a woman's headful of foils, waved across and smiled.

'Right there, honey,' she called.

There was a lot about Tiffany Wills that reminded Alice of Dolly Parton. The boobs, for one thing. The big hair, for another. But even more than that, it was the American accent that did it, a kind of exaggerated Southern drawl that somehow lent itself well to compliments. 'Don't you just look peachy,' was one of Tiffany's favourites.

'Alice, I swear to God you don't change,' she now said, kissing her on both cheeks, although Alice wasn't sure whether this was a good thing or not. After all, Tiffany was in the business of change.

'How are the boys?' Alice asked after Tiff had exalted over the tiffin, which Jinx had at least had the courtesy to tell her was Alice's creation.

'Terrorists,' Tiffany said in a deadpan way. 'But then they always were. But at least they're working. That's something, I guess. Max is at the gym and Elijah is an actual bouncer now. Like his father. Not that I ever wanted either of them to have anything to do with that scumbag, but I guess he's their daddy so what's a girl to do?'

Tiffany had indulged in a fling with a nightclub bouncer when she'd been twenty-two and had produced two enormous twin boys, who Alice and Jinx had first met when they were still tiny. Alice had babysat them once when they'd got older and bigger and Tiffany had picked them up with a knowing look on her face. 'I know. I know. I should hire them out as contraception, right?' she'd said.

But that was then, and once her sons had left home, thanks to her tenaciousness, exceptional energy and sheer force of will, Tiffany now had what she'd always dreamed of, her own little beauty empire where ladies – and some men – in the know, came for an array of the latest treatments.

'I was telling Tiffany about the Messents,' Jinx said.

'Quite the toast of the town,' Tiffany said. 'Apparently, their house is stuffed to the gills with priceless art.'

'It is. I went there,' Alice said.

'Did you?' Tiff looked impressed. 'When?'

She told Jinx and Tiffany about her visit to Enya and how she seemed to have fitted right in.

'Apparently, they're having a big New Year's Eve party,' Tiffany said. 'I'm booked out solid.'

'I know.'

Jinx stuck out her bottom lip at Alice. 'Why do you always know everything first?'

'Enya was on the phone to Charles Tavistock,' Alice admitted.

'Oh, typical! Of course, *he*'d get the gig. But did you know Alex Messent also owns an art gallery?' Jinx said, clearly having only just learned this from Tiffany herself.

Alice decided not to trump Jinx again in front of Tiffany, so didn't admit she'd just come from snooping round there too.

'Here. Look. I got a screenshot of their Christmas card,' Tiffany said, opening her large phone in its gaudy leopard print case.

Alice took it and examined the picture of the Messents in their study. Alex Messent sat below a beautiful watercolour painting, with the same woman in the photos in the house, his wife Camille, his hand on her shoulder.

Sitting on the front of the desk, nearer to the camera, was Laura. She was wearing ripped fishnets above twelve-hole Doc Martin boots.

'She looks like trouble,' Jinx said, grabbing the phone to zoom in on Laura, whose eyes were scornful and sullen. 'I was a nightmare at that age.'

'As I well remember,' Alice said to Tiffany.

Jinx laughed and handed the phone back to Alice who studied the picture for a moment more.

'They've hired in caterers for the party, apparently,' Tiffany said, sliding the phone into her tunic pocket. 'Justin. You know, Justin Ellis?'

'Hmm,' Jinx said. 'So, there's obviously going to be no expense spared. Oh, and Alice, guess who's on the guest list?'

'Everyone who is anyone, I should imagine,' Alice said. Although she knew from experience that someone, somewhere, always got left off the guest list and took offence.

'That's as may be, but I heard that Laars Tredeaux is on the list.'

'Laars as in . . . ' Alice began.

'My no-good dirty ex,' Jinx confirmed.

Husband number two, then, Alice remembered. He hadn't stuck around for long. In fact, all Alice could really remember about him was that he'd worn a white tuxedo with a black frill to some event. Oh yes, that was it. His wedding. A frou-frou affair in Holland Park, as she recalled.

'He's living in London? I thought he buggered off to Hong Kong?'

'He did. But he's back and apparently footloose and fancy free again, after whoever it was he married next,' Jinx said, taking an angry swig of her champagne glass. 'After they no doubt discovered what an unfaithful, dishonest—'

'It was a long time ago, Jinx,' Tiffany interrupted. 'We're over that. Remember, hon?'

Jinx put her glass down and nodded. Alice smiled, knowing that Tiffany doubled as a shrink for most of her customers.

'I mean, when I think back . . . ' Jinx said, staring off into space, 'I knew from the get-go it was doomed. He always wore socks in bed.'

Tiffany laughed. 'Maybe he got cold feet.'

'I'd say socks in bed is admissible after a good twenty years of marriage, but keep the flame alive, boys.'

'You have very high standards, Jinx,' Alice said.

'I resent that.'

'Darlin', I don't care a rat's hoot about the socks,' Tiffany said. 'Just a man in bed. That's good enough for me.'

She made eyes at Alice, whose eyebrows shot up.

'Oh, Alice, don't look like that, honey,' Tiffany said, stretching a manicured hand towards Alice. 'You got all those frown lines. You want me to give you a little pep whilst you're here, hon?'

'Thank you, but no. I'm fine as I am,' Alice said, ducking backwards. She felt protective towards her wrinkles. They'd been years in the making. 'Come on, Jinx, we can't be late for lunch.'

'Orders from the boss, I gotta run,' Jinx said, hopping down off her chair and kissing Tiffany goodbye.

'Aren't you two just my favourites,' Tiffany said, hugging them both before they left. 'Oh, and I got a feeling good things are coming your way, Alice,' she said.

Jinx squealed and for a moment Alice wondered why, before remembering that Jinx believed wholeheartedly in Tiffany's clairvoyant abilities, even though Alice suspected these made-up suppositions were just a sales ruse.

'You mark my words, honey,' she said, before tapping her perfect nose and pointing at Alice. 'This year all your dreams will come true.'

9.

Alice's car might have had a recent service, but it really wasn't up to dealing with the 'beast from the east', as the papers were dubbing this weather system. The heater of the tiny MG was barely making any difference against the freezing conditions as she drove south out of London. The song on the ancient crackly radio was about driving home for Christmas, but Alice was seriously worried that, at this rate, she wasn't going to make it at all.

Sitting forward, she gripped the black steering wheel, her teeth chattering, as she peered through the vortex of slushy snow coming towards her as the motorway gave way to the A23. Agatha, oblivious to everything, slept soundly on the passenger's seat, tucked up beneath Alice's scarf. The flashing lights of an AA van up head blinded her momentarily as she passed a slewed lorry, which had crashed into a car.

'Oh God. Poor people,' she muttered, gripping the wheel even tighter and glancing anxiously in the rear-view mirror.

The back seat was crammed full of her bags, presents and a teetering pile of Tupperware boxes containing all the Christmas food. She'd had such a bad hangover yesterday after her Christmas lunch with Jinx, which had gone on late into the evening, that she'd had to cook all of last night and her eyes now pinched with tiredness.

The visibility got even worse once she'd turned off into the winding country roads, so much so she almost missed the turning for Hawthorn. She tensed, knowing there was a terrifyingly steep bit of hill to come.

She changed gear into first and put her foot down, willing the car to the top of the hill. She only just made it and veered dangerously left, the back tyres slipping out beneath her on the black ice as she turned into the last lane that would lead her home. The jolt woke Agatha who barked, immediately alert, and Alice reached behind her to stop the boxes tumbling. God only knew if her plum pudding had made it intact.

'Almost there,' Alice reassured Agatha, who now had her feet on the dashboard, her tail wagging. The snow was battering down in thick flakes, the little windscreen wipers struggling to keep up.

The car clanked as Alice navigated the potholes, fretting that they were going to get stuck at any moment. She knew the trees in this lane like the veins on the back of her hand, but in the dark, everything seemed unfamiliar, and it gave her a little shock when she arrived at the drive.

When Pop-Pop and GG were alive, the large wrought-iron gates, with their swirls and spikes had always been locked, the key hidden behind a brick in the small gatehouse. In her parents' day, they'd always been closed but kept unlocked, mainly because there were too many visitors going back and forth. But now the old gates were rusty and off their hinges altogether and propped up against the stone pillars. There was the start of what looked like some wiring work going and she remembered Jasper talking about an elaborate plan for electric gates. Another project that had clearly been abandoned.

Alice turned into the drive and drove past the high privet hedges, which had once been splendidly sculpted, but were now overgrown and unkempt.

The front part of Hawthorn – or 'the money shot' as Jasper crudely liked to call it – had been built in 1652. With snow covering the mossy tiles on the roof, it looked picture-perfect, and Alice's heart gave a little leap of joy when she saw the lights on behind the familiar latticed windows. She exhaled dramatically and tickled Agatha's ears. They'd made it.

She stopped the car outside the front door and got out, her legs shaking from having been cramped in the cold. Agatha trotted over to the iron boot scraper. With no security, there was no way anyone inside would have realised Alice had arrived and she took a moment to turn her face up into the snow and enjoy the distinct smell of Hawthorn – fresh air laden with a tang from the tall pines and ancient yews. She did a girlish twirl. Snow in London was one thing, but here in the country it was an altogether more exciting affair.

She grabbed her handbag from the car and walked up to the iron-studded oak door, noticing that the wreath on it was gaudy and modern, with . . . *plastic* ivy? Alice peered in closely at the aberration. With the fields lined with hedgerows, Hawthorn was a Christmas wreath-maker's paradise according to Mrs Doulton. But that was Sassy all over. She rarely saw what was beneath her nose.

Alice resolved not to be critical, or at least not verbally so. She rapped the large iron knocker with her signature rat-a-tat-tat and, a few moments later, the door opened.

Sassy, who tried to always live up to her name, was wearing skinny white jeans and black high heels, and her face was plastered in full make-up. Her honey-blonde tresses hung in waves over the shoulder of her fitted red Christmas jumper.

'She's here,' she shouted, pulling Alice towards her onto the doorstep and enveloping her in a cloud of pungent perfume. Alice winced, not least of all because Sassy's surgically enhanced breasts crushed into her like pound bags of flour, but also because she always felt so shabby by comparison.

'You made it then. Come in,' Sassy said it as if there'd been speculation that Alice might not have. When had she ever not done exactly what she said she would? Alice thought, cautioning herself not to take everything Sassy said the wrong way.

Agatha sniffed the doorstep suspiciously, before hopping over the threshold and past Sassy, nose snootily in the air. The door closed and Alice stamped the snow from her boots on the mat.

'There she is,' Jasper boomed, coming out of the library door. His cheeks were ruddy. He was four years younger than Alice but looked a decade older. He was dressed as a 1950s country squire might – in tweed trousers and a jacket, with a maroon jumper and clashing red cravat. He strode over, embracing her in bear hugs, lifting her up off the floor as he always did. He'd inherited their mother's tall genes and red hair, whilst she was petite and dark, like their father.

'Oh, God, put me down,' she managed. She hated it that he always picked her up like a child.

'Boys,' he boomed, looking towards the wooden staircase, almost deafening her. 'Aunty Alice is here.'

'They won't hear you,' Sassy tutted, before confiding to Alice,

'They have these new headsets and, mercifully, it keeps them quiet. Except when the internet drops out. Which is *all the time*,' she added pointedly, shooting a withering look at her husband. 'Another thing on our list that Jasper has promised he'll fix.'

And that I'll have to pay for, Alice thought, although she couldn't voice it. Sassy didn't have the first clue that it was Alice keeping her whole lifestyle afloat. She'd been tempted on so many occasions to blurt out the truth, but Jasper had begged her not to let slip. He had every intention of returning everything he'd ever borrowed from her, he'd repeatedly promised – with interest . . . twice over.

But these assurances were running thin. And she'd already firmly impressed upon him that the last time had been *the last* time. What she'd not yet told him – probably out of pride as his older sister – was that she'd been forced to secure this final chunk of money from a private lender at hideous interest and with the threat of escalating late payment penalties, which was still a worrying possibility. She needed to have 'the chat' with Jasper about exactly when he was paying her back.

But now, as they walked to the kitchen and Jasper put his arm around her, their financial relationship was clearly the last thing on his mind. She let herself be cajoled by his cheeriness, keen to hold onto the flutter of Christmas cheer that was building up inside her. But then, she stopped in the doorway, her mouth falling open.

The kitchen at Hawthorn Hall had always been her happy place. The place she most associated with Mrs Doulton. The place she'd learnt to cook. But the familiar cupboards and surfaces had been replaced by a modern kitchen in an ugly brown melamine, which didn't go at all with the grey flagstone floor.

'Isn't it wonderful!' Sassy exclaimed, leaning forward in

a conspiratorial whisper. 'We got it . . . ' she mouthed the next words silently, fanning out her hand with their long red gel nails, 'for free.'

'Someone was throwing out a whole kitchen. In the manor up the road. And it's virtually brand new,' Jasper added, with a delighted guffaw. 'Can you imagine? Chucking out a perfectly decent kitchen?'

'It's elephant's breath,' Sassy added, as if Alice might know what that meant. Although to Alice's mind, now realising she must mean the colour, she decided it might be much more readily associated with the other end of the aforementioned beast.

'What happened to the old kitchen?' Alice asked, trying to recover.

'Oh, that old thing,' Sassy said, waving her hand and laughing, her cleavage bulging up and down beneath the V-neck of her jumper. 'We had to pay someone to take it to the dump.'

Alice fought down another lump in her throat. Those antique wooden butchers' blocks, and marble slabs were probably worth a fortune. She stared at the cast-iron range. Probably too heavy to move. So at least they hadn't got rid of that.

'Chop chop. Open the champers, darling,' Jasper ordered, and Sassy trotted over to the fridge.

'Look! American style,' Sassy said, with a giggle. 'An icemaker and everything.'

Alice could really have done with a cup of tea after the long drive, but something stronger might get her over this feeling that something precious had been lost forever.

'Boys,' Jasper bellowed. 'Boys!'

A moment later, Alice heard her nephews bounding down the stairs, scuffling as they did so.

Woody, who was holding his brother Baxter at arm's length, came in laughing, clearly having won some sort of race. He was fourteen and already as tall as Sassy in her heels, and was sporting bumfluff and spots. Sassy got hold of his chin, turning him to face Alice.

'Can you believe this one?' she said. 'Look at this acne. And Alice, a moustache!'

He broke away to hug Alice.

'I've grown one too, but don't tell anyone,' she whispered and he laughed.

Darcy, the family's fat grey and white cat, darted into the room, hissing viciously at Agatha, who quickly hid behind Alice's legs, quaking.

'Oh, don't mind Darcy,' Sassy said. 'She'll get used to Agatha.'

Baxter put his arms around Alice's waist and squeezed her tightly and she hugged him back.

'Hello, you,' she said, her heart swelling with love. He was nearly twelve and yet to have the growth spurt of his brother. She kissed his mop of strawberry blond curls. He'd always been a cherub and it made her happy that at least there was one person in the house that was smaller than her.

'Come and help with Aunty Alice's things,' Jasper said.

'Did you make Christmas cake? The proper one?' Baxter asked.

'Of course.'

'Hurrah,' Jasper said, clapping his hands.

'And plum pudding?'

'It is Christmas, isn't it?'

'You're a marvel, Alice,' Jasper said. 'What would we do without you?'

Sassy wrapped her hand with its flashy red nails around the champagne cork.

'Give it here,' Jasper said, making to grab it.

'Too late,' Sassy laughed as the cork popped. 'Let the festivities begin.'

10.

As usual, Sassy had declared that Alice 'did Christmas Day best', allowing her to delegate all of the cooking and the responsibilities that went with it, whilst simultaneously sounding like she was doing Alice a favour. And whilst Alice didn't mind being in charge of the kitchen and knew it was better for everyone's stress levels if she saved Sassy from trying to cook, by half past twelve on Christmas Day she was starting to resent that she'd been stuck in the kitchen since the crack of dawn with very little help. Baxter, to be fair, had half-heartedly peeled a few sprouts a couple of hours ago, but Sassy had called him away to help with the table arrangements and he'd made a hasty getaway.

Half an hour after that, Sassy's parents and sisters had arrived to join the festivities, but Alice had only heard their raucous arrival. They were pleasant enough people, but unlike Alice, they'd arrived empty-handed and had followed Sassy's lead in treating Alice as if she were staff. Worse, they'd brought their two unruly Rhodesian ridgebacks, who'd frighted the living daylights out of Agatha. Already on red alert for ambushes from Darcy, Agatha had retreated to Alice's room near the old nursery on the top floor and Alice hoped she was OK up there.

She knew that Sassy wanted Alice to be thrilled that there was a new kitchen 'just for her', but it wasn't nearly as good as the old one and now, coming up to the most crucial part of the whole meal timing-wise, Alice puffed out a hot breath. Her apron was smeared with grease and her forearm smarted from where she'd burnt herself twice putting the China dishes in the bottom oven to warm. And to top it all, she'd only just remembered the pudding. It was going to need to go on now for a two-hour steam.

'Where's the bloody trivet?' Alice asked, rummaging in one of the drawers as Jasper came in with the ice bucket. He was serving pre-lunch drinks in the library.

'What are you talking about?'

'The little thing? You know? For the plum pudding. To stand in the pan? Mrs Doulton kept ours in the right-hand drawer here. When there was a drawer here . . . '

'I know you're upset about the kitchen, Alice,' Jasper said, exasperated, 'but please stop being so annoyed. You can't stop progress and what's done is done.'

Progress? Pah! Alice bit her lip. 'But you don't understand. The pudding will stick.'

'Stand it on something else.'

'Like what?' she asked, annoyed that she was being overtaken by another hot flush. Behind her there was loud rattling. She turned and consulted the orchestra of pans on the stove, lifting up the lid of the red cabbage and seeing it was done. The turkey was already resting on its platter on the side, under several tea towels and foils.

'It's five minutes away. Could you get everyone seated?'

'Yes, yes,' said Jasper. 'Calm down. All in good time.'

'Do *not*,' she finally snapped, 'tell me to calm down. I've been cooking for hours. The least you can do is ensure your guests get to enjoy it all whilst it's hot.'

Rolling his eyes, he saluted her as if she were a bossy sergeant and departed, booming that there were 'orders' from the kitchen for everyone to take their seats.

It was Woody who saved the day, procuring a couple of huge bolts from the shed to stand in the heavy-bottomed pan. He and Baxter helped serve everything, carrying through the beautiful china terrines filled with steaming carrots (glazed in the proper way, with butter and grated nutmeg), peas, savoy cabbage, stewed red cabbage, brussels sprouts fried with bacon, roasted parsnips, pigs in blankets, sausage-meat stuffing, bread sauce, gravy, and enough crispy roast potatoes to keep an army happy.

Alice watched Jasper carry the bronzed bird through to the dining room, and then washed her hands and took off her apron, wiping down the surface and checking the pudding was simmering.

Even if she did say so herself, it was a job jolly well done.

Ducking upstairs, she applied some lipstick and cajoled Agatha off the bed to come and join in.

She smiled as she entered the dining room where her family sat, serving themselves.

'Finally, you're here,' Sassy said, as if she was a teenager who'd been lolling around in their room glued to a screen. 'We can do the crackers now.'

Sassy insisted on everyone pulling their crackers at the same time and Agatha barked at all the noise, setting off the two ridgebacks, who were then banished to the library, thank God.

'Cheers,' Alice said, accepting the glass of champagne from Sassy with a smile, before tucking in, realising she was starving.

Sometime later, Alice was feeling full and rather fuzzy from the delicious Pinot Noir that Jasper had served when she remembered the pudding. She hurried through to the kitchen and gingerly unwrapped it, before sending Woody to fetch a bottle of brandy from the drinks trolley in the library. As she poured it over the top of the steaming pudding, she told him about how his distant ancestor Mrs Beeton had been uncharacteristically modest when she'd placed the words 'Very Good' under her recipe.

Christmas Plum-Pudding
(Very Good)

INGREDIENTS – 1 1/2 lb of raisins, 1/2 lb of currants, 1/2 lb of mixed peel, 3/4 lb of breadcrumbs, 3/4 lb of suet, 8 eggs, 1 wineglassful of brandy.

METHOD – Stone and cut the raisins in halves, but do not chop them; wash, pick, and dry the currants, and mince the suet finely; cut the candied peel into thin slices, and grate down the bread into fine crumbs. When all these dry ingredients are prepared, mix them well together, then moisten the mixture with the eggs, which should be well beaten, and the brandy; stir well, that everything may be very thoroughly blended, and press the pudding into a buttered mould; tie it down tightly with a floured *cloth, and boil for 5 or 6 hours. It may be boiled in a cloth without a mould and will require the same time allowed for cooking. As Christmas puddings are usually made a few days before they are required for the table, when the pudding is taken out of the pot, hang it up immediately, and put a plate or saucer under to catch the water that may drain from it. The day it is to be eaten, plunge it into boiling water, and keep it boiling for at least 2 hours; then turn it out of the mould, and serve with brandy-sauce. On Christmas Day a sprig of holly is usually placed in the middle of the pudding, and about a wineglassful of brandy poured round it, which at the moment of serving, is lighted, and the pudding thus brought to table encircled in flame.*

Time – 5 or 6 hours the first time of boiling; 2 hours the day it is to be served.

Average cost, 4s.

Sufficient for a quart mould for 7 or 8 persons

Seasonable on 25th of December, and on various festive occasions till March.

Note – Five or six of these puddings should be made at any one time, as they will keep good for many weeks, and in cases where unexpected guests arrive, 'twill be found an acceptable, and, as it only requires warming through, a quickly prepared dish. Moulds of every shape and size are manufactured for this pudding, and may be purchased of Messrs. R & J Slack, 336 Strand

She'd just lit the match to set the pudding on fire when Sassy trotted into the kitchen.

'Oh, let me, Alice,' she said, more of a command than a question, grabbing the flaming dish. 'Tell Daddy to get the lights,' she instructed Baxter.

She clip-clopped across the hall to the dining room on her high heels, a little wobbly from all the wine, and Alice heard the table-full of people erupt into a round of 'We Wish You a Merry Christmas'. They'd almost finished by the time Alice had joined them at the table, the last of the blue flames dying out.

As she sat down, she caught Woody's eye and he rose to his feet, surprising everyone. He tapped his spoon on the edge of his Coke glass.

'Can we raise a toast to Aunty Alice, please,' he said. He looked accusingly at his parents, who after the briefest of embarrassed pauses, lifted their glasses and the table chimed with 'To Alice'.

Too little, a little too late, but Alice supposed it would have to do. Smiling round the table, she blew her nephew a grateful kiss.

11.

Boxing Day was traditionally Alice's favourite of all the Christmas days, when she'd finished all her kitchen duties and could finally relax and crack open the chocolates. But this year, she was on edge having failed to have the necessary chat with Jasper about their finances. She started the day full of apprehension and with a fuzzy head from the booze-fuelled game of Articulate that had gone on until midnight.

The snow was melting as she donned her wellies for a bracing walk with Baxter and Agatha to clear her head. But seeing more and more of her brother's half-finished projects scattered around the grounds only made her more nervous. She knew Hawthorn always looked a little skeletal in late December, but she couldn't help feeling sad at the aberration of the kitchen garden, which had once been Mrs Doulton's pride and joy. It was now both patchy and overgrown, not to mention the half-demolished stone wall and the rotting greenhouse with its broken glass panes.

When they went through the squeaky gate in the hedge to the fields beyond, her sense of dismay and disappointment only increased when she saw that the Christmas tree crop that Jasper had assured her was a winner, was in fact – owing to the trees' stunted heights and their continued presence here on Boxing Day — yet another financial flop.

After a late lunch of turkey sandwiches and mince pies — a meal rustled up by Sassy with much fanfare — Alice spotted her opportunity to retreat to the library. The interminable goodbyes with Sassy's parents and sisters were just too much and Agatha, having been harassed by their dogs all day, was clearly in need of some sanctuary too.

With her back to the door, Alice sunk into one of the ancient wing-backed chairs in front of the fire, glad to be finally alone. Agatha did little circles on the threadbare silk rug and slumped down with an exhausted sigh and was almost instantly asleep. Alice settled back, looking around the familiar room, fiddling with her spinner necklace.

Along with the grand hall next door, this room had a higher ceiling than the rest of the house and always felt stately. It was particularly magnificent now with the late afternoon sun streaming in through the latticed windows. But the russet-toned William Morris wallpaper their grandmother had put up was speckled with mould and the matching curtains were tattered and frayed. Above her, the incongruous Louis XIV chandelier on the ceiling was so dusty and the ceiling so cracked, it looked like it might cascade smashing to the floor at any moment.

Working as she often did with people who'd come into extreme wealth, Alice had secretly staved off her own sense of inferiority by drawing the age-old distinction between old money and new. Old money, in her book, had always been more respectable, although after several heated debates with Helly in the office, she'd realised that this received view didn't really bear much scrutiny. Helly was quick to point out that the people with 'old money' often had it because they'd exploited other people down the generations, from slavers onwards. Alice's ancestors' money had come from the noble profession of printing, but even so, Helly's arguments had stuck.

Besides, what did 'old' or 'new' money mean anyway in regard to Hawthorn? Wasn't 'no money' discomfortingly more on the nail? It was simply shabby. Falling to rack and ruin. The house that her grandparents had lovingly restored was now tatty with plaster cracks, its roof tiles missing, its outbuildings collapsing, and its guttering falling off at weird angles. In the corner of her bedroom upstairs, the mildewed paint bubbled like a medieval plague, and the bathroom walls flaked like sunburn. It was a travesty that Sassy and Jasper had let it get into this state, despite her pouring money into it. But it had been like pouring it into a sieve, she realised now.

A few minutes later, Agatha raised one eyebrow, as the door quickly opened and closed, but Alice couldn't muster the energy to greet whoever it was who'd also decided to seek sanctuary in here too.

Jasper peeped around the chair and grinned.

'Oh, good. It's you,' he whispered. 'Won't they ever leave?'

She smiled as he walked over to the fire, drawing her feet up underneath her out of childhood habit, her knees to her chin.

She'd shown Woody the spyhole behind the fireplace earlier and she looked towards it now as Jasper used the old-fashioned leather bellows to reinvigorate the flames. She wondered if her nephews were already spying on them, like she and Jasper had done once on their parents.

'Can I offer you a sharpener?' Jasper asked, pouring himself a hefty scotch from the crystal decanter.

'No, thanks,' she said, watching him squirt a little soda from the syphon they'd once had a spray fight with. It was one of the only times Alice could remember Mrs Doulton shouting. This room had always been out of bounds when they'd been children and it still felt special to be in here.

She watched as Jasper came to sit in the leather wing-backed chair opposite and there was an awkward pause.

'So, now that we're on our own . . . ' she began.

'Oh,' he sighed. 'I know what you're going to say, Alice.' He held up his hand like a belligerent policeman. 'I've been waiting for this, but it's not my fault about the trees. I was misinformed. You'd have made the same mistake. How was I to know when I planted them that the damn things would only make it to a metre tall?'

'Have you tried to get your money back?' Alice said.

Jasper jumped up, pacing in front of her. 'Of course I have. But it's hopeless. What's done is done.'

'But, Jasper, you promised you'd have the money by now. By Christmas.' She tried to keep her tone gentle, but a sense of panic was rising. She'd convinced herself that Jasper's laid-back manner over the last couple of days might be because he'd found a solution, but now the scales fell from her eyes.

'I know I did, Sis, I know.' He said it sadly, as if it were some divinely miserable fate they were both discussing, and nothing of his own making. She knew he only called her 'Sis' when he was trying to get on her good side.

'You're the one with a job,' he said, as though she'd somehow

75

lucked out on this, while he'd been unfairly denied. 'You don't know how expensive this place is, and *they* are—' he nodded towards the door '—to run.'

Alice bristled. Her nephews weren't engines. They were people. 'You could get a job. It's not that hard,' she said.

'Doing what? I don't have a qualification to my name. And anyway, nobody wants to employ a white middle-aged man these days. We're *personae non grata*, if you hadn't heard. Cancelled, I think is the modern term.'

What rot, Alice thought. He just needed to get off his arse.

'And I've cut back as much as I can. I mean, have mercy, Alice. The boys go to state school. *State school*,' he said, in a mortified whisper.

Again, ridiculous. But his big concession, she knew, because Sassy still hated the fact.

'As they should,' Alice said, curtly. 'That high school has splendid results and all the facilities they'd get at a private school.'

'I knew you'd be like this,' he said, petulantly.

Alice felt an indignant flush break out. 'I'm not "being" like anything,' she said, her voice quivering. 'I've helped you as much as I can. You know I have. Maybe it's time you faced the inevitable.'

He looked at her. 'What do you mean?'

'Much as I hate to say this . . . maybe you should . . . I don't know . . . *sell* the place.'

The sentence hung between them like a thundercloud. There was a lump in her throat as Jasper's eyes met hers, but before he could respond, the door burst open.

'I hate these bloody things,' Sassy said, breaking the moment.

She was holding some sort of remote control. 'The backs always disappear, and they lose their sodding batteries all the time. Have you got any AAs, Jas?' She looked between Alice and Jasper. 'What?' she said, picking up on the tension.

'Nothing,' Jasper said, breaking away and walking towards her. 'I'm all out. The kids raided the last lot for their controllers,' he said.

'World War Three is breaking out up there.'

'I'll go to the shop at the garage,' Alice suggested.

Alice was glad to get away and Woody offered to come with her, clearly happy with the break too. He sat in the front of her MG with Agatha on his lap as Alice negotiated the piles of slush in the lane.

'I like it when you're here,' Woody said as they turned out onto the road. He tickled Agatha's ear tips, making her make a sound like a cat's purr. Alice didn't know if he was talking to her, or Agatha.

'We like it here too.'

'It's just they behave when you're here.'

'Who?'

'Mum and Dad. Otherwise, they bicker and fight all the time.'

This was news to Alice. 'Every married couple argues,' she said.

'I suppose. But they really shout. Mum gets very cross.'

'I love your father dearly, but he can be rather frustrating.'

'She's always banging on about how she wants to get away. How she needs a "proper holiday". Not that she really does anything to deserve one.'

Alice felt a dart of love for her astute nephew. It was gratifying to see that he'd noticed Sassy's indolence, but even so, she felt compelled to defend the grown-ups.

'It's a difficult house to run,' she said.

'I know. She says she wishes she had a modern house.'

Alice bristled. And all this time she'd been busy ruining Hawthorn without even wanting it? Sassy didn't realise how lucky she was. But now Alice panicked that her comment to Jasper might get back to Sassy. About selling Hawthorn. Because what if they actually did? What then? Seeing it as a financial solution was one thing, but losing it forever was something else entirely — something that would break her heart.

She drove into the little town and parked in the Spar, getting cash out of her purse and handing it over to Woody.

'Buy yourself some sweets,' she said, feeling silly. She'd always spoilt the boys when they'd been little. But now she realised that Woody was too old for sweets. 'Or chewing gum. A can of Monster. Whatever,' she said, raising an eyebrow as he blushed. 'And don't forget the batteries.'

'You don't have to. I've got money on my card—'

'Go on. It's fine.'

He reluctantly took the ten-pound note and she watched him walking to the shop, her heart aching for the little boy who'd long gone.

Her phone rang and she jumped, picking it up to look at the screen. It was an unfamiliar number.

'Hello?'

'Miss Beeton?'

'Yes?'

'It's Enya. Enya from the Messents'.'

'Oh, hello, Enya. How are you?' Alice smiled, realising that she'd almost completely forgotten about work for the last twenty-four hours.

'Oh, Miss Beeton, I'm so pleased to have got you.'

'Is everything all right?'

'It's Justin. Justin Ellis.'

'What about him?' Alice asked, thinking of the suave celebrity caterer.

'He's had an accident. Skiing.'

'Oh dear. That's terrible.'

'Yes, but he's also just called to say he can't cater the New Year's Eve party and Madame is very distressed. I said you'd probably know someone who could help at short notice?'

Alice felt a warm glow at the compliment. At least someone thought her advice was worth listening to. 'Actually, I do happen to know someone,' she said. 'Jacques.'

'Who?'

'Don't worry. He's wonderful. Really, the best chef I know. Leave it with me.'

'Oh, thank you so much.'

'You're welcome.'

'Oh, but Miss Beeton, do tell him that Thérèse is extremely allergic to seafood.'

'I'm sure that won't be a problem. He caters for all sorts of diets.'

'Oh, I knew you'd help,' Enya said, gratefully, and sounding deeply relieved. She was about to ring off, but Alice stopped her with a question.

'How was your Christmas?' Alice asked.

'Oh. Fine. I was mostly with Laura. We had dinner on our laps in front of a film.'

'A TV dinner?' Alice couldn't keep the horror from her voice.

'Monsieur Messent was partly away on business and they don't seem to spend much time together as a family.'

The poor young girl, Alice thought. In that art gallery of a house. Thank goodness she had kind Enya for company.

When she hung up, Alice's phone pinged again, this time with a message from Jinx. **It's been liked more times than anything she's ever posted**. Alice was confused for a moment until she opened the screenshot of Sassy's Instagram.

'Christmas traditional style!' Sassy had written over a still from a video of her bringing in Alice's plum pudding.

12.

Alice was relieved to get back to London.

Things with Jasper had been strained after their conversation and Alice had left an evening earlier than she'd intended. She didn't want to come to blows with her brother about money, but after Sassy's post, she'd felt annoyed in a way she couldn't shake. It was the sense that she'd been taken advantage of – and worse, that she only had herself to blame.

She threw herself into distraction techniques, tidying up her office, deleting emails and checking that Jacques was doing a good job for the Messents. But by New Year's Eve, she'd recovered her sense of humour and Barney accepted her invitation to spend the evening playing Scrabble, although they'd both agreed that they were going to be in their separate beds by 10.30 p.m.

Alice had made her fake foie gras pâté to start, a recipe she'd torn out of a magazine, made a few adjustments to and squirrelled away in her *Book of Household Management* for just this occasion.

Fake foie gras

INGREDIENTS – 1 shallot, finely diced, 4 cloves garlic, thinly sliced, 4 tbsp good olive oil, 2 tsp rosemary finely chopped, 2 tsp sage, finely chopped, 2 tsp thyme, finely chopped, 24 button mushrooms, 2 tbsp cognac, 2 tbsp soy sauce, 400g cooked puy lentils, 150g toasted walnuts, 2 tbsp beetroot purée, 2 tbsp butter, salt and pepper.

METHOD – sauté the button mushrooms in half the oil until translucent, add the chopped garlic and chopped herbs. Turn up the heat and add the cognac, then add soy sauce and cook on low heat for 6 minutes. Let the pan cool. Tip the mixture into a bowl and use a stick blender to blend. Add the cooked lentils, the rest of the oil, walnuts, beetroot pureé and black pepper until smooth. Add a glug more cognac to loosen if desired. Place in glass jar and pour over melted butter. Refrigerate for 2 hours.

Serve with slices of homemade sourdough bread.
Seasonable at any time.

The pâté was a hit, as was the partridge pie made with the game Jasper had come back with from the shoot on the estate next door just before she'd left. She'd served it with champ and kale and had followed it with a simple blackberry compote for dessert. Barney had brought a delicious cheese platter, a miniature bottle of special Spanish port to go with it and some exquisite truffle chocolates that a friend in Paris had sent him for Christmas.

Fully replete and sitting by the small fire in her sitting room, Alice lolled against the sofa next to Agatha, who was laid out on the rug fast asleep, her soft pink belly in the air. As Barney's delicious port hit her system, she found herself off-loading about Sassy and her selfishness and the post about the plum pudding, which had been the final straw. It sounded petty as she recalled it, but it still rankled. Particularly the hashtag #SugarPlumFairy.

'Families are always tricky,' he said, looking from the board and back to the letters on his wooden tray, lifting them close to his face and wrinkling his nose in concentration. 'My sisters used to drive Honey up the wall.'

'I know I'm being mean. And I guess that Sassy is a good mother in her way. I don't know . . . I just always come away from Hawthorn feeling so used.'

Alice took another sip of the port, as Barney thoughtfully placed his word to make a stack.

'Oh, very clever,' she said, secretly cursing him for stealing her next move.

'Seventeen,' he said.

'You're missing the double word score,' she said, which she knew full well he hadn't.

'Oh, yes. So, I have,' he said, sitting back, and Alice totted up his score and wrote it in pencil on the little spiral-bound notepad resting on the deep-red velvet ottoman. As usual, he was trouncing her. But she didn't mind.

JOSIE LLOYD

'And then there was the thing Woody said – about his parents not getting on.'

Barney sighed. 'It seems to me, Alice, that you're spending a lot of time worrying about something over which you have no control.'

'I know. You're right. But it was gratifying to know that he realises how lazy she is. She's just not a very good housekeeper.'

Barney smiled at her. 'And that is the perfect point on which to give you your present.'

Alice had already spotted the package when he'd come in and left it on the low table beside the sofa. She'd been eyeing it all evening.

'It's rather a special one, if I say so myself,' he said, handing it over.

'Intriguing.' Alice smiled. It was flimsy and thin and, below the red paper, she realised it was a magazine wrapped in crisp tissue paper. Alice gasped. It was an original *Beeton's Christmas Annual*. The title on the front was 'A Study in Scarlet' by A. Conan Doyle, with a picture of a young man in red switching off a lamp by a desk.

'It was published in eighteen eighty-seven,' Barney said, smiling at Alice's reaction. 'Most copies of his first four stories were found in people's homes in the *Christmas Annual* and not as novels.'

'I knew the Beetons published him, but it's wonderful to see this.'

'They gave him his start. We wouldn't have Sherlock Holmes without your ancestors. They were the ones who recognised that we all love solving crimes.'

'It's the perfect present,' Alice said, grinning at Barney. 'Spot on.'

'Oh, and there's one more little thing,' he said, handing her a tiny package. 'For your collection.'

'Oh, goody,' she said, already guessing it must be one of the tiny models he specialised in making from matchsticks. Carefully unwrapping the silver crepe paper, her smile grew even wider. 'It's Agatha!'

And it was. A freakishly lifelike rendition of her little dog made from tiny, trimmed pieces of wood. Kneeling up, she kissed Barney's cheek, then still walking on her knees, went to the small Christmas tree by the bookcase, bent over and took out a present from underneath it.

'And I have something for you,' she said.

'What is it?' Barney asked, taking the package she'd wrapped in bubble wrap and gold paper.

'Guess.'

'It feels heavy. Like a pan. But why the long handle. And what's this?' he asked, feeling the dome in the centre.

He unwrapped it and laughed at the bag of netted chestnuts and the chestnut roasting pan, which was very much like a frying pan, except with holes in the bottom.

'Oh, how marvellous. Let's give it a try, shall we?'

Taking the penknife he always carried in his pocket, Barney slit the net bag and the chestnuts rattled into the pan. Alice put them on the fire and Barney knelt next to her, looking at the red coals. She thought of the lyric of the Christmas song about chestnuts roasting on an open fire and Jack Frost nipping at your nose, and acknowledged this cosy moment as probably her favourite of Christmas so far.

Suddenly there was a loud popping noise and Agatha leapt to her feet, barking in alarm.

'It's OK.' Alice laughed, picking up the long handle of the chestnut pan and giving it a shake. 'They smell good,' she said, looking at the charred nuts.

'Did you know that chestnuts are from Castanea in Thessaly, which gives them their Latin name?' Barney asked, going back to the board and picking the overturned letters one by one from the lid of the scrabble box. Barney never missed an opportunity to bring up his knowledge of the Latin names for plants and trees.

'No, I didn't,' Alice said. 'I know the Romans brought them over to Britain, though. It's a shame they're rather out of fashion in food. They've got the least oil and the most fibre of all nuts.'

'According to Mrs Beeton,' Barney teased.

'Yes, according to Mrs Beeton,' Alice said, before taking the pan and laying it gently on the green hearth tiles, keeping Agatha away so that she didn't burn her nose.

They ate the chestnuts and finished the game, the scores satisfyingly into the three hundreds. Barney won by twelve points.

'So, any resolutions?' she asked as she helped him put on his coat. Outside it was snowing heavily again.

'Oh, I never make resolutions,' Barney said, leaning down to kiss her on both cheeks. 'Life is too short. But you should make a resolution if I might suggest it?'

'What's that?'

'To let Jasper grow up and make his own mistakes.'

'Easier said than done.'

'Perhaps you should give it a try for once.'

Back inside, Alice cleaned up and made the kitchen spick and span, washing the floor as well. She knew she'd be much happier to wake up in the new year with it all fresh. Hopefully the plumber would be coming to sort out the leak in the ceiling, although Mr Mantis had questioned the owner upstairs who'd still sworn blind that there wasn't anything leaking in his flat. Even more annoyingly, Mr Mantis had refused to come and see the evidence himself. She glanced up. The dripping had stopped, but the ugly brown stain that had spread in concentric circles out from the ceiling rose looked grim.

She got into bed to read her book, but after the big meal and Barney's delicious port, her eyes were soon heavy and she must have dozed off, because when she woke up the phone was ringing and her light was still on.

'Hello?' she asked, blearily, turning around the little clock to see that it was 2 a.m. Who on earth called at 2 a.m.? Unless it was Jinx, squiffy and wanting to wish her a happy new year.

'Miss Beeton? Miss Alice Beeton?'

It was a man's voice. Gruff and impatient.

'Yes?'

'This is Detective Rigby of the Metropolitan Police.'

Alice struggled to sit up in bed, suddenly wide awake.

'Oh, goodness. What's happened? What's going on?'

'Miss Beeton, I'm sorry to disturb you in the middle of the night, but do you know Enya Fischer?'

'Enya. She's one of my staff. On my agency's books,' she stumbled. 'She's at the Messents' in Oxley Square.'

There was a small pause and Alice thought about her last communique with Enya, just yesterday, who'd been very pleased that Jacques was working out so well.

'I'm afraid there's been an incident,' the detective said.

'What kind of incident?' Her voice sounded husky.

'Miss Fischer has been . . . found dead.'

'What do you mean *dead*? How? Where?'

13.

Jinx finally picked up the third time Alice rang.

'Alice!' she shouted into the phone, causing Alice to wince and pull the phone away from her ear. 'Happy New Year, Happy New Year,' she sang in a silly voice. 'You're a dark horse, aren't you? You said you were going to have an early one,' she slurred. 'Don't tell me you let Barney have his wicked way. I'm sure he fancies you—'

'Where are you?' Alice asked, cutting her off.

Jinx laughed. 'You want to come and join us? I'm just at Ricardo's. We're playing drinking Jenga. Everyone's a bit smashed, to be honest.'

Alice regretted calling Jinx now, but she'd been so shocked by what Detective Rigby had just told her that she'd simply had to tell someone. She hadn't considered the fact that Jinx would still be out partying.

'No, it's not that. Jinx. Listen. I've had a call from the police.'

'What?' Jinx still had a laugh in her voice.

'The police,' Alice said loudly.

Jinx's voice changed. 'What did you say?'

'A Detective Rigby just rang.'

'Hang on . . . '

Alice gripped the phone as she listened to Jinx leaving the kitchen and shutting the door. The voices in the background were suddenly muffled.

'Did you say police?'

'Yes. This man . . . a detective. He rang. Asking questions about Enya. He wanted to know about her next of kin . . . ' Alice found her voice catching as she thought about Enya's parents. Intelligent, lovely people who were probably celebrating the new year with friends, or with other family members, not knowing that already this year might be the most awful of their lives. And did Enya have brothers, sisters, cousins, nieces and nephews? If Alice was this shaken up with only a small connection to Enya, how were those people closest to her going to feel?

'What? What do you mean?'

'Jinx, she's dead.'

It was such a relief to tell Jinx the shocking news, but saying it out loud herself made a sudden sob escape. This couldn't be happening. Not to poor, sweet Enya.

'Oh my God.' Jinx sounded suddenly very sober.

'I'm going to the Messents' now.'

'Are you OK, Alice?'

'No, not really.'

'I'll be right there.'

'Thank you,' Alice whispered, relieved that she could rely on her best friend.

★

Alice dressed quickly in tweed trousers and a cashmere jumper, her shearling coat and fur hat, but just as she was leaving, Agatha started barking, refusing to be left behind.

'Come on then,' Alice told her little dog. 'But I'm warning you. It'll be cold.'

At this time on New Year's morning there was no chance of a cab and really no point in calling for one, especially as it was snowing heavily. Out on the streets, there was hardly anyone around, but occasionally she'd hear raucous laughter as a door opened and a group of revellers spilled into the night. Otherwise, it was unnaturally still in these pre-dawn hours, her footsteps muffled in the snow. Agatha trotted dutifully by her side, her head down, as determined as Alice.

And all the while, Alice couldn't help picturing Enya and her lovely grey eyes and long blonde hair and intelligent smile. How could she possibly be dead? And more to the point, how could it have happened? The detective hadn't said accident, but rather had described what had happened to Enya as an 'incident'. Alice, a stickler for language, knew that in circumstances like these, there was an awfully big difference.

As if to confirm her worst fears, as she rounded the corner into Oxley Square, she saw two police cars parked at an angle and yellow police tape across the front of the Messents' porch. An officer was guarding the front door. Alice hurried towards her but suddenly Agatha yanked on her lead and shot down an alley at the side of the house.

'Agatha, what are you doing? Come back,' Alice said, her voice sounding strained and too loud at the same time. But Agatha was pulling most insistently, and she found herself hurtling past bins and drainpipes, until she came to the end of the alley, where a closed gate led into a large walled garden, pristine beneath a blanket of snow.

Looking through the gate, Agatha started whimpering and Alice saw why. Jacques was standing outside a basement service door in a gully at the back of the house in a square of orange light, smoking a cigarette, peering up through the curtain of snowflakes.

Agatha stopped and turned to give Alice a haughty look, but Jacques, spotting them now, hurried over to unlock the gate.

'Here, come in, quietly,' he said. 'I've been told to keep this locked. Oh, Miss B, I can't tell you how good it is to see a friendly face.' He led them back down the gully towards the basement door.

'Jacques, what on earth happened? A detective called me. Rigby? He said Enya's . . . '

But she couldn't say the word. Not again. Not to someone else who'd known her. But she didn't need to. Jacques nodded grimly and ground out his cigarette.

'I thought you'd given up?' she said.

'I only ever have the one. But come on. Come inside,' he said, taking Alice's arm. 'It's freezing out here.'

He led her through the back door and into a storage room piled high with caterer's crates, and Agatha pulled on her lead, nosing into an old-fashioned boot room on the left. Alice could see a couple of Barbour jackets hanging on the brass hooks and some pristine Hunter wellies on the worn bench below. To the right was a bigger room filled with two industrial-sized washing machines and two dryers. Alice shook off her coat and hat, both covered in snow, and hooked them on a peg.

Jacques led her on, past two giant wine fridges, into an industrial-sized kitchen. Alice presumed that there must be a more homely domestic kitchen for the Messents upstairs, because this one was rigged up for catering.

There were two induction ovens and two separate gas hobs, all with steel extractor fans above them, as well as state-of-the-art air fryers, several kitchen mixers, and a walk-in fridge and freezer. But any traces of food had long since been cleared away and the surfaces were gleaming.

With Agatha's nails skittering across the stone-flagged floor, Alice followed Jacques into a little office area separated from the rest of the kitchen by a glass divide. The walls were a stylish dark blue and there was a desk and some chairs. She suspected that this must have been where Enya had spent some of her time as housekeeper. There was a filing cabinet and a calendar on the wall, plus a laptop and several phones.

Jacques told Alice to sit down, but she was too jumpy to. Instead, she leant back against the wall, watching Jacques as he animatedly recounted what had happened earlier.

'I know there were lots of people here, but I didn't see any of them. Trudi, one of the service staff, who kept coming back for more trays of canapés, said there must have been two hundred or more in the ballroom. There was music and dancing, then at nine o'clock Camille Messent made a speech about her refugee charity. She called for a minute's silence to honour everyone killed in the war. But then everyone heard a terrible thud upstairs. Alex Messent went up to investigate and found Enya in his study. Dead.'

He shuddered and looked at Alice. 'I'd only seen her fifteen minutes before.'

'And how was she?'

'Totally normal. I didn't know her that well, but we shared a joke. She seemed fine.'

'So, what happened?'

'I don't know. I don't know why she was up there. Everyone else was either in the ballroom or here in the kitchen with me. It's strange because I know the study is out of bounds for the staff.'

'Out of bounds?'

'And always locked. I haven't been here long, but from what I can gather, the Messents seem to be quite paranoid about security. I suppose it's because they have such valuable art.'

Alice bit her lip, thinking, her eyes wandering to the door. Agatha had been there a moment ago, but now the door was open a crack and she'd gone.

'Hang on. Agatha?' she called, looking through the doorway to the kitchen and then the other way. 'Oh God, where's she gone?'

'Agatha?' Jacques called, joining Alice in the doorway in time for them both to see the small dog disappearing up a flight of stairs, her lead trailing behind her.

'Oh no,' Alice exclaimed, looking in horror at Jacques.

'Quick. Go grab her,' Jacques said. 'The police up there said they didn't want to be disturbed.'

Alice raced up the stairs, bursting out into a second kitchen – the family one, this time – startling several people already gathered there.

'Have you seen a—'

One of them pointed along the corridor and Alice took off. 'Agatha,' she hissed, spotting her beloved now dashing for the main staircase – the one with the glass sides.

A police officer stood resolutely on the half landing as the dog scampered towards him.

'Quick, grab her,' Alice cried.

But as the officer lunged for Agatha, she gave him the slip and scampered on up towards the first floor. The officer put out his arm to stop Alice doing the same, but she copied Agatha's manoeuvre, flattening herself against the wall, slipping past in hot pursuit.

'Madam, come back,' he yelled after her.

But Alice was too fixed on catching up with Agatha to listen.

'Whose bloody dog is this?' a woman called out, as Alice bolted up the last of the stairs.

'I'm so sorry,' she said, dashing past another police officer, after Agatha who'd just done the same.

Chasing Agatha down a long corridor, she arrived outside an open doorway out of breath, only to see that her little dog had finally been apprehended and was now upside-down in the arms of a man who looked rather like he'd unexpectedly just caught a rugby ball.

14.

Alice put her hand on her chest gasping for breath.

'Yours, I presume?' said the man. He was wearing jeans and black shoes and a black shirt beneath a navy duffel coat. He must have been around her age, Alice thought, his face craggy and lined and sporting a shadow of stubble.

'Oh, I'm so sorry—' Alice began, then stopped, covering her mouth as she looked past him into the room and towards the fireplace.

Pink fifty-pound notes were scattered across the floor. Enya was sprawled on the carpet amongst them, a hideous bloody wound on the side of her head, and a livid bruise on her cheek. For all the crime fiction Alice had read, she'd never seen an actual dead body. And certainly not one belonging to someone she knew. She'd read about people swooning upon seeing corpses in books and had always dismissed it as rather histrionic, but she actually did have to grab onto the doorframe just to stop herself from sinking to her knees.

'Hands off the doorframe, and for God's sake, don't faint,' the man said, a thunderous expression on his face. 'This is a crime scene. No one's allowed in until forensics arrive.'

Steadying herself, she looked at him instead. He was rugged in a possibly handsome kind of way, but deplorably scruffy. His shaggy salt and pepper hair curled down just past his collar, suggesting a trip to the barbers was long overdue. His accent was London – or more likely Essex, if the flat vowels were anything to go by. This must be Detective Rigby, to whom she'd spoken to on the phone.

'I'm terribly sorry,' she said. 'About the dog. She's normally much better behaved, you see, and—'

But Rigby wasn't interested. Even though Agatha was trying her hardest to be cute now, staring up at the detective with her tongue lolling, panting enthusiastically, it was clearly much too late. Rigby unceremoniously shoved her into Alice's arms.

'And you are?'

'Miss Beeton. Alice Beeton,' Alice said, noticing that his eyes were a disarmingly lovely shade of hazel.

'Ah, yes. You *placed* Enya here. Is that the right word? For getting someone a job somewhere like this?'

Nodding mutely, Alice found herself gazing once more past the detective and around the room. A window led out onto a fire escape and snowflakes flurried outside. An open doorway opposite her led into an adjoining room. A personal gym, it looked like. Alice could see the edge of what appeared to be a state-of-the art bench press and a running machine and free weights on the floor.

Other than the obvious exceptions – Enya, the money – what struck Alice most about the study was how perfectly tidy it was. Like these three cushions neatly fanned out on the beautifully upholstered button-back chair. And those art books on the shelf ordered in ascending size. And these five pens in a regimented line on the burnished teak desk.

Her eyes were drawn to a watercolour of a pirouetting nude male dancer on the wall.

Detective Rigby stepped in even closer towards her, deliberately blocking her view of the room and backing her up even further away from the door.

'What happened?' Alice asked. She couldn't help herself.

'It's too early to say. Now if you'd just wait downstairs with the rest of the staff. Then once the pathologist's been, I'll be down to ask a few questions.'

Staff. She wasn't staff. But she supposed she knew what he meant.

'But . . . you do suspect foul play?' she said. Because he must do, looking at the state of that room.

Immediately, she regretted the question – or perhaps, more specifically, the antiquated phrase – seeing the long-suffering look on Detective Rigby's face. That same look she had to stop herself giving new staff who asked questions about duties that were simply not their business.

'I'm sorry,' she said. 'It's just that I've read an awful lot of crime books and have probably watched far too many detective shows on TV too,' she added with a nervous laugh. 'Although, as far as I'm concerned, there's really no such thing as too many of either.'

But Detective Rigby clearly didn't give a stuff about her reading and viewing habits, or like her little joke. As his eyes locked with hers, she experienced an odd sensation in the pit of her stomach, as if she'd just been told off by a teacher. He breathed out, as if it was all too much to keep up the façade of being cross, and for a second, she thought he might be about to impart some precious nugget of information, or some idea as to what the police might be thinking, but then he looked right past her and his whole demeanour changed.

Alice turned to see two figures in baggy white paper suits, plastic over-shoes, latex gloves, face masks and protective glasses had arrived, carrying steel briefcases. She'd read enough to know that these people were Scene of Crime Officers, or 'SOCOs' in crime book lingo, here to carry out the forensics. Shuffling sideways, she hugged Agatha to her chest as they swooped past.

She wondered if Detective Rigby might be about to introduce her, but, 'The kitchen,' was all that he said, pointing her firmly in the direction of the stairs.

15.

Back in the staff kitchen in the basement, Agatha wriggled free from Alice's arms, as she firmly closed the door to the staircase behind her. Alice was about to reprimand her naughty scamp of a dog, but Agatha was intent on running towards Jinx who was now chatting with Jacques outside the little office.

'Hey baby,' Jinx said in her usual silly voice, scooping up Agatha and striding towards Alice, her free arm outstretched. 'Oh, Alice,' she said, her heavily made-up eyes huge with concern. She was wearing a long leopard print fake-fur coat over a shiny pink fitted mini dress and a pair of animal print shoes with statement platforms. 'I came as soon as I could. Couldn't find a cab for love nor money. Let me tell you, these shoes are not designed for the snow,' she said, setting Agatha down, before hugging Alice tightly. She smelt of booze and perfume, but she was here and that was all that mattered.

'I'm glad you made it,' Alice said.

Jinx put her hands on Alice's shoulders and stared down into her face, her expression full of concern. Somehow facing a crisis was always easier when Jinx was by her side.

'You OK?'

'Just about. Although that one . . . ' Alice said, pointing down to Agatha crossly.

'What happened? Where did she go?' Jacques asked.

'She ran straight to the crime scene upstairs. I don't think Detective Rigby was too pleased.'

'So, it is an actual crime scene?' Jinx asked. 'As in a crime has been committed?'

'Poor Enya is just . . . lying there and . . . ' Alice's throat tightened. 'It's so awful. It's not the same when you actually know the person. The side of her head is all . . . ' Alice waved her hand around her own head and shuddered at Jinx and Jacques who crowded around sympathetically.

'So, they don't think she fell? What do they think happened?' Jacques asked.

'It's hard to see how she could do that much damage by simply toppling over. It looked to me like she'd been hit with something.'

'Hit?' Jinx asked. 'As in *murdered*?'

Alice nodded, remembering the sight of Enya.

'Poor Enya,' Jacques said, tutting and shaking his head. 'She was so sweet, you know. And so kind to Laura.'

'Oh yes, that's the daughter?' Jinx checked.

'They were close. I could see that,' Jacques said. 'Laura thought the world of her.'

'Where are the family now?' Alice asked.

'They're all upstairs. The guests were questioned, but they've gone home.'

'Someone must know something,' Alice said. Because what if Enya had been murdered? Maybe by a guest at the party? And the police had just let them go?

'I should imagine the Messents are in shock,' Jinx said. 'What a terrible end to a party.'

Alice frowned at her. Surely Camille and Alex Messent's feelings about their party was a somewhat secondary point. Alice thought about them, somewhere in this house, having been questioned. She wondered briefly if it would be very inappropriate to seek them out. With her personal connection to Enya, she wanted to introduce herself and to offer her condolences. But putting herself into the forefront of the situation might be unwise, seeing that she'd already made a very bad first impression with Detective Rigby.

Or rather Agatha had.

It was another half an hour before Detective Rigby arrived in the kitchen and Jinx had to grab Agatha to stop her greeting him like a long-lost friend.

They all waited as he stood at the door by the little office and introduced himself and thanked everyone for their patience. Jacques fetched him a chair and Alice offered him a cup of tea.

'I know it's not my house, but you look as if you could do with one,' she said, trying to sound friendly, but something about him made her feel all flustered. Probably the fact that she'd made such a numpty of herself upstairs.

'There's teas over there,' Jacques said, waving his hand at a corner cupboard.

It was such a modern kitchen that Alice felt self-conscious as she tried to work out how to actually open the cupboard door.

'Just push it,' Jacques called over.

'Real good,' Jinx giggled, before remembering herself and pulling a serious face, and mumbling, 'Sorry,' to Detective Rigby.

'And again,' Jacques called, seeing Alice still hadn't got it open.

But even though she now finally did, she found herself blushing even harder. What must Detective Rigby think of her? She looked like she couldn't even make a cup of tea.

'What would you prefer, Detective Rigby?' she called, trying to get a grip, pleased to see that at least there was a decent array of teas here to choose from.

'Earl Grey, if they have it. Milk, two sugars.'

Alice smiled, opening the Earl Grey tin, thinking this would have been her choice too if she'd been asked. She found a modern teapot and filled it with water straight from the boiling water tap next to the sink. She'd never get used to such a modern contraption and tried to imagine owning such a thing herself. She liked her old-fashioned kettle with its comforting whistle much better.

When she came back to the table, Detective Rigby was already making notes.

'You're quite sure it was a quarter to nine, when she came down?' he asked Jacques.

'*Oui*, I had a plan for the canapés, you see,' Jacques said, reaching into the back pocket of his chef's trousers and unfolding a sheet of A4 covered in scribbled words. 'The timings were quite specific and, see here, I'd just finished preparing the last of the mini wagyu beefs. I remember Enya saying that they looked delicious, and I said I'd try to save her one for later. Then I went for a quick cigarette out there.' He nodded towards the back door, then glanced guiltily at Alice. So much for him only having one cigarette a night. 'I don't remember seeing her after that . . . '

'That's very helpful. Thank you,' Detective Rigby said, nodding politely to Alice as she poured his tea.

'Is that too strong?' she asked.

'No, it looks perfect. Anything warm and wet is appreciated. It's been a very long night already. And it's only going to get longer.'

'I can imagine,' Alice said, passing him the sugar bowl. 'I must say how awfully sorry I am about earlier. Agatha can be quite the little tyke.'

'Agatha? Odd name for a dog,' said the detective.

'After Agatha Christie,' Jinx said in a loud aside, and Detective Rigby gave a long and weary nod again.

'So, um, regarding Enya,' he said. 'I gather it's a new placement?'

Alice explained about Enya's interview and Madame Messent's call and how Enya had been a perfect candidate for the job, but all the while she felt a blush rising. She'd taken Enya's word for it that she had the necessary skills for the placement at the Messents'. Alice had been so won over by her, she'd skimped on the usual checks, hadn't made her fill out the questionnaire she usually did, and she and Jinx both knew it.

'These were her referees,' she said, pulling up Enya's CV on her phone. 'I spoke to two women. One at The Dorchester and one in Klosters. They couldn't have spoken more highly of her.'

'What about her family?'

'In Switzerland,' Alice said. 'I think. She said her father was German and her mother French.'

'Do you have a number for them? Someone should inform the next of kin.'

Alice scanned the CV, then looked at Jinx, stumped.

'She gave The Dorchester as her last address,' Jinx said. 'I don't think I . . . we, er . . . ever took an emergency contact, did we?'

'I see,' Detective Rigby said, in a way that made Alice feel rather judged. It hadn't occurred to her to get a more permanent address for her, although it should have done, of course. 'And what was your impression of her?' Rigby said.

'We liked her.' Alice glanced at Jinx, wanting her to back her up.

'She was so well presented,' Jinx said. 'Smart and respectful. I hate to think she was actually *murdered*.' The way she said it, it was a wonder she didn't press the back of her hand to her forehead and swoon.

Detective Rigby looked up sharply at Alice. Then Alice sent the exact same look Jinx's way. Because Jinx really had just made it sound as if Alice had been gossiping about the crime scene – which of course, she had. But Jinx now drunkenly blabbing about it in front of the detective made Alice look even more of a busybody than she had done upstairs.

'Well, hold on there. It's far too early to know anything for sure . . .'

'It's just I was telling them about the study, you see,' Alice said, deciding it was better to speak her own mind than let Jinx am-dram translate it for her. 'About the drawers and the money on the floor. I thought that perhaps Enya might have . . . you know . . . disturbed a burglar.'

'Yes. Maybe she heard something?' Jacques said.

'That would figure,' Alice said. 'If she had, she would have almost certainly gone to check it out. She was that type of person. Thorough.'

'Miss Beeton, it seems you're intent on doing my job for me,' Detective Rigby said, with a sigh.

At least he didn't actually seem offended by the fact.

'But how would they have escaped? The burglar, I mean?' Jacques asked, 'with all the people downstairs . . . '

'The window was open,' Alice said. 'And there's a fire escape outside.'

'So whoever did it, hot-footed it after whacking poor old Enya over the head . . . ' Jinx slurred morosely, miming donking herself with a hammer.

'Is that what you think happened, Detective?' Alice asked brazenly.

'I couldn't say. The pathologist will give me their report in due course.'

'But that would make sense, wouldn't it?' Alice persisted. 'I mean, she could have just tripped and hit her head on the fireplace, or even have been thrown by someone to the floor. Given her injuries, it does seem much more likely that she was hit with something. Something heavy and yay-big—' she made a circle with both hands '—I'd say, judging by that wound . . . '

Rigby's eyes narrowed, but he neither denied nor confirmed this.

'And where exactly did you say *you* were this evening, Miss Beeton? At the time of the . . . death.'

'Me?' Alice asked alarmed. 'I didn't say, but now that you ask, I was at home having supper with Barney. My friend. We were playing Scrabble. You can call him if you like.'

'And you, Miss . . . ?' Detective Rigby asked, writing some notes and then turning his attention to Jinx, who now described her haphazard evening of drinking in a bar, followed by a house party. Alice noticed the detective giving up on writing notes.

'So now that it's established that neither of us were involved, I do wonder, Detective, whether you've found a weapon yet?' Alice asked, taking a sip of her tea.

'If it's here, my officers will find it,' Rigby let slip.

Ah, so they *were* already looking for whatever she might have been hit with.

Right on cue, two more officers swept downstairs and into the kitchen.

'We should leave them to get on with their job,' Rigby said. 'I think that's all, so I'll let you good people get home for some sleep.'

More than a little disappointed that they couldn't stay here chatting for longer – after all, she felt, she was just warming up – Alice took the tea things over to the counter to wash up, as Detective Rigby spoke to his colleagues.

She caught herself whistling in the low-lit kitchen. Inappropriate, of course, considering the deeply grim circumstances, but talking to Detective Rigby just now really had given her a bit of a buzz.

Jinx lurched over, leaning drunkenly against her, yawning that she'd called an Uber and could drop Alice home.

'I was just wondering,' Alice said to the detective as she shrugged on her coat and pulled on her hat. 'What you thought about the timing of it all?'

Detective Rigby's hazel eyes narrowed again as he checked his pad. 'Like I said, we think she died at around five past nine – during the speech.'

'No, I mean the whole coincidence . . . '

'What coincidence?'

'That whatever was going on up in that study was going on at the exact same time that everyone else in the house was fully occupied . . . '

'Go on . . . ' he said. There was something else in his eyes now. He wasn't just indulging her. It seemed he genuinely wanted to know what she was thinking.

'Isn't it much more likely that whoever else was up there knew about the party and already had the information about the timings and when the best time might be to strike?'

Detective Rigby's eyes narrowed and then he pulled out his phone.

'Would you mind if I took your number again, Miss Beeton?' he asked.

'Of course.' She watched him tap it into his phone.

'And here's my card,' he said, reaching into his jacket pocket. 'In case you think of anything else.'

As she took it, she noticed that he wasn't wearing a wedding ring.

'Thank you,' she said, and there was an awkward moment as she wondered whether it was protocol to shake his hand, but decided against it. She'd never read about detectives or policemen shaking hands or touching very much at all for that matter. She picked up Agatha's lead and, as the detective watched her walk towards the back door, she could have sworn that Agatha, the naughty little minx, gave him a flirty backwards glance.

16.

Alice knew that bad news travelled fast, but when she opened up the office two days later, she was still surprised by the sheer number of unannounced visitors who popped in to hear Alice and Jinx's version of the New Year's Eve murder. A version that became more embellished every time Jinx told it. Even Tiffany paid them a visit, determined to get her facts straight, before her clients demanded all the latest from her too.

Alice passed on what she saw fit, but remained mindful not to 'speculate', as Detective Rigby had put it. She'd always prided herself on her professionality in the rest of her life and this was no exception. She tried her very best to be discreet, but the facts were the facts: she had placed Enya at the Messents' and it did look very much like Enya had been murdered, although frustratingly this had yet to be confirmed. Alice had spent every waking hour scouring the police websites and the local papers, but so far there'd been no other information released.

Alice herself had appeared in the papers, being the only person willing to comment on Enya's personality in the small article that appeared. She'd been quoted as saying that 'everyone at The Good Household Management Agency was devastated by the tragic loss of an upstanding, intelligent young woman'. Jinx had been very impressed that Alice had got a plug in for the agency, not that Alice had meant to. Besides, she was telling the truth. Enya's death did feel rather devastating, and Alice felt distinctly shaken as the new year got under way.

On Tuesday, Alice told Helly to fetch the scones for their tea break and to dig out the jam and cream from the fridge, but Jinx tutted and gave her a filthy look. They always had a row about whether one should smother each side with butter then jam then cream, or cream then jam as Jinx insisted was correct, but with Jinx's January diet in place, Alice could see she was taking the arrival of scones as a personal slight.

Scones

INGREDIENTS – 1 lb of flour, 1 oz sugar, 2 oz of butter, 2 tsp cream of tartar, 1 tsp bicarbonate of soda, $\frac{1}{2}$ tsp of salt, $\frac{1}{2}$ pint of milk.

METHOD – Rub the butter into the flour, mix in the sugar, salt, and cream of tartar. Dissolve the bicarbonate of soda in the milk, stir to form a smooth dough. Knead lightly, roll until 1 inch thick and use a cutter to make rounds. Place on a greased baking tray. When half done brush over with milk to form a glaze. Bake for about 30 to 35 minutes.

Alice retreated into her office and shut the door, keen to eat her scone in private and without Jinx staring daggers at her. Besides, with everyone gossiping about the Messents and Enya's murder, she was keen to write down the things that she'd seen herself, just to make sure the facts stayed set in stone. She flicked the silver spinner on her necklace, knowing that it always helped her to think. Then, grabbing a black Sharpie and a bundle of spare index cards from her box of contacts, she started writing a timeline for the circumstances surrounding Enya's death. But by lunchtime, the cards had become so muddled that she popped over to the stationery store for a large whiteboard. She'd always thought of the incident room corkboard, as an unnecessary trope in TV crime shows, a kind of cheap visualisation of what was going on in the detective's mind, but she was surprised to find out that it was actually rather a handy way to 'see' the facts.

Just as she was perfecting her handwriting in the marker on the board, Alice saw Helly flapping her hand excitedly, having taken a call. Alice got up and opened her office door.

'It's her, Alice,' Helly stage whispered, covering the receiver. 'Madame Messent.'

Alice felt Jinx and Helly watching as she picked up the call.

'Oh, Madame Messent,' Alice said, annoyed that the condolence card she'd posted wouldn't have reached their house yet. 'I've been meaning to telephone. I'm so terribly sorry about what happened. About Enya.'

'Thank you,' Camille Messent said.

'I was wondering if you'd been able to talk directly to her mother?' It was a nosy question, but Alice couldn't stop herself asking it. That poor woman. Wherever she was, she must be distraught. She'd assumed that the detective must have found a way of contacting the relatives, but she wanted to make sure Madame Messent had remembered to as well. It always made such a difference when one's employer showed an interest in one's home life. Even more so, in an odd way, when one was dead. Enya's parents would appreciate it and anything that might make them even remotely less miserable was worth encouraging.

'I asked the detective for the next of kin,' Madame Messent said, 'but he's been unable to trace them. This is one of the reasons I'm calling. Do you have a number for them?'

This was a turn-up, Alice thought. Why on earth hadn't Detective Rigby been able to track them down? She picked up her Sharpie, delighted that at last she could do something to help.

'I haven't right now but leave it with me.' Really, how hard could it be?

'*Merci.*'

'Have the police said anything more?' Alice asked, unable to stop herself.

'No. Nothing. They were at the house for several days, but they've gone now. They say they are waiting for the post-mortem.'

Alice shuddered, thinking of Enya under a sheet in a freezer at the morgue.

'And I know this is – how you say, delicate?' Madame Messent said. 'But life must go on and, you see, I have a trip abroad . . . I'm taking my assistant, Thérèse, with me . . . and these commitments I cannot change . . . '

'Right . . . '

'So, I need someone to look after the house – *tout de suite*, you understand? And to take care of my daughter.'

Alice had been so preoccupied with Enya's death that it hadn't even occurred to her that the Messents might need a replacement housekeeper. She should have been on the case already.

'Yes. Yes, of course. I'll get on it right away.'

'Perhaps someone English this time,' Madame Messent said. 'To help Laura with her conversation.'

'Absolutely.'

'But someone sensitive. You see, my daughter is very shaken.'

'Understandably.'

'She cannot be left alone in the house. And I have to have someone here to make sure there are no further break-ins and to supervise her going back to school. My husband is very busy at the moment also, you see.'

'I quite understand,' Alice said again, trying to sound reassuring, but at the same time feeling sorry for Laura Messent too. She knew exactly what it was like to have parents who prioritised their own agenda. To feel that you were always an afterthought, a problem to be dealt with. She couldn't remember her mother ever coming to her parents' evenings or taking an interest in Alice's academic work, even once. That had fallen to Mrs Doulton, who'd been paid to do the things that Alice's parents should have wanted to do themselves. And now, when Laura probably needed both her parents, the Messents were delegating their responsibility to a stranger.

But then, who was Alice to judge? She'd built her life on supplying staff to do things that, quite frankly, a lot of rich people should have been doing themselves.

'I know she left quite suddenly. But I'm wondering if Katy

might reconsider her decision to leave?' Madame Messent continued.

'Katy?'

'Katy Ellison. I already tried the last agency, but they said they couldn't get hold of her.'

'I'll see what I can do,' Alice said. 'If we can't track down Katy, we'll find you a replacement straight away.'

'Thank you. That's such a relief to hear. And I can trust you completely with this, yes?'

'Yes, of course,' Alice said.

'Then *à bientôt*,' Madame Messent said and rang off, before Alice had even had the chance to mention that she had in fact been to her house on New Year's Eve.

'Well?' Jinx demanded, standing in the doorway.

'She sounds . . . ' Alice tried to put her finger on it, but she hadn't quite been able to gauge Madame Messent's mood. Perhaps because she couldn't quite interpret the nuance of her intonation, but she seemed more weary than sad. Inconvenienced and harassed rather than genuinely sorry. But then how exactly did Alice expect her to behave? She'd hardly known Enya and it must be terrible having someone die in your own home. Especially in front of everyone you knew. She was probably absolutely mortified.

'Yes?' Jinx pressed.

'Busy. She says she's got a business trip.'

'She's going away?' Jinx asked. 'After what happened?'

'She says she has to. She can't cancel.' She stared down at the pink Post-It note on which she'd written Katy's name. 'I need to get hold of Katy Ellison. She was the Messents' last housekeeper.'

'They want her back?' Jinx asked.

'Possibly. They certainly need someone,' Alice said. 'I'm sure it's been quite an ordeal for the family.'

'There's no need to state the blummin' obvious all the time, Alice,' Jinx said, in a rather snappy tone.

Alice raised her eyebrows. 'Are you sure you don't want a scone?' she asked.

'No, Alice. That's the last thing I want,' Jinx snapped and Helly, behind her, pulled a face at Alice.

Fortunately, the tension in the office was broken by a visit from Jacques.

'How are you feeling?' Helly asked, as he marched in and put his moped helmet down on her desk.

Jacques looked tired. 'Shaken up. I can't stop thinking about what happened to Enya.'

'I know. I'm shaken up too,' Helly said, offering Jacques a sympathetic hug.

Alice could have sworn she saw Helly breathing deeply in as she pressed her face to his shoulder. Jacques sat down on the sofa and Agatha jumped up next to him, snuggling in as Jacques tickled her ears.

'Horrible to think that whoever did it is still out there,' Jinx said.

'*If* she was murdered,' Alice said for the umpteenth time, 'because it's still speculation, remember?'

'Yes, but it's still bloody horrible, whether she was actually clobbered or not.'

'I just spoke to Madame Messent,' Alice told Jacques. 'I'm trying to trace the last housekeeper, Katy Ellison. She went to the Messents via Elite.'

'I could call Christian there, if you like?' Jacques said.

Christian was Alice's counterpart at the rival agency and she doubted he'd give her the number if she called to ask for it herself.

'Really? Do you think you could wangle some contact details out of him for her?' Alice said. 'Only, subtly. And obviously without mentioning me. Make it a personal thing.'

'*D'accord.*' Jacques nodded and took out his mobile and pressed a few buttons, casually passing the time of day with his other boss there, before asking the favour and then, mercifully, springing up to grab a pen off Helly's desk and jot down a number and address.

'There,' he said, satisfied, when he'd rung off. 'At your service. Don't say I'm not a pivotal part of the team.'

'You would be even more if you weren't on Elite's bloody books as well,' Jinx said.

'I have to get work wherever I can. You understand, Jinxy? My sister. You remember she's deaf? I pay for her extra tuition and it's so expensive.'

She harrumphed. 'Just remember who looks after you the best,' she said, peeved. She turned on her heel and started angrily ripping down the Christmas cards she'd put on display.

'What's up with her?' Jacques asked Alice.

'Dry January. No carbs,' Alice whispered back.

'Oh,' he said. 'Leave that with me.'

17.

Alice went back into her office and called Katy Ellison, but there was no answer. Keen to persevere, she tried several times over the next hour, until she finally got through.

'Hello?' a woman's voice said. She sounded sleepy.

'Katy? Katy Ellison?'

'Who wants to know?' The girl sounded guarded, but Alice was so relieved to be speaking to her.

'This is Alice Beeton of The Good Household Management Agency.'

There was a small pause.

'Yes?' Katy sounded wary.

'I understand that you used to work for Camille Messent?'

There was a long pause. 'Yes . . . but I left.'

'I know, but you see, I was wondering if you wanted your old job back,' Alice said, trying to sound friendly. 'With the Messents.'

'But they've already employed somebody else. Enya . . . '

'I know. I placed her there myself.'

'So why would they want *me* back?'

It was a good point. Alice felt a blush rising in her cheeks.

Somehow, she'd assumed that Katy must know about Enya, but she clearly didn't. 'I'm not sure if you've seen it on the news . . . '

'Seen what? I only came back from abroad late last night.'

Oh, so *that* was why Elite hadn't been able to get hold of her for Madame Messent. 'Oh, well I'm very sorry to be the bearer of bad news, but Enya is . . . well, you see, Enya is no longer with us.'

'What do you mean?'

'She's um, well . . . I'm afraid she's dead.'

'What?' Katy's voice was tremulous. 'Are you joking?'

'I'm afraid I'm not.'

'That's terrible. What happened?'

'It's not something I want to discuss on the phone. Could we possibly meet?'

There was a pause and Alice was fully expecting Katy to give her instructions to do just that. Instead, she heard a sharp intake of breath. 'No. No, I don't think so.'

'But—'

'I really don't want anything to do with this, or them.'

'But—' Alice tried again, flabbergasted.

'Please don't call me again.'

The phone abruptly cut off.

Alice was still staring at it in disbelief, when Jacques marched back in the office with four cardboard soup pots, and shouted, 'Lunch!'

'I'm not eating lunch this month,' Jinx said, huffily folding her arms.

Jacques winked at Alice as she came through to join them in the kitchen. 'But it's my Chankonabe,' Jacques said.

'Your what?' Alice asked.

'Japanese sumo wrestlers' soup,' he explained.

Jinx let out a high-pitched 'pah'. 'As if I'm not big enough already,' she complained.

'Nonsense. These wrestlers, they eat this with tonnes of potatoes and noodles, which is what leaves them on the large side, but this version is carb-free and possibly the most healthy soup there is. Come on, try it.'

He lifted the lid off a carton, smelt it and passed it to Jinx.

'Please, Jinx,' Jacques goaded. 'Just for me. I'll be so unhappy if I have to throw it away.'

Jinx snuck another peek – and her nostrils quivered and flared.

'And besides, Jinxy—' Jacques smiled, already seeing he'd got her hooked '—it's too sad a time to be depriving oneself of comforts. If we've all learnt anything, then surely it's that life's too short not to enjoy the good things, *non*?'

Chankonabe

INGREDIENTS – 1 medium chicken, boned and cut into chunks, bones reserved. 2 leeks, sliced into rounds, 4 carrots cut into chunks, 1 daikon shredded, 1 cake of tofu, cubed, 12 shitake mushrooms, 2 medium onions, quartered, 1 savoy cabbage, shredded, 8 baby corns, cut into chunks, 150ml soy sauce, 4 fl. oz mirin.

METHOD – Put the chicken bones, leeks and carrots in large pan of water and bring to boil. Simmer for 3 hours then strain. Parboil the daikon in lightly salted *water and drain. Put the chicken meat, tofu, mushrooms, onions, cabbage, corn, and strained stock into large pan and add soy sauce. Simmer until chicken and veg cooked, then add daikon, mirin and 1/2 tsp salt.*

Soon, they were all tucking in happily and Alice recounted the phone call with Katy.

'Don't you think that's a bit of a strange reaction? Especially when you find out someone is dead?' Alice asked Helly and Jinx.

'I suppose. Maybe it's a shock thing. Fight or flight,' Helly said.

'Now I think about it . . . how did she know that the Messents had employed Enya?' Alice asked. 'I didn't give her that information. And if she knew about Enya, or even knew her personally, why wouldn't she want to know what happened to her? She just shut me down.'

'People are weird about death,' Jinx said, slurping her soup noisily. 'God, this is so good.'

'But . . .' Alice pondered. 'It's just so strange. To be offered her job back. And not just any job. It's a well-paid job. She said she didn't want anything to do with "this" or "them". Washed her hands of the whole business.'

'That's her choice,' Helly said.

'But what's she got against the Messents?'

'Who knows. They probably had a row when she left. Madame Messent was rather desperate that day, wasn't she?' Jinx said.

But Alice had a hunch there was more to this than Katy had let on. She listened to Jacques tell Helly how he'd made the soup, but she could hardly concentrate. When she'd finished her pot, she jumped up and put her spoon in the sink with a clatter.

'I'm going to go and pay her a little visit,' Alice said, looking at the piece of paper with Katy's address on it.

'Who?' Jacques asked.

'Katy Ellison.'

'You can't just turn up on her doorstep,' Jinx said, her spoon paused halfway to her mouth.

'Why not?' Alice asked, grabbing her coat. 'Enya was killed. I feel it's my duty to find out whatever I can. And that girl . . . I'm telling you . . . she was just . . . weird.'

Agatha barked in approval and Jinx rolled her eyes.

'It looks like Agatha agrees,' Jacques said, and they all laughed as she trotted to the corner and picked up her lead in her mouth.

18.

Alice caught the bus to Fulham and sat with Agatha on her lap, looking out through the steamed-up window at the streets and the piles of slush on the grass verges. It was always so dismal when the snow started to melt, Alice thought, watching the pedestrians with their heads bowed against the wind, and the back-to-work grind of January somehow palpable in their stances.

She rarely came out this way these days, but still remembered the pub, The White Horse, nicknamed The Sloaney Pony, where she and Jinx had hung out in years gone by. How long ago and how carefree those times seemed now.

It was a lot smarter around here than it was back then, Alice noticed, as she and Agatha got out by Parson's Green. Alice checked the address that Jacques had written down. Katy's flat was in a nice terraced street that led down from the green. She walked along the black and white tiled path to the porch and rang on the buzzer. Soon a woman's voice crackled out of the intercom. 'Hello?'

'Is that Katy? Katy Ellison?' Alice asked, cocking her ear to the metal box.

'Yes?' The girl sounded suspicious.

'Oh, I'm so glad I caught you. It's Alice Beeton. We spoke on the—'

'I told you. I don't have anything to say.' The intercom went dead. Alice buzzed again, but Katy didn't answer.

Alice just stood there, staring at the door. Then turned to walk away, because really, what else was there to do? Only Agatha sat resolutely on the doorstep, her little head cocked at Alice.

'Oh, you think we should try again?' Alice asked. 'I agree. Let's pop round the block and come back.' Because of course, Agatha was right, they'd never been much good at simply giving up. And best for Katy to think Alice had gone, in order to catch her off guard next time.

The ruse worked, because just as Alice was about to ring the buzzer again, she heard footsteps thundering down the stairs inside. The door swung violently open and a young woman about the same height and build as Alice stood, her mouth falling open with shock. She was dressed in dungarees and had dark hair poking out from beneath a black beanie. Her face was suntanned, and her nose was peeling. The tell-tale sign of someone just back from a trip.

'Katy?' Alice said, with what she hoped was a friendly smile. 'I'm Alice Beeton. We spoke—'

'If you don't go . . . I'll . . . I'll . . . ' But the young woman didn't seem to know what she might do. She was younger than Alice had thought she'd been on the phone, barely twenty.

'I only want to ask you a few questions,' Alice told her, as gently as she could. Agatha sat neatly by Alice's feet, her head cocked, looking her most cute, and Alice saw Katy glance down and her fury falter. She let out a low sigh, and her shoulders slumped.

'OK,' she said. 'You'd better come in.'

Alice followed her inside and Agatha scampered past the bikes in the hallway and up the narrow flight of stairs to the first floor. Katy unlocked the door and pushed inside.

'Oh, how lovely. I do admire anyone who can grow a monstera like that,' Alice said, following her and nodding at the sprawling plant that almost filled the open plan kitchen-cum-living room. 'I don't have very green fingers, but then you have such lovely light in this room.' Alice took in the IKEA sofas and cushions. 'I live in a basement and I do hanker after light, especially at this time of year.'

'Look, can we just get this over with?' Katy said. 'What exactly is it that you want?'

'Right. As I said on the phone, the Messents were rather hoping you'd go back to them. They are in somewhat of a bind.'

'I can't. I've got another job,' Katy said, her eyes shifting away to the right. She was clearly lying.

'Right,' Alice said again, nodding. 'I see. But you said you knew Enya?'

'I didn't say that.' Katy's eyes met hers briefly and then slid away again.

'But you knew the Messents had employed her? You said that on the phone?'

Katy pressed her lips together, colour rising in her cheeks.

'Katy . . .'

'I didn't think it would end in something like this. Not with her dead.' Katy's voice rose a little, both defensive and scared.

'I looked it up online after you called. I had no idea. Am I in trouble?'

'Why would you be in trouble?'

'Because she wanted me to . . . ' She trailed off.

'She? Enya, you mean? Wanted you to . . . ?'

Katy looked over at the wall, her knee bouncing nervously.

'So, you do know . . . *did* know Enya?'

Katy was silent then nodded once reluctantly. Alice realised she was going to have to tread carefully to get this skittish girl to open up, but warning signals were flashing in her mind. Katy was hiding something, something important enough to be scaring the living daylights out of her.

'I know this is presumptuous,' Alice said, in her most gentle tone, 'but is there any chance I could trouble you for a cup of tea?'

Katy nodded quickly. She lifted down two mugs from the cupboard and put a teabag from a jar in each one. PG Tips by the looks of it, Alice thought. Totally fine in the circumstances.

'How do you have it?' Katy's voice was weak.

'Oh, the normal. Builders,' Alice said. 'No sugar.'

Katy stayed facing away from her as the kettle boiled. The silence stretched and Alice twiddled her necklace, looking at Katy's tense shoulders, but eventually she made the tea and placed a steaming mug in front of Alice on the counter.

'Thank you.'

She noticed Katy looking at her necklace, and when she met Alice's eyes, Alice smiled gently. 'Why don't you start at the beginning and tell me how you met? You and Enya?'

'It was in a coffee shop. In South Ken.'

'When?'

'A couple of months ago,' she said. 'Maybe less. The first time we just chatted. She was so friendly. She said she was a house-keeper too and we seemed to have a lot in common. I told her about the Messents. She was just so easy to confide in.'

'Go on.'

'I bumped into her a few times after that. It was uncanny, the coincidence. We joked about it.'

Unless Enya had been following her, Alice thought. 'What happened then?'

'In December, she called. I'd given her my number and she asked me to meet her. So, I did. She said she had a proposition that couldn't wait.'

'A proposition?'

'I'd told her about wanting to go skiing, you see. I'd just said it casually and had explained how I hadn't really expected to get time off from my job and how I'd only half-heartedly asked for it, but I really wanted to go as my friends were going and this guy . . . a guy . . . ' She fizzled out. 'It was just a little piece of information I'd shared, nothing more. But when I met Enya that time she said she had it all worked out. She told me that I should go skiing and that she could replace me. She'd finished her placement, you see.'

'Oh? Did she say where she'd been working before?'

'Just for some family, but that now she was free. She could take over from me. She said she liked the sound of my job. I'd told her it was an easy gig, you see.'

'So the plan was for her to cover for your holiday?'

'No, to take the job full time.'

'But if it was an easy gig then why would you give it up? Didn't it bother you? The thought of being unemployed?'

'Yeah, but I don't know . . . she was kind of persuasive. She convinced me that I'd be able to get another job easily once I was back from skiing. That it was outrageous that the Messents wouldn't give me time off at this time of year and that life was too short not to spend it with friends. She made it sound so easy. She said there were tonnes of jobs around. Ones that were even better than the one I had.'

'So you quit?'

'Yes. Madame Messent wasn't very pleased.'

'No, I can imagine she wasn't.'

'I told her that there were other people – experienced people – who could replace me. Right away. She just had to ring the agency.'

'Elite?'

'No, not Elite. They would have been furious about me quitting. Enya told me that. She gave me a number. It must have been your number. For your agency. She told me to give it to Madame Messent and to tell her to call straight away.'

Alice let out a slow breath, a new understanding suddenly dawning. Enya booking her appointment with Alice on 21 December . . . it had all been part of some elaborate set-up? She'd come in knowing that Madame Messent would be phoning and that she'd then be right there on hand to offer herself up for the job.

'And how could she be so sure Madame Messent would hire her?'

Katy shrugged. 'She'd asked me about what kind of

qualifications I'd needed to get the job there when we first met. She said she was putting together a more up-to-date CV. And I told her that first-class references were always the most important thing. Languages would help.'

Exactly what Enya had pointed out to Alice on her CV. She'd obviously done her research on Alice too, coming to the office and being so charming about Mrs Beeton. Alice felt a rising sense of indignation that she'd been duped.

Katy shrugged, as if trying to make sense of it herself. 'I wanted to go with my friends so badly and Enya, she . . . '

'She what?'

'She . . . well . . . she made it worth my while.'

Katy looked down at her hands and Alice saw more guilty fidgeting. 'Worth your while how?'

'She paid me.' Katy's voice was small.

'*Paid you?*'

'Just . . . she made it sound like a Christmas bonus. The one I wouldn't be getting from the Messents. She said she had plenty of spare cash, and it would help me have the skiing holiday of my dreams.' Katy looked down, shamefaced. 'You must think I'm awful.'

Enya had *paid* Katy to leave. 'How much?' Alice asked, trying very hard not to sound judgemental.

'A couple of thousand. In cash. Euros. Enough for the trip to Courchevel.' She nodded at a packed bag in the hallway, her cheeks reddening even more. 'I just got back.'

'I see.'

So Enya had engineered it so that Katy had left and had thrown in cash to sweeten the deal. *Interesting.*

Alice took a long sip of her tea. 'If you don't mind me asking, what was your impression of the Messents?'

'I spent most of my time with Laura and supervising the cleaners. Monsieur Messent was very particular. Wouldn't have anything out of place. Wanted the whole house to be spotless at all times. It was quite stressful living there.'

'I see.'

'But I hardly knew him – or Madame. They were away so much. But she's a good kid,' Katy said, looking wobbly again. 'Laura, I mean. Just a shame she's got the parents she has.'

'Oh,' Alice said, 'what do you mean?'

'Just that, they might look perfect on the outside, but you never really know what people are really like, do you? Behind closed doors.'

'I suppose not, but then someone in your position of privilege would be party to exactly that, wouldn't they?'

'I guess.'

'So I'm just wondering how they differed from other families you've worked for? The Messents?' Alice probed.

'Something about them . . . it never felt quite *right*. Nothing specific. Just too many heated conversations . . . slammed doors . . . that sort of thing.'

'I suppose it's good you're not going back there, if you feel like that,' Alice said. 'And, as you said, you've got another job now. So, it seems that Enya was right.'

Katy's eyes slid away. She realised she'd burnt her bridges now.

'I won't take up any more of your time,' Alice said, getting up and calling for Agatha.

'That's it?' Katy asked.

'Why? Is there more?'

'No, but how did she die?'

'The police aren't yet certain.'

'I mean . . . do you think it was quick?'

'Yes, I think so. But I'm afraid *not* very pleasant.'

'Poor Enya.'

'Quite.'

Alice smiled without warmth and opened the door.

'You won't tell them . . . about what I just told you, will you?' Katy asked, looking terrified.

'Who?'

'The police.'

'No, but perhaps you should,' Alice said, looking Katy right in the eye. 'If you think it's relevant. If I were you, I'd report exactly what you've just told me to Detective Rigby. In fact,' she said, opening her bag, 'here's his card.'

19.

Alice was still reeling from Katy's bombshell about Enya as she hurried back towards the office. She couldn't wait to tell Jinx what she'd found out. But the second she stepped through the agency's doorway, she sensed a weird atmosphere. Something was up.

'There's someone here to see you,' Jinx whispered, nodding to Alice's office, where Alice could now see a well-presented, middle-aged woman in a denim skirt and polo neck under a Harris tweed jacket sitting in the chair opposite her desk. Only her boots gave her away – square toed and rubber soled. Most definitely a utilitarian European brand.

'Miss Beeton?' she asked, standing up, as Alice came in.

'Yes. Hello. How can I help you?'

'My name is Gerda.' Her accent sounded vaguely Germanic and vaguely familiar. A faint alarm bell started ringing in Alice's mind. She was absolutely sure she'd never met this person before, so why did she feel this recognition? 'I am . . . was . . . a friend of Enya's.' She sniffed loudly, rubbing her nose. The poor woman clearly had a dreadful cold. Alice recoiled. She could really do without getting ill herself.

'I read about what happened,' Gerda said, proffering Monday's copy of the paper, Alice's quote outlined in red.

'Oh, I'm so sorry for your loss. It's really quite awful,' Alice said.

Gerda sniffed loudly again and let out a shuddery breath. Alice looked through the glass at Jinx, making wide eyes. She came in with a box of tissues and handed them silently to Alice and then backed out again.

'Excuse me, sorry, but how exactly do you know each other?' Alice said. 'You and Enya?'

Gerda sneezed, accepting the tissues gratefully.

'We used to work together. As au pairs. Then for hotels. She was younger than me, but she was my best friend.'

'I see,' Alice said, remembering her manners. 'Please. Sit down.'

'But now she has been . . . ' Gerda seemed to be steeling herself ' . . . murdered.'

'The police aren't exactly sure that—'

'Murdered,' Gerda repeated. 'I know this as fact.'

'But how?' Alice stared at her, alarmed.

'On the night she died . . . she called me. She said she was frightened for her life. She was scared.'

'Of whom?' Alice asked, shocked.

'I don't know. That's why I'm here.'

Alice swallowed, feeling completely out of her depth. 'I'm not entirely sure why you think I can help. Surely this is a matter for the police?'

'I can't go to the police.' Gerda vehemently shook her head.

'Why not?'

'They don't like people like me. I have the wrong visa. And Enya . . . ' Gerda said, looking up ' . . . she was the same . . . '

Alice nodded. She thought about the CV printed on the thick paper that Enya had handed over from the very spot that Gerda was now sitting in. How perfectly official and above board it had looked.

'She was such a fine person,' Gerda said in a small voice and the lightbulb pinged on in Alice's head. *The voice. It was her voice.*

'Was that you I spoke to on the phone? Pretending she'd worked for you at The Dorchester?' she asked.

Gerda nodded, her cheeks now burning. 'She begged me to. She said she'd found the perfect job. One that was easy and paid well and she was determined to get it.'

Alice slowly shook her head. She really had been made a fool of, hadn't she? She was half-tempted to tell Gerda to get out there and then, or even call the police, but what was she guilty of? Other than having tried to help a friend out in need?

'Why did she want the job so badly?' Alice asked, because the events of the past few hours had made it very, very clear that Enya Fischer had wanted the job at the Messents' very badly indeed.

'For the money, of course.'

'She needed money?' Alice asked. This didn't tally with what Katy had said.

'Her mother. She was sick. Is sick. She's dying,' Gerda said. 'The money was for an operation.'

'Do you have a number for her mother? A real number,' Alice warned.

Gerda shook her head. 'No, nor for any other family. But then, I don't think Enya was her real name. A lot of us, we take on fake ones. To keep the authorities at bay. That's why the police . . . they won't be interested in what's happened to her either . . . not once they find out she was an illegal worker,' Gerda said. 'They never are.'

'I'm sure that's not true. They're taking this case very seriously.' Alice couldn't help rushing to Detective Rigby's defence.

Gerda shook her head and coughed. 'They will drop it. There will be no answers.'

'I'm sure that's not true at all—'

'So, you must find out,' Gerda said, leaning across the desk to grip Alice's arm. 'Please.'

'Me? But I, I . . . ' Alice stumbled. 'I can't.'

'You met her.' Gerda's bloodshot eyes bored into Alice's. 'How would you feel if the person closest to you was cut down in their prime? Wouldn't you want answers too? What if it was your friend out there?' Gerda nodded through the glass towards Jinx, who, caught out staring, turned quickly on her Manolo heels. 'We were this close,' Gerda said, crossing her fingers, her voice breaking. She dabbed at her eyes with a scrunched-up tissue.

Alice looked at Jinx, standing in the kitchen, her heart tugging with sympathy for this poor woman. Because if something happened to Jinx, wouldn't she do everything in her power to get answers?

'But . . . but how?' Alice said. Because how *could* she help?

'Talk to the other staff there.'

'But Enya was the only person I placed. Other than Jacques. And he's already told the police everything he knows.'

'But the cleaners. And others. Please,' Gerda said. 'You surely must be able to find a way to find out more?'

Maybe she was right. It wasn't like Alice didn't know anyone in the industry. She should be able to track these people down and talk to them. 'I'll do what I can, but I'm not promising anything.'

'You know she's very sweet,' Gerda observed. She reached down to stroke Agatha's ear.

'She's also very spoilt,' Alice said, as the dog gently wagged her tail.

'She's like your family?' Gerda asked.

'Yes, I guess so.' Alice smiled down at Agatha. 'Although she can be very naughty at times.'

But it was only after Gerda had left that Alice realised she'd totally failed to get her full name, address or telephone number.

And neither had Jinx or Helly.

20.

On Saturday morning, Alice was wide awake at five, still mulling over her encounters with Gerda and Katy. Agatha whined, clearly annoyed at being woken up so early, and Alice let her jump up onto the bed, where she turned and slumped down on the duvet and was snoring within seconds.

Alice hadn't often had cause to feel that someone had pulled the wool over her eyes, as Mrs Doulton would say, but that's exactly what had happened. Who had Enya really been?

But Alice was still determined not to hate her. Who knew what struggles she'd gone through to get here or how hard her life had been? And as desperate as she'd clearly been, she'd remained a charming, intelligent young woman who really hadn't deserved to die in such terrible circumstances. Not that *anyone* deserved that. Alice couldn't shake the image of her lying on the study floor, or the horrible sight of her bloodied head.

In the kitchen, Alice waited for the kettle to boil. Noticing that the waterlogged plaster on the ceiling was sagging dangerously, she made a mental note to call Mr Mantis again as soon as the hour was reasonable. He really was being utterly awful about the leak. Alice's eyes narrowed as she stared up at it, thinking how oppressive it felt having it hanging over her – a kind of ceiling of Damocles. It infuriated her that Mr Mantis still refused to take responsibility when she paid a fortune in building maintenance. Would he dare to be so dismissive if she weren't a woman on her own?

She made a cup of tea and turned on the radio, but the cheery music only made her mood worse, and the news was no better.

The only thing that might distract her was a spot of baking. She looked in the cupboard, seeing half a packet of the delicious fat currants she'd been given by Massoud and three eggs. Opening a drawer, she pulled out her personalised wooden spoon that Jinx had given her for Christmas and smiled. She knew just what cake would cheer her up.

Soda-Cake

INGREDIENTS – 1/4 lb of butter, 1 lb of plain flour, 1/2 lb currants, 1/2 lb of moist sugar, 1/3 pint of milk, 3 eggs, 1 teaspoonful of carbonate of soda.

METHOD – Rub the butter into the flour, add currants and sugar and mix these ingredients well together. Whisk the eggs well, stir them into the flour along with the milk, in which the soda should be previously dissolved, and beat the whole lot up together with a wooden spoon or beater. Divide the batter in two, put them into buttered moulds or cake-tins, and bake in a moderate oven for nearly an hour. The mixture must be extremely well beaten up, and not allowed to stand after the soda is added to it but must be placed in the oven immediately. Great care must also be taken that the cakes are quite done through, which may be ascertained by thrusting a knife into the middle of them: if the blade looks bright when withdrawn, they are done. If the tops acquire too much colour before the inside is sufficiently baked, cover them over with a piece of clean white paper, to prevent them from burning.

Time – 1 hour.
Average cost, 1s. 6d.
Sufficient to make 2 small cakes.
Seasonable at any time.

It was only when the cakes were out of the oven, that Alice realised that she'd made two for a reason.

A small cake might be the perfect thing to offer as a gift. Yes. To Detective Rigby. Surely a visit was in order. To check that he was still actively investigating the case, and not just letting it lie like Gerda had feared.

After lining a Fortnum's tin with greaseproof paper, she put one of the pleasingly golden cakes inside and dusted it with icing sugar. She had a shower and dressed in a skirt, then trousers, then jeans and a jumper, then back to her first outfit. Having tried and failed to style her hair in a funkier version of its usual bob, she gave up, put on a hat and woke up Agatha.

'Come on,' she told her bleary-eyed dog. 'Let's find out what's what.'

She caught the Tube to South Kensington, but it was only as she approached the front of the police station that it occurred to her that it might have been better to call to make an appointment. It was all very well her hoping that the detective might be up for sharing information with her, but now faced with the brutal bureaucratic façade of this building, her certainty was rapidly evaporating. Maybe he was just being polite when he'd asked her to stay in touch.

If he was even at the station today. He might be out solving all sorts of crimes, with this case already way down on his list. Or maybe he didn't even work on weekends but spent Saturdays at home with his family. *If* he had a family. *Did* he? Just because he didn't wear a ring didn't mean he didn't have a partner. Why was she even thinking about this at all?

But, it was too late to back out now. She forced herself to walk in and introduce herself at the front desk. The uniformed young man took an age to write down her name and request correctly. He looked no older than Woody. Chiding herself for being so ageist, she waited on a hard plastic chair, looking over the tired old 'Wanted' posters on the chipped wall and the chewing-gum-dotted laminate floor. This place really could do with a lick of paint, or at the very least a decent scrub.

'Ah, Miss Beeton.' She looked up to see Detective Rigby coming through the green wooden door and her heart gave a little leap. 'To what do I owe this pleasure?'

Agatha barked once and, in a most uncharacteristic show of affection, managed to manoeuvre herself so that she was nuzzling up against the detective's leg, gazing up at him with adoring eyes.

He was wearing black jeans and the same scruffy duffel coat he'd had on the last time she'd seen him, and she wondered if he'd just got in, or had been on his way out. But no matter, at least he was here and that was all that mattered.

'She's rather a fan of yours,' Alice said. 'Honestly, she's never usually like this. You should be flattered.'

'Right,' Detective Rigby said.

There was a small pause and, again, Alice felt herself losing her nerve. 'I'm sorry to drop in. I know you must be busy,' she blustered, 'but I was wondering if we could have a chat. About Enya?'

'I suppose you'd best follow me,' he said, and Alice felt a wash of relief. 'Just to warn you, though, the inspector doesn't like dogs, so we're going to have to sneak Agatha in undercover, understood?'

Understood. The way he'd said it, it made her want to salute. But bravo to him. He'd remembered Agatha's name. How wonderful. Or was it? What if he'd memorised all the names of those men and women on the 'Wanted' posters too?

Without any warning, he scooped Agatha up and hid her beneath his coat. As he marched deeper into the station, Alice stuck close – she had no choice, seeing as she was still holding Agatha's lead, attaching her to the detective now like an umbilical cord. She tried her very best not to laugh as Rigby started quietly whistling the theme tune from *The Great Escape*, Alice's father's favourite film.

From all the thousands of scenes she'd watched and had read in novels, Alice had always assumed that behind the 'cop shop's' front desk, she'd find a kind of *Hill Street Blues* and *Brooklyn 99* hubbub of activity and banter, a cluster of desks populated with swaggering, larger-than-life characters, a volley of scrunched-up papers flying through the air.

But there was no one around. The bland offices could have belonged to any other business, and certainly not the kind of place where crimes were solved, and criminals brought to justice. Maybe her fictional view of the police was just that, a load of made-up nonsense. The disappointment hit her hard.

'Welcome to my humble abode,' Detective Rigby said, opening the door of his office, before following her in and releasing Agatha onto the worn grey carpet.

The office had a small window half-covered with a wonky venetian blind and the dimly lit space was filled by a giant brown Formica desk, littered with teetering folders. A shelf behind the chair was piled high with box files and a dead spider plant. The bin to one side of the desk was overflowing and she noticed a greasy McDonald's wrapper. In her opinion, fast food was the devil's work, but she reasoned that Detective Rigby must have to eat at strange hours, and there was a distinct lack of affordable restaurants in the nearby streets. One couldn't expect him to survive solely on Michelin stars. He flicked a switch and an unpleasant strip light buzzed into life.

'Can I offer you something? Tea, perhaps?' he said, walking over to a small cabinet behind her, where she saw a kettle and mug tree.

She almost declined. If this was the state of his office, she didn't dare guess as to the cleanliness of those mugs, but she could tell he was trying to be polite.

'Earl Grey, OK?' he asked, and she nodded, noticing the box

of premium teabags that he now got out of a cupboard. There was a tiny fridge in the cabinet too, and he reached into it for a pint of milk, which she saw him undo and surreptitiously sniff. 'Milk, no sugar, am I right?' he checked.

So, he'd remembered that too. Very impressive. But then, Alice did suppose that noticing things was rather his job.

Agatha jumped, rather cockily, onto the chair behind his desk.

'Agatha, get down,' Alice said, ashamed. She stood up to shoo the little dog, but Detective Rigby just chuckled. He seemed much more relaxed on his home turf than he had at the Messents'.

'It's OK,' he said. 'She's just nosing around.'

'Are you a dog owner, Detective Rigby?' Alice asked, finally corralling Agatha under her own chair.

'I was,' he said. 'But it's a long story. The shaggy dog kind.'

'Oh, I see,' Alice said, although she didn't really see at all. Was he making some kind of joke? Or just saying he didn't want to talk about it? It being his home life.

Shuffling some papers, he cleared a space on his desk to make room for the two mugs of tea.

'I hope you don't find this too presumptuous, but I brought you a cake,' she said.

'A cake? It's not my birthday.'

Alice felt ridiculous. 'I had a spare. I like to bake, you see. It relaxes me.'

She handed over the tin and he looked inside. 'That smells wonderful.'

'Fresh out of the oven. I hope you like it. I've already cut it,' Alice said. 'I wasn't sure whether it was wise to bring a knife into a police station.'

'No, probably not. I might have had to arrest you.'

Another joke? Yes. He was even smiling this time. Thank goodness, Alice thought. Not about him not arresting her, more that they really did seem to be getting along.

Rigby took a slice of cake and bit into it. Then another. And another. 'Delicious,' he said. 'Your own recipe?'

'A distant relative's, actually. Mrs—'

'Beeton,' he finished her sentence for her.

'Yes, but how did you know?'

'Let's just call it an educated guess. I like to bake a little myself as it happens,' he admitted. 'But you said you wanted to chat about Enya. Have you some information?' he asked.

'Not . . . not exactly. Just some things have come to light. About the circumstances of her employment.'

'I see.'

Alice shifted uncomfortably. 'That may or may not be relevant.'

'Oddly enough I had a call about exactly that. Yesterday, in fact,' he said.

'Katy?' Alice said, too enthusiastically, putting her hand to her chest in relief. 'Katy Ellison? She called you.' He moved his head, in what Alice took as a nod. 'Oh good. I so hoped she would.'

Alice smiled at the detective, feeling a glow of satisfaction that she was personally responsible for bringing a source of information to the investigation, but his face gave nothing away. He could at least thank her for pushing a lead in his direction.

'I feel a little duped. I'm not sure Enya really was all she seemed to be.'

'Go on.'

'Well, if you've spoken to Katy, you'll know how Enya engineered an elaborate plan to work at the Messents'.'

The detective took a bite of cake. Was he agreeing with her? She couldn't tell.

'I mean, is that relevant? Did Enya have a motive to be working at the Messents'? Other than the obvious?' Alice persisted.

'The obvious?'

'Money. The fact that the job was a cushy one.'

'Easy?'

'Not that being a housekeeper is easy. It's a lot of responsibility,' Alice blustered, feeling that she was getting off track.

She paused, unsure how to continue. The detective seemed to be pondering what she had said. What had he made of Katy's revelations? She was desperate to know, but she could see he wasn't about to divulge any details. She decided to cut to the chase.

'And . . . well, I wondered if you'd had any leads? About her death? Because maybe . . . and I'm speculating here, maybe she could have been working with whoever broke in.'

'Why would she do that?'

'Perhaps she was up to something.'

'Up to something?'

Alice was convinced that the detective was toying with her.

'Maybe she knew about the valuable art in the house. Maybe she'd tipped off the burglar?'

'But no art was taken.'

Alice swallowed. Stumped. But at least that was a tiny nugget of information. Maybe, just maybe, Alice's original theory was correct and Enya had unwittingly foiled a burglary and paid a terrible price for her diligence.

'But you must have found something else out?' she asked, unable to mask the frustration from her voice.

The detective sighed and looked at Alice.

'I suppose you'll see it on the news anyway,' he said, 'but the pathologist has now officially concluded that Enya didn't die from a fall – accidental or otherwise.'

'That was obvious.'

'Nothing is *obvious*, Miss Beeton,' he said. 'Until the evidence says it is.'

Alice blushed.

'Cause of death was blunt force trauma to the head,' he said.

'So have you found it? The murder weapon?' Alice asked.

His silence spoke volumes.

'So you're still no closer to finding out who did it?' *Done it.* She'd nearly actually said *who done it.* Like she really was in a TV detective show.

'No,' Rigby said gruffly. 'Everyone in the house that night was either in the kitchen or in the drawing room,' he said. 'We know that from the photos.'

'Charles Tavistock's?'

Detective Rigby's bushy eyebrows shot up.

'And *everyone* is accounted for? There was nobody else who came in or out of the building?' Alice said. 'Only when I called round to check on Enya after she'd first started, I noticed a CCTV camera at the front of the house.'

'Yes, but no one other than guests or staff used that door. And, again, they're all accounted for at the time of Enya's death.'

'So, it really must have been someone who broke in through the window,' Alice said. 'A thief. Who Enya disturbed. Then again, we don't know where she was between Jacques seeing her at quarter to nine and when she died. That's a whole fifteen minutes unaccounted for. Is there CCTV at that side of the house covering the fire escape, or the gardens below?'

Detective Rigby shook his head.

'So there's no way of knowing who came in or out of that window? And no footprints because of the snow,' Alice surmised. 'No way to know how many intruders there might have been or how they might have escaped?' She felt so hopeless, she couldn't help sounding indignant. How could the police be so useless? And how could anyone get away with such a heinous crime with so many people in the building? *Someone* must have seen *something*, but Detective Rigby's inscrutable face told her that they hadn't. Or not that the police knew about.

Rigby stared down at the messy mosaic of papers on his desk, Alice thought back to the whiteboard on her office wall, on which she'd been continuing to scribble down any facts she'd discovered that she'd considered pertinent to the case. And something was nagging her about it. Now, what was it? Ah yes.

'Jacques told me that the study was out of bounds,' she told the detective, 'and was *always* locked. So why was the door open? I don't remember it looking like it had been forced.'

'It wasn't.'

'Meaning, what? That Monsieur Messent left it unlocked?'

'Possibly. Or it was picked.'

'By Enya?' Was that really what the detective meant? That he thought Enya had left the kitchen after speaking to Jacques and gone up to pick the lock?

The door opened and a police officer came in, shooting Alice a look. 'Sorry, Darren, but Inspector Travis is asking for you,' she told Rigby.

Darren . . . it wasn't her favourite name, she had to admit.

'Right ho,' he said, quickly getting up.

The young officer looked at Alice curiously and then at the mugs of tea and the tin of cake. Alice suddenly felt caught out, and clearly so did Detective Rigby, who walked to the door, making it clear their meeting was over.

'So, what will happen now?' Alice asked, once his colleague had gone. 'What about a funeral?'

'Enya's body has to remain in the police morgue whilst the investigation is ongoing.'

'That poor girl's family,' Alice said. 'Do they know? That she's dead.' She almost said, *or whoever she really is,* but she decided that she wasn't going to share what Gerda had told her about how the police treated cases involving immigrants on the wrong visa.

Rigby sighed, then looked squarely at Alice. 'To be honest with you, I don't know.'

'You don't know?'

He shrugged. 'The case is no longer mine.'

'What?'

'It's gone upstairs.'

'Upstairs?' What on earth did that mean?

He shrugged. 'You can make of it what you will, but my guess is that the Messents have friends in high places.'

'Like who? Who's in charge? Who can I speak to?'

'I'm sorry, I can't give you that information,' he said.

Alice pursed her lips. It was on the tip of her tongue to say that she smelled a rat. Wasn't it more likely the Messents would want a scandal attached to their property to be hushed up? 'She was murdered. That lovely young woman.'

'I know and I'm really sorry, but I can't help you. I'm just following orders.'

'I see,' Alice said, although she really didn't see at all.

'But listen, as much as I appreciate your help – and your cake,' he said, with a bashful face, 'if you want my advice, I think you should leave it well alone.'

He was shutting her out. But what had she really expected? She ran a domestic staff agency, not a crime bureau, for God's sake.

He walked her back out to the reception, but her emotions churned at how unfair this was, how awful it was that the detective was prepared to let the case drop. That a terrible crime had been committed and nobody was going to pay for it.

But as Alice turned away, Agatha stayed rooted to the spot, staring up at the detective, who now crouched down and gently stroked her face.

'Go on, you, hop it,' Rigby told her. 'Or I'll have to arrest you too.'

Alice pulled on Agatha's lead, but Agatha wouldn't budge. Rather embarrassingly, Alice dragged her towards the door, sliding her bottom across the floor. Rigby laughed and shook his head and turned away.

Outside, Alice pulled on her gloves and looked at the door, half tempted to pop back in. But to say what? Hadn't they just said everything there was to say? About poor Enya, at least.

And now it hit her. Was that it? The last time she'd see the detective.

She blew out a frustrated breath, annoyed that this whole

business made her feel so impudent with rage. An old phrase of Mrs Doulton's now sprang to her mind, her mantra that 'if you want something doing, then it's best to do it yourself'. And letting out a determined hurrumph, she set off for home.

21.

It started to rain as Alice made it to Waitrose, and she left Agatha with Jim, *The Big Issue* seller who was huddling under the dripping canopy. She bought a pint of milk, some cream with a yellow reduced sticker on it, an onion, potatoes, leeks and some chives. She'd make some hearty soup, she decided, then light the fire and spend the afternoon with her library book. After the few days she'd had, a nap would probably then be in order.

LEEK AND POTATO SOUP

INGREDIENTS – 50g butter, 450g potatoes peeled and cubed, 1 small onion, 450g leeks, dark green parts removed, cut into rounds, 2 pints chicken stock, 142ml whipping cream, 125g full-fat milk.

METHOD – melt butter until foaming and add potatoes, onion and leek. Stir until all well coated. Season with salt and pepper and toss again. Put a disk of greaseproof paper *over the vegetables to keep in the steam. Cover pan with lid. Cook gently for 10 mins. Uncover pan. Discard paper. Add stock. Bring to boil and simmer for 5 mins. Purée in blender until smooth. Return to pan and add cream and milk.*

Serve with drizzle of cream and chopped chives.

Back outside the supermarket, she smiled, seeing Jim petting Agatha.

'Bet you're pleased the cold snap's over?' she said, buying a magazine and taking Agatha's lead.

'Yes, it's been horrible. I hate this drizzle. Gets right in your bones.'

'Spring's not too far away,' Alice said cheerily, but Jim looked sceptical. They both knew that these long winter months were going to be gruelling and hard.

As she walked back to her flat, she thought about Jim standing in the cold and how awful it was that he had to stay in the hostel several Tube stops away, which he called his temporary home. She often wondered whether she should just invite him to stay with her, not that she had the room, but she still always felt so mean walking away. She resolved to make enough soup to bring him a large flask of it.

Life was often so complex, the right path not always so easy to spot. Like with Enya's death. Alice had so hoped for answers when she'd set out this morning but now she had more questions than ever.

She wanted nothing more than to hop into a warm bath and ring Jinx to tell her all about it, but she couldn't admit that she'd baked the detective a cake without opening herself wide to a level of teasing she wasn't quite feeling robust enough to take.

The more she thought about it, the more she worried she really had now done all she could to help find Enya's killer. But her promise to Gerda weighed heavily on her mind. She'd promised she'd find out exactly what had happened to Enya, but what if the police proved Gerda right by ditching the case? The way Detective Rigby had said that it had gone 'upstairs' had made Alice suspicious. Who was 'upstairs' and what exactly were their powers? It was all terribly unclear.

As she rounded the corner onto her street, all thoughts of Enya were instantly forgotten when she saw two large red fire engines parked outside her building.

'Oh, goodness,' she said to Agatha, upping her pace. What was going on? Please don't let anyone be hurt.

A crowd had gathered in front of the engines, and Alice recognised several of the tenants from upstairs amongst the looky-loos. But there was no sign of any smoke.

'What's happened?' she asked the fireman standing at the edge of a cordon.

'Sorry. I'm afraid you can't go any nearer,' he said. 'We're not sure how safe the building is.'

'But that's my . . . that's where I live.'

'Please, madam, just stand back,' he said, his radio crackling.

Spotting Mr Mantis, Alice shouldered her way through the crowd towards him. The man from the flat above was with him too and, astonishingly, shot Miss Beeton a smile.

'Look, she's here,' he said, jerking Mr Mantis round to face her.

Mantis gave her a flash of his yellow dentures. 'Oh, thank God, thank God, you're OK,' he said.

'But why wouldn't I be?' Alice asked.

'Because we thought you were inside. You and your dog.'

Mr Mantis reached down to stroke her, but Agatha, who had a long – and vindictive – memory, viciously bared her teeth.

'Please,' Alice said, 'will someone just tell me—'

'Your ceiling. His floor,' Mantis said, jabbing a fat finger towards the man from upstairs, who was now looking anywhere but at Alice and talking rapidly into his phone. 'The whole thing's collapsed.'

Alice gawped at Mr Mantis and then pushed forward with Agatha barking by her side. Reaching the front of the small crowd, she saw several more members of the fire crew at the bottom of her steps, surrounded by shards of smashed terracotta pots.

Dusty smoke billowed out from her open front door, which looked like it had been smashed in. She couldn't see through her kitchen windows, but above, through the windows of the first-floor flat, she could see the same dust.

'It's all right, it's all right,' Mr Mantis shouted down to the fire crew, pointing at her. 'She's here.'

A burly crew member with a huge handlebar moustache rushed up to talk to Alice, grinning to begin with, before shouting back down to his crew to call off the search. He started asking a lot of questions, which rushed over Alice in a wave.

As he spoke, she could only look at the smoke and her flat. Her lovely little flat. Her home in ruins. And her things . . . all her beautiful things . . .

'I'm afraid you're not going to be able to get into your property for some time,' she heard the burly fireman telling her. 'At least not until a structural engineer has deemed it safe, which, judging from the damage, isn't going to be any time soon.'

'How bad is it?' Alice finally managed to say.

'The kitchen ceiling's fully down and there's some damage in the other rooms too. One of the old mains pipes burst, so that's the bedroom wrecked as well . . . '

She thought immediately of her prized Agatha Christies.

'But you can just thank your lucky stars you weren't inside,' the crew chief said. 'Or you'd probably be a goner.'

Yes, yes, he was right, of course. She picked up Agatha and squeezed her little dog extra hard.

'You're probably in shock, Miss, if you don't mind me saying,' said the crew chief. 'Do you have somewhere else you can stay? We'll make the door secure for you again. But you really should leave it a day or two to let the dust settle before going in.'

Dressed in a Japanese kimono, with her hair wrapped in an orange turban, Jinx was framed by a riot of colour, being the angels and cherubs on the designer wallpaper of her kitchenette. The cacophony of colours was giving Alice a headache.

'So, what happened then?' Jinx asked, as she plopped slices of lemon into the two large gin and tonics on the worktop.

Rain lashed against the skylight and window, which opened onto a small terrace with a view of the west London cemetery. The view was framed by mint silk curtains Jinx had purloined from one of her previous, larger homes. They ballooned excess material on the floor, which Agatha padded at with her paw.

'Agatha, come here,' Alice said, worried her little dog might mistake the plush green for foliage and decide to cock her leg.

Wriggling her hips past an art deco drinks cabinet, Jinx handed one of the glasses to Alice.

Alice sniffed loudly, dabbing the kitchen roll into the corner of her eye and gratefully taking the glass, as Jinx sat beside her, ruffling Agatha's ears.

'So much for dry January,' Alice said.

'Ah, but this is an emergency,' Jinx told her, 'wouldn't you say?'

She smiled sympathetically and Alice nodded and they clinked glasses. Then she took a big, grateful swig.

Alice was over the worst of the crying, but she felt embarrassed now for losing control so comprehensively in front of Jinx when she'd turned up on the doorstep, bedraggled and angry, with Agatha in her arms.

'You can stay here for as long as you like,' Jinx said. 'Honestly. *Mi casa* and all of that.'

'No, Jinx, I can't. You don't have space.'

The tiny kitchen had a door off it to the bedroom, which also housed inappropriately large furniture, along with a life-sized cast-iron gorilla, which Jinx had adorned with sunglasses and a green feather boa.

'You can have my room,' Jinx said.

'No.'

'Or just camp down in the sitting room.'

Her sitting room where there was barely room enough to sit. 'I'll book into a hotel.'

'You can't afford a hotel.' Alice blushed. Then, as if weighing up whether or not to say it, Jinx added, 'I saw Jasper's text.'

'What text?' Alice said, searching around for her phone.

'It just flashed up when you were in the loo. I didn't mean to read it.'

Alice picked up her phone from the ornate side table. She'd called Jasper earlier. She'd been in such a state that she'd just wanted to tell someone what had happened, but he hadn't picked up. And now she read the text that Jinx had seen.

Still working on the money. Sorry Sis xx

So that's the only reason he'd thought she'd been ringing him – to harass him. Not because she might have been in trouble herself. Jinx cocked her head sympathetically and Alice felt her eyes fill with unwanted tears again.

'He's still ducking you over that money, then?' she said.

Alice shook her head and dabbed away her tears. She wanted to defend Jasper, but right now she couldn't find the words. She hadn't wanted to face it, but the interest on the loan was going to really bite this month. Panic started to rise again as she thought about her home insurance policy, knowing she'd taken out the cheapest one possible. And, pleased as he'd been that she wasn't actually dead, Mr Mantis had already started making noises about leaving the matter of wider building insurance in his solicitor's more than capable hands. In other words, he was going to fight her over every penny.

'I've got a spare duvet somewhere,' Jinx said, going through to her bedroom.

Alice followed her and stood in the doorway as Jinx opened the sliding door of her closet. In spite of her dour mood, Alice had to stop herself from gasping out loud. She'd never seen so many things crammed into one space.

'Wow!'

'Don't judge. I know it's a bit much.'

Alice walked over and surveyed the vast volume of clothes, hats, scarves, shoes and accessories before her.

'You know, you could make a fortune selling some of these?' she said, touching the jammed-together dresses.

'Over my dead body,' Jinx said. 'These are my babies. They all have memories and meaning. They're the very fabric of my life.'

Alice pulled out a slinky white satin jumpsuit. 'Even this one?' she asked.

'Oh, now that *is* a treasure. There was this cute little shop in the meatpacking district in New York. This was back in the day, long before it became as trendy as it is now; 2002 or 2003 and I was with—'

'You've never even worn it,' Alice interrupted. 'Look, it's still got all its labels on.'

'I know but—'

'And it's tiny. Does it actually fit?' Alice asked. 'Be honest.'

'No, but if I went on a diet . . . '

'Oh, for God's sake, Jinx. You're still gorgeous, but you'll never be a . . . ' Alice consulted the label. 'Two. Not unless you get seriously ill.'

'It's not that bad. It's American so a six, not a two.'

'I rest my case. You'll never be a six. Well, I hope not. So why not let her have another lease of life,' Alice said, knowing that Jinx liked to give her clothes a sex. Most were women, but a few odd pieces were male. Alice had yet to fathom the formula. 'What about Pandora? The dress agency. You know by the V&A? I know Bridget who runs it. She'd sell this and give you half of what she makes. Then you could buy something you really want. And that fits,' she added.

'Hmm, maybe,' Jinx said. 'I'll think about it.' Digging deeper into the closet, she hauled out a duvet from the very back. 'Oh, dear,' she said, recoiling at the slight smell of mildew.

'You need a saucer of quicklime,' Alice said. 'That's good for damp.'

'And preserving bodies,' Jinx joked. 'Don't worry, I've got fresh sheets and you probably won't even smell this after a while. Let's set up the sofa bed. It'll be just like old times.'

But as determinedly cheery as Jinx was, and as much as Alice suspected she was just trying to help, Alice knew that sleep was going to be elusive. She felt Agatha's warm body coiled up against hers and put her hand on her soft ears for comfort. Where on earth were they going to live? Whatever was Alice going to do?

22.

On Monday morning, as Alice and Jinx caught the Tube to the office together, Alice realised how important her usual daily walk through the park with Agatha was for getting her headset right for the day. She couldn't fault Jinx, who'd rallied around and had been the perfect host, but Alice felt crumpled and worried in a way she couldn't shake.

Matters soon went from bad to worse. She left three increasingly irate messages for Mr Mantis, who wasn't picking up his phone, requesting his lawyer's details, but she heard nothing back. Her own insurance company was equally unhelpful, a bored woman putting her on hold for ages, only to then tell her she'd have to wait in a queue for the claims department, who promptly dumped Alice into another automated system, which spat her right back out at the start of the loop. Three quarters of an hour later, and Alice was ready to smash the phone against the desk.

Marching into the reception to try and calm herself down, she found Helly chewing the end of her pen, reaching the tail end of the list of potential housekeepers for the Messents that Alice had given her earlier.

' . . . moved to the States . . . ' Helly was muttering out loud, crossing another name off. ' . . . just had a baby . . . ' She ran a red line through the next name too. ' . . . joined a rock band . . . ' With a resigned flourish, Helly struck off the last name on the list.

'What, little Mary Dawes?' Alice could hardly believe what she'd just heard, picturing Mary. She still remembered her acting like a frightened mouse when the family she'd been placed with had invited her to Royal Ascot and Jinx had had to lend her a hat.

'They're called Wobbly Gristle, apparently. Drum and bass,' Helly said. 'Oh, and before you ask, Calista Stubbs is on a yacht with her family in the Bahamas, so she can't fill in either.'

Helly knew Alice too well. She had just been about to suggest Calista, even though she'd not done any real work for them in years.

So that was it. They'd gone through every single one of their reserve list and still had no one. Right on cue, the phone rang. And Alice knew, just *knew*, on a day like today, just who it was going to be.

'Hello, The Good Household Management Agency,' Jinx said, before frowning and clamping her hand over the receiver.

'Let me guess . . . Madame Messent?' Alice said.

'Close.' Jinx pulled a face. 'Thérèse Clement, actually. Her personal assistant.'

'OK, put her through.'

Alice marched back into her office. She'd break the bad news herself.

'Hello, Thérèse, Alice Beeton here,' she said, picking up the phone, feeling some sense of relief, at least, that she wasn't dealing directly with Madame Messent.

'The replacement for Enya? Where is she?' Thérèse cut straight to the point, her tone positively oozing stress. 'We need her here already. We have to leave this afternoon.'

'Oh, right, well, we have been working on it, only—'

But Thérèse wasn't listening. 'And already the monies have been transferred to your account.'

'But we still have to find the right person . . . '

'You're saying you haven't?'

'No, but . . . '

'You said your agency would provide someone. *Tout de suite.* Those were Madame's exact words. And, yes, you agreed. You said it would not be a problem.'

Madame Messent had said *tout de suite*, but Alice hadn't thought she'd meant it literally. She'd assumed she'd still have a few more days to make this right.

'You assured her your agency was to be trusted,' Thérèse snapped.

'Yes, and of course we are, but—'

'*Très bien*,' Thérèse said, 'because a reputation like yours, I'm sure can be broken just as quickly as it can be endorsed.'

Alice felt her cheeks burn at the threat.

'I shall expect the new housekeeper here by three.'

Then the line went dead. Not even a bloody *au revoir.*

Alice slowly put down the phone.

'Wow,' called out Jinx, who Alice now realised had been eavesdropping on the other line. 'What a total and utter *chienne.*'

Alice's phone pinged and a quick glance at its screen confirmed a sizeable deposit had just hit her banking app. A lifeline from the Messents. Meaning so long as she did supply a housekeeper, she could still afford to advance herself her salary so that her loan repayment wouldn't bounce.

In the kitchen, Jinx was stabbing the remains of the frozen tiffin dejectedly with a knife.

'What the hell are we going to do?' she asked. 'We're well and truly snookered.'

'Let's all calm down a minute,' Alice said.

'We've been through everyone. There's no one to send,' Helly said.

'I was thinking . . . ' Alice began, twisting her lips, Mrs Doulton's mantra coming to mind again. Louder this time.

Jinx paused, the knife in her hand and her eyes narrowed.

'Oh no. You've got that look on your face,' Jinx said. 'Out with it.'

'Well . . . ' Alice paused, feeling like she was bouncing precariously on a diving board. She couldn't even really believe what she was about to say, but what other choice was there? 'Why don't I go?'

'Go? Go where?'

'To the Messents'. As their housekeeper.'

'You?' Jinx asked, aghast. The knife clattered onto the counter.

'It's actually not a completely mad idea, you know,' Helly told Jinx, quietly. They were both staring at Alice. 'I mean, she can cook and clean. How hard can it be?'

Alice nodded. 'Hard, I should imagine. But we're out of options.' She nodded to the whiteboard in the office. 'And if I go in as the housekeeper, then maybe, just maybe, I can find out what happened to Enya.'

'But didn't your detective tell you to leave the case alone?' Jinx asked. Alice remembered telling her this, last night over their second – or was it their third? – G and T. 'Isn't it all a bit of a risk?'

'Thérèse and Madame Messent are going away, and Laura will be back at school,' Alice reminded her. 'Surely, it's as good a time as any to have a snoop around that house?'

'She's right,' Helly said. 'You're more thorough than anyone, Alice. You're bound to spot something they've not.'

'Won't they find it weird that someone who runs an agency has now taken the job?' Jinx asked.

'No!' Alice exclaimed, seeing that she'd got the wrong end of the stick. 'I won't be *me*,' Alice said, shaking her head. 'No, that wouldn't be right at all.' It'd be a complete betrayal of all the principles of their agency.

'You mean you're going in undercover?' Helly asked.

'Yes. That's what I had in mind.'

'They haven't met you, the Messents, have they?' Helly asked.

Alice thought about the agency's website, remembering how she'd deliberately refrained from using photos of her staff. She'd used a picture of the front of the building and tastefully framed quotes from satisfied customers. A few framed quotes from Mrs Beeton's book. And since she'd always shunned social media, Alice didn't have a profile online. So, yes, she could potentially get away with being undercover. 'But, actually, now I come to think of it, Thérèse and Madame Messent have heard my voice.'

'If you go in as a housekeeper, they'll never put two and two together,' Helly assured her. 'As you always say, staff are invisible.'

Jinx's eyes were narrowed, but Alice could see she was on board. 'She's right. The Frogs probably think us English all sound the same, anyway. *Les rosbifs*, isn't that what they call us?'

'We'll knock up a fake CV and cobble together some references, just like Enya did,' Helly said. She looked at her watch. 'There's just about time.'

'But . . . oh Alice, it's a bit of a risk,' Jinx said, holding her elbows and staring into her eyes. 'Are you absolutely sure?'

Alice smiled and nodded, touched that Jinx cared about her so much. 'I'll be fine. And anyway, it'll get me out of your hair at the flat. It rather kills two birds with one stone, now that I'm homeless, wouldn't you say?' And besides, Alice thought, what other choice did they have? 'And, not to put too fine a point on it, you heard the woman. She'll ruin our reputation if we don't send someone. You know what Mrs Doulton always said about London . . . '

'It's a small bloody town, so mind your p's and q's!' They laughed together.

Agatha barked excitedly, getting in on the action too. Then cocked her head to one side, as if she'd been asked a question. Alice looked from her little dog's expectant gaze to Helly and Jinx.

'Don't worry. You're coming too,' she told Agatha.

23.

Thérèse Clement was one of those immaculate women who somehow seemed to have a presence much greater than her petite physique.

She was dressed in a stylish light-blue trouser suit with soft leather boots. She had a long silk tie knotted loosely around her neck and her jet-black hair was cropped, the front swept up and away from her high forehead. Her skin was flawless, her large hooded brown eyes set above razor-sharp cheekbones, and she smelt intoxicatingly expensive.

She was, Alice thought, utterly intimidating as only French women could be. But she'd also been utterly rude.

Alice sat with her knees turned in neatly on the pink silk sofa in the Messents' drawing room, acting like she hadn't ever set foot in this house before, and thanking her lucky stars that neither Thérèse nor the Messents had seen her when she'd been summoned here by Detective Rigby on the night of Enya's death.

She felt self-conscious in the black suit that Jinx had chosen for her and tried to still her trembling hands, clasping them tightly together in her lap – making her feel worryingly like a nun. She longed to touch her necklace for comfort, but Jinx had told her not to wear it and she couldn't help feeling that a part of her was missing.

Thérèse was reading the dodgy credentials Helly had printed for her. She wondered whether her alter ego, Caroline Doulton – a cobbled-together identity made up of an old school friend and her former mentor – was going to work.

She'd almost lost her nerve twice on the way here, but Jinx had dropped her a street away in a cab and had assured her that she'd be right there on the other end of the phone. Despite her earlier confidence, Alice had started to get cold feet and she'd clung to Jinx feeling unexpectedly jittery for a whole second or two before letting her go.

But she was here now, she told herself. She just had to hold her nerve and bluff it out, even if Thérèse's silent scrutiny still felt unbearable. In the hall, a rather splendid antique-looking grandfather clock ticked loudly.

'I hope you don't mind about the dog. I came at such short notice from the agency, you see,' Alice blurted, with a nervous smile. Agatha was sitting by the sofa, Alice's foot firmly on her lead. 'I can arrange for her to stay elsewhere, but um . . . Miss Beeton – er, yes, at the agency – she told me to come straight away.' It felt ridiculous, referring to herself like this. She was going to have to get better at this charade if she was going to last.

'I don't think that'll be necessary, as long as she's trained and does not um . . . how do you say it . . . do the business . . . on any of the carpets.' Thérèse didn't look up.

'Good,' Alice said, 'and she most certainly would not.' Or at least Alice would most certainly clean it up sharpish if she did.

Jinx and Helly had been horrified that Alice had insisted on bringing Agatha, but Alice needed an ally in the house otherwise she'd lose her nerve.

The front door slammed and, through the open drawing room doorway, Alice saw a girl dash across the hallway in long strides and up the central stairs.

'Laura,' Thérèse called out.

Reluctantly, Laura reversed back down the stairs and walked over to the door. She was a pretty girl, wearing an ugly sports hoodie that was far too big and black jeans with ripped knees and huge, clumpy boots. Large headphones were slung around her neck, the tinny sound of angry music coming out. As Thérèse spoke to her sharply in French – something about being pleasant to the new lady was all Alice's O-level French picked out – Laura lolled against the doorframe in bored resignation, and all that was missing to complete the stroppy French teen look was a flick of cigarette ash and a pop of pink bubble gum.

'Laura, meet Caroline.' Thérèse switched seamlessly back into English. 'She's our new housekeeper.'

Laura's heavily outlined eyes briefly met Alice's. She was wearing a lot of foundation but it didn't conceal the spots on her forehead. Lack of fruit, vegetables and hydration, thought Alice, seeing the dullness of the child's skin. She'd be sorting that out for starters. Then she checked herself.

Had she heard right? Had Thérèse given her the job? Just like that?

It stunned her that Thérèse was so trusting. It was only now, seeing this process of recruitment 'live' for the first time, that Alice realised how important her agency's reputation was. Because Thérèse had accepted that Alice had come pre-vetted by the agency. An agency whose reputation would be in tatters if this went wrong.

'Hi,' Laura said, with an insincere attempt at a smile, holding up her hand.

Agatha barked once and Alice shushed her.

'Oh! Is that your dog?' Laura asked, only noticing Agatha now.

'Yes. I didn't have anywhere to leave her, so I brought her along. I hope you don't mind?' Alice let go of the lead and Agatha scampered over.

Laura crouched down to pet her. 'She's cute.'

'You can pick her up,' Alice said. 'If you want. She likes a cuddle.'

Laura turned off her headphones and cradled Agatha over her shoulder like a baby, then laughed as Agatha snuffled her ear.

'*Bonjour, petite*,' Laura said with a smile.

Thérèse raised her eyebrows. She'd clearly expected Laura to be a lot more obstructive.

'Can I take her?' Laura asked. 'To my room. I want to show my friends.'

She meant on the phone, Alice realised, taking a second to keep up. Thérèse shrugged, indicating that the decision was Alice's.

'If you'd like.'

Laura turned and walked upstairs with Agatha, who looked over her shoulder at Alice, and Alice wondered whether she actually winked.

And that's when she noticed the hardly perceptible lowering of Thérèse's shoulders. It must be fairly stressful to be tasked with finding a trusted housekeeper at such very short notice,

Alice thought. Especially considering what had happened to the last one.

Handing back Alice's CV, Thérèse smiled for the first time. A smile that revealed that she was wearing one of those plastic braces that were all the rage. Alice, whose own teeth, although rather overlapping in places, were perfectly passable, was fascinated by the fad for adult orthodontics. Although, Eva, one of her housekeepers, had got her teeth done on holiday in Turkey a few years ago, and had come back looking like a completely different person. Oh! Eva, Alice thought. She would have been perfect for this job. Why, oh why had she had to fall in love with that bodyguard from New York?

'You're just what we need. And it seems that Laura is on board. It's tricky dealing with a sixteen-year-old. She's not always so . . . agreeable. So, thank you for coming, Caroline,' Thérèse said.

Alice looked around. Who on earth was she talking to? Oh gosh! She rapidly swivelled back.

'Wonderful.' She grinned, because, of course, Caroline was now her.

'*Très bien*.' Thérèse clapped her perfectly manicured hands together. 'Let me show you around. The first thing you must know is that Monsieur Messent – and we have cleaners in three times a week to ensure this is so – he is very exacting . . . '

'Exacting?'

'Insofar as he likes everything to be—' she threw her hands up in search of the right phrase '—just so. You know. Tidy. Neat.'

Like his study had been, Alice remembered. Or at least until Enya had been killed.

The next hour passed in a blur, as Thérèse took Alice on a whistlestop tour of the house – with the notable exception of Monsieur Messent's study, which she told Alice was 'strictly private and not for you to go into' – before announcing that she and her boss, Camille Messent, would be leaving shortly.

Alice hardly had time to take in her cramped little staff quarters in the attic, before Thérèse whisked her down to the family kitchen. There was no food, Thérèse explained, in an exasperated way, opening the cupboards and fridge, so Alice would have to order supper in tonight.

Hurrying downstairs to the staff kitchen where Jacques had worked on New Year's Eve, Thérèse led her into the little back office there – which she referred to as the ''owskeepers office' – and presented her with an iPad, explaining that it was already set up for doing all the household shopping and food delivery orders from Harrods.

Alice was about to protest that she was perfectly happy to go to actual shops to stock the kitchen, but Thérèse cut her off, looking at her phone and pulling a face.

'I must go, but there's nothing to it,' Thérèse said, with a look as if to say that being a housekeeper was a doddle.

'Are there any alarms I need to know about? In case I go out and there's no one else here? Or spare keys in case anyone loses theirs?' Alice asked. Any that might fit a certain study? she was actually thinking.

'Ah, *oui*. We are very security conscious, particularly after . . . ' Thérèse looked Alice up and down. ' . . . I'm assuming your boss lady . . . the very stiff upper lip one . . . '

'Miss Beeton,' Alice said, trying not to sound offended.

' . . . yes, your Miss Beeton,' Thérèse continued, 'I assume she has told you all about our – how shall I put this? – *troubles* over New Year?'

Troubles. Hardly the phrase Alice would have used. More like *murder most foul.* Only from the testy, if determined, little smile on Thérèse's face, it seemed this whole episode was already something to be glossed over in this house.

'Yes . . . Enya . . . ' Alice said.

'The burglary,' Thérèse corrected her, like Alice had simply mispronounced the word. 'The family . . . I suppose all of us . . . and particularly for the child . . . we all just want to move on.'

'Yes, I'm sure,' Alice said. To move on and forget. Like Enya's life hadn't been worth anything at all.

'You must of course always put the alarm on if there's no one in the house,' Thérèse said. 'I'll WhatsApp you the codes and the instructions. Obviously, you read French, no?'

'*Ah, oui, un pois*, or at least I'm sure I'll be able to figure it out,' Alice said, already worrying now whether she had just said *pois* and not *peu*? 'And the keys?' she reminded Thérèse.

'Here.' Dipping into her purse, she pulled out a jangly set of twenty or so keys on a brass ring. 'Everything you'll need.'

Back upstairs in the hall, Camille Messent was striding down the stairs in heeled boots, carrying a small overnight case with a large gold double-C on its side. She was talking on the phone in French. When Thérèse pointed Alice out, she smiled apologetically and held up a finger, which was adorned in a rather funky square-cut aquamarine ring, a gesture that Alice interpreted as pausing their introduction until she had more time.

Alice smiled back, thinking how extraordinarily beautiful Camille Messent was in person. The photographs that Alice had studied when she'd visited Enya really didn't do her justice. She was wearing a midnight-blue silk jumpsuit with a collection of thin gold chains, and a leather coat with a fake fur collar. She had the kind of soft but commanding voice that made Alice want to listen to her all day. Not that she could understand what she was saying. No wonder this woman had an amazing job and a hectic life. She must be in demand everywhere. Alice suddenly felt ashamed that she'd been so judgemental about her leaving her daughter at this time. Perhaps her husband needed to be doing more to step up? Though she remembered the warning Katy Ellison had given her about them as a couple too. Who knew what lay beneath this smart veneer?

Thérèse suddenly seemed much less glamorous in the wake of her boss. She was busy shoving papers and chargers into a stylish leather case and barely managed the most hurried of goodbyes to Alice, who babbled several pressing questions about her actual duties. Like, were there any social functions she needed to be preparing for? And when would Monsieur Messent next be home? Oh, and where did Laura even go to school?

But Thérèse told her to message any queries. And with that, she was gone, trotting down the front steps after Madame Messent and into a waiting black cab.

24.

Closing the heavy black door, Alice leant back against it and blew out a pent-up breath. Tea, she needed tea. Hopefully she'd feel better once she'd familiarised herself with the kitchen.

She was strangely jittery as she walked along the corridor, and not just from all the subterfuge, but because it was only now that it was dawning on her what a huge responsibility this job was. She would stay until Laura went back to school and then Jinx and Helly simply had to find someone else to take over.

Unlike the impersonal industrial kitchen in the basement, the family kitchen was cheerily sociable, with a large marble island housing an induction hob and high stools around one end. Against one wall stood a double-sized fridge, which was almost empty except for a Tupperware box full of cheese and a few lonely vegetables in the chiller. Next to it was a packed Swisscave wine fridge. She thought of Jinx and how much she'd relish the expensive bottles inside.

Having had a good rummage through the cupboards and a look in the freezer, where she was pleased to find some bags of frozen herbs, Alice could see the basics of several hearty meals, despite Thérèse's declaration that there was no food. Besides, she was a great believer in the art of 'using up', something the great Mrs Beeton had promoted too. The need for economy was greater then, perhaps, but no less relevant today, even in a wealthy household like this.

Alice took out the rice and the remains of a packet of orzo from the slide-out larder, remembering that marvellous Turkish restaurant in Brighton that she and Jinx used to go to on their weekends away. And having gathered together as many ingredients as she could, she was pleased to see there was sufficient for her store cupboard pilaf.

Store Cupboard Pilaf

INGREDIENTS – 4 tbsp olive oil, 1 tin of chickpeas, drained, 2 tsp chilli flakes, 1 tsp cumin seeds, 200g long grain rice, 2 tbsp butter, 80g orzo, 1 onion, finely chopped, 1 clove of garlic, finely chopped, 500ml hot chicken from a cube, juice of 1 lemon, 3 tbsp chopped flat-leaf parsley, 3 tbsp chopped dill, 1 jar of red peppers, drained and finely sliced, handful of toasted flaked almonds, half tub plain yoghurt, 1 tbsp harissa

METHOD – Heat the oven to 180 degrees C. Pour half the olive oil into a roasting tray and add the chickpeas. Toss to coat and season with half the chilli flakes, cumin seeds, sea salt and pepper. Roast for 30-35 min until crispy and golden.

Wash the rice until the water runs clear. Heat the remaining oil with the butter in a lidded non-stick frying pan over *a medium-high heat. Add the orzo, coat it in the fat and toast it, stirring for a few minutes until golden. Turn down the heat slightly, slide in the onion and remaining chilli flakes, and sauté with the orzo for 5 min until it starts to soften. Add the garlic and rice. Stir until the rice is bright and opaque. Pour over the stock and bring to a simmer, then turn the heat down to low, cover with a lid and cook for 18-20 min until all the stock is absorbed. Remove from heat and leave to sit with the lid on for 10 min until the grains are plump. Stir through the lemon juice, herbs, peppers and chickpeas, and season to taste. Garnish with the nuts.*

Mix the yoghurt and harissa to serve on the side.

Satisfied that supper was in hand, Alice went upstairs and knocked on the door of the room she thought was Laura's, although she could hardly remember, her tour had been that fast.

'Supper will be ready in ten minutes,' she said when she got no answer.

'You can just bring it up,' Laura shouted back from inside.

'Oh no. That's not possible.' Alice turned away. 'And do bring Agatha down when you come. She'll be hungry too.'

Back in the kitchen, she laid the countertop with placemats, glasses, and the correct cutlery, and was just lighting some candles she'd found when Laura came in wearing a slouchy tracksuit, which was cropped to show off her tiny midriff. She let go of

Agatha who shook herself out — a sure sign she'd been over-cuddled — and trotted happily over to the bowl of water Alice had put down for her.

'What's this?' Laura asked, gazing in confusion at the place settings.

'Supper. What does it look like?' Alice said. 'Please take a seat.'

Laura's eyebrows shot up, but she nonetheless sat down at the counter and Alice smiled, spooning the pilaf into a bowl that she'd warmed in the oven.

'Surely your last housekeeper ate with you?' Alice asked.

'I suppose. Sometimes.' Laura pursed her lips. 'You didn't hear? About what happened to her?'

'Only the bare details.' It stood to reason that anyone taking on this position here would have been told something about it. Alice reached for the bowl of marinated tomatoes she'd prepared with the lovely bottle of Greek olive oil she'd found, keen to leave Laura space to say more. 'I'm so sorry. It must have been dreadful?'

'Maman and Papa, they don't talk about it,' Laura said.

There was a crack in her voice and Alice suddenly felt her heart go out to this young woman who was clearly trying to be as diplomatic as she could. She thought of Jacques and how he'd said on the night of Enya's murder that Laura had thought the world of her. She couldn't imagine the trauma of getting to know someone and them then being killed. In your own home. It certainly wasn't something any teenager should have to experience. Alice found it worrying that her parents had left Laura in the care of a stranger — at such a traumatic time. Even if that stranger was herself.

'What was she like?' Alice asked.

At first, Laura said nothing, just took a spoonful of her food. 'This is good,' she said, then after a few thoughtful bites, 'Enya was always nice . . . particularly to me . . . '

'But?' Alice prompted. She'd worked with too many staff members discussing too many thorny clients over the years not to sense when one was in the air.

'But there was something . . . I don't know, funny about her . . . '

'Funny how? As in haha, or strange?' Another one of Mrs Doulton's sayings and one that now made Laura smile.

'A bit of both, maybe.'

'Was it her language or accent?' Alice asked.

'No. Her English was perfect.' Laura looked surprised.

'What sort of strange then?' Alice asked, heaping another spoonful of pilaf into Laura's bowl.

'I don't know . . . just sometimes she didn't seem to know how to make things or do things. Like the Pacojet ice cream maker,' she said, nodding at the sleek stainless-steel machine in the corner of the kitchen. 'Everyone who's ever worked here knew how to use that, but not her . . . '

'How odd,' Alice said, hoping to God that Laura didn't ask her to whip her up anything using the notoriously tricky machine now.

Laura shrugged. 'I guess I just had a feeling, you know? That there was more to her than she was letting on.'

Alice nodded. 'Agatha's like that,' she said. 'She can always tell when someone's not being completely up front with her.' Hmm, like I'm not being honest with you now, Alice thought, hoping that Laura wasn't quite as good a mind reader as her little dog.

'She's lovely,' Laura said. 'My parents would never let me have a puppy. They don't let me do anything I want to.'

Alice picked up on the note of anger in her voice.

'Agatha can have her moments, believe me. It's not that easy looking after a dog. Oh, I forgot the yoghurt.'

Alice retrieved the bowl of harissa yoghurt she'd mixed earlier from the fridge.

'This is nice too,' Laura said, tucking in.

'Good,' Alice said, genuinely pleased.

'I'm not used to home-cooked stuff. I mostly get Deliveroo – something else Enya was very happy for me to do too – so long as Thérèse isn't eating with us, because she's so allergic . . .'

Right, Alice thought, because she probably only knew about five recipes – if the rest of her housekeeping credentials were anything to go by.

'And my parents eat out all the time,' Laura continued. 'Papa goes to the same few restaurants again and again. Because they have good hygiene and always cook his food and present it just so.'

Just so. That same phrase Thérèse had used about him.

'It's some kind of OCD, only we're not allowed to mention it,' Laura said.

Ah, well, that made sense, Alice thought. About the house too. How clean it had to be all of the time.

'And Maman . . . Maman would have a fit if she could see me having carbs in the evening.'

'Really?'

Alice shook her head. If she knew one thing about teens, it was that they needed feeding. She longed to tell Laura about Mrs Doulton and about her common-sense advice about eating three square meals a day and a little bit of everything in moderation, but she sensed she would have to get to know her a little better before she started dispensing such nuggets of wisdom.

'She's not here, and whilst I am, I intend to give you a balanced diet,' Alice said with a friendly smile.

Laura paused, as if someone actually caring about what she ate was a joke.

Spreading her napkin out over her lap again, Alice tried hard not to glance too obviously at Laura's terrible table manners. The poor girl couldn't shovel it in fast enough.

'Do you cook?' she asked Laura, but Laura pulled a face as if the suggestion was absurd. At her age, Alice had regularly made supper. But then she'd had Mrs Doulton to show her how.

'Never. But I met a chef recently. He was kind of cool.'

Was she talking about Jacques? She must be.

'He was working here on the night that . . . ' Laura's voice trailed off.

'Oh,' Alice said, 'I see . . . ' She meant the night Enya had been murdered, of course.

'And what was Enya doing that night? Was she busy helping with the party?'

'Yes.'

'Only I think . . . yes, I'm sure, Miss Beeton at the agency . . . she mentioned to me this morning that Enya was up in your father's study when she died . . . '

'Yes,' Laura said, 'but before that she had been helping . . . at the beginning when we were welcoming the guests . . . '

'Only then she went down to talk to your chef friend. Just a bit before your mother's speech,' Alice said.

Laura looked her over curiously for a moment, leaving Alice worried she'd started pushing this all a bit too hard.

'Just something else Miss Beeton mentioned,' she lied. 'Because I think the chef was one of hers. On her books.'

'Ah, yes. OK, I see,' Laura said, accepting the logic of this. 'Yes, she was there.'

'Right, because you went down there too, didn't you?' Alice smiled innocently, already knowing from Detective Rigby that this was true. 'Just something else Miss Beeton said,' she lied again – in fact, *was* it a lie, because she was saying it right now?

'Yes.' Laura blushed.

'Did you talk to Enya?'

'No, well, not down there . . . when I last saw her, she was already on the stairs going back up . . . '

Ah, a further sighting of Enya. This was news. 'Back up to the party?' Alice asked.

'No, further up. I think – yes, now I remember – she said she was popping to the upstairs bathroom . . . the staff toilet downstairs, it was occupied.' Laura's eyes glistened. 'Something as silly as that. That really was the last thing she said to me.'

Alice's mind raced. Laura must be referring to the guest bathroom on the half-landing near Monsieur Messent's study that Alice had seen on her tour. But what then? Had Enya heard something in the study that had lured her to her doom? Meaning she'd had a perfectly good – and innocent – reason for being up there after all?

'You know you ask a lot of questions,' Laura said.

'Ah, yes.' Alice managed to smile. 'I suppose I do have something of an inquisitive mind.'

Laura's phone tinged. Rapidly. Three times in a row.

'Goodness. Who are all those messages from?' Alice said, grateful for the distraction, worried Laura might have already come too close to working out that Alice wasn't quite what she seemed.

'Friends. Just talking about going back to school,' Laura said, relaxing. 'But I've been looking at the trains. It doesn't look like they're running. There's a strike.'

'Isn't your father taking you? Is he away too?' Thérèse still hadn't replied to any of the queries Alice had messaged her.

Laura pulled a face, as if Alice were crazy. 'Oh no, he's in town. But he's, like, way, way too busy.'

'I can get someone to give you a lift, if you like?' Alice said, thinking of Massoud.

'No, it's OK,' Laura said.

She remembered what Jinx had been like at that age and how she'd always wanted to bunk off school. She didn't trust Laura to actually get there, if left to her own devices.

'Oh, I insist. I promised I'd get you back to school so that's what I'll do,' Alice said with one of her firm smiles just to let Laura know that the subject was closed.

25.

In her old flat – her *poor* old flat – Alice had been used to the distant rumble of traffic, the chatter of pedestrians on the pavement, and most definitely the *boom-boom* bass of her neighbour upstairs.

The room she'd been given in the Messents' attic was eerily silent in comparison. But lovely too, she supposed, in its small but perfectly formed way, with its sash window overlooking the trees in the back garden, and its large, comfortable bed with linen in muted greys. The en suite bathroom was the cleanest and most modern Alice had ever used and was stocked with expensive toiletries and the fluffiest of towels.

Perhaps Enya had been similarly impressed at this level of luxury after living wherever she previously had – which certainly hadn't been The Dorchester, Alice now knew. She hoped she'd at least had a few decent nights' sleep before her life had been cut short in the deplorable way that it had.

Alice sighed under the heavy duvet and picked up her telephone. It was 2 a.m. She missed her little alarm clock and her own bed. In fact, she missed everything about her old life. Apart from Jinx's slightly pongy duvet. But even surrounded by all this luxury here, and exhausted from faking her new role as housekeeper, she still couldn't sleep, her mind anxiously whirring.

She glanced at the little black suitcase she'd brought with her. She'd filled it with essentials after visiting what was left of her flat. The fire chief had been as good as his word and had made the front door secure for her and had left the padlock key for it with Mr Mantis. She could barely believe the devastation she'd witnessed inside.

So many of her lovely little things had been ruined or outright destroyed. And big things too. The ceiling had come down in whacking great clumps of plaster, all over her sofa and ottoman. But what had broken her heart the most was her bookcase face down in the soggy mess. Fortunately, her Christies, being on their own separate case, had been salvageable, and were now holidaying on Jinx's bookshelves. And her Mrs Beeton tome had been protected by having its own kitchen cupboard. But so much else had been lost.

Mantis himself had been next to useless, somehow managing to stonewall just as much in the flesh as he had done on the phone and online. He'd hidden behind his lawyer again, another odious creature, Alice had learned now she'd finally spoken to him. Alice had been given no option other than to employ – again, at vast expense – her own lawyer to deal with the matter from here on in.

She turned on the night light and picked up her book, but Barney had been right about it. The detective was in the 'scratching their head phase', as Alice liked to call it, ruminating on clues and going round in circles. Alice was tempted to skim forward – although she knew she'd miss something vital if she did. Being stuck in the middle was part of the process. Like the point you got to when mixing a cake, when one's arm was aching and it was tempting to give up, but you still knew that the extra effort to get all the ingredients combined to their proper consistency was going to be worth it in the end.

Alice got up and put on the dressing gown that had been hanging on the back of the bathroom door. Thrusting her hands deep into its pockets, she momentarily wondered whether Enya had worn it and if she might find something she'd left. But they were empty. In fact, the entire suite seemed to have been cleared of all traces of her predecessor. Leaving it now as impersonal as a hotel room.

Solving the real-life crime of who'd killed Enya was looking like it was going to be a lot, lot harder than Alice had anticipated. How she wished she could just set up her whiteboard in here and somehow magically figure it out. But living in the very building in which Enya had been murdered was having the reverse effect of the one she'd expected, blurring the details, rather than clarifying them.

She needed clues. Clues, that, if she were in a crime novel, would almost certainly turn out to be right under her nose. Detective Rigby would already have searched this room with his team, of course. But Jinx was right. How thorough had they really been?

Turning on all the lights, she surveyed the room. Agatha growled from where she was curled up on the little chair in the corner, clearly annoyed that her beauty sleep had been disturbed, as Alice set about searching under the bed, and through the empty wardrobes and drawers.

Finding nothing, she turned her attention to the cubbyhole

shelving opposite the bed. Many of the books on display in the compartments were the kind of random second-hand hardbacks that Alice already knew interior designers bought as job lots.

What was the name of that delightful young designer Alice had once got in for one of her clients? Ah, yes. Belinda Monteray. She'd been all the rage ten years ago and Alice had once accompanied her to a car boot sale to buy books just like these – ones with stylish spines and covers that people hardly ever opened, but that added an artistic or cultured feel to a room.

But whilst these books might once have been on proud display in, say, the drawing room downstairs, they were now evidently deemed sufficiently out of fashion to have been relegated to the staff quarters.

One by one – well, you never could be too thorough, could you? – Alice pulled each out and examined them, flicking through their unloved pages, rather hoping that a clue might simply fall out and land in her lap.

It didn't. She'd almost given up hope of finding anything interesting, when she noticed a clutch of what she at first thought were clothes shop labels simply staring right up at her from the floor beside the little wicker bin, next to a lollipop stick – all presumably spilt there by whoever had last cleaned this room.

The labels turned out, in actual fact, to be ticket stubs. And for London museums, of all things. The top one was for the Tate Modern and was dated . . . just after Enya had started working here. Then there was one for Tate Britain a day later. Then one for the Victoria & Albert Museum dated just a couple of days after that.

What to make of them? Had Enya simply been an art fan? Or

maybe she'd been meeting someone? A friend – or maybe even a lover? Alice thought, her pulse now starting to race. Because it hadn't occurred to her before, but someone as attractive as Enya could hardly have been short of attention, could she?

Blimey, what if she did have a partner and they didn't even know what had happened to her? Or what if they did? What if they'd somehow been complicit in her death?

Whoa! *What if what if what if . . . What if,* Alice reprimanded herself, *instead of letting your imagination run away with you, you simply try sticking to the facts instead?*

Doing just that, she put on her glasses and turned the Tate Britain stub over to see if there was any other information that she'd missed, like perhaps some credit card details printed there. But whilst there was nothing like that, which might reveal Enya's true identity, her heart did skip a little beat, as she noticed that something was written there, in tiny handwriting.

Trying to decipher the slantways scrawled words, she could just about hazard they weren't written in English, but beyond that she was flummoxed. Even when she used her phone's magnifying glass app, the handwriting was too difficult to read. Then she remembered – Barney had that whopping great illuminated magnifying glass he used for making his matchstick models and examining all those stamps he was obsessed with collecting. That would probably do the trick. And he'd once worked for GCHQ, so he'd probably cracked all sorts of codes. Surely he'd have no trouble with some scrawled handwriting like this?

Alice called up Enya's CV on her phone, to see if she'd included painting or art history amongst her interests, but she hadn't. Plus, Alice promptly reminded herself, this whole CV was probably no more than a pack of fibs.

But what if – go on, surely she was allowed just one more? – the reason for Enya's interest in art was not just personal, but something to do with the Messents themselves?

26.

At half past seven the next morning, Alice was in the kitchen packing away the last of the online order that had been delivered. She'd never been one for internet shopping herself, so she was impressed with the speed at which an entire grocery shop had been delivered. She took out the notepad from the pocket of her tunic and saw that every item she'd requested was here.

She still couldn't quite get used to the feel of the black and white tunic and trouser combinations that Thérèse had left her. She hadn't worn a uniform since she'd been a Girl Guide. But Thérèse had explained that Madame Messent was a real stickler for formalities like this that distinguished family and guests from staff. Leaving Thérèse herself as what, exactly? Alice hadn't been able to stop herself wondering. Because, of course, Thérèse dressed, quite literally, like a lady in waiting – clearly aiming on being every bit as important as her boss one day.

But no matter, Alice told herself now. A uniform was a helpful armour of sorts. Now, more than ever, she needed to blend into the background. In this strange kitchen, in a strange house, with a new persona, she felt reassuringly unrecognisable as herself. Even Agatha was giving her the side eye.

Alice could have done with her trusted radio to help her feel a bit more relaxed, but her ears strained for signs of life in the house. After finding the museum tickets last night, she couldn't help but wonder what other clues Detective Rigby and his team might have missed.

And what about Alex Messent's study? The scene of the crime itself. Alice was itching to get up there and have a good snoop around.

Laura came in and slumped against the counter, texting. Alice cleared her throat, until Laura looked up and said good morning. When Alice enquired what she'd like to eat, Laura shrugged and said she didn't 'do' breakfast, to which Alice replied that that wouldn't 'do' at all. Not taking no for an answer, Alice went through the options and to her astonishment discovered that Laura had never had eggy bread before.

Eggy Bread With Fruit Compote

INGREDIENTS – 2 medium eggs, 1 tbsp milk, 2 slices white bread, 1 tbsp butter, 1 bag frozen berries, 3 oz golden caster sugar.

METHOD – put berries in the saucepan with caster sugar. Allow berries to defrost, then gently heat. Beat the eggs in a bowl with salt and pepper. Add the milk. Dip each piece of bread in egg mixture. Heat frying pan and add butter. When foaming, add bread and fry.

Serve the eggy bread with fruit compote and yoghurt.

Whilst she fried the bread, Alice tried to engage Laura about her preferred morning routine and, trying to be as subtle as she could, checked on her father's whereabouts. Laura informed her that he'd come back late last night but had probably already left for the gallery this morning. He never ate breakfast either, it seemed.

Laura then said, when quizzed on her own plans for the day, that she was going to meet friends and then study at the library – an excuse to leave the house that Alice, even with her limited knowledge of teenagers, suspected was entirely spurious. Nevertheless it was one that was most welcome.

As soon as she'd left, Alice made herself useful clearing up the breakfast dishes, before heading down into the basement to the office, where she methodically opened every drawer and flicked through the diaries and notebooks on the shelves. Then she sifted through the paperwork, looking out for anything that might be pertinent to the case.

Case. Yes, she really had just thought that. And why not? Because of course now Enya's death really was a case that she was trying her best to solve. But there was nothing much of interest, just items like an unpaid bill from December from Grass 'n' Gutters. She put it to one side with a little shudder. What kind of person put an 'n' in their business? Then she spotted the invoice from Charles Tavistock for his services at the New Year's Eve party.

'Ah yes. Charles.' She took her little notebook from her tunic pocket, flipping to a fresh page and writing down, 'Charles', then a 'J' in a circle. She'd get Jinx on that one right away. Because who knew what the great society photographer might have seen?

Next, she checked out the CCTV system, working out from

the instructions that the footage was stored on the iPad. She flicked through it, looking at the grainy black and white images taken at the front door, surprised to see her own visit to Enya just before Christmas. She quickly erased it and fast-forwarded to New Year's Eve and the days after, the police coming and going and then a few frames of Alex Messent and Thérèse together on the doorstep. They seemed to be arguing, her face drawn and upset. She showed him a phone and he recoiled. She said something and he shook his head and covered his eyes, then looked down at her before speaking.

Alice reversed the frames and recorded the whole scene on her phone. Jacques had a sister who was deaf. He was an expert on lip-reading – especially in his mother tongue. Perhaps he could make out what they were saying to each other and if it had any relevance at all. Whatever it was, neither of them looked very happy about it.

Right. She checked her watch. Telling Agatha she'd be back down in a few minutes, she shut the little dog in the room. Stealth really had never been Agatha's forte.

Armed with a very complicated-looking, but surprisingly light, designer vacuum-cleaner as cover, Alice headed to Monsieur Messent's bedroom and knocked loudly on the door.

Nothing.

Good. As Laura had suggested, he must have gone out already.

She walked quickly along the corridor towards his study, listening at the various other rooms which she passed, noticing the sun from the domed skylight above casting shards of kaleidoscopic light on the cream and gold carpet runner. The clock in the hall ticked loudly, but otherwise, the house was silent.

Edging closer now to the study itself, she peered up at each of the framed watercolours, thinking that they must be very valuable indeed to have little brass lights above them and to be protected like this behind security glass. Were they alarmed? she wondered. A naughty part of her was almost tempted to take one down to see.

If only she weren't so dreadfully ignorant about art. She'd always thought that one day, she'd go to night school and study art history, but time seemed to have crept up on her and now the fantasy had popped. But focus! she told herself. There might not be a future at all if she somehow got caught breaking into Monsieur Messent's study like this.

Not that it proved as easy as she'd hoped. After pressing her ear to the door and listening very quietly for upwards of a minute, she tried the handle. Of course the door was locked. Still, no matter. Taking her big brass keyring from her belt, she slid the first likely-looking key into the lock. No dice. She tried another then another after that.

Then matters went rapidly from bad to worse. The last key she tried – the very last key that she had – got stuck. And wouldn't come out. No matter how hard she twisted it and rattled it about. Only then it did. Gripping onto it with both hands, Alice found herself falling slap bang onto her bottom in the corridor – where she let out a little yelp.

Before she could even get up, another key turned in the lock. Quickly, all the way round – from inside. The door flew open and a half-naked man glared down.

'*Qu'est-ce que vous faites?*' he shouted, striding towards her.

Crikey. This had to be Alex Messent. Yes, she recognised him from the photographs. He was wearing only running shorts and trainers, with a white towel around his neck. His body was toned and sweat glistened on his brow, as he breathed heavily.

'Oh, Monsieur Messent,' Alice said, her voice catching. She felt herself flush, but she had no choice but to 'style it out', as Jinx would say. She smiled brightly, her back teeth clenching with the effort, as she managed to get back up onto her feet.

'And who are you?' he said.

'I'm Al . . . um . . . I mean, I'm Caroline, the new housekeeper. Thérèse must have told you about me?' Risking another smile, she held out her hand.

But Alex Messent was clearly not impressed, continuing to stare down his long Gallic nose at her, until she let her hand fall awkwardly to her side.

'I was cleaning and—' she started to explain, waggling the vacuum's nozzle hopefully at him by way of an explanation.

'This is my study.'

'Oh, is it?' Alice said, but the sheer level of her own disingenuousness only made her blush.

Alex Messent was a lot taller than he'd appeared in the photographs and he towered over her even now that she was upright. And, just as she'd seen in his photograph – there was the dimple in his chin.

'Thérèse must have told you that this is,' he then said, shaking his head in disbelief, as he searched for the words in English, 'off limits.'

And, of course, yes, Thérèse had.

'Ah, yes, I suppose, um, that must have just got lost in translation,' Alice said. 'And you're quite sure it doesn't need a clean?'

Alice asked, her throat dry — because, heck, nothing ventured nothing gained.

'Perfectly sure,' he said. 'What was your name again?'

'Caroline,' Alice said. 'Caroline Doulton.'

He nodded once, like he'd just memorised it. And walking away, she glanced back, to see him still standing there in the doorway, watching her. Hurrying back downstairs with the vacuum cleaner, she pictured his brooding, dark eyes.

She'd have to be much more careful in future. Alex Messent looked like the kind of person she really didn't want to make a habit of crossing.

27.

Alice spent the rest of the day dealing with the various maintenance people Thérèse had organised to visit the house – a man
to service the boiler, a florist who refreshed the flowers, and the
cleaners.

Just as she'd promised Gerda, Alice talked to all of them in
turn, but although they'd been here to help set the house on the
day of the party, they'd all left long before the first guests had
arrived. And none of them had anything useful to say about either
the Messents or Enya herself.

She turned her attention to the laundry, noticing that Alex
Messent wore black silk socks with a small gold motif, which
needed a cool wash, and there were a few white shirts that would
need a much hotter wash. None of them were actually very dirty,
but Alice noticed that one smelt different – although she felt
rather ridiculous for sniffing one of his shirts – definitely more
like perfume than aftershave.

By the time Laura came back, Alice was exhausted. The
Messents' daughter had already eaten at a pizza place with her
friends so Alice left the simple salmon and vegetable supper
she'd prepared for her in the fridge. She must have found it,

though, because at midnight, when Alice came down to make a camomile tea, she saw the dirty plate beside the dishwasher. Or perhaps that had been her mysterious father, who as far as Alice knew, had not left the house all day.

The next morning, Monsieur Messent finally did leave, but without a word to either Alice or Laura who were both in the kitchen. Alice noted the way Laura's cinnamon toast paused midway to her mouth, as they heard the front door slam. She continued eating, but she seemed somehow relieved that he'd gone. What a strange and frosty relationship they had. But then Alex Messent was a very chilly person. Alice couldn't imagine having a father like that or living in this mausoleum of a home. No wonder poor Laura didn't want to spend any time here.

When she left shortly after breakfast with her backpack full of books to meet her friends, and with no clue as to when Alex Messent might suddenly arrive back home, Alice felt unnerved. Standing in the big hallway, she felt simultaneously alone and observed, in a way she couldn't quite put her finger on.

'Come on, Agatha,' she said. 'Let's get out of here.'

Fifteen minutes later, when Alice and Agatha alighted from the bus in Sloane Square, she waved at Jinx who was waiting for her outside Peter Jones. She was wearing a baby blue fake fur coat, a leather skirt and zippy ankle boots and – rather optimistically given the dull day – large Dior shades. It was only seeing Jinx's friendly face that made Alice realise how much tension she'd been under, and she felt unexpected tears prickle in the corners of her eyes as her friend hurried towards her and pulled her into a tight embrace. Only Agatha barking caused Jinx to break away.

'Oh, you jealous girl,' Jinx said, smooching Agatha, who practically swooned with love.

They set off towards the mews where Charles Tavistock had his studio, Jinx linking her arm into Alice's.

'So? How is it? Being on the other side?' she asked.

'It's not a game, Jinx,' Alice said, miffed by her tone. 'I'm taking a serious risk.'

'I know you are, darling, I know.'

'I mean, to be honest, it's awful. I don't have a second to myself. And Mr Mantis finally got back to me, but I was so busy yesterday I couldn't take his calls. You know how he goes on, and I can't risk anyone overhearing my conversation. Honestly, I'm on eggshells, Jinx. What if someone realises that I'm not Caroline Doulton? The tension is unbearable.'

'You can do it,' Jinx reminded her. 'You've done the hard bit. They've employed you. And . . . ' Jinx probed. 'More importantly, what have you found out?'

Alice gave her a blow-by-blow account of everything that had happened since she'd arrived at the Messents' house, including her encounter with Alex Messent himself.

'What's he like in the flesh?' Jinx asked as they arrived at the mews, waiting for a black cab to reverse out of its narrow entrance.

'Hard to describe,' Alice said, remembering how his physical presence had been so intimidating. She didn't want to tell Jinx she'd been scared.

'Don't give me that. Come on. In two words . . . ?'

'Inscrutable and French.'

'And his wife?'

'She's ridiculously beautiful and glamorous, but we haven't been properly introduced. I have to say, I'm astonished the Messents are both so trusting. Just leaving me in the house.'

'Why? You came highly recommended. Helly and I worked hard on those fake references.'

'But I could be anyone.'

'Not if you're recommended by The Good Housekeeping Agency. You haven't built a reputation for years for nothing.'

They walked down the cobbled mews, past the row of expensive cars, until, near the end, Jinx stopped and pointed.

'It's this one,' she said and bounded up to the red door and knocked loudly. Agatha sniffed around the planters and then the door opened.

'Ay ay. Double trouble,' Charles Tavistock said with his cockney drawl.

He was tall and rangy, his straggly shoulder-length curls styled to cover a thinning patch. His extremely white teeth contrasted his slightly orange fake tan and he was wearing a grey, loosely knit jumper with a whole array of silver pendants on a leather chain. His tight jeans were frayed at the bottom, just above his fur-lined biker boots.

'Hey, Charlie. Long time, no see,' Jinx said, kissing him on both cheeks. 'Wow. This place hasn't changed a bit.'

'And neither have you,' Charles said, with a lascivious guffaw and a wide smile. Goodness, those gnashers really were quite something, Alice thought.

He was clearly waiting for Jinx to return the compliment, but instead, she noticed his balding head, smiled and made a 'huh' sound, before swishing past him into his studio.

With a jovial shrug, Charles turned his attention to Alice, greeting her like a long-lost friend, even though he'd only met her once, briefly, years ago, when he'd only had eyes for Jinx.

Inside, the ground floor of the mews house had been hollowed out into a cavernous space, the brickwork painted black with matt black floorboards to match. In the centre of the room was a vinyl backdrop in a vivid mustard yellow, with two huge umbrella lights facing it.

'You still got my gorilla?' Charles asked Jinx. 'She nicked it off a shoot with the Stones,' he told Alice.

'You gave it to me,' Jinx said.

'Did I, though?' he asked. 'That's not how I remember it.'

'You were rather stoned yourself,' she joked.

'You should give it back,' Alice told Jinx, ignoring her wide-eyed glare of betrayal. 'It completely overtakes your flat. Plus, she's recently committed to de-cluttering,' Alice told Charles.

'Yes, I suppose I did get rid of one very annoying thing a couple of days ago,' Jinx sniped, pointedly.

Agatha sniffed around the floorboards.

'You can let him off the lead,' Charles said.

'Oh, Agatha's a girl.'

'Right. She can smell the cat, probably. He's around here somewhere,' he said.

'So . . . what can I get you?' Charles asked, rubbing his hands together. 'Coffee? Or something more bubbly?'

Alice agreed to a coffee, but Jinx was straight in there with the champagne. 'I'm just greasing the wheels,' she whispered to Alice, who had to forcibly stop herself from eye-rolling as Jinx set about flirting with Charles as he poured a long-stemmed glass of fizz. She subtly pressed her shoe on Alice's toe and Alice bit in her cheeks, knowing she had to trust that Jinx would eventually turn the conversation in the direction they needed it to go. But as the minutes ticked by, Jinx laughing at Charles's lame jokes, Alice became increasingly impatient. Fortunately, Charles's cat made an appearance, hissing at Agatha who practically leapt into Alice's arms and it took quite a while to calm them both down.

'Come on,' Alice whispered to Jinx as Charles put his cat outside. 'I don't have much time. Get on with it.'

When Charles came back, Jinx leant on one hip and smiled at him. 'So, you're still very much on the society scene,' she said. 'I heard about a party at New Year's Eve you were photographing.'

'Oh yeah, that,' Charles said, giving nothing away.

'Only . . . and I know this is probably a long shot,' Alice said, 'but my niece was at the same party.'

Jinx's eyebrows shot up, but Alice gave her a reassuring look. 'And the thing is, she was so hoping to get a photo that night. She was wearing a dress by a young designer, you see. And she'd kind of promised she'd get a good snap in return for the dress.'

'But then the woman who hosted the party . . . ' Jinx said, riffing on Alice's bluff, 'who was it, Alice?'

'Oh, er, Camille . . . er the Messents, right?' she said, as if trying to remember.

'Yeah, well she never showed any of the pictures.'

'She um . . . ' Charles said, rubbing the side of his face. 'She never ordered any prints.'

'But you've got them all?' Alice pressed, innocently.

'Sure. They're on there,' he said, nodding towards a big

desk in the corner with a computer screen the size of an aircraft window at its centre.

'Oh, Charles,' Jinx said, folding herself around to stand in front of him, 'you wouldn't be an absolute darling and let Alice take a look, would you?'

He looked unsure and Alice smiled.

'Just to see if there's any shots of my niece . . . '

'Lucretia,' Jinx said and Alice caught the glint in her eye. Surely she could have come up with a less ridiculous name for Alice's invented relative?

'I mean, you may remember her from that night,' Alice said. 'Tall. Blonde.'

'Amazing figure . . . ' Jinx embellished.

Charles was interested enough now. 'OK, you can have a look, but only in the strictest confidence.'

'Absolutely, of course,' Alice said, with what she hoped was a grateful smile.

Leading them over to his computer, he clicked through a bunch of folders and then opened one full of jpeg files. He gestured for Alice to sit in the black leather office chair in front of the screen.

'There you go,' he said. 'Knock yourself out.'

Alice put on her glasses and leaned in towards the screen. Jinx, being the star she always was, drew Charles away, skipping over towards the yellow backdrop.

'So what's this for?' she asked, doing a pose, although Alice noted that Charles didn't pick up his camera.

Alice tuned out as she opened the folder. The pictures of the Messents' New Year's Eve party were all timestamped, and Alice went through them one by one, noting the shots of the partygoers arriving in their finery, of Camille and Alex Messent greeting them, with Alex's hand on his wife's arm, and then of Camille – with diamonds glittering at her throat, dressed in a spectacular long blue dress, with a lace skirt studded with sparkling embroidery – her head back laughing. They looked perfect. The kind of gracious, cultured couple who had no idea that the peace of their luxurious home was about to be shattered.

Alice methodically scrolled through more and more shots – of delicious-looking canapés on silver trays, gleaming flutes of champagne, and giant pedestals of chrysanthemums and roses. Alice could almost hear the atmosphere of relaxed yuletide chatter ringing out through the screen.

As suavely relaxed as Charles was in person, he was obviously a real stickler for detail too, as all these shots had been arranged here in chronological order. 20.45 . . . 20.46 . . . 20.47 . . . And now their timestamps got closer to the moment of Camille Messent's speech, her guests gathering into a semi-circular crowd before her, while she stood on the slightly raised stage area at the back of the vast drawing room beneath that raging seascape in oils.

And now here was Camille addressing the crowd. One shot captured her extending her hand to her husband . . . another showed him stepping towards her, staring adoringly up. 20.57 . . .

Charles had clearly turned the camera on the guests at this point, using some kind of wide-angle lens to capture the entire crowd – and this was probably the image that the police had used to eliminate everyone as suspects, Alice supposed. But looking now across the sea of smiling faces, she spotted someone who was neither really in the room or out. Thérèse was standing in the doorway to the hall, staring in, with her face set and determined.

But did her being in the doorway mean she'd just arrived? Or was she about to leave? From her stance, it could have been either, but it oddly looked like the latter. But why would she be going out in the middle of Camille's speech? And where? In less than four minutes, Enya would be dead. Murdered by someone upstairs. *Could* Thérèse have got up in the time to have either seen something, or been somehow otherwise involved? Or, again, was Alice simply letting her imagination run away with her? Sadly, there was no way to tell.

She went through the rest of the pictures, but Charles had stopped taking photos altogether, it seemed, during the minute's silence, and then there were only a few shots of the ceiling and floor, possibly taken accidentally in the panic and the confusion that must have followed.

Glancing up, she saw Jinx was still posing against the lurid yellow background, with Charles's encouragement. Clicking back through the photos of the crowd, Alice double-checked to see if she'd missed anything. Just as she was zooming in on another snap of Thérèse right near the start of the party, she was interrupted by Jinx.

'I've been keeping him distracted,' Jinx said, swishing her hair over her shoulder. 'But I can't for much longer.'

'Yes, you can. You're a natural,' Alice said.

'He says I could still do a bit of modelling if I wanted.'

'For what? *Saga* magazine?'

Jinx huffed and tutted and came around the desk. 'So, any joy? What are you looking at?'

'Thérèse. The Messents' secretary. That's her,' Alice said, pointing to the screen.

But Jinx's look darkened. 'Typical. Look whose hand she's holding.'

Alice hadn't even realised. But yes, Jinx was right. Subtly, in fact even barely noticeably, Thérèse did seem to be touching her fingertips against a man's as he stood back-to-back with her, talking to somebody else.

'Why typical?' Alice asked.

Because, look, you ninny,' Jinx said, her expression turning positively thunderous now, 'that's bloody Laars, of course.'

28.

The following Wednesday, Laura was due to go back to school and Alice was pleased to see Massoud's sparkling limo pull up outside the Messents' house nice and early. As Alice hurried down the front steps, his face broke into a smile.

'Well, well, well,' he said, stepping out. 'This is exceptional above and beyond the call of duty service, to not only book me but to be here to meet me on behalf of your client too.'

'Shh,' Alice said. 'I'm not myself.'

'You're feeling ill?' Massoud frowned.

'No, I mean I'm pretending to be someone else. Caroline Doulton,' she said.

'Who?' Massoud asked, looking even more concerned.

'Listen, it's a long story and I'll tell you about it later, but for now please don't give me away,' she said, squeezing his arm imploringly. 'As far as you know I'm just the new housekeeper here.'

'Whatever you say, Miss . . . Doulton. Or should that be Mrs?' Massoud smiled.

A clattering sound. Alice turned to see Laura lugging a large rucksack down the stairs, before a sharp voice behind her stopped her dead in her tracks. Alex Messent appeared, looking first at

Laura, then Alice, then Massoud in his starched chauffeur uniform, and finally at his car.

'What's going on?' he said.

'Laura's going back to school.' Alice had assumed they'd have already said their goodbyes.

'Yes, but this limousine . . . ' he said.

'Oh, that. I ordered it,' Alice said.

'But she always gets the train.'

'They're on strike,' Alice said. 'And Massoud here was more than happy to—'

'So you just thought you'd book a limousine for her . . . for a child?' he sneered.

'Papa, I'm not a—'

'Silence,' he snapped, actually clicking his fingers at her, like she was some kind of disobedient pet. His face was turning red, enraged.

'Massoud drove for the last family I worked for,' Alice said, standing her ground. 'He's a hundred per cent trustworthy and will get her there on time. Particularly as you're not able to take her there yourself,' she added pointedly.

Massoud smiled, tipping his cap.

'But she doesn't need a limousine. She can . . . get a lift from a friend . . . or, I don't know . . . take an Uber instead . . . '

'OK, no problem. I'll send him away. If you'd like to call one, or take Laura yourself?' She smiled charmingly at him, calling his bluff.

He scowled with an accompanying growl, and, clearly not wanting to do either, waved his consent towards the car.

'Jolly good,' Alice said, as Massoud went over to help Laura with her bag.

Alex Messent stopped Laura following and whispered something into her ear. Something that made her skin burn red. Some sort of judgement, it looked like. Or threat. Then his phone rang, and he marched back into the house, without even saying goodbye.

Alice gave her a hug instead, then stood on the threshold to wave her off. But Laura Messent didn't even notice her. Her little face in the back of the huge limo just looked sadly past Alice to where her father had been.

Alice busied herself sorting the laundry, but all the time her mind was mulling over the scene she'd just witnessed.

Putting fresh towels in the various bathrooms, she ended up in the small downstairs staff loo. It was in the service corridor that ran off the hall just to the side of the drawing room.

'Oh, this simply won't do,' she said aloud, seeing how grubby it was.

She caught her grimace in the reflection in the heart-shaped silver mirror. What were the cleaners thinking of? If Monsieur Messent saw how dusty and messy it was in here, he'd have a fit. But then that was the point, she supposed. The cleaners already knew that someone of Monsieur's elevated status would never come in here. Peering out of the window, she saw that it looked down over doorway just outside the staff kitchen below.

Folding a fresh towel into the handrail, she picked up the dirty one of the floor. That's when she noticed it. Something gleaming just there in the gap beneath the wooden sink unit.

Leaning in closer, she saw it was a mobile phone. She tried turning it on, but the screen remained black. It must have been dropped there. But how long ago? And by whom? No one had mentioned any missing phones since she'd been here at the house.

Turning it over in her hand, she didn't recognise the brand.

Spurred on by finally finding something of potential use, she quickly finished her laundry round. Back down in the staff kitchen, she tried her own charger on the phone, but it didn't work. Next time she was out of the house, she'd call in at the little electronics store on Tottenham Court Road.

She then headed back upstairs into the ballroom, because one of the cleaners had said there was a problem with the rug. They weren't wrong. Alice straight away noticed a moth flying in the giant space and, suspicious, she knelt to examine the silk rug. If it had carpet moths, that was a serious problem. She thought of Mrs Doulton and how she'd used to steam-iron the rugs with a huckaback towel in Hawthorn, but this rug was too huge for that old remedy.

Behind her, she heard a sound in the hall and opened the door a fraction. Alex Messent was shrugging on a cashmere overcoat, looking at some letters she'd left for him on the hall table. He glanced in the direction of the door, and Alice realised he'd seen her.

'Oh, Monsieur Messent,' she said, as breezily as she could. 'Would you like me to cook you some lunch?'

'*Non, merci.* I shall be out for the rest of the day.' He was wearing a grey suit with a white, perfectly tipped handkerchief pointing out of its breast pocket. 'Did Madame Messent leave any messages for me?'

'No,' Alice said, smoothing her hair behind her ear.

'And you'll be here all day?'

'Yes, of course,' she said, but now she wondered if he'd noticed she'd gone to Charles's studio yesterday. It was on the tip of her tongue to tell him about the potential moth problem, but she suspected that a man like Alex Messent wouldn't be the least interested in such a domestic issue. He continued staring at her, his dark eyes seeming to bore into hers and she got the distinct impression that he really didn't trust her.

'That painting . . . the seascape,' she said, quickly changing the subject and pointing at the door she'd just come through. 'I think it's . . . I've never seen anything quite like it. I'm not much of an art aficionado myself, but your collection is breath-taking, if you don't mind me saying.'

He nodded but didn't reply. In fact, he ignored her altogether, his attention suddenly switching to a smaller portrait by the door. Reaching out, he adjusted it until it was perfectly square, before nodding to himself, pleased.

How did Camille put up with him? Being around him felt like walking on eggshells. Perhaps just another effect of the OCD Laura claimed he suffered from.

Alice retreated to the kitchen to start on the soup she planned to make. One of her favourites from Mrs Beeton, who was quite the magpie when it came to her recipes. It was no secret that she used recipes in her book that she'd 'borrowed' from other cooks as well as her readers, but Alice was pretty certain that this recipe was one of her own inventions. Mrs Doulton maintained that in the horribly harsh winter of 1858, Mrs Beeton had set up a soup kitchen from her own home and served this up to the hungry masses. But whether for paupers or kings, Alice knew that this 'glue-your-insides-together' meal was undoubtedly good for the soul. She'd adapted the recipe over the years, but it remained essentially the same as Mrs Beeton's, and she always made a big vat of it and kept the leftovers in the fridge.

Useful soup for benevolent purposes

*INGREDIENTS – 2 ox cheeks, 1 large swede cubed,
4 stalks of celery, roughly chopped, 8 carrots, chopped, 4
brown onions, chopped, 6 leeks, sliced, 3 turnips, chopped,
a savoy cabbage, shredded, a large bunch of fresh
herbs including rosemary, coriander, flat-leaf parsley,
thyme and 4 bay leaves, 1 cup pearl barley, 1 cup red
split lentils, 500ml beer or cider, 2 beef stock cubes, 3
stock cubes, 3l water. Salt and plenty of black pepper.*

*METHOD – cut the meat into cubes and chop all the
vegetables. Put the meat in a large pan and add salt.
Cover with water and put lid on pan. Bring to the boil
and remove any scum. Crumble in the stock cubes and
add all the vegetables and herbs and beer. Replace
lid. Simmer for 2 hours, then add the lentils and pearl
barley and simmer for another hour, until pearl barley
is softened. Add the cabbage and simmer for a further
10 mins. Season generously with salt and pepper.*

Serve in large bowls with crusty bread and butter.

She'd just got everything simmering, when her phone rang.

'Oh, Barney. How was your holiday?' she asked. She'd missed him.

'Marvellous. A real tonic. Just what I needed. But I got your message, asking me to call you as soon as I got back.'

'Yes, there's something I wanted to show you.' Those museum ticket stubs, with the writing she'd not been able to read on the back. 'Only now, it's more like two things,' she said, thinking of the phone she'd just found.

'Oh,' Barney said, 'what?'

'I can't talk about it now.'

'Why ever not? Where are you?'

'I'm not at home. In fact, home's not really there either. But, of course, you haven't heard, have you?'

'Heard what?'

'Oh, my goodness, there's so much to tell you. Hang on.'

Alice hurried down the stairs to the bottom kitchen. She didn't feel right divulging what she was up to when there were people in the house.

Grabbing one of the Barbour jackets from the boot room, she slung it over her shoulder and stood outside the back door, lowering her voice.

'Alice? What's going on? Why are you talking so quietly?' Barney asked.

'I'm worried I'll be overheard.'

'What do you mean?'

In a hushed voice, Alice recounted everything that had happened since New Year's Eve – starting with the phone call in the middle of the night from Detective Rigby. She told him too about visiting Katy and what Gerda had said. And her discoveries here at the house – the museum stubs and the phone.

'I can't believe you've actually gone, well . . . ' for once, Barney seemed lost for words ' . . . *undercover*,' he hissed, as though someone his end might be listening in on him too. 'Rather a bold move, if you don't mind me saying.'

'So far, I'm getting away with it, but I'm worried they're going to rumble me any second. I can't help thinking that Alex Messent is suspicious already. He gives me the creeps.'

She looked up behind her at the Messents' house looming down and told him how strange it was to be sleeping in Enya's room.

'But so far, the only hard clues you've got are these museum tickets and this phone.'

'Yes, and I was hoping you'd let me use your model-making stamp collector's magnifying glass thingy to look at the stubs.'

'Right, although I'm not sure that's its exact technical name,' Barney laughed. 'How about you swing by on Saturday? I'm down here in Dorset at my sister's until then.'

Dorset? Drat it. Alice was itching to know what those notes had said and had been hoping she could pop over tonight. She just about managed to keep the disappointment from her voice.

'Great. Yes. Thank you. I'll see you then.'

'Just one other thing,' he said. 'Would you like me to run a little background check on the Messents for you? I mean, it won't be the full Monty, not like I could have got when I was still at work. But I've still got a few contacts who owe me some favours,' he said, cryptically.

Ah, Barney. Alice smiled, feeling a warm glow enveloping her in spite of the chill air. Even on the rare times when he let her down on one thing, he always came good on something else.

29.

On Friday morning, after she'd heard Alex Messent leave, Alice hurried upstairs and along the corridor to his study door. She tried the handle, just in case. But again, it was locked. Did he keep the key on his person? she wondered. As in always? Or sometimes might he leave it somewhere else, like his room?

Tempted as she was to go and have a dig around in there right now, she had to admit she was doubtful she'd find it. Equally, she had to admit she was scared. He'd caught her trying to get into his study once already; what would he do if he found her snooping round his bedroom? Again, she pictured his brooding, dark eyes – and the vicious way he'd whispered into Laura's ear.

But as chance would have it, she was saved from indecision by a message. It was Jinx, a snap of her wearing dark glasses like she was in a spy film, telling her she was already waiting round the corner in a black cab. Alice read the words below the photo.

Today's the day! Pandora. I have a plan.

Alice typed back. **Roger that!** Then, she quickly got changed out of her black and whites and hurried round to meet Jinx who was in the waiting cab half-buried beneath a pile of bulging black bin bags.

'We're going to have to be quickish,' Alice said, climbing in with Agatha under her arm. 'An hour, tops. I've no idea what time Monsieur Messent's back and the cleaners are coming again.'

'Oh, I was rather hoping we'd have lunch after.'

'Can we take a rain check?'

Jinx pulled a face, but then nodded. 'Hit it, Paul. And don't spare the horses,' she told the driver.

The handsome young man smiled back at her in the mirror before screeching away up the road. Jinx patted the one bit of her knee still visible, and Agatha daintily hopped across to perch.

'I have to say, I'm impressed. I never thought you'd do it,' Alice said, looking at all the bags.

'You laid down the gauntlet and I could feel the pressure from you even a page of the A–Z away,' Jinx said.

Alice laughed.

'It's no laughing matter. Even now I'm not sure I can bear to part with them.' Jinx patted the bags, a look of pre-mourning in her eyes.

'Nonsense,' Alice said. 'You'll feel totally different once you've met Bridget.'

They chatted about the office and everything Alice had missed, as they drove towards Knightsbridge and past the iconic steps of the Natural History Museum and then the V&A. Alice tapped on the glass in front of her.

'Left here,' she instructed the cabbie, and they turned out of Rutland Street and into Cheval Place. 'And just along there.' She pointed to the striking turquoise blue building on the corner of Montpelier Walk.

The cab drew up outside the familiar black signage, and Jinx, craning her head to look through the window, smiled at the lovely arch of flowers above the doorway.

Alice had first come here years ago with the thrifty Mrs Doulton. Back then, June and Roma, two fabulously eccentric women, were running the dress agency, having come up with a fine business plan to recycle unwanted designer clothing for money, decades before vintage or pre-loved became such a popular thing.

'I can't believe you've never been here. You're going to love it,' she assured Jinx now, as she helped her haul her bags out of the cab and up the steps, with Agatha trotting behind.

The shop was a lot bigger than it looked from the outside and was crammed with long rails full of clothing in a riot of colour and textures. Jinx stopped and clapped her hands over her mouth.

'Have I died and gone to heaven?' she asked, clutching Alice's arm and walking forwards to reverentially touch the day dresses on the nearest rail, before pulling a red felt hat from the shelf above onto her head.

Bridget, a small woman, with a comforting northern accent and a no-nonsense attitude, greeted Alice and Agatha warmly. She was wearing a blue turtleneck jumper and practical black trousers. She might work with designer clothes all day, but Bridget hailed from a rag-and-bone background, and this venture was purely commerce.

Whilst Bridget and her colleague Sona set about emptying Jinx's bags and displaying her clothes on the hanging rail to assess them, Alice joined Jinx where she was already leafing through the other stock on display nearby.

'Look. Oh, God. I've always wanted one of these.' She held up a Vivienne Westwood blue and red woollen dress against her.

'We're not here to buy, but to sell,' Alice reminded her firmly.

'But what about this?' Jinx said, picking up a white leather crossbody bag. 'That's so cool.'

'Is it? It looks like one of those Eighties bum bags.'

'Well, that's exactly what it is. It's all the rage. You're always losing things in your handbag, you should get one. It's really quite spacious. Try it on, go on.'

Alice put the bag over her shoulder and realised Jinx wasn't wrong.

'It suits you. I'm getting it for you. No questions asked.'

Alice laughed and shook her head, knowing full well Jinx wouldn't take 'no' for an answer. 'Now what's the plan you mentioned?'

'Ah yes, well that's why I thought it was a good idea to come here. You see, we have to find you an outfit for tomorrow night.'

'Tomorrow?'

Jinx turned her attention back to the clothes, in a way that Alice knew meant she wasn't going to like whatever it was she said next. 'Yes. It's to do with Laars.'

After seeing that photo of Thérèse possibly holding hands with Husband Number Two in Charles Tavistock's studio, Alice had told Jinx to try and track him down to see what he might be able to tell them about that night. He might be able to say whether Thérèse had been in the room at the time of Camille's speech. Or whether she'd been absent at the exact time of the murder. Alice had no reason to believe that Thérèse wanted to do Enya any harm. But her whereabouts was still a missing part of the puzzle. Who knew what Laars might know? And what exactly was their relationship anyway?

'Good. You've spoken to him, then?' Alice said.

'God, no. The number I've got for him is well out of date. He's always switching phones. A deliberate tactic. It makes it easier for him to hide from the latest trail of destruction he's left in his wake.'

'Charming.'

'But what I *have* learned is that he's in town and, even better, I now have it on good authority that he's going to be in his usual lair.'

'Lair?'

'Annabelle's,' Jinx said, as if it was obvious.

'The nightclub? Is that still a thing?' Surely, Alice assumed, it would have gone the way of the dodo by now.

'Very much so. So, we're going to go and "accidentally"—' Jinx made inverted commas with her fingers '—bump into him. Surprise is always the best tactic with Laars, believe me. Just like trapping snakes.'

Alice smiled in spite of herself. Because of course this last phrase wasn't just a simile. Jinx really did know what she was talking about. She'd spent part of her honeymoon with Husband Number Three – or was it Four? – trapping copperheads in the grounds of his colonial mansion beside the opal mine he owned near Coober Pedy in South Australia.

'Right,' Alice said, trying to think of the logistics. 'But how? I'm supposed to be at the Messents'. What are you suggesting? That I sneak out?'

'Exactly. Like at school, remember? Giving old Thunder Britches the run-around. Don't look like that. We never got caught, not once.'

No, but they'd come damn close a few times and their old housemistress wouldn't have hesitated to expel them if they had been. While Jinx had thrived on the adrenaline of all this, Alice had hated it to her bones.

But Alice saw that Jinx was right. She was going to have to find a way, because Laars might be her best chance to find out vital information about that night.

'But Annabelle's?' Alice said, her mind racing over the practicalities. 'I have nothing to wear.'

'Ta-da!' Jinx grinned and held out her arms. 'Fortunate for you that we're in the right place. What about this?' Jinx asked, suddenly full of enthusiasm and holding up a sliver of a dress against Alice.

'Don't be ridiculous. I'm not wearing that.'

Sona came over. 'What are you looking for? Can I help?'

Jinx explained and Sona looked Alice up and down thoughtfully then headed to the middle rail. 'Take the Arlington,' she said, plucking out a green sequinned dress.

'I can't wear that,' Alice said. 'It's only got one arm.'

'It looks fantastic on,' Sona said.

'Shoes . . . shoes . . . ' Jinx said, casting her eye around. 'She's a five.'

'The green Pradas then,' Sona said. 'Or the Miu Mius. Or both? I'll put them in the changing room. Oh, and you need a bag. I'd say a Judith Leiber.'

Bridget, overhearing all of this, walked over to the handbag section and lifted out a small oblong clutch from the tray below the glass-topped counter.

'This will be perfect,' she said, as Alice and Jinx came over to inspect it.

'How much is it?' Alice asked.

'This one? Er, let's see,' Bridget said, unlocking the clasp to reveal the sumptuous silk interior. The label read '£899'.

'Seriously? And it's second hand?' Alice was aghast.

'Judith Leibers always hold their value,' she said. 'Look at the crystal work. You know every first lady in America is given one.'

'Hold the phone,' Jinx said, excitedly. 'I've got one. In that bag, over there. It was a present from the Shit, so I've never used it.'

'The Shit?' Bridget asked.

'One of the ex-husbands,' Alice told her in an aside.

'If you've got one, that's very exciting.'

'So, you can borrow mine,' Jinx said. 'Before we sell it. Because at that price, I'll be selling it for sure. Oh, Alice, this was such a good idea.'

Jinx grabbed Alice's arm, still transfixed by the rails. She skipped to the back, drawn like a magpie to the shiny long dresses. Alice joined her, wanting her to focus, but Jinx was already swirling around with a multicoloured crocheted sheath dress.

'Missoni. You can always tell by the print. Can you just imagine wafting around a Caribbean villa in this?'

Alice laughed. She could imagine it all too well.

'Or this baby. Oh, simply divine,' Jinx said, holding out a flared Prada jumpsuit.

Alice, despite being tight for time, rifled through a few herself because Jinx's enthusiasm was kind of infectious. Then a ball dress laid out on a counter to one side caught her attention. It was midnight blue with a sheer lace skirt dotted with hand-embroidered crystals, and as she reached out to touch it, she felt a jolt of recognition. It was exactly like the dress that Camille Messent had worn on New Year's Eve. The one she'd seen the close-up of at Charles Tavistock's studio.

Sona came back from the changing room. 'It's all in there for you. Oh, and you saw that, did you?' She smiled, seeing Alice with the ball gown. 'It's just been dropped off. Elie Saab. One of my clients always brings in her pieces once she's worn them. The money she raises goes straight to her charity.'

'Oh, Alice,' Jinx said, loudly. 'That is just exquisite.'

'Can I try it on?' Alice asked.

Jinx looked surprised. 'Yes, you *should*. Just for the hell of it.'

Sona picked it up and led Alice over to the changing room.

'I'm not a hundred per cent sure,' Alice whispered into Jinx's ear on the way, 'but I think this is the dress Camille Messent wore at New Year's Eve. Can you find out?'

'Oh! Really?' Jinx whispered.

Alice was no friend of dressing rooms and always found the lighting or the mirrors, or, in most cases both, to be hideously unflattering, but this changing room was different. Considering the original value of the clothes, it felt reassuringly down to earth. There was ample space, and the mirror was beguilingly flattering. Probably tipped forward a little, Alice surmised. Clever.

The dress was surprisingly light, and up close it was even more beautiful than she'd first thought. Quickly getting changed, she carefully slid down the hidden zip from the bodice past the skirt and stepped inside. It was a little tight around the bust and way too long, but as she looked at herself in the mirror, turning one way and then the other, Alice tentatively held up her hair at the back, pulled a face, pouted and then smiled. She rarely appraised her reflection, except to assess whether she had food on her face, but this show-stopping dress made her feel powerful in a way that she'd never have imagined.

Yes, even if she said so herself, in the right light, and in the right clothes, she might actually scrub up quite well.

She heard a knock on the door and Jinx hissed, 'It's me.'

Alice opened the door a crack. She passed her crystal clutch through the gap.

'The dress *is* from Camille Messent,' she said in an excited stage whisper. 'Well spotted, you old sleuth.'

Jinx left and Alice turned back to her reflection.

Now that she knew this was the dress that her boss had been wearing, her moment of self-appreciation burst into something much stronger. A kind of visceral connection to that night. She thought back to the photos of Camille she'd seen on Charles's computer, and for a second, she closed her eyes, imagining herself in that ballroom, giving that speech, commanding a whole room full of people to be silent for her.

The second she opened her eyes, the spell broke, but she couldn't stop thinking about Camille. All this time, she'd been dumbfounded that the Messents had simply moved on, but now she had a glimmer of understanding for what it must be like to be Camille Messent. How Enya must have been so far down her thoughts before she had unexpectedly taken centre stage.

Alice appraised herself again. She rubbed her hands over her hips and felt something – a deep hidden pocket in the skirt. Reaching inside, her fingers touched something. It was a small square of black plastic, she saw now, as she pulled it out.

She turned it over in her hand. What was it? It looked like it was part of perhaps a phone or something like that. Deciding that it might be important, she slipped it into her satchel. Then unzipping the dress, she stepped out of it reverentially, putting it back on its silk padded hanger.

'What did you think?' Bridget called.

'Fun to try it on, but it didn't fit,' Alice called out, handing the dress on its hanger through the door.

'Come and show us when you're in the Arlington,' Sona called.

Alice consulted her phone, panicking about the time, quickly changed into the green dress and stepped out of the changing room, wobbling on the high Prada heels, Judith Leiber clutch in her hand. She wriggled the dress around her hips. It felt very structured with a ruched shoulder on one arm, but even she had to admit that the bodice was beautifully cut.

Jinx came over and adjusted the shoulder, then Bridget tugged at the hem. They both stood back and then laughed.

'Cinders, it seems you shall go to the ball,' Jinx said.

'Are you sure it's not . . . ?'

'Alice, I swear you look ten years younger.'

'Yes. Knockout,' Bridget agreed.

30.

Camille Messent arrived back from Paris that evening, startling Alice who heard the front door slam. When she came downstairs, she found Camille in the living room, her coat discarded on a chair, her case abandoned by the door.

'We haven't met properly. I'm so sorry,' Camille said, extending her hand with its glistening rings towards Alice. 'But Thérèse has been keeping me informed and tells me you've been remarkable.'

Had she? Alice was unaware that Thérèse had any feelings towards her other than mild irritation. Camille smiled and Alice felt warm inside.

'How was your trip?'

'Tiring. Seeing the refugees . . . it's difficult. When there's all this,' she said, putting out her hand to the sumptuous living room. 'The hardship people live with and yet . . . they are so kind. It's humbling, you know?'

'It must be,' Alice said, watching Camille sink onto the sofa. She watched her plump up a pillow and lean back. She might be feeling guilty about her home comforts, but she certainly appreciated them.

'But . . . oh, I am exhausted.'

'Shall I draw you a bath?' Alice asked and Camille laughed.

'Draw a bath. That's so funny.'

'Oh,' Alice said, realising that she'd taken her literal meaning.

'No, Caroline. It's OK. I don't need you to be . . . how you say, like a servant,' Camille said, her eyes warm and friendly.

But she was a servant, Alice thought. 'Are you hungry?'

'No, I'm fine,' Camille said, snuggling back on the sofa, as if supremely happy to be home. She was like a sleek cat. She somehow filled the room with her presence, and now that she was here, the house felt as if it had come to life. 'Perhaps a camomile tea, then? I took the liberty of buying some new teabags from my favourite supplier.'

'OK,' Camille said. 'That would be lovely. Thank you.' Alice turned to leave. 'Oh, and Caroline? How was Laura?'

'Charming.'

'Really?'

'Yes,' Alice said, a little defensively.

'I'm so glad,' Camille said, putting her hand on her chest. 'I've been so worried.'

'You needn't be. Laura is a lovely girl,' Alice said, meaning it. 'A credit to you, in fact.'

But Camille wasn't listening, her attention now on her phone.

How could Camille be married to Alex Messent, Alice wondered. She seemed so warm and genuine and was clearly doing her best to help those in need.

She made some tea, putting a slice of the Bakewell tart she'd made on a side plate for Camille. She knew the recipe by heart – one from a later edition of Mrs Beeton, but a failsafe pudding or snack to have on hand.

Bakewell Tart

INGREDIENTS – Shortcrust pastry made with 6 oz
flour, 3 oz butter, a pinch of salt and enough cold water to
form a dough. Filling ingredients: 3 tbsp raspberry jam,
2 oz butter, 2 oz sugar, 1 egg, 2 oz ground almonds, 2 oz
cake crumbs (crushed biscuits suffice), 1/2 tsp almond extract,
3 tbsp sliced almonds, powdered sugar for dusting.

METHOD – to make the pastry, sift the flour and salt
together in a large bowl. Cube the butter and rub into
the flour to form breadcrumbs then slowly add the
water until the dough is formed into a ball. Press out
into a 7-inch buttered tart dish. Place a good layer of
raspberry jam on the bottom. Cream together butter
and sugar until thick and white. Beat in the egg, then
add ground almonds, cake crumbs and almond extract.
Spread the mixture on top of the jam. Top with sliced
almonds. Bake in hot over for 30 minutes. Sprinkle
powdered sugar on top and serve hot or cold.

Serves 5 to 6.

But by the time she'd returned to the sitting room, Camille's eyes
were closed. As Alice got closer and placed the tea tray on the low
ottoman, she saw that she was fast asleep. Alice carefully eased
off her shoes, and put her legs up on the sofa, before covering
her with a blanket. She hardly stirred as she settled on her side.

Alice tiptoed out and put her case upstairs, folding down the pretty eiderdown cover. She knew Camille would be much more comfortable in the enormous French wooden bed, but when Alice went down later on to wake her, she was in an even deeper sleep and, reluctantly, she decided to leave her.

It wasn't until much later that Alex Messent came home. It was the raised voices that woke Alice. She opened her bedroom door and heard Camille's voice rising in accusatory French and Alex's gruff reply. Then feet stomping up the stairs. Alice tiptoed to the top of the staircase from where she had a view of the corridor below. Camille's voice was strained now with tears. Alex shouted something that sounded like an insult and slammed a door. Alice jolted. She heard a hissed insult from Alex, then his footsteps retreating back downstairs. She hurried back into her room and silently closed the door. Katy had been right about the strained atmosphere. Alice's heart went out to poor exhausted Camille having to deal with a row at the end of her long day.

The next morning, there was no sign of Alex Messent and Camille didn't look flustered when she came down in her dressing gown. She looked so effortlessly chic as she stood in front of the complicated Gaggia coffee machine, her hair in a loose plait over her shoulder. Even without make-up she was beautiful.

She made no mention of the previous night and smiled at Alice, who was folding the tea towels she'd recently ironed.

'Why don't you take some time for yourself today,' Camille suggested. 'I want to spend some time with Laura when she's home.'

'She'll be home at lunchtime. I've made a pie,' Alice replied, delighted that she'd been let off the hook and could go and see Barney. 'You just need to heat it up.'

'Thank you,' Camille said, squeezing her arm. 'I've been hearing wonderful things about your cooking.'

Alice smiled, feeling gratified. It was nice to be thanked after the past few days.

Soon afterwards, she set off with Agatha to catch the number 52 bus to the top end of Ladbroke Grove. Barney lived in a pleasant Victorian terraced street and whilst most of the white, four-storey buildings had been converted into flats, Barney still had a whole house. They often chatted about how he should downsize, but the prospect of parting with some of his treasures in order to move was too much. As Alice walked in through the front door and past the dining room, she could see that the table had been given over entirely to Barney's modelling projects.

Downstairs, in the cosy basement kitchen with its rickety floorboards, Alice sat at the wooden table, resisting the urge to cup the crumbs away from the sticky surface, as Barney filled up the kettle. Meanwhile, Agatha made herself at home, panting delightedly as Barney gave her one of the treats he always saved for her. She settled herself on the padded pew by the window and was almost instantly asleep.

'So, how's the investigation?' Barney asked.

'I'm going round in circles, to be honest. I certainly don't have any answers.'

'Yes, but on that note . . . ' Barney said with an encouraging smile ' . . . as promised, I've done a little digging into your Monsieur Messent.'

'And?'

'He's certainly very distinguished,' Barney said. 'Notably so. He's cited in lots of academic art articles.'

'Up until a year ago, he had a job as *Directeur Général* of one of Paris's most exclusive private art collections,' Alice said. Barney wasn't the only one who'd done some research.

Alice remembered Alex looking down his nose at her. It was no surprise that he hadn't risen to her feeble attempt at art appreciation.

'Yes, until he left without warning and came to London to open his own gallery. He's considered to be one of the most knowledge-able art connoisseurs in the world and clearly has a little black book full of high-net-worth individuals, but his art business – at least from what I've been able to ascertain – doesn't seem to be the huge hit everyone expected it to be.'

'Interesting,' Alice said, thinking back to the 'closed' sign on the gallery door just before Christmas.

'I've also heard from a friend at Oxford – and this is very much on the QT, because I've seen no hard evidence yet myself – that Messent has something of a side hustle as a gambler.'

'A gambler?'

'High-stakes poker games.'

'I suppose he's got to spend his money somehow,' Alice said. 'And he's got a good poker face. I'll give him that.'

'But I'm wondering if a gallery in London, particularly one not deemed to be performing particularly well, is enough for a man like that.'

'What do you mean?'

'If I know anything about the psychology of gamblers, it's that they're always after a thrill of some kind. And also, invariably, money itself.'

But where did Camille fit into all this? Alice wondered. She thought back to the very separate lives that Camille and Alex Messent seemed to live and the erratic hours he kept. Was that what their disagreement had been about last night? Perhaps she knew about his gambling habit? Did she disapprove of it – indeed, of him? Was it possible that their marriage was actually in trouble? That behind the public appearances where they had to look united, they were papering over the cracks?

'Oh, and look, these are the receipts I found in Enya's room,' she said, taking them out of her bag, where she'd carefully placed them in her notebook. 'It seems she was interested in art. But as far as I know, she wasn't an artist herself. And as I told you on the phone, she made some notes, but I can't make out what they say.'

Barney pulled the stubs right up close to his face and peered over his glasses. 'Let's have a look.'

'Your model-making stamp collector's magnifying glass thingy?'

'Precisely that.'

In the dining room, Barney switched on a light on the complicated-looking contraption and slid the receipts inside its display drawer. Peering over his shoulder, Alice watched excitedly as he snapped it shut and the stubs swung into heavily-magnified view.

'Even up close, that's terrible bloody handwriting. Worse than my doctor's,' Barney said. 'But, uh-huh . . . definitely, definitely Dutch . . . '

Dutch? But why would Enya have been writing in Dutch? She hadn't mentioned that amongst her languages.

'They're comments on various works by Rembrandt, Caravaggio and Da Vinci,' Barney said.

'The Great Masters . . . '

'Quite so.' He flipped the tickets over. 'There must have been paintings by them on show at these various exhibitions or in the museums' permanent collections.'

'What kind of comments?'

'Sort of ratings. Things like "perfect", "wonderful" and "ephemeral". The sort of thing any art lover might write.'

Alice couldn't help feeling a surge of disappointment. Maybe that's all these precious, so called 'clues' of hers really were . . . not clues at all, just evidence of a dead woman's hobby. Yet Alice still couldn't help feeling that they were somehow connected to Alex Messent. Perhaps they even were his? But no, Alice remembered that Enya had told her when she'd called round that he'd been abroad for these dates.

'Do you think Enya could have been Dutch?' Alice said.

'Quite possibly. I mean why else write in it? It's such a confoundedly tricky language to learn.'

Though clearly not so confoundedly tricky that Barney hadn't mastered it himself . . .

'Then there's the phone I told you about,' Alice said. Please God, she thought, let there at least be something concrete on here that might help her work out what had gone on in that house.

She explained how she'd already bought a charger for it at the little place she used on Tottenham Court Road, but even though it was now charged, and was showing a photograph of a flash red sports car on its screen, she'd tried every combination she could think of, she'd not been able to get in.

'Sorry,' Barney said, turning it over in his hand and then giving it back. 'Much as I'd love to help you, phone tech's not really my bag. I'm sure I'll be able to find someone if you can't . . . '

'No,' Alice said. 'You know what? I think I might already have the exact person I need.' Hadn't Massoud said that his grandson, Wisam, was good with computers and phones?

She put the phone back into her pocket and sighed.

'What?'

'Just it's hard, this detective lark. It seems to be one step forward two steps back. I mean, everything . . . *everything* . . . it still comes down to the question of why she was in the study in the first place,' Alice said.

'You haven't been able to get in?'

'No. I can't find a spare key. Monsieur Messent seems to have the only one. But I'm convinced,' she said, 'that if I can get in, then I might be able to find other things that the police missed. Just like these stubs and the phone. Why else would Alex Messent keep the door locked and alarmed. What is he hiding?'

Barney was smiling broadly at her. Why? Because she was being an idiot? Because that's suddenly how she felt, with her cheeks now burning too. What must he think of her? He'd spent most of his career working with real spies at GCHQ. Or possibly been an actual spy himself. And now he was forced to listen to her prattling on like the very worst kind of amateur detective there was.

Only Barney wasn't thinking this at all.

'You know, I've always been a bit partial to lockpicking,' he said.

She stared at him dumbfounded. 'Seriously. You'd actually have a go? At getting into the study?'

'My dear Alice.' He grinned. 'I thought you'd never ask.'

31.

That night, as the kitchen clock ticked increasingly closer towards the time Alice needed to leave to meet Jinx, she busied herself with a cupboard stores audit, getting increasingly apprehensive about getting caught sneaking out.

Monsieur Messent was once again absent, having not been back since he'd left just after dawn. But Camille remained working in her study, meaning Alice was still on call.

Finally, at just gone ten, Camille did appear, in stylish yoga attire, and informed Alice that Laura was staying at her friend's house for the night.

'But I thought you wanted some time with her?' Alice asked.

'I did, earlier on,' Camille replied, with a shrug. 'But she's a sixteen-year-old and she clearly got a better offer than her old mother.'

Alice smiled. Camille was most definitely not old.

'But, you know, maybe it's for the best. I'm going to take that bath you suggested and a sleeping pill.'

'Not before the bath,' Alice warned. 'You can't fall asleep in the water.'

'Ah, but you are sweet,' Camille said. 'No, I just need a proper sleep. I'm so tired.'

As Alice wished her a pleasant night, she felt wretched. Not just about all this sneaking around, which was unavoidable, but about what she'd learned from Barney about Camille's husband. What kind of man was he not to be there when his wife had come back from a gruelling trip, or to leave her home alone on a Saturday night? She wasn't one to judge, but Alex Messent didn't seem remotely up to scratch as a husband in her opinion.

Upstairs, with Agatha snoring quietly, and now knowing that Camille would be unlikely to wake up, Alice attempted to make up her face in her little room's en suite bathroom, but only succeeded in feeling like a clown.

At eleven o'clock, Alice took the green sequinned dress from the plastic carrier bag she'd hidden under her bed and changed. Taking Jinx's handbag, she checked out her reflection one last time in the mirror on the back of the door. The clothes looked great, but as for her . . . gosh, she really wasn't sure if she was up to this. What if when she got there, everyone just stared at her for all the wrong reasons? She slipped on her spinner necklace for courage.

Agatha, stirring, cocked her head on one side. Alice sat beside her, tickling her ears as she explained that she would be out for an hour at the most and Agatha was not to breathe a word.

'Shh,' Alice said, putting her finger to her lips, before backing out slowly from the room.

Out in the corridor, she stood still for a moment, listening to the house, silent except for the distant tick of the clock. Then, blowing out a breath of resolve, she tiptoed along the corridor and down the stairs, high heels in her hand.

'What on earth do you look like?' Jinx asked, peering down at her from the pavement, as Alice climbed out of the cab onto Berkeley Square. She tugged at the collar of the coat that Alice had thrown on top of the dress in case she'd bumped into anyone on the way out of the house – and to make herself feel less self-conscious. 'Take that off immediately. You're not Inspector Clouseau.'

'But it's freezing.'

'Yes, well sometimes the cost of being fashionable is being bloody cold,' Jinx said, as if this were a given fact. 'Come on, get with the programme. You've been to clubs before.'

'Not for a hundred years.'

Alice tried to look calm and cool as she stared up at the flower-studded Georgian façade of Annabelle's. But the thud of the music coming from inside only matched her racing heart as they waited in the roped-off guest list queue. At the front, smart bouncers flanked a young woman wearing a black suit and an earpiece, who was checking each guest off against a list on her iPad.

'Stop tugging at the hem and stand up tall,' Jinx said. 'Honestly, you look sensational, but we're going straight to the loos so I can fix your face.'

'What's wrong with my face?' Alice asked.

'Everything. You need way more make-up.'

'Do I?' Alice asked, alarmed. She'd given it her best shot, but Jinx gave her a look as if she was crazy.

Jinx herself was wearing a black sculpted mini dress, which showed off her legs, and her chest was covered in a subtle sheen of glitter. Her hair was perfectly coiffed in a side up-do and her eye make-up was heavy and shiny, her lips glossy. It must have taken her hours to look like that.

When they finally reached the front of the queue, Jinx dropped the names of some old staff members that were clearly lost on the young woman. For one dreadful moment, Alice thought they might be turned away, but then she caught the eye of the bouncer behind her.

'Elijah? Is that you?' she asked, squinting.

The bouncer's face lit up into a grin, just like when he'd been a little boy. He looked exactly like his mother.

'Miss B! Jinx!' Tiffany's son said, stepping forward and unclipping the rope. He nodded at the girl with the iPad who instantly turned her attention to the people in the queue behind them. It was on the tip of Alice's tongue to tell him that he'd grown – although that would only be stating the bleedin' obvious, as Mrs Doulton would have said. He must have been at least six foot four now. After a quick chat he ushered them through the door and pointed out the cloakroom. 'So nice to see you two,' he said. 'Anything you need. Anything at all, just holler.'

'Holler,' Jinx said, laughing. 'He sounds exactly like Tiff.'

They went straight to the plush ladies' cloakroom, where Jinx set her cosmetic bag out by the mirror and quickly set about sorting Alice's eye make-up.

'You see,' Jinx said, after five minutes, 'gorgeous.'

Alice stood back and appraised herself in the long mirror. She had to lean forward to check it was really her. Her eyes were enormous, surrounded by green glitter.

'Ready?' Jinx asked, as she pushed through the doors, and

walked into the main club, feeling suddenly as if she were twenty again.

As they walked past the dance floor – a sea of throbbing bass and bodies – it was all Alice could do not to laugh. Because nobody seemed to spot what an imposter she was. In fact, from where they stood in various clusters, the other women seemed to be looking her up and down with approval. So this was it, the real power of designer clothes, she supposed.

'I'm old enough to be a mother to some of them,' she said to Jinx.

'So? Age really doesn't matter as much as you think it does. And, you don't look it really.' She grinned. 'Neither of us do.'

Jinx continued to survey the crowd, hauling Alice further round the edge of the dance floor. Alice had no idea how to look cool like the couples moving beside them in the strobing lights and her feet were already killing her in her high heels.

'Can't we sit down?' she begged Jinx. 'Those booths look good.'

'Uh, uh,' she said, still cruising around until she stopped suddenly. She turned round to face Alice, her eyes wide as she clutched Alice's arm.

'He's there. Behind me. Twelve o'clock to you. And he's alone. Look. Very end of the bar.'

Alice glanced over Jinx's shoulder, and there was Laars. He was wearing a shiny navy suit and a black pin-striped shirt, sat in a casual man-spread with one foot up on the bottom of the next stool, his soft navy suede loafer revealing his bare ankle.

Alice shuddered and pulled a face at Jinx.

'Come on then,' she said. 'We'd better get on with this.'

'Oh, no, Alice. I'm not sure I can face him. He might

be . . . cross with me.' Jinx, clearly having cold feet about confronting her ex. 'It'll be better if it's just you.'

'Really? You're sure?' The disco ball made little squares of light dance over Jinx's face. She was serious, so Alice made her way over to the bar, until she came to a stop a couple of bar stools away from Laars.

She watched in the mirror behind the bottles on the bar as he tugged on the collar of his shirt and then shook his arm. Alice noticed the flash of his chunky watch.

'What can I get you?' the bartender asked Alice.

'I'm . . . er . . . my friend's getting a booth I think, but a glass of—'

'Another flute for the lady,' Laars interrupted, and she turned to see him flicking his finger at the bartender. In a second, he'd moved, with alarming speed – rather like one of those velociraptors from that film she'd watched at Christmas with her nephews – and was next to her holding a sweating bottle of Veuve Clicquot in his hand. 'Allow me.'

Alice smiled nervously and fiddled with her spinner necklace, as Laars grinned and poured her a glass. His sandy hair was in the same style as it had always been, but his face was even more tanned than she remembered and a lot craggier. It was interesting how men aged in such a different way to women, Alice thought. Laars was almost wearing his wrinkles like a badge of honour. If only women were allowed to do the same.

'Er . . . thank you,' Alice said. He clearly didn't have a clue who she was, but she could feel him appraising her – her shoes, her legs, her dress, her hair and make-up. Despite herself, it felt sort of thrilling to be admired.

'May I?' he asked and before she'd had a chance to answer, sat on the bar stool next to her. Boy, he was a smooth operator.

'Cheers,' he said, tipping the rim of his glass towards hers, giving her a flirty upward glance. Was it really this easy to get chatting to a man? All these years she'd been single and all it might have taken to meet someone was to dress up and sit at a bar on her own in a racy club. What had stopped her? Why hadn't she done this before? Because she was definitely getting a buzz out of this.

But then, if she had, the person she might have met might have turned out to be someone like Laars. No, this wasn't the place for her – or ever had been, but that didn't stop it being fun to pretend to be someone she wasn't for one night only.

'Cheers.' She smiled.

'That's better. A smile on that lovely face.'

Ick. Alice grimaced awkwardly and took a sip of the champagne, the fizz stinging her tongue. She and Jinx hadn't really made a plan about exactly how to extract information from Laars about the night of Enya's murder. But the fact he was clearly already squiffy would probably help. A little shock and awe probably wouldn't hurt either, Alice thought. Put him firmly on his back foot.

'You don't remember me, do you?' she said, adding what she hoped was a steely little squint to her eyes.

'Erm . . . ' His own eyes narrowed, as he looked her up and down. 'No . . . did we, um?'

'No,' Alice said, cutting him off, 'we most certainly did not. But you do remember Jacinda, don't you?'

'Jinx?' His lewd grin was back, his eyebrows bobbing

knowingly. 'Oh yah, like a million years ago.' He guffawed and shook his head as if was about to say something derogatory before Alice quickly cut him off again.

'She's a friend. My best friend. We were at school together. I'm Alice Beeton,' she said. 'Now do you remember me, Laars?'

'Alice . . . ' Blinking, he peered in even closer. 'Yes . . . hell's bells, yes, of course . . . it's all coming surging back now . . .'

'The wedding . . . ? I was her maid of honour.'

'Ha. My God.' He rubbed his chin, like he'd just fallen for a particularly clever magic trick. 'I'd never have recognised you.' In light of his earlier attempt to chat her up, she could now see a sharp dose of awkwardness dawning on him too – leaving him torn between the person he thought she was and the person before him now. 'And I don't just mean because we're older. Just . . . you know . . . you look . . . great. I mean, seriously. Like, wowzer.'

Alice, despite herself, felt the compliment fan her ego. She looked away to hide her rather inappropriate smile, but turning back then saw that Laars was pointing his phone at her . . . well, not all of her, just her . . . legs.

'Did you just photograph me?' she asked.

'No.' He shook his head vigorously.

She didn't believe him for a second, but demanding to see his phone would only bring this conversation to an end. He really was creepy.

'Isn't it funny that we're still moving in the same circles?' she said through gritted teeth instead, quickly turning her mind back to the matter in hand. 'Because I thought I saw you at the Messents' at New Year. I wanted to say hi, but I wasn't sure it was you.'

'Yah, yah, I was there,' he said, sliding his arm around the back of the seat behind her.

Alice stiffened but forced herself to smile. 'You were with Thérèse, weren't you?' she probed, taking another sip of champagne. 'You know, Camille's secretary?'

'Who?' Laars screwed up his nose.

'Thérèse.' Alice spelled the two syllables out nice and slowly, so even Laars couldn't fail to understand. 'Yes, you seemed pretty preoccupied with her, actually. That's why I didn't approach you.'

Laars pulled a face, as if he didn't know what she was talking about, then puffed out his cheeks as if trying to remember a past transgression. 'Maybe, I don't know. I was pretty smashed by that point, to be honest. I'd been out for lunch and had been mainlining champers all afternoon. But, you know, I do remember some broad flirting with me. Never been a fan of the French ones, though, *entre nous* . . . '

'I wasn't at the party long,' Alice said. 'I *missed what happened.*' She said these last few words in a stage whisper right into his ear. She'd remembered how much Laars loved gossip – particularly when he had the inside skinny himself. 'Were you there?' She leant towards him. 'Only I heard it was dreadful. That poor girl . . . '

'Christ, yes. I mean, what can I tell you?' Laars was now leaning forward too.

'Oh, everything,' Alice said.

'I remember the Messents were both at the front of their ballroom, and she was banging on about her charity. Camille Messent, that is. Yadda, yadda. Starving kids or immigrants or some such. You know, the usual.' Laars took another glug of his fizz. 'And I kind of slipped out then. Got bored. Went to the loo or for a smoke or something . . . and then, when I got back, everyone was going bloody nuts . . . and, yah, the police were called and we were told to wait around . . . I mean, the whole evening went pretty much tits up after that . . . ' He rolled his eyes. 'And all over some maid, apparently . . . you know, just some nobody in the wrong room at the wrong time . . . '

Some maid. It was all Alice could do not to throw her champagne in his face. But then she'd be betraying how interested she was and he'd only clam up. God, what a bloody awful human being he was.

'It's just ironic it happened at their party, that's all. When they're all about being perfect,' he said, topping up his glass.

'Perfect?'

'Yah. You know. It's all about the virtue signalling with those people. I've seen it all before. A room full of sycophants . . . '

When Laars himself surely qualified as the biggest sycophant of the lot? Another thought Alice kept to herself.

'Oh,' she asked instead. 'You don't approve?'

'Let's put it this way. While the Messents clearly act like they're chocolate, I've heard some things.' He tapped the side of his nose.

'Oh? What?' Alice felt her pulse starting to race. Maybe something useful might come out of her conversation with this idiot after all.

'He's . . . well . . . they say he's dodgy.'

'Dodgy? Alex Messent, you mean?'

'I don't think even I'd do business with him, if you know what I mean?'

No, Alice did not. But she said nothing, just let the silence run. Because the other thing she'd remembered about Laars was just how much he loved the sound of his own voice. Meaning it was only a matter of time before he'd fill the void.

'Russians,' he said.

'Russians?'

'Yup, that's what the word is. That he's in bed with the swine. Oligarchs. The unsavoury ones.'

Like there was another kind. 'Oh?'

'Just rumours. I mean, you can't prove anything. Someone like Messent keeps things squeaky clean, but still waters run deep, eh? Yep, he's connected. Right to the top of the rotten pile. And with all the protection that comes with it.'

'Protection?'

'Good God, yes. These aren't Boy Scouts we're talking about here. The only law they respect is their own. And you go messing with them . . . mark my words, there'll be blood on the floor.'

But what kind of blood? Alice wondered. That of rival gangsters and businesspeople? Or innocents like Enya too?

Laars drained his glass and hid a revolting little belch behind the back of his hand, as though drawing a line under the conversation.

'But enough about them,' he said. 'What about you, babe?' He tried that eye smouldering thing he'd actually been rather adept at in his youth – partly what had first drawn Jinx in, she'd always sworn – but it now just made him look like he was squinting. 'You know, I never realised you were so attractive,' he said. 'You were always so mousey, back in the day. I could never understand why a wildcat like Jinx kept you on as a friend, but I'm beginning to see now.'

He leant in to touch her hair, but Alice flinched out of the way, so much so that his lunge turned into a lurch and he had to grab onto the bar to stop himself toppling off his stool.

Alice stood up. 'I think I'd better go. Thank you for the champagne,' she said, looking at her barely touched glass and back at him.

Having righted himself, Laars was now trying to recover his cool by leaning on the bar as if nothing had happened.

'Oh, don't be like that,' he said. 'Stay. Have another. We're only just getting to know each other again.'

But Alice was already walking away from him as fast as she could.

Back on the dance floor, out of sight of Laars, Jinx hooked her into a tight embrace.

'What did he say?' she shouted over the music.

'I can't believe you married him,' Alice shouted back.

'I know. I know.' Jinx shrugged. 'But he really was rather splendid in bed.'

'Even though he wore socks?' Alice said, reminding her of their conversation.

Jinx laughed.

'Let's get out of here. I can't hear a bloody word,' Alice said.

'Oh, come on. Let your hair down. Now that you're here, let's dance,' Jinx implored, clearly pretty squiffy herself, pulling Alice back towards the dance floor.

'I can't. I snuck out, remember?' Alice said.

But a man half Jinx's age was now rushing up to them, and from the way Jinx giggled, they'd clearly been chatting already. He was holding two shot glasses, one of which he handed to Jinx. She clinked his glass and they downed the shot. Jinx laughed and patted her chest and as she breathed out, Alice caught a waft of the alcohol fumes. The man took Jinx's hand now, pulling her away from Alice and luring her onto the dance floor and Alice saw that a serious chat was going to be impossible.

'I'll call you tomorrow,' Alice said, making an old-fashioned hand gesture for the phone.

'Come and dance.'

'No,' Alice said, shaking her head, then gesturing to the door.

Grinning, Jinx blew her a kiss, before allowing herself to be swept away.

After she'd called a taxi, Alice grabbed her coat from the cloakroom and squeezed out past the queue of people waiting to go in. Elijah, surprised she was leaving but polite enough not to enquire why, got the rope for her as if she were a celebrity. He really was a lovely boy, Alice thought.

It was a sheer relief to be outside. Away from all that noise. And, more importantly, away from Laars. She didn't stop until she reached the corner of the street where she'd arranged to be picked up, shivering, with the night air cold on her bare arms. She was just about to put on her coat, when she became aware of someone crossing the road towards her.

'Miss Beeton?' a familiar voice said. 'Alice?'

Detective Rigby. Yes, it really was him. Alice felt a little rush of adrenaline course through her. Because he'd just caught her red-handed, dressed up to the nines and still interfering with the case he'd told her to leave alone? Or because, well, just because he was here, and smiling, at her?

He pointed his keys at a black Mercedes on the other side of the road and its headlights blinked twice as it locked. He must have stopped in a hurry, as it was parked on a red line.

'I thought it was you,' he said. 'I was driving past and . . . ' his eyebrows knitted together, and she felt a blush starting in her toes and rising up to her cheeks as he took in her attire ' . . . and so . . . yes . . . ' he looked suddenly awkward, like he might have overstepped some mark ' . . . so you look like you're having fun? A special occasion?' he asked.

'A friend's birthday,' she fibbed. 'I've left them to it, though,' she added, nodding towards the club. 'I'm just going home.'

'I'm on duty,' he said. 'But I can call you a cab.' He smiled down at her Prada heels. 'They don't exactly look built for hiking.'

'Thank you, but I've already got one coming.'

There was another awkward beat as she thought about what she'd just found out about Alex Messent from Laars. And what she'd learned from Barney too. In fact, maybe the two things were related. Perhaps Messent owed gambling debts to these Russian gangsters. But even if this were true, what could it possibly have to do with Enya's death?

Rigby was the last person she could confide in anyway. He'd already banned her from having anything more to do with the case. And God only knew how much trouble she'd be in if he found out what she'd been up to.

But even so, there was no denying it either. She was enjoying the thrill of it all. Including right here, right now, with Rigby again looking her over like he might have misjudged her and was now seeing her in a completely different light.

'You don't have any more information . . . about Enya, do

you?' she couldn't help herself asking, as he started to walk away. 'From the powers that be. *Upstairs?*'

'No. Sorry,' he said, with a shrug.

'Shame,' she said and there was a beat as his eyes met hers. Was he going to say more? For a moment, she thought he might, but then he smiled bashfully and pointed back towards his car.

'I'd better go . . . ' he said. 'Good to see you, Alice. Get home safely.'

He left her to cross the road and she saw him look back, not once, but twice. Still shivering as she was, she kept her coat draped over her arm. Did he glance her way again as his car pulled out into the road? Yes, she was certain he did. She put her hand up in an attempt at a wave.

But gazing down at her dress and shoes, she smiled, enjoying the thrill of this too, of being here, in disguise. Because right now, she wasn't just a cake-baking busybody at all, but a sequin-clad *femme fatale*. And it felt . . . ?

It felt tip-top.

32.

Fortunately, back in Alice's attic room, Agatha had hardly moved a muscle. As Alice flopped onto the bed and reached down to squeeze her ruined feet, she felt excitement and adrenaline course through her. She longed to tell Jinx about her encounter with Detective Rigby, but she would still be at that dreadful club.

The next morning, she took Agatha for a trot around the block to do her business, but the whole time she was thinking about Detective Rigby's face. She was being vain, she knew, but the fact that he'd seen her all dressed up and outside Annabelle's felt like a kind of victory. Gosh, wasn't it wonderful not to feel dull?

When she got back, she found Camille Messent making coffee in the kitchen.

'What's that on your cheek?' Camille asked, reaching out a finger. Pressing it to Alice's skin, she then held it up. 'Is that glitter?'

'Blimey. Yes.' Alice felt her stomach lurch. 'But I can't think from where . . . ?' She quickly turned away to the sink. 'Are you going to be in for lunch?'

'No. I'm going to a friend's,' Camille said.

'Will Monsieur Messent be here?'

'No, I don't think he'll be back until well after lunch.'

Alice detected a hint of weariness in her voice, but then Camille smiled.

'Is there anything you need me to do whilst you're out?' Alice asked.

'It's Sunday. Try and relax, Caroline,' Camille said with a smile. 'You've organised everything so well so far. Take some time for yourself.'

'Very well. Thank you.'

'Have a lovely day,' Camille said, as she left the kitchen with her coffee, leaving a trail of perfume behind her that Alice happened to know the French called *sillage*.

Alice stared after her, feeling a momentary flicker of guilt, before picking up her phone to text Barney, the second Camille's footsteps had faded down the hall.

We're on.

Half an hour later Alice hurried down to the basement door.

'Come in,' she whispered, quickly ushering Barney inside.

'Why are we whispering? I thought the coast was clear?'

'It is, but . . .'

'You never can be too careful.' Barney smiled. 'Relax, Alice. We'll be in and out in a jiff.'

She was used to seeing him in grandpa shirts and cardigans. But today, he was dressed in dark blue overalls, as agreed. They'd come up with a ruse to cover their tracks. If anyone came back, Barney would pose as a workman here to fix one of the blinds that Alice had deliberately broken in Laura's bedroom. He even had a blue metal toolbox with him to complete the disguise.

'Oh, very thorough,' she said. 'Very Bob the Builder.'

'Ah, yes. My box of tricks.' He shot her a wide grin, and Alice realised that it wasn't just a prop, that Barney clearly relished the challenge ahead.

She led him through the kitchen and up the same route she'd taken the first time she'd come to the house on New Year's Eve. When they arrived in the central hallway, Barney whistled softly.

'You weren't joking. This place is spectacular.'

'But extremely unhomely, wouldn't you say?' Alice said. 'It's like a museum.' Or a gallery, of course. 'Here this way.'

They walked quietly along the first-floor corridor and Barney peered above his glasses at one of the gilt-framed watercolours.

'Look at these. If these are originals, they're worth a fortune.'

Outside the study door, Barney politely asked her to stand back, then got busy with the contents of his toolbox. Turning on a very small torch, on an elastic strap around his head, he crouched down, his knees cracking loudly.

Alice watched, fascinated, as he jabbed and twisted a variety of tiny, hooked metal instruments into the lock with surgical precision. Finally, he made a small grunt, as if confirming his suspicions and stood up.

'That should do it.'

'Golly, that really was quick.'

'Easy when you know how. Over to you,' he said, stepping aside and putting his tools away.

Alice stared at the door handle for a second before turning it Please, please, please let this work, she thought. Then, twisting the door handle, she grinned as it opened with a click.

Alice pushed the door wide open and lingered on the

threshold, remembering the last time she'd stood here on New Year's Eve. Everything had remained so vividly locked in her mind – almost like a photograph, she thought – possibly due to her shock.

There'd been the body, of course, and Detective Rigby holding Agatha, and his scruffy coat. And the fifty-pound notes scattered across the rug. But so much of what she'd seen was the same now. The lovely Edwardian chair with its upholstered buttons and three cushions. The neatly ordered art books on the shelf. And the five pens laid out in a perfect row on the desk. All exactly as she remembered them from that night. All perfectly neat. *Just so*, as Alex Messent would have no doubt said.

'Right, shall we?' Barney asked, passing her a pair of latex gloves and snapping a pair on himself.

They started in the room next door, the personal gym that Alice remembered glimpsing on the night of the murder too. The small room was dominated by a bench press, with a variety of free weights, now neatly stacked on a metal rack beside it. Next to this was a running machine with a huge TV screen in front of it. What was wrong with jogging around a park? Why sweat on a hideous contraption like this, filling one's head with depressing rolling news?

She stood on the machine, wondering what it felt like to be Alex Messent. Picking up the TV remote, she saw its back had been taped up. Before she had a chance to see if it worked and to see what Alex Messent might have been watching, Barney cleared his throat.

'Quick, give us a hand, over here,' he said. He was standing on a bench, prising off the grille from an air conditioning outlet. 'If you're going to search, search everywhere,' as my old boss used to say.

He passed the grille down to Alice then clicked back on his tiny torch.

'Anything?' Alice said.

'Bah. Afraid not,' he said, and screwed the grille back into place.

They checked beneath the machines and behind the weight rack, and inside the shower room too, but found nothing. Methodically, they searched the actual study next. First up, were the desk drawers. A few documents written in French, which Barney quickly read, before dismissing as old utility bills and the like from Paris, plus a box of clear plastic gloves, which Alice assumed Alex Messent used to handle precious artworks.

Then Alice finally found something. A key. But for what? It was too big for the desk drawer. Barney nodded to the study door, and sure enough, when Alice tried it, it fitted.

'So he does have a spare, after all,' Alice said. 'Isn't that just typical? The one thing we do find, we no longer need.'

'Never say never,' Barney said, reaching into the pocket of his overalls for a little tin. He carefully pressed both sides of the key into the plasticine-like moulding gum inside, then he filled both sides with something from a small white bottle and pressed the sides of the tin together. He waved it around, as if performing a magic trick then handed Alice a flimsy replica key. 'There you go. Now you can get a copy made.'

'Good thinking,' Alice said. She'd ask Shilpa's husband at the dry cleaners next time she was passing.

They continued with their search. The bookshelves. The wardrobe. Barney even looked under the rug.

It was slow work. One of the problems, of course, was that they didn't actually know what they were looking for. Just something, anything that might help to explain what Enya had been doing up here that night, or why she'd been killed. According to Gerda Enya had been 'frightened for her life'. What had prompted Enya to call her friend and tell her that? What had happened that night?

And what exactly had the unsuccessful burglars been after? Rigby had told Alice that nothing had been taken, so maybe they had just used the study as their way in and had been planning on burgling other rooms in the house.

Unless . . . unless there really had been something else here of interest to them. But what?

The painting of the nude dancer was still staring at Alice. Or, rather, she was still staring at it. Because now she remembered something else from New Year's Eve. In contrast with the chair cushions, the art books and the pens on Alex Messent's desk, this painting had been hanging off centre – *hadn't* it? Yes, in fact, she was almost certain she'd noticed it, just before Detective Rigby had blocked her view of the room.

Whereas now it was perfectly straight. *Just so*, in fact. Exactly like the painting Alice had seen Alex Messent correct downstairs. Why then was it misaligned on the night of the murder?

'There,' Alice said, 'look behind it.'

'Why, do you want to see his bottom?' Barney said. 'Only I don't think paintings really work that way.'

'It wasn't straight like that on New Year's Eve.'

'Ah . . . ' Barney said, his smile growing even wider. 'Let's take a peep.' He unhooked it from the wall entirely. 'Well played, Alice. Well played.'

Behind the picture was a wall panel. Now sliding it across, Barney grinned, revealing an old-fashioned safe.

'Hmm. A Milner List 3, Size 2 Holdfast safe. I haven't seen one of these for quite some time,' Barney said, peering over the top of his glasses.

'What if it wasn't just the money in the desk drawer the killer came here for? What if there was something in there they were after?' Alice said.

'My thoughts exactly.'

'Can you . . . crack it?' Alice almost didn't have the temerity to say it. Did people actually *crack* safes? Here in the real world outside her precious books and TV shows . . .

'I'll give it my best shot,' Barney said, already rummaging in his toolbox.

He set to with his little curved tools again. Only this time, there were a lot more 'dashits', 'bolloxes' and 'wellwhodhavethunkits' involved. Alice was hideously aware of the time. What if Barney took too long? What if he couldn't get in at all? What if he wouldn't give up? But most of all . . . what if Alex Messent came back?

And yet her thirst for what exactly they might find inside still overrode her fear.

'Done it,' he finally announced.

They twisted the handle of the safe and, together, heaved it open. She didn't know what she expected to see, a diamond necklace at the very least. Surely that was the kind of thing that wealthy people like the Messents would keep in their safe? As well as possibly a weapon of some kind. She'd been imagining a Dick Tracy .38 Colt detective special.

'There's nothing much. Just these,' Barney said, putting his hand right into the back, and pulling out a couple of passports. 'Both Brazilian,' he said, examining the covers.

Alice flipped open the first one. 'This is Alex Messent,' she said, although his hair was different. 'But it says Alexandre da Silva. Do you think it's some kind of fake?'

'Or he is,' Barney said.

'And this one is Thérèse, Camille's secretary,' Alice explained, checking the next passport. 'But, look, she's got a different name as well.' She felt butterflies in her stomach. 'Crikey, so what does this mean? That they're somehow involved?'

'Steady on, old girl,' Barney said. 'You can't go jumping to conclusions. Just because there's a couple of false passports, it doesn't mean they had anything to do with Enya's death. For one thing, you said they were both downstairs when it happened.'

'It still looks dodgy, though,' she said. 'Because why would they both have false passports? Maybe they were involved some-how indirectly.'

'What? With whoever else might have been in this room?'

'It's possible, isn't it?'

'Yes, but that's just the trouble,' Barney said. 'So many ruddy things are.' He reached back into the safe. 'But look, here's some-thing else . . . ' He pulled out a brochure.

'Oh, Audley Manor,' Alice said, examining the cover. 'I know that place. Jinx and I went to school with the girl whose family owned it.'

Alice saw that there was a date written on its cover in the

corner. The Saturday after next. But so what? It was hardly the kind of case-busting clue she'd been hoping for, was it? She couldn't help feeling terribly disappointed.

After photographing the passports and brochure, Alice returned them to the safe. They were just replacing the picture to make sure it was perfectly straight, when there was a sound of a door closing downstairs. They both froze.

A second later, they heard the rising noise of an argument between a man and woman in increasingly loud French.

The Messents.

Barney put his finger to his lip, as Alice faced him in abject terror. Without saying anything he picked up his toolbox and led Alice out into the corridor. Gently closing the door, Barney knelt and quickly fiddled with the lock from the outside. It was all Alice could do not to scream, with her eyes transfixed on the end of the corridor, expecting to see Alex Messent appear at any second. But Barney remained utterly calm.

Then, finally, *click*. He'd done it. They both crept as fast as they could down the corridor, all the while hearing Alex and Camille's voices getting louder and louder.

Camille was shouting now, but Alice couldn't understand what the row was about.

Ducking into Laura's room, just as Camille and Alex neared the top of the stairs, Alice pushed the door closed. Pressing themselves to the wall, barely daring to breathe, she and Barney listened to the Messents pass them barely inches away, still arguing. Then a door slammed.

Alice opened Laura's door and peeped around the corner to check the corridor was clear.

'Go, go, go.' She and Barney tiptoed to the staircase and down into the hall. For someone so old, Barney was certainly stealthier on his feet than Alice had given him credit for.

They didn't stop, or even talk until she'd got him to the back door. Alice shut the door behind him, but her legs were trembling as she walked quickly to the housekeeper's office and let Agatha out, then hurried upstairs to busy herself with emptying the dishwasher in the family kitchen. She didn't look up as she heard footsteps approaching.

Her heart was thumping so hard, and her hands and face sweating so profusely, that it took every inch of her composure to behave normally as Camille appeared in the doorway. She was still wearing her long cashmere coat, black trousers and a stylish silk blouse beneath it.

'Oh, hello,' Alice said, with an attempt at a friendly smile. 'I wasn't expecting you back so soon. I was just about to make tea. Would you like some?'

Camille Messent didn't reply for a moment. Her face was drawn, her cheeks flushed. 'Everything OK?' she asked, holding eye contact with Alice for a little longer than necessary – but probably just wondering if Alice had heard their little fight.

'It's been very quiet. I was thinking about what to prepare for supper?'

'I shan't be eating tonight.'

'And Monsieur Messent?'

She bit her lips together. '*Non.*'

Alice smiled. 'As you wish.'

Camille turned to leave then stopped and turned. 'Would you mind making up the spare room please, Caroline?'

'Certainly.'

Alice watched her leave, seeing the determined stride, but her hand going to her head as if she had a headache. Alice looked down at Agatha who had her head cocked to one side.

'Oh, Agatha, that really was too jolly close by half,' she said.

33.

Thérèse was back in the house on Monday morning. If she was aware of the row between her employers, she didn't hint at it as she briefed Alice in the study at the back of the hallway on the ground floor. The office had a large wooden desk and was painted in a stylish dark teal with contrasting patterned wallpaper. There were some lovely abstract oils on the wall as well as a huge art deco mirror, which reflected the light from the windows with their stylish silk curtains.

Alice scribbled in her notebook, trying to keep up with the list of tasks for the week. Amongst them was sourcing new linen samples for a dinner party Madame Messent was giving for her charity backers next Friday. Thérèse also said that whilst Laura was at school Madame Messent wanted to refurbish her room, so Alice was to put together a mood board, whatever that was. Alice nodded, making a note to ask Helly.

Alice couldn't stop herself from glancing up at Thérèse, and seeing not just her face in the flesh here, but also in that fake passport in Alex Messent's safe. What did it mean? That they were somehow in on something together? And did Camille know? Did she have a fake passport too?

And what was the Brazilian connection? Were they planning on travelling there incognito? But why? Or, could those two passports be real and Alex and Thérèse's identities here be fake? Perhaps Thérèse had no idea that this second passport even existed? Cripes, the sheer array of possibilities was making Alice's head spin. But maybe there were answers here in her study, she thought, eyeing the desk. As soon as she could, she'd find out.

'Ah, *putain*,' Thérèse said, taking a sip of her coffee and spilling it on her cream cardigan. She dabbed at it, ineffectually.

'Give it to me. I'll get the stain out,' Alice said. 'It'll mark.'

Thérèse shrugged off the cardigan. 'I had a late night. I'm being clumsy today,' she said, handing it over with a grateful smile. Alice folded it over her arm and stood to leave. 'Oh, and Caroline, Laura has her orthodontist appointment on Thursday. I forgot to sign her form, so if you don't mind, could you go to pick her up and sign her out? The school is being difficult . . . ' she sighed. 'There have been problems with Laura before, so they won't allow her to go there alone.'

'Problems?'

Thérèse pressed her lips together in a way that Alice knew meant she was determined not to say too much. Thérèse leant in. 'Put it this way . . . she can't get expelled from this school, too. It's her last chance.'

Alice was shocked. 'Laura has been expelled from other schools?'

Laura had seemed a rather well-behaved teenager to her, but Thérèse seemed to think she was problematic. *Quelle surprise*, Alice thought. She was probably doing all she could to get the attention of her parents. Even Alice herself had indulged in a fair bit of that as a child – though, admittedly, more in the realms of pinching the odd cheeky cigarette and ducking off Latin than getting expelled.

'Is it OK if I book the same car that took her to school when the trains were on strike?' Alice omitted to mention the stink the previous booking had caused with Alex Messent, because having a legitimate reason to be with Massoud in the car for the whole journey to Berkshire and back would also give her the opportunity she'd been looking for to visit Audley Manor.

'Of course,' Thérèse said.

'Is there anything else?'

'Yes . . . actually, can you pick up my dry cleaning?' Thérèse asked, handing Alice a slip of rough red paper from the pages of her diary.

Alice was barely able to hide her smile. She'd already recognised the logo on the slip as belonging to Shilpa. Meaning she could drop that moulding Barney made with Shilpa's husband and get a spare key cut for Monsieur Messent's study. Not that she could currently think of any reason she might need to get in there again. But you never knew.

'Of course.' Alice nodded. 'No problem.'

'Oh, I'm sorry,' Thérèse said, shooting Alice one of those pointed little smiles. 'I've been so busy. I forgot to ask, how are you finding things here?'

Alice felt wrong-footed. Did she suspect something? 'Everything's fine.' She beamed.

Thérèse nodded. 'I don't need to remind you, of course, that anything you see going on in this house is strictly confidential?'

Ah, so she *did* know about the row, Alice concluded. But did she also know that Alex had been banished to the spare room?

'Absolutely,' Alice said.

'*Très bien*,' said Thérèse, returning to her phone – leaving Alice now genuinely dismissed.

As Alice walked into the corridor, she examined the stain on Thérèse's cardigan and couldn't help lifting the garment to give it a sniff. It smelt very strongly of a familiar perfume.

As Alice set off with Agatha to Shilpa's, she phoned the office.

'Hang on, you're on speaker. Helly's here,' Jinx said.

'Hi Alice,' Helly said, and Alice felt a little pang in her heart for her old life. As intriguing as all her recent chicanery was, a part of her still yearned for normality to return. But, she reminded herself, this wasn't just about her. This was about Enya and Enya's family and hopefully finding out the truth.

She told them both about Barney coming to the house, breaking into the safe, the false passports and the brochure for Audley Manor, and how they'd nearly been caught.

'Bloody hell,' Helly said. 'You're so brave.'

Alice felt her spine straighten a little, glad that her ordeal had been appreciated.

'Hang on. Audley Manor, you say? Sodding Dilly Harrington's place?' Jinx said.

'Exactly,' Alice said.

'Who's Dilly Harrington?' asked Helly.

'She was my nemesis at school,' Jinx said. 'She was captain of everything. And wanted everyone to know it.'

'It was a long time ago, Jinx,' Alice said, recalling nonetheless the spiteful school bully, her signature black ponytail forever swishing in Alice's face as she cut in front of her in the dining room queue. 'I'm sure she's perfectly pleasant now.'

'Bee–atches like that never change,' Jinx said, ominously. 'But thank God for you, Alice. I'd have beaten her up and ended up expelled ten times over if you hadn't talked me out of it.'

'I'm just looking her up on Instagram,' Helly said. 'Oh, my. She's quite the . . . powerhouse . . . '

'Brick shithouse, more like,' Jinx cackled. 'She's on Facebook all the bloody time, banging on about her boys playing hockey and her place in Gstaad. Yes, look, here she is just yesterday, jiggling on the beach in Cavalière. She says she's going to be there all week, the lucky cow.'

Alice smiled, picturing Jinx's face. 'That's perfect,' she said. 'That means there'll be no danger of her being there at Audley in person if I call in on Thursday.'

'Thursday?' Jinx asked.

Alice explained how she was picking up Laura from school with Massoud. 'Can you call whoever manages the hall and make up an excuse for me to visit? Only obviously not *me* me. Just make me up a name and tell them I'm some party planner looking for venues.'

'Roger that. Consider it done,' Jinx said. 'Another alias coming up.'

It only occurred to Alice, as she walked through the familiar door of the dry cleaners that she would have to explain her uniform to Shilpa so she quickly drew her trench coat tighter across her body, feeling even more like a spy.

They chatted about the usual things – the weather and their respective businesses, then Alice said, 'Actually, one of my house-keepers forgot to pick up some dry cleaning and I said I'd do it as I was passing. Long story, but . . . ' She fished in her purse for the pink ticket Thérèse had given her. 'Oh, and I don't know if you can cut a key right this second, but I've got this,' she said, handing over Barney's little dummy key.

'No problem,' Shilpa said, taking it over to her husband, who inspected it and nodded. A second later, he started grinding out a key with his cutting machine. Agatha whimpered at the noise and hid behind Alice's legs.

Shilpa took the ticket and pressed the button on her remote control and the rail of plastic-clad clothing began to move around. She plucked out the item corresponding to the slip and brought it over to the counter.

'This is it. For Thérèse, yes?'

'Yes.' Alice smiled, more easily this time, because at least this time she wasn't telling a fib.

'Could you tell her that I tried my best and I think I've got most of the blood out.'

'Blood?'

'Yes, there was a bit of blood on the trousers. She said she'd had an accident.'

But it wasn't just the mention of blood that was making Alice's heart race. She now remembered walking past Alex Messent's gallery just before Christmas. And she remembered him laughing and handing a woman in a trouser suit a glass of champagne. A suit identical to this. And hadn't Thérèse been wearing a white trouser suit on New Year's Eve too? Yes, she had. Alice was sure of it.

'Are you OK, Alice?' Shilpa asked.

'Yes, um, yes, sorry,' she said, handing over her card to pay. 'Oh, and Shilpa, do you mind not mentioning that I was here? I don't like to get the housekeeper into trouble.'

'Of course,' Shilpa said.

With the spare key in her pocket, Alice carried the white suit in its plastic sheath over her arm, Agatha trotting beside her, but she could barely concentrate on where she was going.

Should she take the suit to Detective Rigby? What if the blood that Shilpa had so skilfully got out of the white fabric had been Enya's? What if Thérèse had made it up to the study and bludgeoned Enya to death?

More *what ifs* . . . But the plain fact of the matter was that the blood had already been cleaned off. It was no longer proof of anything at all.

Camille, Alex and Thérèse were all out by the time Alice got back to the house.

After feeding Agatha, she took the trouser suit to Thérèse's office and hung it on the back of the door, before partially closing it. With a bit of luck, she'd have time to have a good snoop around.

Moving stealthily behind Thérèse's desk and opening the drawers, she thought about the mounting evidence. It seemed Thérèse was not just up to something dodgy with Alex Messent, but perhaps knew more than she'd let on regarding New Year's Eve.

Thérèse had been standing by the door in Charles's photos, so she could easily have slipped out of the room when Camille had started her speech. But to do what? Murder Enya? It hardly seemed likely, did it? She'd hardly known Enya and her death certainly hadn't benefited Thérèse in any way. But then those fake passports *were* jolly sinister. The sheer . . . *couple-ness* of the his 'n' hers – and, yes, she would allow herself just this one 'n' – passports. Were she and Alex Messent somehow together? Having an affair? Could that be what she'd glimpsed that evening in his gallery? And, of course, the blood on the trouser suit. Enough blood to have made a fuss to Shilpa . . .

Spiralling into full fantasy mode now, Alice imagined walking into the police station and laying out her case to Detective Rigby. He might even let Alice accompany him back to the house as he arrested Thérèse and possibly Alex Messent too, whereupon Alice could reveal her true identity and this whole ordeal would be over. With the case solved, and having fulfilled her promise to Gerda, she could then go back to the office and her old life. Bravo.

Only real life was never that simple. There were no blood-stained murder weapons waiting for her as she searched the room from top to bottom. And Detective Rigby wasn't even on the case anymore. But Alice *had* to find something, or Enya's death would just be swept under the carpet. Now, as she sat in Thérèse's chair and tried the desk drawers, she remembered Enya's lovely hair and intelligent smile. She would not let her down.

The bottom drawer was sectioned with file dividers. She scanned through their headers. 'D.T. Holdings', she read, flicking through the papers inside. The name kept coming up again and again. Some sort of London-based property company, in Alex Messent's name.

Then she saw an envelope with Thérèse's name on the front.

There was a note, written in French, and a set of keys inside. Alice took out her mobile phone and opened Google Translate.

Dear T – here's two sets of keys to your flat. Number 19, Park View, South Kensington. With our kind wishes, C and A.

So the Messents had rented Thérèse her flat, it looked like. And in quite the location. Very decent of them. Quite the action of a model employer. And yet . . . Alice weighed the keys in her hand for a moment. Thérèse must have the other set, but these spares would do just fine for Alice's next mission – namely to search Thérèse's actual home as well. She slipped them into her pocket.

Feeling a buzz in her other pocket, Alice pulled out her phone.

'Can you get back to the office?' Jinx whispered when she answered.

'Why?'

'She's here.'

'Who?'

'Gerda. I told her you were out, but she said she's prepared to wait all day. She's . . . well, you'd better come and see for yourself . . .'

34.

When Alice arrived at The Good Household Management Agency offices with Agatha, Jinx met her in the corridor and gave her the spare clothes she now kept for her in the closet. She was grateful that Jinx had remembered that she would be dressed in her uniform – one that Alice now realised she'd become completely used to.

'Just act normal,' Jinx said in a worried hiss, pressing the clothes against Alice with an ominous look. Jinx ignored Agatha for a moment, who made a disappointed whining noise until Jinx picked her up and gave her a smooch. 'Oh, and that appointment's booked by the way. For, ahem, nudge, nudge, wink, wink—' Jinx, rather unnecessarily mimed both these things too '—Martina McKlusky at Audley Manor on Thursday. Noon.'

'Martina McKlusky?' Alice said. 'Was that the best you could come up with?'

Alice quickly changed in the loo. Ignoring Agatha who was barking and running around in little circles of joy, Alice picked up some post from Helly's desk, as if she was just breezily getting back from a meeting, then went in to meet her visitor. She felt bad, but she'd already decided that she didn't want to go getting

Gerda's hopes up by sharing her theories with her, at least not until she'd made full sense of them herself.

Gerda was standing, inspecting the framed print from Mrs Beeton's book. The one Enya had looked at too.

'Gerda? How can I help you?' Alice said, briefly shaking her hand, before rounding her desk and sitting down. 'Your cold is better?'

'Yes. Thank you.'

As Alice met her clear gaze, a shiver went down her spine. She understood why Jinx had been so nervy now. There *was* something off about Gerda. She was different to before. Business-like, but steely too.

'I'm glad,' Alice said. 'Please do take a seat.' She gestured to the chair opposite her, but Gerda remained standing.

'I demand to know if you've uncovered anything about Enya's death. As you promised?'

'I'm afraid I can't say I have,' Alice said, taken aback by Gerda's confrontational tone. 'Although I've been trying, of course. Asking around . . . '

'You haven't been to the police?'

Alice felt herself blushing, recalling how she'd given the detective soda cake. But she hadn't told him about Gerda. She'd been discreet about that.

'Er . . . no, but um . . . I don't think they have many leads . . . '

She tried to meet Gerda's eye but failed. As the silence stretched between them, a ripple of apprehension ran through her.

'You're a terrible liar, Miss Beeton.'

'I beg your pardon?'

'Shall we be straight?' Gerda said. 'You see, it's true that Enya and I were friends . . . but in a professional sense.'

'Yes, you told me you used to work as au pairs together . . . and then in hotels . . . '

'No, I mean we're colleagues now. Or at least we were, until she was killed.'

'I'm sorry, I don't quite follow . . . '

'We both work for Interpol.'

Alice stared at her. 'Interpol . . . as in . . . ?'

'Yes, the International Criminal Police Organisation,' she said.

Alice was thinking about James Bond and the various spy thrillers she'd read. Gerda was actually from Interpol? And Enya had been too?

'We've been working to recover a missing Rembrandt painting called *The Storm on the Sea of Galilee*, which was stolen from a gallery in the United States in nineteen ninety. It has an estimated value of two hundred and forty million dollars.'

'Two hundred and . . . oh, my goodness,' Alice said, her mind reeling.

Gerda leaned forward, putting her strong hands on the edge of Alice's desk. 'A couple of months ago, we received intelligence that the art dealer Alex Messent was to be involved in the sale of this stolen masterpiece.'

'But surely that's impossible? Who would buy it? *Could* buy it?'

Gerda let out a humourless chuckle. 'Oh, Miss Beeton, you have no idea how nefarious the art world can be. It may come as a surprise to you, but at least half the Rembrandts on display in museums across the world are fakes.'

My God, Alice thought, was that what Enya had been doing

visiting all those exhibitions? Looking to see which of the Great Masters on show could be counterfeits? Was that what her comments on those stubs had been? Ratings of how well they'd been faked?

'There are plenty of people – private collectors – from all over the world, who'd happily compete at auction in order to pay handsomely for these missing originals to be in their homes.'

'But that's so . . . *selfish*.' Alice really couldn't think of another word.

'That doesn't bother them one bit. But that's the rich for you. They believe themselves to be above the law and entitled to whatever they want. Trust me, if this sale goes ahead, then this Rembrandt will most likely vanish forever.'

'I really don't understand what any of this has to do with me?' Alice felt another shiver of fear as Gerda's eyes locked with hers.

'I'm afraid it has everything to do with you. It's only thanks to your help that we were able to engineer Enya being "placed" at the Messents' home to begin with.'

'Thanks to you tricking me, more like,' Alice said. And tricking Katy Ellison.

'Enya's job was clear,' Gerda continued, as though Alice being duped was by-the-by. 'To find out whatever she could about the Rembrandt's current whereabouts and when and where it was going to be sold.'

'And that's why you think Enya was up there in Alex Messent's study?' Alice deduced.

'Quite possibly,' Gerda said.

'And working alone?' Alice asked, thinking of the open window.

'Yes.'

All of which rather shot down the theory that she'd disturbed some burglars. She'd been breaking and entering herself.

This might also explain why the painting had been askew – because she'd found the safe. But then what? Had she been able to break into it like Barney had? Had she taken something from it? Or had someone found her there and killed her before she could?

But who? Not Alex Messent. He'd still been downstairs with his wife. Thérèse, then? Yes, she'd had the opportunity. And, yes again, she seemed to be involved in some sort of skulduggery if that fake passport of hers was anything to go by. And, thrice yes, there'd been blood on her trousers.

But could Alice picture Thérèse doing it? Actually clubbing Enya to death with whatever weapon it was the police had failed to find? And what about motive? Unless she too was involved in this Rembrandt scam. Or had done it to protect her lover – if she was even seeing Alex Messent, for which Alice still had no hard proof . . . And what about the money on the floor and the open window? How did they fit into this?

'What you told me about Enya fearing for her life? Was that even true?'

'Call it an added incentive to get you to look as hard as you could.'

'And her mother dying?' Alice didn't even wait for a reply. She could already read the answer on Gerda's face. More twaddle. 'So, who was she? Really?' Alice asked, thinking of Enya's family. Would Gerda have even told them she was dead? 'Enya wasn't her name, obviously?'

'I'm afraid I can't tell you.'

'You should at least tell the police.' Alice couldn't begin to imagine what Detective Rigby was going to make of this new development. But now it started to dawn on her . . . if Gerda was Interpol, then no wonder Detective Rigby had been pulled off the case. There were clearly higher powers at work.

'That's not going to happen,' Gerda said.

'But why?'

'Because we have our own forces attached. If we send the English police bumbling in now, we'll lose whatever slim hope we still have of recovering the Rembrandt. I don't believe for a second that it's being kept at Alex Messent's house or his gallery. He must have it in a security deposit somewhere.'

She stared at Alice, who felt herself blushing. 'I'm not sure what you think I can do to help you,' she said. 'I've done what I can.'

'Seriously, Miss Beeton? I asked you clearly to talk to the other staff to find out what they might know, but you . . . you went one better, didn't you? You decided to join the staff yourself . . .'

Alice felt an icicle drop into the pit of her stomach. She knew. *Of course* she knew. Gerda had probably been following her every move. Alice had felt that she was being watched and now she realised it was actually true.

'I . . . I can explain,' she said, although of course she couldn't. She'd been such a fool, thinking she could solve Enya's murder herself, but she'd had absolutely no idea of the gravity of the stakes involved and now her head was reeling.

'You don't have to. I've decided that it's for the best having you at the Messents'.'

Gerda had *decided*. Alice suddenly felt as if she were on

quicksand and all the control she'd had was just an illusion. She was in way over her head.

'So this is what's going to happen,' Gerda said, her voice so steely that the force of her words seemed to pin Alice to her chair. 'You're going to keep digging. We already know from our own sources that the sale of the Rembrandt is imminent. I need you to work out where and when it will be.' Gerda was staring at her, unblinking. 'Because if you don't . . . then Enya will have died for nothing, and the Rembrandt will be gone for good . . . '

'But I *can't*.' Alice's voice betrayed her panic. Because she *couldn't*. Not now *knowing* that Alex Messent was a bona fide crook. Connected to God knows who. No, she needed to stop. To pull out. Now. This was all just too bloody *real*.

'I'm afraid "can't" isn't an option,' Gerda said.

Alice stood, red-faced. She just wanted this woman gone. God, she wished she'd never met her. She wished she'd—

'I hoped it wouldn't come to this,' Gerda sighed. 'But you do need to understand, Miss Beeton, that I can put in any number of anonymous calls . . . yes, to the police . . . but to your clients as well . . . to let them know what you've been up to . . . to make your business not a business worth having anymore . . . '

'You wouldn't . . . ' But already, Alice knew that she *would*.

'I'm sorry,' Gerda said, 'but too much work . . . and yes, blood . . . has gone into this to fail now. So, you will do exactly as I say. Yes?'

Alice nodded and sat with a thud. Because – good grief – what other choice did she have?

'Good. And you'll be discreet and not let any of this slip? To anyone?'

'I won't.'

'*Including* your staff and friends . . . ' Gerda glanced back towards Helly and Jinx.

'I won't,' Alice repeated, even though she already knew that she would.

'And the reason I know you won't is because I'll be keeping Agatha until you get me the information I want.' She smiled back at Helly playing with the little dog.

A jolt of fear coursed through Alice. 'I beg your pardon?'

'Your dog will be staying with me. Let's just say . . . as insurance. To ensure your dedication. But don't worry. I'm very fond of animals. In fact, at home I have two dogs of my own.'

She wouldn't . . . couldn't take Agatha? *Could* she? Yes. She could. This awful woman had her over a barrel.

'And when you find out who killed Enya, you will get her back.'

Alice was speechless.

'So, pay attention,' Gerda said, with a cold smile. 'You are going to stand up and shake my hand, as if we've had a satisfactory meeting.' Gerda held out her hand and Alice shook it, limply. 'Then out we'll go.'

Alice walked out of the office, Gerda's gaze like a gun on her back.

'Alice?' Jinx asked as Alice grimly walked straight past her to retrieve her uniform. She made wide frightened eyes at Jinx and shook her head to let her know she couldn't talk.

She couldn't even bear to look down at Agatha.

'Alice?' Jinx asked more urgently.

'I'll be going,' she said, her voice breaking as tears blurred her eyes. 'Gerda has agreed to look after Agatha.'

'But we'll keep her here,' Jinx said, as if Alice were mad.

'She'll be perfectly safe with me,' Gerda said, picking up the small dog. 'For a while.'

Jinx and Helly gawped in horror as Alice and Gerda walked out.

35.

Alice coughed as she opened the oven door and waved her hand at the acrid smoke. The smell of burned flapjacks filled the Messents' kitchen. She cursed, annoyed that the treat she'd made for Laura was ruined. And now there weren't enough ingredients to make more.

She dumped the flapjacks in the bin, then, feeling utterly defeated, retreated to the office downstairs and sat with her head in her hands. She dug out the spinner necklace from under her uniform and held it like a crucifix against her lips, but for once it wasn't giving her any clarity or strength.

At least when her parents had died, Mrs Doulton had scooped her up in her warm arms and comforted her, but for this – possibly the biggest crisis of her entire life – Alice felt completely alone.

Why hadn't she seen through Gerda the first time she'd come to the office? Or Enya, for that matter? Hindsight was a fine thing, but she couldn't believe she'd been so naïve. So trusting. So happy to take them both at face value. And all these years she'd thought she was a good judge of people. And that she had the smarts to chance her arm at being an amateur detective. How spectacularly wrong she'd been.

And being the fool she was, of course Gerda had been able to blackmail her so easily. Obviously taking Agatha would be the simple way to ensure Alice would comply. Now Gerda held all the cards and Alice had no choice but to play by her rules.

But her heart physically ached whenever she thought of Agatha. Where was her darling dog right now? Would Gerda have given her tea in a saucer for breakfast? She sincerely doubted it. And where exactly had she been taken? Alice tried to imagine Agatha in somebody else's home with people talking to her in a language she didn't understand, and it made her want to weep.

She wished she could blow the whistle on this whole terrible business, come clean to Detective Rigby and enlist his help in bringing the Messents and Thérèse to justice, but she knew that was impossible. She still had no solid proof. Plus, Gerda could kill her business at the click of her fingers. But all of that paled into insignificance compared to the true extent of the danger Alice had unwittingly put herself in.

Because this really was no longer a game. Not only had Enya been cold-bloodedly murdered in this house, but it looked increasingly likely that she'd been killed by someone still working here, possibly with the compliance of one of the owners. If Thérèse and Alex really were behind Enya's death, then what would they do to Alice if they caught her snooping around too?

All last night, she'd battled with her instinct to call Jinx. She must have been going out of her mind with worry after the way Alice had left the office, but Alice had kept her phone switched off. Not only because of Gerda's threat that she was watching her – quite how, Alice had no idea, but people who worked for Interpol could probably listen in on phones, couldn't they? And what if what Gerda said was true and the Messents were involved in this huge, despicable fraud? Wouldn't involving Jinx – and Helly – any further only put them in danger too?

'Where is your dog?' Thérèse asked Alice, startling her. She was peering in through the office doorway, dressed in stylish black trousers and a mustard roll-neck jumper, her phone, as ever, in her hand.

The same hand that smashed Enya to the floor in Alex Messent's study? The same hand that held his during some romantic tryst? The same hand that signed that fake Brazilian passport?

'Um . . . my sister is in town,' Alice lied, trying to keep the panicked, choked-up feeling from her voice. 'She always likes to look after her.'

'Ah, yes, very convenient,' Thérèse said, in such a way that Alice at first took it for sarcasm. What? Surely she couldn't have somehow already worked out what was going on? 'Because you're getting Laura from school today, *oui*?' Thérèse said.

'Yes, yes, exactly.' Alice smiled, relieved, remembering like a burst of light in the darkness that Massoud would be here. Massoud, who would whisk her away. 'Would Madame Messent like to see Laura whilst she's back? For lunch maybe?' she asked.

'*Non*. I don't think that will be necessary. Madame has engagements today,' Thérèse said, turning back to her phone, before walking away. Not looking where she was going, she stepped on the old-fashioned grate and her boot heel became stuck.

She stumbled, her foot coming out of the soft leather ankle boot. 'Oh,' she said, laughing, retrieving her boot and putting it back on. But as she did, Alice saw that she was wearing a black sock with a gold insignia.

★

It took forever for ten o'clock to come around and the chance for Alice to escape. She changed out of her uniform and put on the suit Jinx had given her in the office yesterday, although that already felt like a lifetime ago.

Being out of her uniform helped make her feel marginally less like a prisoner. She strode out of the house, down the stoop and got into Massoud's limousine before he'd even had the chance to get out and open the door.

'Miss Beeton . . . ?'

'Just drive,' Alice said, closing her eyes as the car sped away. Only when they were a few streets away did she let out a sigh followed quickly by a sob.

Massoud leant across to the glove compartment in front of her and extracted a box of tissues, before flicking on the indicator to pull over.

'No, keep going,' Alice said, taking a tissue and wiping her eyes. 'Please. Just get me away from here as quickly as you can.'

'What's going on?' Massoud said. 'Jinx called me. She told me about that woman taking Agatha to stay with her? That doesn't sound right.'

Alice took a deep breath. She'd promised Gerda she wouldn't tell anyone, but in the comfort and safety of Massoud's car, she felt secure for the first time since Gerda's visit.

'Jinx made me promise to get you to call her,' he said. 'And you should. Because that's what friends are for. Particularly in times of need.'

And of course he was right. If the situation had been reversed, she'd have been furious if Jinx hadn't called her. No matter what the risk.

'Use my phone,' he said, picking it up from the compartment between them and handing it to her.

'Oh, Massoud, thank you.'

Alice watched West London slide by from behind the tinted window as she made the call. Once Jinx had calmed down about Gerda, she made Alice promise not to cut off contact again.

'It's not like she's really watching you, not minute by minute and bugging your phone and all that guff,' Jinx said. 'She's just trying to frighten you.'

And Jinx was right, of course. Although, to be perfectly honest, Alice wouldn't put anything past that *dognapper* now.

Massoud didn't say anything when she finished the call, even though he'd looked more and more concerned as the conversation had gone on. Instead, he turned off the A40 and drove past the services and stopped at a roadside café at the edge of a village.

'We need tea for this,' he said, pulling into the car park.

'But we don't have time.'

'Fifteen minutes won't make a difference.'

Inside, he ordered Alice a full English breakfast and a pot of tea. In the corner booth, he leant across the table, pushing the condiments and silver napkin dispenser to one side and took Alice's hands gently in his.

'Tell me all about it,' he said. 'I vow to you, Miss Beeton, it will go no further than here.'

So she did. Holding nothing back. When her food arrived she ate it so quickly she could barely believe it herself. But she was ravenous. She couldn't remember the last time she'd had a decent square meal, she'd been that stressed.

In a soothing tone, Massoud told her that, in spite of Gerda's behaviour regarding Agatha, she was more than likely only doing her job, albeit with grim efficiency. He also suggested that having Agatha out of the Messents' home was no bad thing. Surely, anyone there who might end up wishing Alice harm, could also then use her beloved pet against her? The fact that a professional like Gerda also clearly believed that Alice was her best chance of getting the vital information she needed should give Alice confidence too, Massoud said. In his own former career, which he did not wish to get into now, he'd only ever worked with assets he'd thought were up to scratch.

'Gosh, an *asset*,' Alice said. 'Is that what I am now?'

'Quite so. Your strictly amateur days are now done,' Massoud said, grinning, before looking suddenly serious again. 'You just have to hold the line and see the job through. And then Agatha will be returned, the murder will be solved, and your business will be safe.'

'Just a tiddly wish list then,' she said, nonetheless managing a smile for the first time today.

'Yes, but wishes can and do come true,' said Massoud. 'It just takes a lot of bloody work, that's all.'

And he was right, of course. Alice finished her cup of tea. She would get through this. She had to.

'You're not alone, Alice,' Massoud said. 'Remember that. And the second you *do* feel in any danger, you get the hell out and you call me. Understood?'

Alice nodded and grasped his hands. She'd never been so much in need of a friend. It felt so good hearing him call her Alice.

'Very well then,' she said, feeling much more positively

charged. 'Then let's get back to today's business. Audley Manor. On the double.'

Massoud nodded. 'I'll make up time, don't worry. What's at Audley?'

'More . . . shenanigans, I suspect,' Alice said. 'I'll tell you all about it on the way.' She waved for the bill. 'Oh, and there's something else I need you to do too,' she said, passing him the small phone she'd found in the staff loo. 'Do you think you could get that clever grandson of yours to see if he can open it? I found it hidden at the Messents'.'

'Of course. I'll get Wisam on it right away. He'll make sure "Find My Phone" is off too. So anyone looking for it won't see where we are.'

'Is that really a thing?'

'Yes, it really is.' Massoud laughed. 'You've got a lot to learn if you're going to be a detective for real.'

'Oh, Massoud, I know, I know.' Alice sighed. 'In fact, I don't know, but that's the whole point . . . if this whole adventure has proved anything, it's that I don't know anything at all.'

'Not yet, Alice,' Massoud chuckled, pushing his hand back through his dark, curly hair. 'Not *yet*.'

Yes, Alice thought. He's right. Not yet.

But I *will*.

36.

Massoud found the discreet drive for Audley Manor on the far edge of a golf course, sandwiched between dense copses of ash and beech.

As they wound their way along the tree-lined drive, the grey turrets of the house came into view and Alice checked her face in the visor. She should really have brought some more make-up, because after her earlier tears, she was washed out, but she'd have to do. Thanks to Massoud's kind words and fortifying breakfast, she felt a lot better.

As the hall came into view, Alice thought of Hawthorn and its 'money shot', and her heart gave out a little pang. She longed to confide in Jasper about her predicament, but she knew he'd wade in to try to help – in all the wrong ways. Even with the best intentions, he'd undoubtedly make matters worse. But she wished she could warn him that she was in danger. Because what if this all went wrong? What would happen to Jasper and his boys if she got murdered? Somehow, the thought of them being upset was almost worse than the idea of being killed herself.

No. *No.* She wouldn't even entertain the thought, she told

herself. Massoud was right. She just had to focus on finding out what was going on.

'OK, so remember the plan?' Alice asked Massoud.

'Yes.'

'Ten minutes.'

'I've got the timer on my phone.'

'It doesn't look like much is going on.' There wasn't a person in sight.

'I spotted some cars around the back,' Massoud said. 'So someone's home.'

'Yes . . . right.' It was all very well for Jinx to have made up an alter ego for Alice as Martina McKlusky – owner of Fizz Productions. She didn't exactly look very fizzy today. But she'd got away with being Caroline Doulton. Was this really so different?

'Just relax. You've got this,' Massoud said.

Alice gave Massoud a wobbly smile as he let her out of the car.

'Ma'am,' he said, doffing his cap, his moustache crinkling with a smile. 'Oh, hang on, don't forget this,' he said, handing her an executive laptop case from behind the seat.

Oh goody. A prop. Alice felt like an actor in the movies and TV shows she watched as she walked on her heeled boots across the gravel drive with her empty bag and up the handsome slope of sandstone steps, noticing they were all slightly worn in the middle. She thought of all the people who must have traversed these steps over the years, wondering if the cook here had ever owned a copy of Mrs Beeton's book. She wouldn't mind betting that he or she had. She thought of the dinner party menus for twelve her ancestor had painstakingly planned and presented.

She'd always imagined she'd host a dinner party somewhere like this one day. And if she ever got through this, she promised herself now, that's exactly what she'd do.

She pressed the round white china button in the middle of the moulded stone mount, hearing a bell ring inside, and a moment later, the large oak front door opened.

'Can I help you?' a woman in a navy suit asked in an accent Alice detected as Central European. Polish maybe. She was wearing glasses on a chain, and minimal make-up, and a little gold lozenge badge saying 'Manager', which Alice thought was rather tacky.

'I was hoping to see someone about a booking. My secretary called ahead,' Alice said. She nodded to the limousine, where Massoud stood with his arms professionally clasped behind his back. 'I'm Martina McKlusky.'

The woman smiled and opened the door wider. 'Of course, Miss McKlusky. I was expecting you. Please, do come in.'

Alice followed her into a large, bright hallway with a glass-domed ceiling. A marble staircase ran around the sides of the circular walls. She was sure she'd seen this impressive hallway before on TV. Knowing her taste, a body had probably been pushed down these stairs. But forget that, what about her own murder mystery? Why had Alex Messent marked next Saturday's date on the brochure for here? Since her conversation with Gerda about the Rembrandt sale, Alice couldn't help hoping that it might be for that. Otherwise why go to the length of hiding the brochure in that safe to begin with? But could she actually imagine it? Realistically? A bunch of ne'er-do-well art collectors tipping up here? The setting was certainly grand enough. Yes, she actually could imagine it.

'What a lovely hall,' she said. 'And owned by the Harringtons, am I right?'

'Yes.' The woman smiled thinly. 'Though, actually, it's in the process of being sold,' she added as a confidential aside.

'I see.' So perhaps old Dilly Harrington wasn't quite so minted as she always seemed to be making out. Or maybe she had a Jasper in her family too. 'But it is still available for hire?' Alice asked.

'Very much so. Do take a seat.' The manager offered Alice a brown leather chair opposite her desk. 'Here, have one of my cards.'

She slid one across her desk.

'Thank you, Polga.' Alice slipped the card into her pocket.

'So, Miss McKlusky. How can we help?'

'As my secretary might have told you, I work in events management. With international clients.' Alice was surprised by how fluent and convincing she sounded – even to herself. She'd never considered acting as anything other than a rather childish career, but after her experience at the Messents', she was starting to appreciate the skill of inhabiting someone else, and the odd thrill of confidence and inner recklessness it instilled.

'I see.'

'And some of my clients are looking to hold an acquisitions meeting somewhere out of the city. Audley came highly recommended.'

'I'm so pleased. Our clientele do help us spread the word.'

'I'm afraid it's rather short notice, but the meeting is next Saturday.'

Polga laughed as if Alice were joking. Then frowned, recovering, realising she was not. 'I'm so sorry, but as you can imagine, we're booked up months, sometimes years in advance. No, I'm afraid next Saturday is not possible.'

'I appreciate that, but I have the authority to make it worth your while to move the booking. Money isn't an object,' Alice said, with the kind of 'I dare you to defy me' smile she'd often seen rich people use.

Polga looked momentarily tempted, but then shook her head.

'I'm afraid that's out of the question. Audley is booked for a very special client that day and the preceding days for a thorough security check.'

A security check, eh? Very promising. Exactly the kind of precaution you'd probably have to take if you were conducting an illegal sale. 'Oh, I see.' Alice feigned deep disappointment. 'And there's really nothing you can do?'

'I'm afraid not,' Polga said, before adding in a whisper, 'We've been told there'll be a lot of VIP guests. From abroad. So much so that even the owners have been asked to stay away and none of our own regular staff will be here on site, although I shall be on call from my rooms in the gatehouse, just in case.'

That clinched it for Alice. This really did have to be the sale, didn't it? Either that or Alex Messent had some other secretive event on his calendar.

Suddenly, there was the sound of a piercing alarm outside. Alice just about managed to hide her smile as Polga looked up sharply.

'Goodness, what's that? Can you excuse me one moment?' she said, as the racket continued. 'I'm not sure what's going on out there . . . '

What was going on, Alice already knew, was that Massoud

had set off his car alarm around the corner, just as they'd agreed. With Polga now rushing out, he'd bought Alice a few minutes to nosey around.

When planning this, she'd imagined, at best, being able to get a good look at a calendar or some such on the wall like she used back at the office, or at worst, a laptop or desktop computer, but it was even easier than that. Behind Polga's open laptop was the old-fashioned desk diary she'd been consulting. Sure enough, next Saturday was booked. But not in Alex Messent's name. Alice felt her heart plummet. But only for a second. Because then she saw that the name written down here was 'A. da Silva'. Of course. Alexandre da Silva. The same name on Alex's Brazilian passport in the safe.

She heard footsteps clack quickly towards her across the hall tiles. She pushed the diary aside and then the laptop, but if she tried scrambling out from behind the desk, she knew she'd be caught. Instead, she stood up languidly, leaning on the desk. Blimey, what the heck was she going to say she was doing here when Polga walked in?

But it wasn't Polga. Instead, she found herself confronted by a tall, wide-shouldered woman with jet-black hair.

'Yes?' said the woman, by way of introduction, baring a set of wide white teeth.

My God, Alice thought. It was only Dilly Harrington herself. 'I, er . . . '

'Speak up, woman.' Dilly glared down her nose at her.

Alice felt her entire resolve turn to water. It was just like she was sixteen all over again. 'I, er—'

'God, you really can't get the staff these days, can you?' Dilly muttered under her breath. 'Where's Polga?' she demanded out loud. 'Your man-a-ger,' she enunciated terribly slowly, clearly assuming that Alice's English wasn't quite up to scratch.

'Outside,' Alice said, finally recovering the ability to speak.

'Right, when she's back, tell her that her boss is back from France early with a bad dose of the runs and you and she are to go and fetch and unpack my bags.'

'Yes,' Alice said. 'Ma'am.'

Dilly's beady black eyes suddenly narrowed. 'Do I know you from somewhere?' she asked.

'No,' Alice said.

'No, I can't imagine how I would.'

And with that Dilly Harrington stormed back out, swishing her black ponytail just as she always had.

For the second time in as many minutes, Alice had to hide her smile as she walked back round the desk. Being a nobody next to Dilly at school had felt awful, but it clearly had its advantages too.

37.

After Massoud had dropped Laura at the orthodontist and Alice back to the Messents', Alice's sleepless night was catching up with her. She could kill for another cup of tea, but Camille and Thérèse were talking in the drawing room with the door open and there was no way Alice could sneak through to the kitchen without being seen.

'Oh, Caroline, you're back. How was Laura?' Camille enquired with a warm smile, as Alice stopped at the door.

It was on the tip of Alice's tongue to say that Laura was quite probably going to be driving almost past the door in the next hour or so, so if Camille really wanted to know about her daughter's life, she could ask her herself.

'She's fine,' she said. She couldn't trust her face not to betray the tangle of emotions she felt. She had to get away from them both to think. She turned to leave.

'Actually, Caroline, do you have a moment?' Camille asked.

'Yes?' she said, only just about managing to put on her game face in time.

'We're just discussing staff for an upcoming event,' Camille said.

'Oh?'

'It's for several clients of my husband's art gallery. I'll need a couple of experienced waitresses.'

'Here?' Alice asked.

'No, the venue is in the country,' Thérèse said from the other side of the room, where she sat with a pile of paperwork on her lap.

Alice felt a thud of comprehension. She must mean Audley. Camille must know about the event. And if she knew that her husband had booked Audley under his false name, then she was in on it. Or was Alice jumping to conclusions? It really had nothing to do with the stolen Rembrandt and was for some of Alex's legitimate clients. But then, why would he have kept the brochure for Audley in the safe and booked it under a false name?

'Do you need a chef?' Alice was already thinking of Jacques. Having someone she trusted on the ground was going to be important.

'The venue is providing a few canapés.'

'Oh? If you don't mind me asking, what kind of canapés? The nibbles at these things make such a difference,' Alice said, as casually as she could. But she was also intrigued. What kind of fare was Dilly Harrington planning to muster up?

'The menu from the venue came through,' Thérèse said. 'It's open on my phone.'

Camille picked up Thérèse's phone, prodding it, but it remained blank.

'*Vingt-deux, trente-deux*,' Thérèse said and Camille pressed the screen. She smiled, pleased, and passed Thérèse's phone to Alice.

She took it and scrolled through the menu on the screen, not taking any notice of the canapés, but rather the headed crest at the top of the page. Audley Hall.

'So you'll arrange a few waitresses then? Caroline?' Thérèse asked, coming over and plucking the phone out of Alice's hand. She clearly trusted Camille with it, but not Alice.

'Yes,' Alice said, taking a split second to recognise her own false name.

'But understand,' Camille said, 'this is a very, very sensitive client event. So do not mention it to anyone else. And only minimal details for the staff.'

'Of course,' Alice said. 'I shall be very discreet. And would you like me to come along too?' she quickly added, because she'd need to be there too if she was going to get to the bottom of this. 'To make sure everything runs smoothly?'

'*Oui. Bien sûr*,' Camille said, flashing a look at Thérèse, who clearly didn't share her trust in Alice.

'Well then,' Alice said. 'I'd better start on supper. I'm making my Chicken Florentine,' Alice said. 'Is Monsieur Messent home?'

'I don't think he'll be eating with us, but Thérèse will stay for supper, won't you?' Camille asked with a smile. Thérèse nodded, but Alice noticed a slight look of alarm on her face.

Chicken Florentine

INGREDIENTS – 6 boneless chicken thighs, 8 tbsp plain flour, 1 tsp salt, 1 tsp garlic powder, pepper, 4 tbsp unsalted butter, 2 tbsp olive oil, 2 cloves garlic, sliced, 1 *glass white wine, 1 chicken stock cube dissolved in half a cup of water, 1 250g pack spinach, 50g parmesan, grated, 125ml double cream, 1 tbsp flat-leaf parsley, chopped.*

METHOD – Coat the chicken thighs in the mixture of the flour, garlic powder, salt and pepper and leave at room temperature for 15 mins. In a large skillet, melt the butter and oil and fry the chicken thighs for 6-7 mins each side. Set aside. Add garlic to the pan and fry, then add 1 tbsp of reserved flour mixture. Add cream and stock and wine. Whisk on low heat until thickened. Add spinach and stir in parmesan. Return chicken to the pan. Finish with chopped herbs.

With instructions from Camille to leave the food in the kitchen and that they'd help themselves, Alice retreated upstairs. But just as she was going up the final flight to her room, she heard a faint giggle and she stopped, her ears pricking up.

She peeked around the corner and down the stairs. Thérèse was coming out of the spare room, a smile on her face. Alice gasped and ducked back so that she wouldn't see her. Because one glance up and Thérèse would see Alice spying. Quickly, she took out her compact mirror from her handbag and flicked it open. Wasn't this what they always did on the television shows? Yes, smart thinking, she thought, angling the mirror to get a look at the corridor below.

The spare room door opened, and Alex Messent stood in the

doorway in his gym kit, a towel around his neck. He darted into the corridor and pulled Thérèse back towards him into the doorway and again, the same giggle. Hers. Alice held her breath as she watched them kiss passionately, then Thérèse, shushing him, pushed him back into the door and took a second to compose her face and smother her smile.

Alice snapped the compact closed and pressed herself back against the wall. She'd suspected of course that Thérèse was having an affair with Alex – the perfume on his shirt, the fact she'd been wearing his sock . . . it all added up, but now she'd seen it with her own eyes and anger flared in her chest.

There seemed to be something so sordid and lazy about Alex Messent sleeping with his wife's trusted assistant. Thérèse's swagger took on another dimension now. It was clear that her secret gave her power.

But to what end? Were they planning on selling the painting and running away to Brazil on their fake passports? Quite probably. But where did that leave Camille? Did she know about their affair? Surely not. But she knew about Audley, so she must know about the auction. And what about poor Laura? Because there was a child involved. How could Alex Messent violate her home and her security?

Alice sat heavily on her bed. She'd never missed Agatha so much. Or Jinx for that matter. But there was no time to call her now. *Think*, she told herself. Stay focussed on her mission. The auction. Everything hung on the auction. Because that was the only way to stop Alex Messent.

But now Alice started thinking about the logistics of going to Audley, she realised that Polga, the manager there, had told her she'd be there at the gatehouse to oversee the event. If she saw Alice during the set-up or even the event itself, then her cover risked being blown.

There was only one thing for it, Alice thought, spinning her necklace. She was going to have to do everything in her power to control the situation. But for that, she was going to need help.

Jinx picked up straight away. Without pausing for breath, Alice told her all about Camille and Alex, and about Audley and her suspicion that it was where the missing Rembrandt would be sold and how Camille had asked her to find staff.

'That's progress,' Jinx said. 'Well done, Alice.'

But then Alice explained the risk of being spotted by Polga and her cover being blown.

'Oh, God,' Jinx said. 'What are you going to do?'

'Well . . . I've got a plan.'

'Go on?'

'So . . . hear me out. It's risky, but what if Audley was to fall through? What if the auction had to happen somewhere else? Somewhere we could control?'

'Alice, you can't possibly mean . . . ?'

'Yes, Jinx. I do. That's exactly what I mean. We're going to hold the auction at Hawthorn.'

38.

By Friday morning, the plan was officially in motion, with Jinx and Helly fully on board. And thank goodness, Alice thought. Having them there with her would make all the difference, wouldn't it? She even felt a tiny surge of confidence that this might yet work.

Just one problem. Jasper was proving impossible to get hold of. She'd left yet another message, but her phone stayed infuriatingly silent.

In order to calm her nerves, Alice spent the day cooking, knowing that Laura would be back this afternoon and, wanting to do something nice for her, she made aubergine parmigiana, which was always a huge hit, as well as a tiramisu.

Tiramisu

INGREDIENTS – 400ml double cream, 250g mascarpone, 75ml Marsala, 5 tbsp golden caster sugar, 300ml coffee, 175g sponge fingers, 25g dark chocolate, 2 tsp cocoa powder.

METHOD – Whisk the cream, mascarpone, marsala and golden caster sugar until it forms stiff peaks. Pour the coffee into a shallow dish. Dip in a few of the sponge fingers at a time, turning for a few seconds until they are soaked, but not soggy. Layer these in a dish until half the sponge fingers are used, then spread over half of the cream mixture. Grate over most of the dark chocolate. Add another layer of soaked biscuits using all of the coffee. Add another layer of cream. Cover and chill for a few hours or overnight. To serve, dust with cocoa powder and grate over remaining chocolate.

Will keep in the fridge for up to two days.

As soon as Laura got back from school – after catching the train by herself, her privileges finally restored – she wolfed down a huge bowl of tiramisu, before announcing she was going to a party with friends.

But Alice had bigger things to worry about than Laura's social life, because at six o'clock, an unknown number came up on her phone.

'It's me.' Alice recognised Gerda's voice immediately.

Alice slipped out into the garden, terrified that their conversation would be overheard. She brought Gerda up to speed on what she'd learned.

'The plan to go to Hawthorn is good,' she stated. 'My people can go there and set up.'

Alice felt her stomach lurch. 'I have to square it with my brother first,' Alice blustered, terrified that things were moving so fast. 'I called him last night several times, but he didn't get back to me. And I haven't been able to get hold of him today.'

'Sort it,' Gerda said. 'There isn't much time. Get him out of the way. We need the place entirely to ourselves.'

'I'll try.' Alice couldn't help her tone sounding terse. She'd put herself and her family home on the line for Gerda and she was being rude. 'How is Agatha?' she demanded, annoyed that her voice broke.

'Absolutely fine. You'll be reunited soon. As long as nothing goes wrong.'

The phone went dead and Alice, shaken, went to the kitchen to make herself a cup of camomile tea, but Thérèse was standing in the light of the fridge, eating from the bowl of tiramisu in big, angry mouthfuls.

'Thérèse?'

Thérèse turned to Alice, her cheeks bulging as she frantically tried to chew and swallow what was in her mouth, clearly mortified to have been caught.

Alice walked past her to the kettle, as if Thérèse being at the fridge was an everyday occurrence.

'I'm glad you've had some,' Alice said. 'I can never resist it myself. The recipe says it'll keep in the fridge for two days, but it never lasts that long.'

But Thérèse didn't say anything. She carefully put the spoon in the dishwasher and then leant on the sideboard. It was only then that she noticed that Thérèse was crying.

'Oh, goodness. Are you all right?' Alice asked.

Thérèse shook her head. 'Not really.' Her voice was no more than a whisper.

'What's happened?' Alice peered into her face.

Thérèse's chin wobbled and she shook her head as if trying to shake the tears back into her eyes. 'Nothing. It's not been a good day.'

'Anything I can help with?'

'That event we told you about . . .'

'Oh yes? The one in the countryside?' Alice was impressed by her disinterested tone. She was getting good at this acting lark.

'The venue has just fallen through. There's been a flood apparently. And Alex – Monsieur Messent,' she quickly recovered. 'He is *furieux*.'

Good work, Jinx, Alice thought, feeling a wash of relief and fear. She'd carried out Alice's instructions to the letter. Even so, finessing the cancelling of the booking without raising suspicion couldn't have been easy.

'Oh dear. What are you going to do?'

'Right now, I have no idea.' Thérèse reached for some kitchen roll and dabbed her eyes. Now that Alice knew what Thérèse was involved with, she could see the stress clearly on her face. 'But my job is on the line. I am responsible and . . . Monsieur Messent is . . . I, I can't lose this job, Caroline. It's all I have.'

Despite everything, Alice felt an unexpected jolt of sympathy. She knew exactly how it felt to have one's life on the line.

'Maybe I can help,' she said. 'You need another venue? Is that right?'

'Yes. But not just anywhere. Monsieur Messent wants somewhere very discreet. And it has to look impressive – certainly from the outside, plus there needs to be easy entrances and exits, a helicopter pad, facilities for catering . . . '

'Well, come to think of it, I know a place.'

Alice could tell she had Thérèse's attention. 'Oh?'

'It's in Sussex. So not far away. It's in the middle of nowhere and I know the owners. They don't usually rent it commercially but I'm sure I might be able to persuade them for the right fee. Let me see if I can find a picture.'

Alice took her phone and glasses out of her tunic and pretended to look on the internet, but in actual fact just scrolled through her photo album until she found a shot of Hawthorn last summer. And there it was – taken just before the boys and Sassy came out of the front door. The 'money shot'.

She turned the phone around to face Thérèse. 'Hawthorn House. It's a wonderful place – and very historic.'

'I've never heard of this one. And I'd been looking at suitable venues for months.'

'As I said, it's a private house. Would you like me to make the call to see if it could be free?'

'I mean, yes, but that's just the problem. It's so soon. Next Saturday.'

Alice felt as if she could see herself from the corner of the kitchen. Was she really negotiating with Thérèse over Hawthorn? She wanted to pinch herself. This was actually happening.

'We could pay to make it worth their while. For the venue to be available,' Thérèse said.

'If you don't mind me asking . . . how much were you paying for Audley? Just to give me a ballpark idea?'

'A hundred and twenty-five thousand. For exclusive use, you understand?' she added.

Alice almost choked at the enormous price greedy Dilly Harrington had negotiated. No wonder Polga hadn't been able to move the booking.

'But double it if you have to. Money's not the problem. Discretion is.'

'I'll see what I can do,' Alice said. 'And if you don't mind me saying, Thérèse, you should go home and have a bath and get some rest. Everything will seem better in the morning.'

'Thank you, Caroline,' she said gratefully. 'That's probably a good idea.'

39.

At eight the following morning, as soon as she'd been buzzed in for their early rendezvous, Alice flew up the office stairs into Jinx's arms.

'Oh, Jinx,' she cried.

Helly embraced her too and Alice was touched that she'd come in on a Saturday to help. 'Alice. Oh my God. I can't believe this is happening.'

'I know,' Alice said, glad that she wasn't the only one feeing slightly giddy. 'So? Jinx? What did they say at Audley?'

'You should have heard her,' Helly said. 'Quite the performance.'

'It had to be,' Jinx said defensively. 'First, I pretended to be Mrs Da Silva and cancelled the booking. I insisted that there'd been a death in the family.'

'She wept,' Helly said. 'Profusely.'

'She was going to go to drama school once upon a time,' Alice said.

'Life *is* drama school, darling.' Jinx grinned.

'She had that Polga woman there promising not to disturb the family and that the deposit could be sorted out at a later date,' Helly said.

'Helly's suggestion,' Jinx said, giving credit where credit was due.

'Good thinking,' Alice said. 'Go on.'

'Then I called Thérèse, pretending to be Dilly Harrington at Audley Manor and laid it on thick about a flood. Thanks to your ceiling falling in at your flat, I was up on all the lingo too and so was very convincing about mains pipes.'

'I guess all those years of perfecting Dilly's accent behind her back really paid off,' Alice said.

'She sounded like a right stuck-up cow,' Helly agreed.

'I don't care how you did it, just bravo,' Alice said, clapping her best friend on the back. 'And the Messents are totally on board with hosting the event at Hawthorn. Gerda wants to send her team down there right away.' Alice had already run this particular thorny problem past Jinx and Helly. 'Did you have any joy with Lux and Mark?' Alice asked. She'd tasked Jinx with calling in a favour from Mark De Vere, who ran the high-end luxury travel boutique, to see if he could put together the kind of holiday that would entice Jasper and Sassy away from Hawthorn and keep them well out of the way.

'Oh yes. Worry ye not,' Jinx said, her eyes glittering. 'It's all sorted.'

'You wait until you hear this, Alice,' Helly said, clapping her hands excitedly.

'As luck would have it, Mark's been putting a package together for a holiday company in the Caribbean – flights, hotel, car, transfer, the lot. And here's the thing that made me sit up . . . they had this influencer booked to go out there and shout about it . . . only she's now been caught up in some unsavoury scandal with a football player . . . so they need someone else . . . '

'But we don't know any influ—' Alice started to say, then stopped, understanding dawning. 'Oh.'

'Yes!' Helly grinned.

'But she's hardly that influential,' Alice said. '*Is* she?'

Jinx flapped her hand dismissively. 'Yeah, but they don't know that. I told them that her reach isn't massive, but it's who you know that counts,' Jinx said. 'And I said she knows *everyone who's anyone* . . . and they bought it. They've given me the go-ahead to offer it.'

'And it really is free?' Alice said.

'One hundred per cent. They're even chucking in spending money. You just have to persuade Jasper to go away. Like . . . now.'

They discussed it for a few minutes more, then Helly handed Alice the office phone. She took a deep breath and dialled the number for Hawthorn.

After a few rings, Jasper picked up. Alice imagined him in the kitchen and her heart fluttered with a mixture of love and trepidation. She needed Jasper to come through for her. And she needed it badly.

'Hi, Jasper, it's me,' she said, guessing he hadn't recognised the number – in fact, thinking that's probably why he'd picked up.

'Alice, how's tricks?' he said, but she knew him well enough to know that his usual bonhomie had a nervous edge to it.

Jinx gestured for Alice to put the call on speakerphone. 'So did you get any of my messages?' Alice asked.

'Oh yes, Sass said you'd called. She always checks them for

me. We were out at the Grangers'. Do you know they're going to increase their shoot by—'

'I know you've been avoiding me, Jas, but I've got a proposition I want to discuss with you,' Alice interrupted him. 'Are you alone?'

'Yes, Sass is out. The boys are still in bed. But Alice, before you ask, I've been trying very hard, *very* hard to sort out the money for you. And I know what you're going to say, but this time—'

'Can I stop you there?' Alice said firmly and Jinx rolled her eyes.

'Oh,' Jasper said, deflated, 'but honestly, Alice—'

'Jasper, just listen. I don't have much time.'

'Whatever's wrong? You're not in some kind of trouble, are you?' He laughed, but only half-heartedly. It was something, she supposed, that he knew her well enough to suspect when something was genuinely up.

'Do you remember at Christmas? When Sassy said that all she wanted to do was to go on holiday?' she said.

'She's always saying things like that. Nothing is ever good enough for that one, I tell you.' There was a weariness to his voice.

'Right, OK . . . so hear me out. And this is a weird one, OK? But Jinx is pals with a high-end travel agent and it's a very long story, but the gist of it is . . . '

And Alice spelled it out for him. The whole deal. The free holiday for the whole family. The spending money. The need for an influencer. And the client's desire for that influencer to be Sassy.

'Wowzer,' Jasper said once she'd finished, 'but this sounds almost too good to be true.'

Both Helly and Jinx had to cover their mouths just to stop themselves from laughing out loud.

'Yes,' Alice said grittily. 'But it is. With the one catch being that you'd need to go right away.'

'When?'

'Tomorrow. Tomorrow morning.'

She could hear Jasper blustering, 'Um . . . I don't know what to say.'

'Yes. That's all you have to say,' Alice said.

'I want to, but—' Jasper sighed and Alice could imagine his expression '—Sassy is the boss. She's in charge of the calendar, so I'll have to check. But no, no. No, no, no, it won't work. The boys are at school on Monday . . . '

'It's just school,' Alice said, kind of horrified at herself for suggesting the boys bunk off. 'They're not doing any exams. And it's the worst part of the school year, as everyone knows.'

'Little buggers are both miserable. Yes. Leave it with me. We'll discuss it tonight.'

Jinx rolled her eyes.

'But that's just the thing. I'm afraid there's no time. You see, the client is here, in the office with me right now, just the other side of my door, and I promised I'd do my best to sort it with you – like straight away,' Alice said, as if in a confidential whisper.

'Then it'll have to be a no. You know Sassy. It's always such a palaver when we go abroad. She'll want to get outfits.'

Jinx grabbed the whiteboard and wrote on it and Alice squinted at her hasty scrawl. 'She doesn't have to worry about it. The holiday will include a . . . a . . . um . . . a personal shopper experience in a luxury boutique.'

Alice made anxious eyes at Jinx, who then scribbled something else and turned the board around and Alice saw that there was a big plus sign and '5★Spa'. 'And there's a five-star spa,' she translated. 'She can be pampered to her heart's delight as soon as she gets there.'

'Oh,' Jasper said, sounding non-plussed.

Jinx scrawled something else.

'And a free game fishing trip for you.'

'Really?'

From the look on Jinx's face it was clear that this was most certainly *not* part of the package. But sod it. Jasper could bloody well pay for that bit himself.

Helly made desperate eyes and Alice gave her a sympathetic look. She was right. Just how hard could it be?

'Oh, Alice. I mean, it's tempting, but I don't know . . .'

Jinx hit her head with her palm and Alice shook her head to tell her to be quiet. She knew how to get round Jasper.

'Look. I know you've been working hard. You need a break too. I was worried about you at Christmas. A holiday will give you a fresh perspective. You can come back and hit the spring feeling full of vigour.'

'I suppose.'

'And, Jas, I know this is none of my business, but Baxter let slip that you and Sassy have been arguing a lot. Which is why I thought of you when this opportunity came up. You need some space to reconnect and bond as a family.'

'You're right, you're so right.'

'But most of all, think of Sassy,' Alice said. 'Or—' Alice had to fight not to physically squirm as she said it '—*yummymummyinthehall*, as I always like to think of her these days. And how incredible this will be for her. To be an influencer.'

'But she already is a—'

'No, I mean a real one. Actually, getting paid. Living the five-star life. All because of . . . because of how *talented* she is.'

Both Jinx and Helly were now staring at her, their eyebrows raised. Alice put her forefinger up to get them to wait. She knew what motivated Jasper: the fear of his wife. 'But,' she told him now, taking a disappointed inhale, 'if you do want to pass up this once-in-a-lifetime gift on her behalf I can call someone else, but if Sassy finds out . . . '

'Oh yes, I suppose you're right. There'd be hell to pay,' Jasper said.

Alice bit her lips together, seeing that Jinx was now play-acting hanging herself. But Alice knew Jasper well enough to know he was on the precipice of a decision. Surely all he needed was one more nudge.

'If you take it, you'll make her the happiest woman alive. And it'll be just what the pair of you need. Because you're so good together and I'd hate to think of you coming unstuck. So many couples do, and this holiday will be just glue you need. To stick you all back together.' Jinx pretended to vomit at Alice's cheesy cod psychology. 'Besides, women love men who are spontaneous,' she added for good measure.

'Jolly well, yes then,' he said. 'Why the bloody hell not? Live a little, as you say.' He guffawed and Alice gave Jinx a 'told you so' look. Helly punched the air.

They chatted more about the logistics and how he needed to

get his passport details to the travel agent pronto so they could confirm the flights.

'What can I do? To say thank you?' Jasper then asked.

'Nothing,' Alice said, almost swooning with relief, 'but would you mind if I came down to Hawthorn whilst you're away?' Because, of course, she'd need keys. 'I could do with some country air and I can feed Darcy. And I was thinking I might perhaps bring a few chums, if that's OK?'

'Sure, why the hell not?'

'Like, um, Helly, and Jinx. She's, er, feeling bit low,' Alice improvised. 'So could do with a break.'

'She's been ditched again, no doubt,' Jasper said. 'No idea why a first-class filly like that can't hold down a stallion.'

Helly turned away, laughing, as Jinx threw her arms up and glared.

Alice said goodbye, and she, Jinx and Helly collapsed onto each other.

'I can't believe this is happening,' Alice said, shaking her head and laughing. 'This is just so . . . but why am I even smiling?' It suddenly occurred to her. 'This is bloody terrifying. Because it means we're actually going to try and do it. We're going to try and catch a murderer.'

40.

Come Monday morning, if Camille was worried about the imminent gathering at Hawthorn Hall, she seemed totally unruffled about it.

She appeared more concerned about her dinner party on Friday night for her charity. A clever distraction, Alice guessed. In case anyone was watching. Making it look like life was simply going on as normal, with Camille wining and dining the great and the good in the name of her charity.

Meanwhile, Thérèse was managing the Hawthorn event. Or at least she thought she was. In reality, Alice was pulling all the strings. First on the list were the waitresses. Alice had told Thérèse she'd 'booked' two via The Good Household Management Agency who of course would be Helly and Jinx. She'd also taken the precaution of hiring some 'extra security' for the event – namely Max and Elijah, Tiffany's sons.

Next up was the catering. With Jacques back from his stint on the yacht, Alice booked him for both the dinner party and the Hawthorn event. She wasn't sure yet whether she'd confide in him about the nature of Saturday's meeting. She didn't want to risk him backing out if he knew quite how dangerous the sting operation was, but she was relieved he was on board.

Alice spent every minute she was alone checking her phone for updates from Jinx who assured her that preparations at Hawthorn were fully under way. Alice played her part too – calling out the local electrician, who fixed the gates. They now had a sensor, so they opened automatically when a car approached. When Barney had checked in and Alice told him what was going on, he offered to go down and help. It was just as well that he had, because Jinx had put him to good use trimming the hedges and clearing away all the rubbish.

Then there was Gerda. Alice had been dealing with her too. She'd kept her fully up to date with every step of the plan. She'd even admitted that she'd let Jinx, Helly and Barney in on the action too. But far from being furious and threatening to expose Alice as she'd promised, Gerda had been delighted with the opportunity the Hawthorn event was going to present her with. She was already down there with two of her own staff members, installing surveillance. With a bit of luck, they weren't just going to catch Alex Messent in the act, they were going to film him too, along with any clients who showed up – unless Alice had read this entire situation wrong. But she hadn't, had she? The passports, the secrecy, the way in which Audley had been booked. It could only be for the secret auction, couldn't it? But even so, Alice couldn't help feeling that a huge amount was riding on this and it was all on her shoulders.

By Tuesday morning, Barney had been promoted from clearing the ancient helipad, to helping Gerda's surveillance team. Under Alice's instructions, Jinx and Helly had found Mrs Doulton's old cast-iron flower pedestals in the back of the barn and had been to the florist. Between them, they'd constructed several gorgeous arrangements with hidden cameras in them. But the text messages with running updates became more erratic as the weather closed in and the reception at Hawthorn got worse and worse.

Meanwhile Sassy, who clearly had an excellent Wi-Fi connection, kept sending Alice pictures from their Caribbean holiday, mostly of her lolling, gurning by the pool in various bikinis. She was clearly in hashtag heaven and even Jasper messaged to say they were having the time of their lives.

Alice, meanwhile, feeling completely useless, was in a state of high nervous tension as she envisaged everything going on at Hawthorn. And it was so much worse because she had to act as if everything was completely normal, when it certainly was not. Camille, meanwhile, was fussing over the options for her dinner party and asked Alice what her favourite dessert might be. To which Alice replied that there were many, but her absolute favourite was apple crumble. And, as she set to and the kitchen started to fill with the aroma of sugar and baking apples, her heart yearned for Hawthorn in bygone times when Mrs Doulton used to make crumble every Sunday.

Apple Crumble

INGREDIENTS – 1 1/2 lb cooking apples, 4 oz granulated sugar, grated rind of 1 lemon, 5 oz plain flour, 3 oz caster sugar, 1/4 tsp ground ginger, cubed butter.

METHOD – grease a pie dish and warm oven to 180 degrees C. Peel and core the apples and slice into a saucepan. Add granulated sugar and lemon rind. Add 2 fl oz water, cover pan and cook until the apples are soft. Spoon the apple mixture into the prepared dish and set aside. Sift the flour into a mixing bowl and rub in the cubed butter until it resembles fine breadcrumbs. Add the caster sugar, ginger powder and stir well. Sprinkle the mixture over the apples and press down lightly. Bake for 30-40 minutes until the topping is brown.

Serves 6.

On Friday, Laura came back from school early, running in from the rain, absolutely soaked. Alice had no idea how she'd found out, but she was clearly very excited that Jacques was catering her mother's dinner party. She went off to shower and arrived back downstairs in a new dress that Alice had to cut the label off, balking at the five-hundred-pound price tag.

Jacques himself arrived at four o'clock to cook for the evening's event, along with a young sous chef, Marcel, cowering under two bin bags they were using as make-shift umbrellas, it was raining so hard.

'Hello, I'm Caroline,' Alice said, formally shaking Jacques' hand at the back door of the house and ushering them in from the rain.

'Caroline. Right,' he said, his eyes sparkling, but she gave him a warning look. She'd sent a message briefing him about her subterfuge and how she'd be at the Messents' house and that he was not, under any circumstances, to let slip that he knew her. But now she felt another dart of fear. What if he did give her away? What then?

She showed him and Marcel into the basement staff kitchen. As she was leaving, Laura walked in and leant on the counter.

'How's it going?' he asked, with a tense smile.

Laura beamed at him, and Alice politely asked her to inform her mother that the chef was here.

A few minutes later, Camille Messent came down to the kitchen. She'd been most insistent on meeting the chef when he arrived, keen to talk to him about his plans for both tonight and tomorrow's event.

Camille was in a black dress paired with high heels, but her hair was messy and she was tying it up in a pin.

'My hair isn't behaving,' she said to Alice, annoyed as she continued to try and stab it into place. 'My appointment today was cancelled. I so wanted it to be perfect for tonight . . . and tomorrow.'

'I could get a hairdresser's appointment for you. For the morning, if you wanted?'

'There's no time.'

'I could get you an appointment first thing at Tiffany's?'

'Tiffany's?' Camille sounded surprised. 'Could you? Really?'

'Yes, of course.'

'That would be wonderful.' Walking forward, she introduced herself to Jacques. 'You've been here before?' she asked. 'On New Year's Eve, yes?'

'Yes, that's right,' he said. Alice couldn't look at Jacques, but there was an awkward moment. Nobody dared mention what happened on that fateful night.

'And you've prepared the canapés for tomorrow? For the event?'

'Yes, but some I'll have to do in situ,' he said, sliding across a piece of paper to her. 'This is what I'm making. I'll go down to the venue first thing in the morning, if that's OK with you?'

'Yes. My secretary Thérèse will come with you and help.'

'I can help too?' Laura suggested.

Camille gave her a look. 'We'll see,' she said, but Laura looked put out. Alice hadn't even considered that Laura would be coming to Hawthorn too, but now she could see that Camille was in a bind. There was no way that headstrong Laura intended to be left behind.

'There was that beef one,' Laura said to Jacques, changing the subject. 'I loved that.'

'Yes, that's on the list.'

Camille read down the list of canapés. 'What's that?'

'That's a wrapped scoop of terrine,' he said, proudly. 'And I was going to top it with a drop of this.'

He unwrapped the pouch of bottles he'd brought to the office to show Alice, Jinx and Helly when he'd returned from his trip. Alice wondered if he was going to put some on his fingertip for Camille to try, as he had done with Helly. 'This is a special collection of concentrates.'

'Please tell me there's no shellfish—' Camille said.

'That one is lobster, but . . . ' Jacques turned away towards Marcel for a moment, who wanted to ask him a question.

'Caroline, you have told him about Thérèse?' Camille checked, looking at the bottle and then up at Alice and then at Jacques as he came back.

'Of course,' Alice said.

'My secretary is highly allergic to shellfish,' Camille said to Jacques. 'So please, keep that well away from your cooking.'

'Of course, of course,' Jacques said.

'Come,' Camille said, before talking to Laura in French. Clearly summoned to do her mother's bidding, Laura sulkily pushed off the counter and followed Camille, turning to smile at Jacques.

'Like mother, like daughter,' Jacques said to Alice. 'She's quite something.'

'Jacques, for goodness' sakes. Laura has the almightiest crush on you. Please tell me you haven't done anything about it?'

Jacques pulled a bashful face, but he didn't catch her eye.

'Jacques . . . ?'

'I just let her share a cigarette or two with me. That's all. I promise. She's a kid,' he said, with a dismissive snort.

'She doesn't think so,' Alice replied. 'Just be careful. And for goodness' sake, please don't blow my cover.'

'I won't, I promise,' he said, and Alice nodded, satisfied. And then she remembered what it was she wanted to ask him.

'If I text you something . . . some footage from some CCTV do you think you could lip-read for me? It's of Alex Messent and Camille's secretary, Thérèse. I think they're talking in French.'

'I can try,' he said.

'But don't show it to anyone. Or mention it at all, OK?'

As Jacques got to work with Marcel in the kitchens, Alice retreated to the office to call Tiffany, who was happy to oblige when Alice told her who the client was, although Alice knew she was going to have to juggle several appointments to make space for Camille at such short notice. She made Tiffany promise not to tell her that it was Alice who'd made the booking on her behalf. Then she texted Jacques the clip of the CCTV footage.

At half past six, Alice was called upstairs to help Thérèse and Camille greet their guests, as they darted from their various cabs up to the stoop in the pouring rain. Alex would not be joining them, Thérèse had explained, as he had meetings the other side of town. With whom? That's what Alice wanted to know. Would his prospective buyers already have started to gather? Was he retrieving the stolen painting from its top-secret location? Alice's mind whirred with all sorts of scenarios, but in the Messents' home with its convivial atmosphere, Camille and Thérèse smiling and laughing, Alice almost had to pinch herself. They seemed so charming. So very normal and so good, when beneath the surface, they were both hiding so many secrets.

Alice helped take the guests' coats and umbrellas, but the mood in the house was jolly as Camille held court in the drawing room. Alice brought up a tray of canapés and started circling with it, praying that none of Camille's guests would recognise her, something that had only just occurred to her. She was sure that the couple by the piano were the Delawares from New York. She'd placed two of their nannies and Jinx had helped organise a day at Brands Hatch for their son, but they didn't even look up as they accepted a canapé from the silver tray. It really was quite remarkable how invisible she'd become.

She saw Laura next to her mother being introduced to her friends, clearly on best behaviour.

'Do you need a hand?' she asked Alice, in a rather pleading tone, as she passed. 'I could bring up more food.'

'No. I think your mother likes having you here,' Alice said, squeezing her arm and smiling, but she was distracted by the sound outside. Great sloshes of rain were intermittently battering the window.

Thérèse helped Alice and Marcel bring up the trays of food for the buffet-style dinner in the dining room, and Alice's stomach grumbled as she looked at the trays of sushi and Japanese salads.

But now, Alice was even more distracted by the loud splashing noise, which was even worse in the dining room. What on earth could be going on to make such a din? She clearly wasn't the only one irritated by the sound either, as Thérèse now shot her a filthy look, nodding towards the windows.

Hurrying downstairs, Alice took a Barbour jacket from the boot room and an umbrella and ducked out of the back door, immediately feeling the rattle of fat raindrops on the taut fabric above her head. She walked further away from the house to look at the source of the water hitting the dining room window.

The gutter above was overflowing due to what looked like a blockage in the hopper on the floor above. Water was cascading over its top.

Thank goodness Agatha wasn't here, otherwise she'd dive straight into the puddles gathering outside the drawing room, Alice thought, hurrying back inside. But why on earth would the hopper be blocked? It wasn't autumn and Alice distinctly remembered that invoice from Grass 'n' Gutters from December.

She certainly wouldn't be booking them again, she thought – before remembering she wasn't even really the housekeeper here.

Then something else occurred to her. This particular hopper and downpipe was just below Alex Messent's study window. The study where Enya had been murdered with a weapon that had never been found . . .

Alice shook her head. She knew it was just a hunch, but now the coincidence bloomed in her mind, and once there, she couldn't shake it.

With Madame Messent and her guests busy eating, Alice tiptoed up to her attic room and fetched the key for the study that Shilpa's husband had cut. She quickly headed back down to the first floor, stopping for a moment to listen to the happy rumble of voices coming up from the dining room below. She listened for footsteps on the stairs. None came so with her heart thudding, she crept along the corridor to Alex Messent's study and inserted the key.

Inside, she quickly locked the door behind her and went over to the window onto the fire escape and slid it up. Putting up the hood of the Barbour, she hooked her leg over the windowsill. Outside, the metal platform was slippery, the rain heavy and cold. She shivered, edging further along until she could peer over the platform, her stomach lurching with fear. She hated heights and for a second she felt dizzy.

But then she saw it, the blocked hopper, gurgling away. Clinging onto the slippery rails of the metal ladder, she went down a rung or two, water pouring onto the hood of her coat.

'Alice, you can do this,' she told herself, forcing herself not to panic. 'You're nearly there.' She thought of Agatha then, how her little dog would do circles of joy when they were finally reunited and forced herself onwards.

Two more steps and she was level with the hopper. Water was gushing over its top. Plunging her hand into the cold water, her sleeve getting soaking wet, she bit her tongue, stretched, and then her fingers connected with something. Something round and heavy and sheathed in plastic. She pulled it out of the hopper and held it in her hand, her eyes blinking in the rain.

My God, she thought, peering at it in the light spilling from the study above, could this really be what she thought it might be? Had she actually just found . . . a murder weapon?

With her mind in overdrive, Alice climbed back up the fire escape and in through the study window, where she had the presence of mind to perch on the ledge and take off her mucky shoes, shoving them into her pocket.

But even as she shut the window and padded quickly across the room to the locked door, she knew she was leaving drips in her wake. She hoped to goodness Alex Messent would be staying away tonight.

Once outside in the corridor, with the study door now locked safely behind her, she ran as fast as she could upstairs to her bedroom. Throwing the sodden Barbour into her shower, she stashed what she'd found in her bedside drawer, aware that she had to get back downstairs and pretend that nothing had happened.

She stared at herself in her mirror for a moment, her eyes wide with shock and fright. Then forcing herself to calm down, she dried herself as best she could with a towel and hurried to the kitchens.

She was only just in time to serve the trays of dessert and she was out of breath as Jacques handed her the dainty cakes to take up.

'Are you OK, Alice?' he whispered. 'You look as if you've had a fright.'

'Shh,' she said, giving him a warning look. He shouldn't even whisper her name. She tried to compose her features in a way that didn't give away that she felt so rattled.

And no wonder. The object she'd found pulsed heavily in her imagination, almost as if she could feel the pull of it in her bedroom drawer. Could the murderer really have attacked poor Enya with that? She thought of Enya lying on the floor of the study and of Detective Rigby walking Alice out of the room. If only she could talk to him now and confide in him, but then she'd have to confess everything. And hadn't Gerda told her explicitly not to involve the 'bumbling' British police?

She was just on her way up to the dining room, when she heard voices in Thérèse's study. She stopped to listen at the door. Thérèse and Laura were arguing, with Thérèse clearly telling Laura off about something in French. But then Laura said in a low, mean voice. *'Je sais ce que tu as fait.'*

Alice pressed herself against the wall. A moment later, Laura stomped out of Thérèse's study and up the stairs.

Alice continued into the dining room and began serving the dessert, thinking about the phrase she'd just heard. *I know what you did.* That was what it meant, wasn't it? But what did Laura know? Could it be something to do with the Rembrandt? Had Laura somehow got wind of that?

She thought again of Alex Messent hissing in her ear. Could

any parent really have involved their own child in that kind of illegality? Yes, he was capable of anything, Alice decided, if he was capable of conducting an affair with Thérèse under the same roof as his wife. And what about Thérèse? What did Laura know about her? That she'd killed Enya?

Alice watched Thérèse closely now as she came into the dining room, but her face showed no signs of the altercation that had just taken place and Alice marvelled at her implacable manner. Because if she could hide her emotions so convincingly, what else might she be capable of?

Alice thought of the letter from the Messents in Thérèse's desk and the flat they'd given her. She thought, too, of how much Camille trusted her and how infatuated Alex was. Thérèse was clearly embroiled with the Messents in a way that made Alice wonder if she might even kill for them.

But at that moment, Thérèse turned and stared at Alice as if she'd been reading her thoughts. 'Where have you been?'

Alice nodded at the window.

Thérèse followed her gaze, then turned, her eyes boring into Alice, who had to hold her nerve as she returned her stare. Because did she know what Alice had had to do to stop the gushing water? Did she know what Alice had found jamming the hopper?

41.

Alice was up at six, having been awake most of the night fretting about how exactly the day was going to play out. She'd already checked in with Jinx who assured her that everything at Hawthorn was proceeding according to plan. Alex Messent's security team had checked the house the day before to their satisfaction.

Blessedly, they hadn't found any of Gerda's cameras. They had already been installed but hadn't yet been activated so hadn't shown up on the sweep. Nor had they found Gerda herself, her two operatives and Barney, who were now ensconced in the attic. But who knew how close they really were to getting found out? Alice felt almost physically sick with nerves.

As soon as Camille left for her appointment at Tiffany's, Alice checked that she still had the spare keys to Thérèse's apartment that she'd taken from the file in the drawer. They were safely nestled next to her phone in the white crossbody bag Jinx had given her, which Alice had decided was just the ticket for the day ahead.

Thérèse had told her yesterday that she'd be heading off first thing, so she should be long gone by now, which gave Alice time to have a quick look around her apartment, before she needed to get to Hawthorn herself. She was determined to sniff out some proof. Proof that Thérèse was Enya's killer. Proof that would mean Alice would get Agatha back.

Fortunately, the skies had cleared and Alice managed to hail a cab on the street. Ten minutes later, it dropped her outside Park View, Thérèse's smart apartment block. Using the fob on the keys, Alice clicked herself into the building and took the lift to the third floor. She walked along the corridor and knocked on the door of flat number 19, seeing the peephole beneath the numbers.

'Hello? Thérèse?' she called, thinking she could always claim she'd come here to ask her something about the event if Thérèse was home. But there was a resounding silence. Thank goodness.

Alice let herself in, sighing with relief that there didn't seem to be an alarm. Inside, it was dark and, as she walked into the sitting room, she could see that the blinds were still closed. She could smell stale food, and as she turned on a lamp, she saw that in front of the stylish black leather sofas, there was a glass table and on it were the remains of a Chinese takeaway – two foil tins and a set of chopsticks. Noodles spilled over out of the containers and there was a glass with an inch of red wine in the bottom.

Alice frowned. Surely Thérèse had eaten at dinner last night? Hadn't she told Alice she didn't want a dessert because she was full? It didn't seem likely that she'd come home after the long day she'd had and binged on takeaway. In fact, she'd never have binged on a takeaway at all. Because of her seafood allergy. Alice remembered Laura saying as much.

So maybe she'd had a guest staying who'd eaten here in her

absence? What if Alex Messent had been here? But surely Thérèse wouldn't have wanted him eating takeaway near her either?

Then on the table, Alice saw Thérèse's phone. She'd never seen Thérèse without her phone practically surgically attached to her hand. What on earth was it doing here if Thérèse was at Hawthorn?

Alice twisted her lips, something snagging on the edge of her hearing — a trickle of running water. She moved towards the bathroom and leant against the closed door. The noise was coming from inside. Maybe Thérèse really was still here?

But when she listened, she could hear no other signs of anyone in there. Just that steady, trickling noise. 'Thérèse?' she called, knocking on the door, trying to get her excuse for being here straight. 'Thérèse?' she tried again, turning the handle now.

Something on the other side of the door was blocking it, stopping her from opening it. Alice pushed hard, finally getting some movement, and stuck her head in through the small gap.

But as she looked down, she yelped, feeling nausea bloom.

Thérèse was lying on the floor of the bathroom, foam around her mouth. Her eyes were wide open and bloodshot, her hand splayed out, an electric toothbrush next to it.

The noise . . . it was the sound of the washbasin tap still running. Alice squeezed into the little bathroom and turned the tap off, then stared down.

'Oh, dear God,' she said, covering her mouth and slumping back against the sink.

Because Thérèse Clement was undeniably dead.

★

Back in the living room, Alice paced back and forth, gripping the spinner on her necklace in her hand. She needed help, she realised. And fast. Her hands were shaking as she fumbled with the zip of her bag and took out her phone.

'Detective Rigby,' she said, her voice trembling when he answered after three rings. 'It's me.'

'Miss Beeton?' Detective Rigby asked and she felt her knees weaken with relief at the sound of his voice.

'Could you come?' she asked.

'I beg your pardon?'

'I'm in a spot of bother . . . ' She glanced towards the bathroom door. 'And I need your help rather urgently. Very urgently, in fact.'

'Where?'

She told him the address and something in her tone must have persuaded him because he said softly, 'Hang tight. I'll be there as soon as I can. Give me ten minutes.'

She rang off without saying goodbye and then texted Tiffany at the salon. Camille Messent would be expecting Alice back at the house soon to travel with her to Hawthorn Hall.

I will pay you double anything Camille Messent pays you, but please detain her as long as possible. And don't say anything at all about this message. Or anything at all.

Alice called Jinx, but she couldn't get through. She started pacing again, her hands on her head as she desperately tried to make sense of what had happened.

Thérèse was dead. *Dead*. But how? By accident? Because, unlike the only other dead body Alice had ever seen – Enya's bloodstained corpse – there'd been no signs of a violent ending or even a struggle here.

But what if it hadn't been an accident? What if she somehow had been *murdered*, like Enya? Because this all just felt like way too much of a coincidence for Alice. This woman who she'd suspected of being involved in a murder and multi-million-pound art smuggling, suddenly ending up dead on the very day of the sale . . .

Alice nearly jumped out of her skin when the door buzzer sounded. She looked through the spyhole and, to her immense relief, saw Detective Rigby's face, his bushy eyebrows and keen hazel eyes staring right back at her.

'What's going on?' he asked, as she opened the door. 'Is this where you live?'

'No, no,' Alice said, pulling him inside Thérèse's flat.

'Are you all right?' he asked. 'You look as if you've seen a ghost.'

'Worse. It's worse than that.'

He looked concerned as she stared at him. She'd never been so thankful to see a familiar face in all her life, but at the same time the enormity of this moment struck her.

'What's going on, Alice?' he asked.

'It's really rather an awful lot to explain,' she admitted. 'But I didn't know who else to call.'

'You said you wanted help and so . . . '

He walked past her, into the living room. Staring down at the remains of the Chinese takeaway, he reached out to take a prawn cracker.

'Don't touch that,' Alice said, remembering how he'd told her not to touch the doorframe of Alex Messent's study on New Year's Eve. 'This is a crime scene.'

'A what?'

'Or possibly. I don't really know.'

He was staring at her even harder now. 'What kind of crime?'

'A murder.'

'A what?' he chuckled, but then his smile faded when he saw her face.

Alice pointed to the bathroom. 'Thérèse. Thérèse Clement.'

'The Messents' secretary?' he checked.

'Yes, this is her apartment, you see.'

In two large strides Rigby was at the bathroom door and stared in. 'Oh, Alice . . . Alice Beeton,' he said, glaring back at her over his shoulder. 'What have you got yourself tangled up in now?'

A minute later, Detective Rigby stood up from where he'd been peering closely at Thérèse on the floor.

'We'll need a pathologist and the SOCOs in . . . again,' he said. 'But my guess is anaphylaxis.'

Alice stared blankly at him.

'An extreme allergic reaction.'

'To what?'

Rigby shrugged. 'Probably that Chinese.'

'But that's just it. She'd never have eaten it,' Alice said. 'She had a severe seafood allergy and she was always extremely careful about it. In fact, she'd never have allowed that in her flat.'

'You certainly seem to know an awful lot about her,' Rigby said.

Alice said nothing. What *could* she say?

'But you think someone else was here?' Rigby said, glancing over at the takeaway again.

'Yes . . .'

'Yes?'

'I don't know.' Alice's mind was racing. 'Maybe . . . maybe whoever it was wanted it to look like she'd died of anaphylactic shock . . . '

'Because she already *had* died, you mean?'

'Meaning we're potentially not just looking at one murder now, but two,' Alice said. 'And with both victims being staff from the same household.'

'That's a pretty strong theory, Miss Beeton. May I ask if you've got any proof for it? Or even a suspect? Or a motive?'

Again, she said nothing. Because once she did speak, once she said the very first word, the whole damned story about what she'd been up to . . . every single word of that would come tumbling out.

'Only from my point of view, you see,' he said, and this time there wasn't anything friendly about him at all, 'you're acting just a wee bit suspicious yourself. What with being here alone with her dead body, in a flat I suspect you have no right to be in at all, after having gone against my explicit instructions not to have anything to do with the Messents . . . '

'But—'

He held up his hand. 'Hold on.' He pressed a number on his phone. 'Rodge, it's me,' he said into the phone. 'I'm going to need backup.'

He looked away from Alice as he gave the details, then turned back to face her.

'So, Miss Beeton. I really think you'd better start explaining why you're here, and before anyone else arrives, because believe me, I'm all ears.'

'If . . . if I tell you everything, will you not speak until I've finished? Please? Because if you hear everything . . . *every-thing* . . . I promise you. I think you'll understand,' she said.

He nodded grimly. 'We'll see about that.'

And so, desperate for him to see things from her point of view and hardly pausing for breath, Alice explained everything – about who Gerda and Enya really were. About how Alice had been posing as the Messents' housekeeper but was in a whole lot deeper than she'd ever anticipated and how a potential auction of the stolen Rembrandt was taking place at Hawthorn Hall this afternoon.

'Fuck a duck. 'Scuse my French,' he said, exhaling incredulously and running his hand back through his hair, as she finished. 'I really have heard everything now . . . '

'If I . . . if I don't go through with this . . . with everything that's going on down there at my brother's home today . . . then goodness only knows what will happen – to me, and the Rembrandt, and poor, sweet Agatha, of course.'

Rigby let out a soft groan, rubbing his eyes. His skin had gone so red he looked like he might pop.

'But, I really do think we might be able to solve the mystery behind both of these deaths by the end of the day.'

'You've given me motive,' he said. 'And several suspects. He flipped through his notepad. You mentioned that chef, Jacques, Laura, the daughter, Alex Messent himself and that fella Laars, but without any proof—'

'Ah, but I do have that too. Or at least I think I might,' Alice said. 'At least as far as Enya's murder is concerned.'

Scrambling in her bag, she pulled out the object she'd found in the hopper outside Alex Messent's study. As she shoved it into the detective's hands, and he looked inside, she explained how and where she'd found it.

'And, look, it's already wrapped in plastic – a glove, I think. So there might even be some blood or fingerprints or even DNA on it. I've been very careful not to touch it,' Alice said.

The detective stared at it for a long time, then made a little grunt and Alice felt hope bloom in her chest. Finally, he was taking her seriously.

'Now, really,' she said, checking her watch. 'I do have to go, Detective. To meet Camille Messent.'

Rigby laughed now, incredulously. 'But . . . but I can't let you *go*.'

'You *have* to,' Alice said. 'And as soon as you've finished here, you're going to have to come to Hawthorn Hall. I'll send you the location on my phone. When you drive in, bear round to the left and drive to the outbuildings. The reception there is terrible, so you'll just have to trust me. But I'll send word as soon as we need you.'

'Oh, you will, will you?' He was now staring at her open-mouthed. 'Do you realise just how crazy you sound?' Detective Rigby asked.

'Yes, but I assure you, Detective, I'm quite sane, so I'm telling you . . . no, I'm *begging you* to trust me,' she said. 'Call your person upstairs. Tell them about Gerda being Interpol if you don't believe me. They know all about this.'

He bit his lip and nodded. 'OK. Excuse me.' He walked away from her then to the kitchen and closed the door. 'Don't you dare leave. Because if you do I'll have every police car in London tracking you down.'

She waited, straining to hear his conversation, her foot tapping, feeling the slow minutes tick by. God only knew if Tiffany had managed to detain Camille long enough for Alice to get back to the house. And then she saw Thérèse's phone on the table. And even though she knew this was a crime scene, she quickly slipped it into her bag. At this rate, she might be a lot faster at gathering evidence than the police.

The door opened and Detective Rigby stood staring at her. For a moment, she thought he was going to say that she still couldn't leave, but something softened, something that reminded her – quite forcibly – of the way he'd looked back at her that night she'd gone to Annabelle's.

'Alice,' he said, 'I don't know how the hell you've got yourself mixed up in this, but . . . '. He swept out his hand in a gesture that told her she could leave.

'Thank you,' she said, physically slumping with relief.

'And for God's sake, try and be careful.' She nodded, heading quickly for the door as the sound of wailing sirens rose in the distance.

42.

Sandwiched between Camille and Laura in the back of Massoud's limo, Alice felt like a defendant going to court. Every fibre of her being longed to be going to Hawthorn without the Messents and to be rid of their horrible, colossal, illegal mess. Because now, the very place that had been a safety net all her life, had inadvertently turned into possibly the most dangerous place on earth – or certainly for her.

She couldn't shake the image of Thérèse on her bathroom floor, or Detective Rigby's reaction. Thank God he'd enough faith in her to let her leave Thérèse's flat. Because, as she'd hurried back to the Messents', it had all slotted into place, and the little experiment she'd performed before they'd left the house just now had confirmed it all.

She thought of the garbled, whispered voice note she'd left for the detective explaining everything she'd discovered and said a private prayer now that he'd listened to it and would soon be on his way to Hawthorn too. But the gulf between what had to happen next – to get to Hawthorn, for Gerda to catch Alex Messent 'red-handed', as was her intention, for Detective Rigby to galvanise his troops and get to Hawthorn on time so that the murderer could be revealed – seemed with each passing mile to be virtually impossible.

'Tiffany did a good job,' Camille said, flicking Alice back to the present.

Camille had her crocodile skin handbag open on her lap like a mouth and was admiring herself in the compact mirror she'd retrieved from inside, flopping her hair over her shoulder, then back again, 'but she really took an age.' She snapped the compact shut. Alice couldn't help but shudder, thinking of her own compact mirror and what she'd seen in its reflection – Alex Messent and Thérèse in a passionate clinch. And now Thérèse was dead.

'I'm sure she was just trying to do the best job possible,' Alice said, covering for the fact that Tiffany had deliberately taken her time. 'She has such a good reputation.' One Alice would do everything to enhance if she ever got out of this alive. Tiffany had played her role in the proceedings to perfection.

'Can you go a little faster?' Camille said, speaking in a louder voice to Massoud.

'It's an average speed check, Madame,' he replied. His eyes caught Alice's for a second in the rear-view mirror. 'There are cameras everywhere.'

'I'll pay the tickets, just hurry up. I should have been there at least an hour ago.' Camille sat back in her seat and, with a grim set of his shoulders, Massoud sped up into the outside lane and Camille made a little grunt of satisfaction at getting her own way. 'You know, it's so strange Thérèse didn't phone,' she said, checking her messages on her phone again and jabbing at the screen.

'I'm sure she had her reasons.' Alice's voice sounded strained.

It was on the tip of her tongue to tell Camille what she'd just witnessed in Thérèse's flat, but she couldn't. And now she heard the faint vibration of the phone in the bottom of her bag. Thérèse's phone. The one Alice had taken from her apartment. The one Camille was texting right now. She quickly had to take her own phone out of her bag to pretend there'd been a text.

Thankfully, she'd turned the ringer to silent after the call she'd made from Thérèse's phone earlier. Remembering the code Thérèse had called out to Camille, Alice had pressed 2232 and the phone had opened. She'd scrolled through the messages – mostly orders from Camille in French, then one from a number without a name attached. One that had simply said: **You have the picture. You owe me.**

Had someone murdered Thérèse because they'd been black-mailing her? And what photo were they referring to? Alice had called the number straight away, but it went through to a voicemail. And she'd recognised the voice immediately.

'You know, between you and me, after this event today, I have the feeling that Thérèse will be leaving our employment,' Camille said in a confidential tone. 'She hasn't said as much, but I think she's going to change direction.'

Alice had a flash of Thérèse's body rigid on her bathroom floor. She wasn't changing direction any time soon.

'Oh? But she seems like one of the family,' Alice said, remembering in the nick of time to use the present tense.

'Yes, of course she is, but she's a young woman. She never says it, but I think she'd like a family of her own. Is that something you've ever wanted, Caroline?'

Alice swallowed hard. 'No, I'm happy the way I am.'

'That's good to hear, because I was thinking, if Thérèse were to leave, then I'd happily employ you as my personal assistant.' Camille smiled graciously at Alice and turned to lay her perfectly manicured hands with their sparkling diamond rings on Alice's arm. 'You've fixed so much for me and, really, just been the best housekeeper I could ever imagine, but your talents are wasted. You'd be a perfect assistant. We'd have to get you enrolled onto a French language course, but I know a great guy who could get you up to speed.' She smiled again, enthused by the idea and looked at Alice, clearly expecting a similarly enthusiastic response.

'I don't know what to say.'

'I would just like you to think about it. Obviously, we'd come to a private arrangement. About your contract.'

'But Miss Beeton should at least be aware,' Alice said, in an oddly automatic little defence of the real her.

'Oh, God. Agency people. I can't bear them. Really don't worry, Caroline. That Miss Beeton person – she's a nothing,' Camille said, flapping her hand and smiling. 'Trust me.'

'OK,' Alice said, pressing her lips together. She didn't dare catch Massoud's eye. 'Well . . . er . . . thank you. I'll think about it.'

Laura sat imperviously tapping her foot to the beats on her headphones. She was wearing particularly heavy make-up today and Alice wondered if that was for Jacques' benefit. But there was something in the grim set of her mouth that made Alice wonder if there was something else on her mind. Despite not wanting to believe it, Alice remembered Laura's altercation with Thérèse. The way she'd furiously stomped upstairs. And Alice hadn't seen her again last night. Isn't it possible she could have got an Uber to Thérèse's flat?

Soon they were off the motorway. On the final approach to Hawthorn. Alice felt her mouth go dry. The gates swung open automatically ahead of them, and Massoud drove through.

On either side of the drive, the sacks of rubble had been cleared away and the tall hedges shaped beautifully. Barney had done a typically fine job.

But the biggest shock of all were the absurdly expensive cars parked in front of the house, including a yellow Ferrari. There was even a sleek grey helicopter on the lawn. Sassy would be beside herself if she could see this, Alice thought.

'Oh, this is lovely,' Camille said, craning her head to look at the house. Laura took off her headphones and looked too as Massoud drove with a crunch over the gravel and stopped the car. 'Laura, remember what I said. You are to stay out of Papa's way.'

'Whatever. I'll go and help Jacques,' she said, getting out of the car.

Camille waited for Massoud to open the other door for her, then she stepped out and stood for a moment, looking at the house. 'How did you say you found this place, Caroline?'

'It belongs to a friend of the family,' Alice said, getting out behind her, glad that Hawthorn had passed muster.

Ahead of them, Elijah stood in a smart black suit outside the front door. He didn't make eye contact with Alice, who was now stopped by Massoud as Camille and Laura strode ahead. He slipped the mobile phone into her hand, nodded and squeezed her arm briefly.

Alice unzipped her bag and put the third mobile phone inside. They were like buses.

Then the front door opened, and Jinx stood in a smart black

uniform with a tray of champagne glasses. Alice's footing faltered briefly and, for the first time all day, she felt just a little bit more grounded. Jinx was here. *Thank God*. Whatever unfolded next, they had each other.

Jinx offered a glass to Camille as they walked in.

'Oh, that's kind,' Camille said, taking one and then sweeping past into the hallway, where there was a giant pedestal of flowers at the bottom of the staircase.

'Where's the kitchen?' Laura asked.

'That way,' Jinx said, eyeballing Alice, urging her to stay silent. 'The guests are just in the hall with your husband,' she said to Camille.

'I'll be there in a minute,' Alice said to Camille. 'I just need to . . .'

Jinx covered for her, putting down the tray on the hall console table. 'Madame Messent, could I take your coat? I hope you don't mind me asking, but is that from the Saint Laurent Autumn-Winter collection?'

'Yes,' Camille said, impressed. 'How did you know that?'

'Oh, I read *Vogue*,' Alice heard Jinx say, as she walked quickly into the kitchen after Laura.

Jacques was bent over the kitchen's central island, squirting something with a blue plastic piping bag onto the row of plates before him.

'Laura,' he said. 'How are you?'

'Fine, thanks,' she said with a big smile. 'Is Thérèse here?'

Jacques shrugged. 'No, I haven't seen her. I thought she was going to meet me here this morning, but she hasn't arrived yet.'

Alice stared at him and he frowned, not understanding, and Alice felt her cheeks flushing. How awful that she'd even considered for one second that Jacques might have anything to do with Thérèse's death.

'Oh, that's weird. I should tell Maman,' Laura said walking past Alice into the hall.

'Is everything OK, Alice?' Jacques asked.

'No, not really. Can you cover for me?' she whispered.

'Sure.'

'Don't tell anyone where I've gone.'

He nodded. 'Got it.'

After slipping out of the kitchen and through the laundry room, Alice peeked through the back door. Outside, there was a sleek Porsche four-by-four and a driver next to it, playing a game on his phone.

She closed the door, pulling the ancient curtain across the glass, then moved stealthily behind the coat rack, pulling it aside, to reveal the damp, hidden corridor that Jasper and Sassy had blocked off, but which the servants had once used to avoid being in the main areas of the house. It led to the back stairs and up to the top floor.

Silently climbing the rickety worn wooden stairs, and batting the cobwebs out of her path, Alice found herself behind a thick red curtain on the top-floor corridor next to Sassy and Jasper's room. She peeked through to check the coast was clear, but a heavyset man in a black suit and a crew cut with a walkie-talkie on his belt stood like a brick wall at the end of the corridor. Another one of Alex Messent's security detail, she guessed, wondering how many of them he had around the property.

When his back was turned, she slipped across the corridor, tiptoeing through the door opposite and up the rickety stairs into the old playroom, then, moving the old rocking horse aside, through the baize door in the corner and up into the even more rickety attic.

Barney turned as she walked towards him across the creaking boards. 'Alice,' he said, putting his hand on his chest. 'Thank God it's you,' he said, coming over to her and embracing her in the cramped space under the eaves.

'Oh, Barney, am I pleased to see you,' she said, hugging him.

'This is quite the thing going on here,' Barney replied, impressed, nodding behind him. Everything in the attic had been shoved to one side and the old trestle table was loaded with laptops. Gerda sat in front of one of them on Pop-Pop's old canvas director's chair with headphones on, peering at the screen. Two men sat beside her, similarly engrossed.

'We've rigged up hidden cameras,' Barney said. 'And we've been filming everyone.' He sounded like an excited little boy. 'Gerda . . . Goodness, Alice. She's quite something.' Barney blushed and Alice saw, with a jolt of recognition, that he was smitten. 'Wherever did you find her?'

'I didn't, remember? She found me.'

Gerda nodded at Alice from the desk, and she longed to ask where Agatha was, but now was not the time. Gerda was speaking in Dutch to the guy next to her, although she did hear the words 'Alex Messent'. Alice moved closer, stooping under the eaves to see the camera footage on the screens. Alex Messent was now in the main hall greeting his guests with Camille, while just off it, two more burly security men stood either side of the library door.

'That's where they're keeping the Rembrandt,' Barney said, before leaning in, 'if it *is* the Rembrandt.'

'You mean, you've still not seen it?' Alice felt a shudder of alarm. She'd been hoping that at least this one particularly important unknown might by now have been taken out of the equation. Because still that other possibility nagged at her. That this might be a perfectly legitimate art sale. And she'd got everyone here for the wrong reason.

'A van arrived last night and unloaded a ruddy great packing case that was then brought through the house into the library,' Barney explained, 'but we haven't got a camera in there and the security's been too tight around it since, for us to get anywhere near it. From all the intel, Gerda is ninety-nine per cent sure that it is, but . . .'

Alice continued to watch the monitor, as Helly, in a smart dark apron and with one hand professionally behind her back, circulated amongst the guests, topping up their champagne glasses. There were about twenty or so people in the hall including a small, elderly Japanese man dwarfed by a towering Nordic-looking woman in very high heels, a couple in white suits who looked like they'd just stepped off a boat in the Riviera, several men and women in business suits, accompanied by several more academic-looking people, along with a sinewy man in jeans and trainers.

Camille and Alex were stationed near the library door, and Camille's smile didn't falter for a second, as she clutched onto his arm. She nodded as one guest, in a well-cut suit, came out of the library with a big grin on his face, patting the back of another man who was carrying a briefcase.

'It's the Rembrandt,' Gerda said. 'It has to be.'

'Yes, a lot of the guests seem to have brought rather less well dressed, science-y types, who could well have been examining it to check on its authenticity,' Barney added.

'Science-y.' Alice smiled. 'If you think you're having that next time we play Scrabble, you can bloody well think again.'

'A shame,' Barney said. 'It could be a fifty-plus word score, that one.'

Back on the screen, Alex gestured for another couple of his guests to go through to the library.

'We're so close, but I'd really like to see the painting for myself before I can give the order to break up his little gathering,' Gerda said.

'There is a way,' Alice said. 'And I'll show you, but Gerda—' Alice's voice broke '—first you've got to tell me that Agatha's safe?'

'Oh, yes, yes, of course she is,' Barney said, looking between Gerda and Alice as if it were absurd that she could think of Gerda as in any way other than a force for good.

'Then you'd better come with me,' Alice said.

43.

Alice was silent as she led Gerda back the way she'd come from the attic, before pulling her through the door behind the coat rack near the kitchen. Then she opened the back door.

Outside, the driver was no longer by the car, but was a little way off, standing by the kitchen garden, smoking a cigarette, looking out through the gate to the stunted Christmas trees. Gesturing for Gerda to keep low, and remembering the many childhood summers she'd played here, Alice scooted under the level of the kitchen window, along the back flowerbed across the rickety terracotta-coloured stone tiles – an original Elizabethan feature that Sassy wanted to raze for an ugly extension.

She hurried down the coal hole steps to the cupboard door at the bottom and slid her finger along the top of it, until she connected with the old crowbar that had been there since Pop-Pop's day. She wrapped it around the edge of the ancient wooden door opposite the coal cupboard and eased it open an inch, wondering why nobody had ever thought to put an actual handle on it.

She passed the crowbar back to Gerda, but somehow, she dropped it, and it clattered loudly on the stone floor and they both froze. Above them, they heard footsteps and the static of a walkie-talkie and someone talking in what sounded to Alice like Russian.

Alice squeezed back against the coal cupboard door, pulling Gerda into the shadow beside her. They both waited, breath held, until the footsteps receded above them. Gerda looked at Alice with wide eyes, then nodded and Alice sprang into action, pulling the door opposite just wide enough for them both to squeeze through.

The air was cool, and damp and it was dark as Alice closed the door behind them. This had once been used as a wine cellar and dusty wooden racks still lined the walls, with a curved brick ceiling above. She took her phone from her pocket, turning on the torch and shone it at the ground, crouching as she started moving stealthily along the low, cobbled corridor.

Soon, they came to a narrower section of the secret passage and Alice peeked through the grate on the wall. Behind it was the walk-in larder in the kitchen, the door of which was open onto the kitchen beyond. Jacques was still bent over the central island, carefully adding the finishing touches to another round of canapés. Helly took another tray from the counter and Alice saw them smile at each other and exchange a few words.

The corridor bore right and it was a tight squeeze between the brick pillars.

'Wait. We can't fit,' Gerda hissed.

'Sideways. Follow me. We're nearly there.'

Alice thought of how she'd shown the boys this corridor at Christmas but hadn't come down this final stretch herself.

It was a lot narrower than she remembered, and Gerda had a considerably portlier frame than Alice, but her face was set in grim determination.

A faint light beckoned them further along and a murmur of voices confirmed they were getting closer. Breathing in, Alice squeezed herself between the cold stone walls, trying not to shudder at their damp stickiness. And then she was out, into the hidden chamber behind the library fireplace.

The tiny priest-hole cell housed an ancient wooden bench along one wall and a crucifix opposite, the date AD 1588 carved into the white plaster.

'There,' Alice whispered, pointing to the tiny hole on the wall, and Gerda squeezed her eye against it, then pulled back and gasped. Then she looked again for a long moment.

She clamped her hands over her mouth then, clearly overcome. Alice moved past her to look through the hole herself.

The library had been spruced up. Jasper's drinks trolley was no longer there, and the dilapidated old chairs had been removed. The rug had been rolled back, the floor polished and there was a wooden lectern by the fireplace. In the middle of the room was a large easel in an ornate gold frame nearly two metres wide and almost as high. Displayed on it was a striking oil painting of a ship on a stormy sea.

'That's it?' Alice whispered. 'You can be sure? Even from here?'

Gerda nodded, her eyes misty. 'Yes. We'll have to have it authenticated but I'm sure that's it. At last. We've got him.'

★

Back up in the attic, Gerda took a deep, excited breath, as on the monitors, she now saw the guests going into the library.

'The auction must be starting,' Barney said. 'Look, they're all going in.'

'Then this is it,' Gerda said. 'I'll give the order.'

'Her guys are in the barn,' Barney said.

'And I think Detective Rigby is on his way. For backup. At least, I hope he is.' Gerda frowned. 'I know you didn't want me to involve the police, but there was a development you see and—'

Gerda nodded. 'There's no time. Tell him to get here now.'

Alice pulled her phone out of her pocket. 'But there's no reception,' she said, panicking.

'Try on the roof,' Barney said.

'Can you help me?' she asked Barney, pointing to the hatch.

He slid across the bolts and pushed the hatch outwards. She put her foot into his cupped palms and he boosted her up.

Jasper used to dare Alice to come up here on the roof when they were kids, but her fear of heights had always stopped her. And now she felt sick as she crawled out onto the tiny ledge and looked down the sloping, slippery tiles. But she still had no signal. Holding her breath, she shuffled up higher towards the terracotta-coloured ornate brickwork of the Elizabethan chimney stack. As she pressed her back against the bricks, a pigeon squawked and took flight behind her. But it worked. Her phone signal bar flicked up. Thank goodness.

'Don't look down. Don't look down,' she muttered to herself as she rang the detective's number.

'Alice?' Detective Rigby answered.

'Thank, God.'

'Are you at Hawthorn?' he asked.

'Yes. You got my latest message?' She checked.

'Absolutely I did. We're nearly there.'

She could have kissed him then. Really? Yes, she really had just thought that. Only, of course, he wasn't here.

'You're not alone then?' she said. 'Only there are guards everywhere — some of them are with the Messents, some of them are ours — so don't use the main gates. There's a security guard there too. But you'll find a farm gate back near the main road. Use that. Then they won't see you coming.'

'Where are you?'

'On the roof. The auction is taking place in the library right now. Just come quickly.'

She put her phone back in the bag, then saw the phone Massoud had given her. She flipped it open and saw the home screen. There were no contacts on the phone or messages, just a few photographs. Alice stared at the latest one, holding her breath. The photograph was blurred, but good enough. Alice looked at the timestamp, but she suspected she already knew when it was taken: 9.04 on New Year's Eve.

'Now it all makes sense.'

And as if reading her thoughts, Thérèse's phone now buzzed and she saw an incoming call and Alice wanted to laugh at the sheer absurdity of having three phones.

'Hello?' she answered, taking advantage of the reception on the roof.

'Thérèse?' the voice was unmistakeable. It was Laars.

'No, it's Alice.'

After he'd got over the shock, Alice explained that she'd read his text.

'Were you blackmailing Thérèse?'

'Not really. I just wanted my phone back.'

'The one you left in the bathroom, you mean? The one with the picture of you and her in a delicate position on New Year's Eve?'

'She wanted a picture. She said she just wanted to make some dude jealous. And, you know when a chick comes on that strong . . .'

Alice shook her head, thinking of poor Thérèse. 'So, you were in the cloakroom during Camille's speech on New Year's Eve. With Thérèse?'

'I guess. Why does it matter?'

Alice shook her head and rang off, then turned off the phone. She had no time for Laars' explanation. She sat for a moment, like a child, her legs stretched out on the tiled roof, everything shuffling into place in her mind.

She stared out across the woods and fields, forcing herself to appreciate the view from this great height for the first time. In the distance, a mile or so away, she thought she could see a line of cars approaching on the main road. Police cars? She could only pray. Her scruffy detective might not exactly be riding a horse, but hopefully he might still prove to be her knight in shining armour before the day was through.

Then she nodded, steeling herself. It was time to reveal the truth, and although there was a certain satisfaction in having worked it all out, it gave her no pleasure.

44.

Gerda pulled at the bottom of her grey jacket and straightened her shoulders, before nodding at Alice as they marched across the hallway towards the closed library doors.

'Who are you?' one of the two guards stationed there challenged them.

'Guests,' Gerda said, smiling at both men broadly – and for long enough, it turned out, for Gerda's two colleagues to creep up from the opposite direction behind them.

The ambush was brief, what with Gerda's two friends having the element of surprise. And met next to no resistance. But then again, Alice thought, you didn't really have much choice than to go where you were told when someone as imposing at Elijah was pointing a twelve-bore shotgun at you at point-blank range.

The ambush had been Gerda's idea. She was still terrified Alex Messent and his guests might somehow escape before the police arrived. But the shotgun had been Alice's suggestion. It was Pop-Pop's old one and didn't work anyway, but she'd thought it might get faster results than having Gerda's colleagues trying to restrain these two men.

As the guards were led off by Max to be locked up in the

larder, Alice and Gerda could hear Alex Messent through the library door conducting the auction himself.

'Do I hear two hundred and thirty million from Mr Kimura?' his voice called out.

'Ready?' Alice asked Gerda, who nodded, then she turned the handle and in two strides, the pair of them walked into the library.

'Stop the auction.' Gerda's voice was loud and clear. She held her hand in the air.

An anxious mumble of voices followed. Alice saw Alex Messent at the auctioneer's lectern look in panic towards the door for his guards. His guests had all been standing in groups around the painting, but now turned towards Alice and Gerda, confusion on their faces.

'What's going on?' Camille said, looking accusingly at Alice. 'I'm sorry, everyone,' she said, trying to appease the crowd. 'Caroline? What the hell is going on?'

Gerda marched up to the painting and studied it up close, her eyes shining, then she turned to the crowd. 'As I'm sure many of you are aware, this is a stolen painting. And, after a very, *very* long search for it, I'm here to claim it for the Dutch government and people.' She produced a badge from the pocket of her jacket and flashed it at the shocked faces.

Alex Messent looked at his wife in alarm, then addressed Gerda. 'What the hell . . . ? What do you mean?'

'It's very simple. You are under arrest, Monsieur Messent.'

Now panic broke out, with the guests all talking at once. Alice saw Camille moving quickly towards the library doors, but just as she got there, Barney stopped her along with Jinx, Helly, Elijah and Max, who stood like a physical barrier, shoulder to shoulder.

As Camille staggered back into the library, Alex lunged sideways at Gerda, who, in a surprising display of agility, quickly twisted his arm behind his back. In all the commotion, Alice then saw Detective Rigby shouldering past Barney. He stopped and stared at the painting and then at Alice and, as his eyes met hers, her heart thudded with relief.

Jinx slotted her fingers into her mouth and wolf-whistled loudly. Shocked by the noise, the crowd fell silent.

'Please can you all stay exactly where you are. I'm Detective Rigby of the Metropolitan Police.'

'This is a misunderstanding . . . ' Alex Messent began to protest, with Camille now beside him.

'Is it?'

Detective Rigby stared grimly at Alex as several other police officers poured into the library.

'I'd advise you all to be as helpful as you can,' Rigby warned the guests. 'Everyone here has serious questions to answer. *And* anyone you might be working for,' he added, glaring at two of the suited men who both had phones to their ears, and had clearly been relaying telephone bids. Rigby nodded to his officers. 'Take them away. All except him and her.'

It was Alex and Camille Messent he'd been pointing to. As his officers started ushering the confused guests out into the hallway, the Japanese man looked desperately, longingly back at the Rembrandt, but Gerda blocked his way.

'You've got this all wrong,' Alex Messent tried pleading again, more desperately this time.

'No,' Rigby said. 'There's no misunderstanding. You see, as well as theft, we're here for another reason: *murder*.'

'What?' Alex Messent looked genuinely shocked.

Detective Rigby turned to Camille. 'Camille Messent, I'm arresting you for the murder of Romee Hoek,' he said.

The two officers nearest now moved towards Camille. 'Who? What? I've never . . . I've never even heard of this person—'

'Also known as *Enya Fischer*,' Detective Rigby said.

Two officers grabbed Camille. 'Caroline?' she asked desperately, as she tried to shake them off. 'Help me.' Her eyes were wide as she appealed to Alice.

'Oh, this isn't Caroline,' Detective Rigby said. 'Allow me to introduce Miss Alice Beeton.'

'Who?' Camille and Alex asked at the same time.

'This is Alice Beeton of The Good Household Management Agency, and it's thanks to her that we know exactly what happened on the night Enya died.'

There was a moment of silence and Alice was aware of everyone turning to face her at once. She had a terrible moment of vertigo – almost as bad as it had been on the roof, but she'd combatted that, she reminded herself.

Even so, she hated being the centre of attention and she locked eyes with Detective Rigby, horrified that he'd turned this onto her. But his hazel eyes were kind and he nodded gently with encouragement. And she saw that rather than landing her in it, he was giving her permission to claim the moment.

'Is it true?' Camille asked, in a whisper. 'You're not Caroline?'

'No, as the detective says, I'm Alice Beeton. I run The Good Household Management Agency. Just before Christmas, Enya Fischer – well, a woman I *thought* was Enya Fischer – came into the office to interview for a domestic position. I was intending to put her on my books, but then you rang, Madame Messent, asking for a housekeeper, and Enya said that she could go to your house straight away. I checked her references, of course, but the timing seemed so serendipitous, I didn't have a moment of hesitation about placing her.'

'But Enya wasn't who she said she was,' Detective Rigby chipped in, clearly keen to keep Alice on track.

'Exactly. I subsequently found out that Enya had paid your last housekeeper, Katy Ellison, to leave her post. In fact, she went to convincing lengths to gain access to your home.'

'I don't believe what I'm hearing,' Alex Messent said.

'She wasn't a housekeeper, but was in fact, my colleague at Interpol and had been instrumental in finding this stolen treasure,' Gerda said, staring venomously at the Messents. 'And a damned good agent she was too,' Gerda added. 'She was a world expert on Rembrandt, you see. If she could only have seen this . . . '

'So, once she was in your employ, she used your New Year's Eve party to gain access to your study,' Alice continued.

'But you saw her, didn't you?' Detective Rigby said, turning on Camille, whose hand fluttered to her throat.

'Me? What? No!'

'You were suspicious and followed her, didn't you? And when you found her snooping in the safe, you hit her over the head, killing her instantly.'

'No, no . . . ' Camille stepped backwards, but into the body of a policeman. 'It's not true.'

'And then you staged the room to make it look as if there'd been a burglary, tossing the cash from your husband's desk around the floor and opening the window. And then, like the cold-hearted killer you are, you went downstairs and joined the party. The perfect hostess. The perfect wife. The compassionate charity patron calling for a minute's silence to honour the suffering of others,' Detective Rigby said. 'The very silence that provided your alibi.'

'It's not true,' Camille shouted. 'How can it be? I was downstairs when she died. Alex, make them stop.'

'This is rubbish . . . nonsense,' Alex began.

'Alice?' Detective Rigby said, holding out his hand towards her.

'Well, yes, the detective is right. You see, it wasn't until this morning that I pieced it all together. Whilst you were at Tiffany's – a friend of mine, who deliberately detained you, I might add,' she said to Camille, 'I went into the private gym, next to your study,' she said to Alex Messent, whose shark-eyes locked briefly on hers. 'To perform a little experiment. You see, on the night of the murder, I went to your house to help the detective here, but my dog, Agatha, ran up to the study, so I saw the crime scene. What I clearly remember was seeing through the open door into the gym, where the weights were scattered across the floor. I hadn't thought much of it at the time, but when I started working for you, and realised how neat and tidy, in fact how like a mausoleum, you like to keep your house, I started to think that it was odd that you would leave the weights like that.'

'I have no idea where you're going with this,' Alex said.

'The other anomaly was that the remote control in the gym had its battery compartment taped up. I'd assumed at first that the remote control was for the wall television, but you see,

I found the back of that very remote control in the pocket of the dress that you wore for your party on New Year's Eve, *Madame*.'

She turned to Camille and saw two high spots of colour blossoming in her cheeks.

'We were selling some clothes,' Jinx chipped in, and Alice realised that Jinx had moved towards her and was now by her side. Alice smiled at her gratefully. 'And that's where Alice saw your dress in Pandora, the dress agency,' Jinx explained.

'Yes, and when I took it to the changing room and tried it on, I found the back of a Bluetooth remote control in the pocket. And I wondered why you'd have had it on you in that particular garment. And then, of course, I remembered the gym. So, I took it there this morning – and when I removed the remote's tape, it fitted perfectly. But I still couldn't understand why you had it. Had you been up there on the night of Enya's murder just watching TV? But then I clicked it on . . . and it wasn't for the TV at all, was it? No, it was the running machine that suddenly jerked into life,' Alice said.

'This is crazy,' Alex Messent protested again.

'No, not crazy, Monsieur Messent, very clever,' Detective Rigby chipped in, nodding to Alice again.

'You see, after killing Enya,' she said, 'your wife piled the weights on the running machine and then from downstairs, during the minute's silence she'd orchestrated, she remotely activated the machine with the Bluetooth control. And when the treadmill moved, the weights flew off the back and thudded on the floor. A thud everyone heard. And everyone assumed was the sound of Enya falling to the floor.'

There was a rumble of voices as everyone started talking.

'Oh, bravo, Alice,' Jinx said.

'And so that was the little experiment I tried myself today. I loaded on the weights and stood in the exact same position your wife had been in while she was giving her speech and activated the machine with the remote. And it *did* sound *exactly* like a body falling.'

'That can hardly count as evidence. This is all ridiculous speculation,' Alex Messent blurted, but he didn't sound nearly so sure of himself anymore.

'I might have been inclined to agree with you,' the detective said, 'but last night Miss Beeton also found the murder weapon.'

He now handed Alice a clear plastic evidence bag with the glass snow globe in it. Was he enjoying this? Alice wondered. It certainly looked like he was. 'Perhaps you'd like to explain how you found it,' he said.

Alice held up the snow globe. 'I found it in a plastic glove stuck in the hopper below the study. Last night, at your wife's dinner party, the rain was intense, and the gutters started overflowing. I thought it odd, as I'd seen a receipt from a firm called Grass 'n' Gutters who'd cleared the gutters recently. So, with considerable difficulty, I retrieved this snow globe, which was blocking the drainpipe. And I recognised it instantly, as it had been on the desk next to Laura on your Christmas card.'

'You saw a screenshot of the card at Tiff's, didn't you?' Jinx said. 'On her phone. I remember.'

'And, you see, I've always been a stickler for details,' Alice said, nodding. 'Meaning I'd also noticed that the snow globe hadn't been on the desk on the night Enya was murdered.'

'And what do you know?' Detective Rigby chimed in. 'It still had traces of Enya's blood on it. *And* your fingerprints, Madame Messent. After you'd used it, you must have rolled it up in a clear plastic glove, of which there were many in the study, and thrown it out of the window, and into the thick snow, where it had been invisible to the officers looking for it. Only as the snow had thawed, it rolled down into the hopper, blocking the drainpipe, causing the gutter to overflow in the heavy rain.'

'Exactly,' Alice said, with satisfaction.

'You might have completely evaded detection too,' the detective said coldly, turning to Camille who'd gone very pale, 'but then you murdered again.'

'Who? Who do you think I murdered now?' Camille said.

'Thérèse,' Alice said.

'Thérèse is . . . is . . . dead?' Alex gasped.

'Oh yes. Very dead.'

'She can't be,' Alex said, his hand covering his mouth and Alice saw genuine emotion in his face for the first time.

'I have to be honest. At first Thérèse was my number-one suspect for Enya's murder,' Alice said. 'On New Year's Eve she was photographed in the drawing room doorway just prior to the speech and so might have had time to get up to the study and kill Enya. And there was blood on her trousers, as I found out when I picked up her dry cleaning, which Thérèse claimed to have been from an accident, but I thought could well have been Enya's blood. Only then I found a mobile phone – and on it were pictures of Thérèse . . . with a man . . . in a very compromising position.'

'Who?' Jinx asked, her ears pricking up at this piece of gossip.

'Laars,' Alice said.

'Oh. That figures,' Jinx said.

'According to him, Thérèse was hoping to make you jealous, *Monsieur*. So she slipped to the cloakroom with a guest at the party, who took photographs of them.'

'Typical,' Jinx said, shaking her head.

'But you know exactly which photographs. She showed you them. A few weeks ago. I saw you on the CCTV at the front of the house having a row. I asked Jacques to translate.'

She turned now to Jacques who stepped forward. 'Oh, yes,' he said, 'I can lip-read and . . . '

'Go on . . . '

'She showed you the phone and you saw the picture of her with another man and she said something like "You see how painful it is? For me? To see you with her?" And you said that you loved her and that it would be over soon.'

Alice stared at Alex Messent, wondering how he could stand there looking so smug when he'd hurt so many people. 'She couldn't bear the charade of watching you and your wife together, pretending to be the perfect couple, you see.' Alice vividly recalled the expression on Thérèse's face in Charles Tavistock's photograph that night. 'Because you promised her a new life. You were planning to escape to Brazil with her along with the proceeds of this sale, weren't you? That's why you had two false passports stashed away in your safe. But sadly, Thérèse will never see Copacabana beach.'

'You mean, this is true? She really is dead?' Alex whispered.

'Oh, yes,' Alice said. 'Very dead. She was poisoned with Jacques' Japanese lobster essence – the one your wife told him not to use because of Thérèse's allergies.'

Now that she'd finally said it, Alice turned to address Camille. 'Whilst Jacques was clearing up, you must have taken the bottle from his pouch, and when you took Thérèse home last night, you used the opportunity to put some of the paste onto her toothbrush, knowing the taste of mint might hide the scent of the lobster oil long enough for her to put the brush in her mouth. Because the second she did, she went into a fatal anaphylactic shock.'

'The cause of death has been confirmed by our forensics team,' Detective Rigby said.

'Then you calmly went out and bought a Chinese takeaway on the corner and set up Thérèse's living room to make it look as if she'd died by accident,' Alice said.

'On the way here, my team confirmed that there's some CCTV footage that clearly shows you at Wonky Wong's at eleven p.m.'

'Proof enough, but then I found this.' Alice now pulled out Jacques' missing vial of lobster oil from her shoulder bag.

'Hey, that's mine,' Jacques said.

'Exactly. I found it in the bin of your en suite bathroom,' Alice told Camille, 'wrapped in tissue, just moments before you arrived back at the house this morning.'

'No, no, no,' Camille said, her head shaking from side to side.

'You see, Madame Messent, that's the problem with assuming that staff are beneath you and are only there to clean up your mess. They're a lot smarter than they're ever given credit for.'

Alex turned on his wife, his look thunderous. Camille let out a tortured sob. 'I did everything for you, to protect you, always. When I saw what Enya had found in the safe . . . those passports . . . I was heartbroken. You were planning on leaving me and going away with her . . . and I couldn't bear it . . . I couldn't bear to lose you.'

Alex roared, breaking away from Gerda in a sudden, violent jolt, at the same time whipping a pistol from the inside pocket of his jacket. He pressed the barrel against Camille's temple, his arm around her neck in a vice-like grip and she screamed.

Half choking her, he dragged her back towards the door, shouting at the police to get back. Everyone dropped to their knees, including Alice, seeing the crazed look in his eye.

Suddenly Laura came running through the library door, tears streaming down her face.

She hurtled into her parents. 'No, Papa!' she cried out.

In the ensuing tussle, a deafening shot rang out from the gun and Alice covered her ears, terrified, but suddenly she was aware of a strange tinkling of glass, and she looked up to see the ceiling plaster crack in a line where the bullet had hit, just next to the rivet that was holding up the ancient chandelier.

Everyone gasped, as with a horrible creak, the rest of the plaster cracked like a broken windscreen.

Alex lunged for his wife and threw her onto the floor, just as the chandelier crashed down on them in a spectacular crunch of glass.

45.

Jinx stood by the long curtains at the library window, looking out at where Alex and Camille Messent, both in handcuffs, were being led onto the front drive and into the back of a police van. Alex had a bloody bandage wrapped around his forehead and Camille had plasters on her face and a bandage on her arm.

'It's a miracle they weren't killed,' Jinx said.

'Thank God. I've had enough dead bodies for one day.'

Alice ran the spinner along its chain around her neck, as she turned back to the room to see Jacques was still holding a sobbing Laura Messent in his arms, but a young WPO was gently prising her away. She sniffed and stared across at Alice, black tears falling down her face. Alice couldn't read her expression, but her heart went out to the young girl.

Through Laura's shocked sobs, Alice had managed to ascertain that in the argument she'd overheard last night, Thérèse had been telling her off for flirting with Jacques and Laura had threatened Thérèse, saying she knew about her and Laars – because she and Jacques had seen them on New Year's Eve when they'd been smoking outside the kitchen and had looked up to see them in the window above. The poor girl was distraught that the last words she'd spoken to Thérèse had been so spiteful.

Gerda was standing in the middle of the library inspecting the painting closely with Barney, as Helly tried to carefully brush up the smashed glass around them. She only broke away when Gerda's colleagues came in carrying thick grey blankets.

'It's not damaged? From the chandelier?' Alice asked Barney.

'No. Thank goodness. Actually, it's in rather good nick,' he said, with a wide smile. 'And Gerda here tells me that there's a very hefty reward for its return.'

Gerda now addressed Alice and, to her surprise, came over and extended her hand. 'Miss Beeton, I can't possibly thank you enough. We're driving to the airport tonight where we'll be meeting with British and Dutch government officials to hash out what happens next,' she said, 'but when the painting is installed back in the Rijksmuseum, there will be a launch. I'm sure you'll be the guest of honour.'

'Oh, I don't care about any of that,' Alice said – although, of course, she secretly did. 'But could you please just tell me one thing?'

'What?'

'Where the hell is my dog?'

Gerda clasped her hand over her mouth and squeezed Alice's arm. 'Oh, I'm so, so sorry.'

'And she'd better be all right,' she said, even though Barney had already comforted her on that note.

'Yes, of course. She's fine. A very fine dog – and a credit to you. I'm very sorry I scared you,' Gerda said. 'But I had to make sure you were with us. I had to ensure your help.'

'You didn't have to go to such dreadful lengths. I help everyone who comes into my agency,' Alice said, rather shirtily. 'Whenever I can.'

'I'm sorry. For being so stern, but . . . '

'Just give her to me,' Alice said, not wanting any more of Gerda's excuses.

'Go easy, Alice,' Barney said. 'She's been under incredible pressure.'

'Really?' Alice said. 'And you think I haven't?'

'Of course, of course,' Barney said, backing down.

'She's out here.' Gerda led Alice through the library and through the kitchen to the back door.

Outside was a grey transit van with the window wound down.

'Just in here,' Gerda said, opening the door. 'We took great care of her.'

But Alice wasn't listening. Her heart lurched as she saw her little dog, curled up asleep. 'Agatha?'

Agatha jumped up on the seat, barking, then did a little circle of joy before Alice picked her up and hugged her in close and let out a little sob. 'Oh, I missed you,' she whispered, kissing her.

Suddenly Jinx was sweeping through the door and lifting Agatha out of her arms. 'My baby, my baby.' She held Agatha aloft. 'Oh, you're here.'

'I don't know about you, but after all of that, I could really do with a cup of tea,' Alice said.

'Or something stronger. I've just discovered Sassy's gin stash if that's any good?' Helly said.

'Oh God, yes,' Jinx said. 'G and bloody T's all round.'

The new kitchen at Hawthorn, which had annoyed Alice so much when she'd first seen it, now felt very similar to the old one, with everyone crowded around the central island, the room filled with the sound of clinking glasses and chattering. Jacques, whose canapés for the guests had hardly been touched, was happily offering them around.

With the last of the late afternoon sun slanting in through the window, and a gin and tonic down, Alice suddenly felt as if an enormous weight had lifted from her shoulders.

She took a moment to watch all of her friends. Helly and Jacques were laughing with Max and Elijah, and Jinx and Barney were chatting with Massoud, who now raised his chin at Alice, and she looked behind her. Detective Rigby was standing in the kitchen doorway.

'That's everything,' he said. 'We'll be off. The Messents are in custody and Laura will be with a relative tonight.'

'Right,' Alice said, and she smiled as he came over. 'We can't tempt you to stay?'

'Sadly not. This is going to be a paperwork nightmare.'

'Sorry.'

'Don't be. I should really be congratulating you.'

Alice smiled. 'I couldn't have done it without the help of this lot,' Alice said. 'You've met Jinx, haven't you? She works at the office. And Helly. This is Barney, Jacques the chef, Massoud, our trusted driver, who has been with the agency forever. Elijah and Max. I used to babysit for them, believe it or not.'

'You'll all be relieved to get back to the day jobs, I'm sure,' the detective said, 'although I should imagine there's going to be a lot of interest after the press get hold of this. Prepare yourself. This story is going to be huge.'

'I do hope the agency will come out of it unscathed,' Jinx said.

'Will The Good Household Management Agency be famous?' Helly asked.

'Probably. But perhaps you should rename yourselves "Miss Beeton's Murder Agency",' the detective joked, winking at Alice, and everyone laughed.

'Oh, that could stick,' Barney said. 'I like that. I like that a lot.'

'I'll see myself out,' Detective Rigby said, but Alice followed him to the front door.

He stepped outside and looked up at the house and then back at Alice. Agatha slipped past Alice and barked and then nuzzled against his legs as he reached down to pet her.

'You've got a good thing going on with that lot. What you pulled off was nothing short of a miracle,' he told Alice and there was a pause and he stared into her eyes.

'I can't thank you enough for getting here in time,' she said.

'You know, I couldn't quite believe what you told me at first, but . . . I'll never doubt you again,' he said.

'That's gratifying to hear, but I sincerely hope there won't be a next time,' she said.

He smiled and rubbed the side of his face. 'Yeah, you're right. Well then. So long, Miss Beeton . . . Alice,' he said.

But now they were interrupted by a van screeching to a halt in front of the house.

'What the—'

'Oh . . . ' Detective Rigby said, 'I knew it wouldn't take long. I think this is my cue to leave you to it.'

More than a little bit sadly, she watched him walk away and he briefly waved as he got into his car, whilst another man with a television camera and a woman in a smart coat rushed up towards her.

She told herself off for being so sentimental, but as Detective Rigby drove around the gravel turning circle, and then away, Alice felt her eyes prick with an unexpected emotion. Why had she said there wouldn't be a next time? It had sounded so dismissive. And that's not what she'd meant. But now it was too late.

'Are you the owner of the house?' the woman asked and Alice saw the record light was on the camera, which was now perched on the man's shoulder.

'Yes. Sort of.'

'Then we'd like to ask you a few questions if we could?'

Epilogue

It was nearly five months since the bust at Hawthorn Hall before life started to get any semblance of normality for Alice.

She stood outside the new offices, as Jinx straightened the 'Now Hiring' sign in the window, and breathed in the spring air, noticing the pretty tree outside on the pavement was in bud. Pigeons cooed and pecked at some crumbs beneath a bench and the busker on the corner strummed his guitar in the sunshine.

'There,' Alice mouthed to Jinx and then put her thumb up and smiled.

She looked along the pedestrianised street, already excited about becoming part of the community of shop owners and cafés. Before Christmas, she couldn't in even her wildest dreams have imagined that The Good Household Management Agency would be in such demand. She'd taken on three new members of staff and many more new clients and had moved to this new office.

The Rembrandt's return to the Rijksmuseum made headlines internationally, and although Alice had played down her role in the whole affair, Miss Beeton's Murder Agency seemed to have stuck, with several newspaper headlines praising her audacious plan to uncover the plot to sell the rare painting. *The Times* ran a lengthy report on how the lost masterpiece had moved in such secretive and rarefied circles that Gerda and her team had been sceptical about ever seeing its return.

Meanwhile, the 'perfect' Messents made perfect villains for the media, who couldn't get enough of the power couple's fall from grace. As far as Alice knew, Camille Messent was still waiting for sentencing at His Majesty's Pleasure in Downview Prison, where she sincerely doubted she'd be able to look so effortlessly chic. Alex Messent, whose arrest had led to an astonishing network of stolen art pieces, was also on remand, awaiting extradition to the Netherlands to answer for his crimes. Alice, unable to resist, had called Laura's school and spoken to the pursed-lipped Mrs Prior, the house mistress who'd told her that Laura had gone back to live with relatives in France. Alice felt truly sorry for the girl.

Gerda, who emailed Alice with regular updates, had personally overseen the repatriation of the body of Enya – or Romee Hoek – to the Netherlands. Alice and Jinx had sent a heartfelt message and flowers to her funeral in the small church in Groningen. They would visit her family when they were over for the gala dinner and grand unveiling of the Rembrandt in Amsterdam at the end of the month. But before then, Alice would be spending the bank holiday with Jinx and Barney at Hawthorn, where she'd be cooking a spectacular twelve-course dinner – just like she'd sworn she would.

Sassy and Jasper had just about forgiven Alice for the mayhem that had ensued on their return from the Caribbean. They'd come back to press swarming all over Hawthorn Hall, and for a second, Sassy had actually thought it was because of her holiday Instagram feed. But there was no doubt that the secret auction at Hawthorn Hall had resulted in a huge boost to Sassy's rep, so in truth she'd still been pleased. And, thanks to Hawthorn's new infamy, she seemed to have fallen in love with the place a bit more properly this time, even throwing herself into refurbishing the kitchen garden, much to Alice's delight.

Alice walked into the office, listening to Jinx training Elliot and Saskia, their new recruits, and sat down at her rather lovely blonde wood desk.

'Oh,' she said, opening the latest email from her lawyer on her computer.

'Anything good?' Helly asked, coming out from the kitchen with a vase full of flowers for the front desk.

'It seems the insurance company have successfully sued the building company,' Alice said. 'Mr Mantis is in a whole world of trouble.' She read further. 'It looks like there'll be some decent compensation.'

'Alice, that's amazing.'

She was still unable to move back into her basement flat, but with the help of Jinx and Massoud, she'd retrieved lots of her things and she'd moved into the place Gerda had been using as a base whilst she'd been in London. Gerda had told Alice she could use it for as long as she wanted for free. Alice, who'd been scared it might have been a dingy bedsit, but was prepared to put up with any free accommodation in London, had been delighted to find out that Gerda had actually given her the use of a charming little house very near the Royal School of Music. Alice rather liked hearing the violins and horns in the practice rooms, and of course Agatha loved being so close to the park, just the other side of the Albert Hall.

'Those are lovely,' Alice said to Helly, who was laying out several crocheted hats next to the flowers.

'You don't mind if I photograph them? The light is so good.'

Alice came across and picked up one of the pastel-coloured hats.

'I'm selling them on Etsy,' Helly said. 'The money I make is going straight into my Japan fund.'

Alice smiled, glad that Helly was galvanised with her plan for a two-month adventure in the summer. For a girl who'd felt anxious about travelling to Leeds last Christmas, she now seemed to be embracing the sheer size of the world, no doubt in large part down to Jacques, who she'd been dating for the last couple of months.

'I love the colours.'

'You should do. They're inspired by that,' Helly said, nodding to the framed plate from the book. It was Alice's favourite page showing the illustrations of all of Mrs Beeton's puddings.

'This one's the pyramid cream,' Helly said, proudly.

'So, it is. Aren't you clever?'

Alice went back to her desk, delighted that Helly had found such unexpected inspiration. Helly took some pictures and then carefully wrapped up the hats in tissue paper.

'What time is it? We're starving,' Jinx said, marching up to Alice's desk, trailed by the new recruits.

Alice got up. 'Actually, I made a cake. A proper sponge. As it's your birthday at the weekend,' she told Jinx.

'Should we sing happy birthday?' Helly asked. 'Are there candles?'

'No, I didn't get candles,' Alice said. 'Lighting that many, we'd only set off the smoke alarm again.'

'Cheeky,' Jinx said, but she laughed too, and Agatha barked.

Victoria Sponge

INGREDIENTS – 6 oz butter, 6 oz caster
sugar, 6 oz self-raising flour, 3 eggs.

METHOD – heat oven to 180 degrees C. Grease two
7-inch cake tins. Cream butter and sugar in a bowl with
wooden spoon, beat the eggs in one at a time with a little
flour each time to prevent curdling. Add remaining flour
and beat well. Pour mixture equally into the cake tins. Bake
for 20 mins until brown and springy. Cool on wire rack.

For the butter icing: 5 oz butter, softened. 10 oz icing sugar.

METHOD – Beat the butter until smooth with wooden
spoon. Add icing sugar bit by bit until smooth.

When the cake is cool, spread one side with butter
icing and the other with jam. Sandwich together. Sieve
icing sugar over the top plus decorations of choice.

They were all tucking in and talking about Alice's menu for the
weekend, when Agatha started making an odd noise and Alice
looked up out of the window. A familiar figure had just walked
past, stopped, and was now retracing his steps. Jinx and Helly
pulled a face at Alice when they saw who it was.

Alice got up and went quickly to the door. The second she

pushed it, Agatha shot out and ran towards the man in the street and jumped up.

'I was just passing,' Detective Rigby said. 'Hello, you.' He tickled Agatha's ears.

'We were having cake. Would you like some?' Alice said, grinning. It was just so lovely to see him. 'Do come in.'

'Oh, I'm OK. I'm on a fitness regime,' he said. 'Plus, I don't want to intrude.'

She stared at him, not quite believing he was in front of her. She'd thought about him so often, but they hadn't seen each since he'd left Hawthorn on the day of the auction.

'I like the new offices,' he said, looking up at the cheerful window.

'They're good, aren't they? So much better than the other ones. And bigger too. Thank goodness. We're busier than ever.'

There was a pause and they smiled at each other. She'd forgotten quite how lovely his eyes were.

'One of the reasons I came past was to give you some information I thought you might like.'

'Oh?'

'You know you told me about Alex Messent being involved with dodgy Russians?'

'Did I?'

'At Thérèse's flat?'

'Goodness, I was in such a state, I can hardly remember what I told you.'

'Yes, it was rather an information dump, when you confessed what you'd been up to,' he said. 'But I remember you saying that they owned Thérèse's flat.'

'Yes, D.T. Holdings.'

'Thanks to you mentioning that the fraud team have uncovered a paper trail to a huge Russian property money-laundering scam. Alex Messent is up to his neck in that too, it seems.'

Alice remembered Laars' warning about Alex Messent being in bed with the Russians.

'I can hardly take the credit, Detective Rigby,' Alice said.

'No, but as you said, it's all in the details.'

'It certainly is. And, as I say, never trust a man with a dimple in his chin.'

The detective laughed. 'I beg your pardon?'

'Alex Messent. He had a whopper.'

'Did he? Oh, I see; well, I'll bear that in mind when I'm next investigating.'

There was a small pause. 'And how is the detecting going?' she asked.

'Fine,' he said. 'I say that, but actually I've got this case on at the moment, and I just can't seem to fathom it.'

'Oh?'

He put his hands in his pockets and scuffed his toe on the paving slab. 'And . . . well, this is a long shot, but I wondered if we could talk it through? It doesn't have to be now,' he hurried on. 'Just sometime. Maybe over dinner?'

Alice's stomach fluttered. 'That would be wonderful.'

'In that case, it's a date,' he said.

And all around them, the pigeons applauded themselves into flight.

Acknowledgements

There are many things that make me happy, but food and writing come pretty much top of the list, so this, my first foray into cosy crime with added recipes has been an utter joy to write. I'm truly grateful to everyone who introduced me to the recipes in this book, but obviously, I'm most indebted to the late great Isabella Beeton. I hope I haven't caused any offence in making Alice a fictionally distant relative.

This book wouldn't have come about in the first place were it not for my insightful, clever agent, Felicity Blunt at Curtis Brown, so a big thank you to her as well as to Rosie Pierce and Tanja Goossens.

I'd really like to thank Clare Gordon at HQ who inherited me as an author, but from the get-go has been my champion and an exceptional editor. It's been such a pleasure to work together. Thank you to the whole team at HQ, especially Jo Rose in marketing, as well as Sophie Calder for her excellent publicity and Donna Hillyer for her copy-editing skills. And a huge thank you to all the bookshops and libraries for getting my book to the readers. Thanks, too, to all my fellow authors for their support.

I'd like to thank Alice Rivers-Cripps my co-host of our *Show*

Us Your Bits podcast, who inspired me to give my fictional Alice a Victorian spinner necklace. Thanks also to Louise Dumas who introduced me to Pandora, the dress agency in South Kensington and thank you to Bridget and her team there. Thanks also to Dawn Howarth, who has been my most trusted first reader since book one, years ago.

And, as ever I'd like to thank my friends and family for their constant support – my sister, Catherine, as well as my daughters, Tallulah, Roxie and Minty. Ziggy, my beloved dog needs a mention too. Without him and all his friends, I'd never have had so much fun writing Agatha.

But most of all, heartfelt thanks to my amazing husband and true partner in crime, Emlyn Rees, who rescued me from several plot cul-de-sacs. Thank you, my love, for all your help and the many, many cups of tea.

Alice Beeton will return in

MURDER MOST PROPER

Read on for an exclusive extract.

1.

In the cosy kitchen of Alice Beeton's basement flat, Barney looked up from the open copy of *Hello!* magazine spread before him.

'And the bodies were never found?' he asked.

'No. Apparently not,' Alice told her friend, peering through the glass of her new oven door, pleased to see that her chocolate fondants had risen to perfection.

She removed them to cool, the kitchen filling with a delicious chocolaty aroma. 'But I suspect that *he* has no idea about any of it. Or would even care if he did.'

She pointed her oven glove at the open pages of the magazine and the picture of Guy Scott looking smug on his megayacht. The same megayacht that Jinx, Alice's best friend and business partner, happened to go to a party on in August, where she was swept off her feet by the flamboyant business tycoon. According to Jinx, who remained as dizzy as a schoolgirl, it was love at first daiquiri.

It had been therapeutic over lunch to confide in Barney how difficult it was running The Good Household Management Agency without Jinx, and certainly not nearly as much fun. Or profitable for that matter. Alice was used to placing high end staff in London's most elite homes and country estates, but she hadn't realised just how much she'd grown to rely on Jinx and her contacts. Contacts that had ensured a steady flow of new business… until now.

It seemed unfathomable to Alice that Jinx had so readily taken a sudden sabbatical from the job she loved for this Guy Scott fellow, who, according to *Hello!* had just bought Rodmell House and was intending on turning the nineteenth century pile into an elite members' country club, with the help of some bigwig investors.

Alice, of course, had immediately done some digging, finding herself down an internet rabbit hole, and had just shared her very interesting findings with Barney. About how Rodmell House had once been an architectural jewel of the Regency era, its owner Edmund Gurnton being a pal of naughty George IV, with whom he'd gone gadding around the world, and how Edmund, just before he'd died, was said to have buried his 'greatest treasure' in the grounds of Rodmell. Rumour had it that the treasure was a colossal diamond that he'd purloined from a Maharaja. For many years after his death, on Edmund's birthday in November, a treasure hunt had been held, everyone from the local village scouring the grounds of Rodmell for the jewel. That was, until two people had gone missing during the hunt.

'How intriguing. So, the treasure has never been found?' Barney asked, as Alice passed him his fondant ramekin. He made an appreciative noise.

'No. Not as far as I know. The annual treasure hunt stopped just before the First World War,' Alice said. 'The house has had various owners since, of course, but it's been empty for years, until lover-boy here came along with his grand plans.'

'Have you told Jinx any of this?'

'I emailed her, of course,' Alice said. 'But I'm not sure she's even read it. She certainly hasn't got back.' She couldn't help sounding miffed. 'I guess she's otherwise occupied. With him.'

Barney chuckled.

Alice pulled a face. He knew as well as she did that Jinx had notoriously bad taste in men. Her four marriages had all been a disaster and Jinx had completely sworn off men until this one had turned her head. 'It's not funny, Barney. I mean, what type of man is he? He has rather eccentric clothes-taste, don't you think? And what's with the blue nail-varnish? Plus, if you ask me, that's an indecent amount of rings.'

'Alice, are you asking me to make some enquiries about this Mr Scott?'

'Oh, Barney, would you?' Alice asked, gratefully, putting down her spoon with relief. She knew he was long retired from GCHQ, but Barney could still call in favours from his old contacts who had access to databases and information that the public never saw. 'Jinx would kill me for meddling,' she added, because it was true and also because it was code for Barney to keep this just between the two of them, 'but I've just got a funny feeling. It's all happened so fast. What if it goes wrong?'

'Oh ye of little faith,' Barney teased. 'Why not let love take its course?' he asked, pouring more cream into the chocolaty ramekin with a flourish. 'Be happy for them.'

'I do want her to be happy,' Alice said curtly, scooping the magazine off the table, dismayed not only that Barney had added such an indecent amount of cream to his pudding, but that he suddenly seemed to have turned into a romantic.

'It's just an adjustment. You'll feel better once you get someone else to help at the agency.'

'Easy for you to say,' she muttered. 'And anyway. All this talk of love. She's acting like she's a teenager.'

'But love is love. Strikes when one least expects it. This is delicious, by the way.'

Alice narrowed her eyes. This again was a very un-Barney-like sentiment. But then he'd also been behaving like a seventeen-year-old rather than a seventy-year-old of late. He'd been utterly miserable after his wife Honey had died, but he seemed to have his pep back. He'd recently discovered a dating app and now Alice felt a pang of alarm. He wasn't suggesting that he was in love himself, was he?

Agatha, Alice's corgi-Jack-Russell-cross, was standing patiently by her bowl and barked twice.

'Alright. I haven't forgotten you,' Alice said, leaning over and dribbling some of the cream from the china jug into Agatha's bowl. 'Don't say I don't spoil you,' Alice added, ruffling Agatha's ear and smiling as her little dog devoured the cream in a very un-ladylike way.

Barney, who'd made fast work of his pudding, scraped out the bottom of the ramekin, lingered indulgently on the contents of his spoon, and then sighed, patting the front of his chunky fisher-man's jumper. As soon as Alice had finished too, he scrunched up his linen napkin and placed it on the table with a flourish.

'Top notch, as ever. But you'll have to excuse me.' He looked at his watch.

'Where are you going? You've only just finished lunch.'

A first-class Sunday lunch at that — a juicy roast chicken,

roasted carrots and parsnips, buttery savoy cabbage, peas, home-made stuffing and glistening gravy. Alice was looking forward to digesting it all over a long game of Scrabble this afternoon as a reward for her hard work. She and Barney had been playing together for years, and she felt confident she might edge ahead in their leaderboard today.

'I've got to get suited and booted. I have my second date tonight with Marie,' he said, grinning and waggling his bushy salt-and-pepper eyebrows with delight. 'She's got tickets for dinner jazz.' He added a flourish on the 'jazz'.

'Oh,' Alice said, failing to keep the disappointment from her voice, but Barney didn't notice.

What even *was* dinner jazz? And on a Sunday night?

'You could have a lot more fun yourself, Alice,' Barney said, giving her a pitying look, as he shrugged on his anorak a few minutes later and kissed her lightly on the cheek.

Alice had always enjoyed the feeling of getting her kitchen ship-shape after a meal. There was a certain satisfaction in knowing that there was 'a place for everything and everything in its place' as the great Mrs Isabella Beeton had once declared. Alice had her distant but much-revered relative's quote framed in needlepoint on the wall. Tonight, however, with a mournful Chopin nocturne playing on Classic FM, she lingered as she scraped the dirty plates into the bin and loaded the new dishwater. Looking out through the basement kitchen window up to the street, her eye was caught by the light drizzle falling against the glow from the lamppost outside.

Was it really nearly a year since the undercover art auction in

Hawthorn Hall and her brief moment in the spotlight? Somehow, it all seemed to Alice like a dream. She glanced up at the ceiling, seeing the proof that it hadn't been. There was a lovely new pendant hanging down from the freshly plastered ceiling, although she missed the shabby ceiling rose. Fortunately, there was no sign of any sinister drips, or any noisy neighbours for that matter, thank Heavens. Persevering with Mr Mantis, the slippery building manager, had been worth it, but her time in the mews house, courtesy of the Dutch government, felt so long ago.

She took the two ramekins from the table, thinking of how Barney had rushed off when she still had so much to discuss with him. She'd wanted to puzzle over the few facts she knew about Rodmell's past and Edmund's treasure hunt. But maybe, as Barney had said, it was just ancient history. She'd hoped, though, he'd have been a little more taken with the story, as she had been when she'd found out about it. Still, at least Barney had agreed to make a few enquiries about Jinx's new beau. *Discreetly*, Alice hoped.

No, she reasoned, she shouldn't be cross with Barney for rushing off. After all, it stood to reason that he'd had other plans before she'd invited him round for an impromptu lunch earlier. She had thought she might be at Hawthorn this weekend, but her brother, Jasper, had cancelled her visit yesterday. Something about his wife, Sassy, doing an influencer shoot in the house, whatever that meant. But with her family, Jinx, and now Barney otherwise occupied, Alice couldn't help feeling a little…well…overlooked.

She remembered Barney's suggestion earlier that she should go on the dating apps, but she really couldn't think of anything worse. How could one possibly make up one's mind about a potential partner from something so superficial and misleading as a photograph? In Alice's experience, men who were aware of their own good looks rarely had a good character to match. The whole 'swiping' thing seemed to Alice to be so distasteful and unromantic. Perhaps, though, it was different for men. Barney was twenty years older than Alice, yet he seemed to have attractive women falling over themselves to listen to him talk about making small animals out of matchsticks.

Without any help from the internet, however, Alice had absolutely no idea where she might meet someone whom she remotely fancied, let alone who might be life partner material.

The only small hint of romance she'd had in years had been with Detective Rigby, who had turned out to be her knight in shining armour at Hawthorn Hall. Months afterwards, he'd come to the agency offices and had asked Alice if she wanted to help him out on a case. She'd jumped at the offer – especially as the dishy, if somewhat shabby detective had suggested that their chat happened over dinner.

Alice hadn't been able to decide whether it had been the opportunity to assist in some real police work that had been more exciting, or the chance to be with Detective Rigby alone in a restaurant. But it was immaterial. Detective Rigby had never called or come through on his offer. And, as the months had passed, Alice had concluded that he'd forgotten her and moved on to better things. *Ghosting*. Wasn't that what people called it these days? *Rude* would be a more accurate word.

She sighed and closed the dishwater, noticing that Agatha had sidled next to her foot, nuzzling into her leg, as if in solidarity. Her little dog always seemed to be in perfect tune with Alice's emotions, and she leant down to pick her up for a cuddle.

'You're right,' Alice said, looking into Agatha's intelligent brown eyes. 'There's really no point in moping, is there? Shall we do a loop around the block?'

Alice placed Agatha gently down and she immediately trotted to the hallway and picked up her lead in her mouth.

Yes. Right foot forward, Alice thought, shrugging on her ancient Burberry mac and pulling her beret down low over her brown bob before checking herself in the hall mirror. There was absolutely no point feeling glum, she told her reflection, smearing on some lip balm. She'd do what her old mentor, the housekeeper at Hawthorn, Mrs Doulton had always said and 'spin self-pity around into self-care'. When she got back from her walk, she'd have a bath with some lovely salts and watch a re-run of *Murder, She Wrote*.

But just as she put her hand on the door, Alice's mobile trilled with an incoming call and her heart did a little leap when she saw Jinx's name.

'Oh, well hello stranger,' Alice said, answering.

'Don't be sniffy, Alice,' Jinx replied.

Having known each other since they'd been at school, Jinx knew every single intonation of Alice's voice and could pick up Alice's admonishment loud and clear.

Chastened, Alice felt herself smiling. Despite all her resolve to be angry, it now evaporated in an instant. 'I miss you, that's all.'

'All the more reason why you're coming next weekend,' Jinx said.

'Where?' Alice asked, remembering in a rush how Jinx always had a knack of railroading her.

'Rodmell, of course. Guy…oh, my God, Alice, he love, love, *loves* your idea.'

Alice frowned and held out the phone and looked at it for a second, as if Jinx might have lost her mind. 'My…?'

'About the treasure hunt, silly,' Jinx said, as if this were something that they'd already discussed. 'We're going to re-instate it. Everyone's up for it.'

'The treasure hunt? For Edmund's treasure?' Alice checked, trying to catch up. *Had* she implied that the treasure hunt should be re-instated in her email? She was pretty sure she hadn't, but, even so, she felt a rush of excitement that Jinx had shared her email with Guy. Maybe Alice had misjudged him from his photograph after all.

'Yes! Do say you'll come. Because I was thinking, didn't Detective Rigby once say you had an eye for detail?' Jinx continued withthat teasing tone in her voice that Alice found so annoying, but she let slide now. 'So, you never know. You might even be the one to find it...'

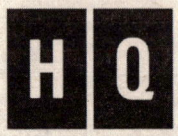

ONE PLACE. MANY STORIES

Bold, innovative and
empowering publishing.

FOLLOW US ON:

@HQStories